MYSTIC EMPIRE

BOOK THREE OF
THE BRONZE CANTICLES

TRACY & LAURA HICKMAN

WARNER BOOKS

NEW YORK   BOSTON

Warner Books and the "W" logo are trademarks of Time Warner Inc. or an affiliated company. Used under license by Hachette Book Group USA, which is not affiliated with Time Warner Inc.

Cover design by Don Puckey and Shasti O'Leary Soudant
Cover illustration by Matt Stawicki

Warner Books
Hachette Book Group USA
1271 Avenue of the Americas
New York, NY 10020
Visit our Web site at www.HachetteBookGroupUSA.com.

Printed in the United States of America

Originally published in hardcover by Aspect
First Paperback Printing: February 2007

10 9 8 7 6 5 4 3 2 1

ACCLAIM FOR

MYSTIC WARRIOR

"Impressive and provocative . . . This emotionally intense novel's meticulously crafted magical system and likable characters evoke an atmosphere both timely and timeless."
—*Publishers Weekly* (starred review)

"An exciting, adventure-filled read from two of the great storytellers and world builders of our time."
—MARGARET WEIS

"Breathtaking . . . something truly special."
—R. A. SALVATORE

"The Hickmans have created a fully realized world with its own legends, traditions, and customs."
—*Romantic Times BOOKclub Magazine*

"Impressive . . . suspenseful . . . a complex, rousing adventure . . . The Hickmans, masters of world building, have created another compelling novel."
—DavisEnterprise.com

"Creative, colorful, and completely original."
—GreenManReview.com

"A very different tale, one that displays a subtlety and sophistication."
—*Starlog*

"An imaginative tale, spun of marvels, exotic magic, and extraordinary dreams, all deftly woven."
—JANNY WURTS, author of *To Ride Hell's Chasm*

OTHER WORKS BY THE AUTHORS

Tracy and Laura Hickman
THE BRONZE CANTICLES
MYSTIC WARRIOR
MYSTIC QUEST

Tracy Hickman

(with Margaret Weis)
DRAGONLANCE CHRONICLES TRILOGY
DRAGONLANCE LEGENDS TRILOGY
DRAGONLANCE: DRAGONS OF SUMMER FLAME
DRAGONLANCE: WAR OF SOULS TRILOGY
DARKSWORD TRILOGY
ROSE OF THE PROPHET TRILOGY
DEATHGATE CYCLE SEPTOLOGY

THE IMMORTALS
REQUIEM OF STARS
STARCRAFT: SPEED OF DARKNESS

Laura Hickman

(with Tracy Hickman)
DRAGONLANCE: DRAGONS OF WAR
RAVENLOFT

(with Kate Novak)
DRAGONLANCE: LOVE AND WAR
"Heart of Goldmoon"

This book is lovingly dedicated
to Our Children

Angel, Curtis, Lani, Tasha, and Jarod
who bring to life joy and magic
far beyond the covers of our books

ACKNOWLEDGMENTS

No book is conjured out of thin air; each bears the touch of many craftsmen and professionals to bring it into being.

We express our deep thanks to Maureen Egen, Jamie Raab, and Beth de Guzman for supporting the sunrise on our worlds; to Bob Castillo and Penina Sacks for smoothing over all our rough spots; and to Devi Pillai for your indispensable aid.

We are also grateful to Jim Spivey for taking the words we sent in and turning them into a real, live book; to Huy Duong, Donald Puckey, and especially Matt Stawicki for his thrilling cover art.

Books do not live until they are read. Our express thanks to all those who worked so hard to get our books in your hands: to Bryan Cronk in online marketing, Rebecca Oliver and Peggy Boelke in subrights, Christine Barba and her fabulous sales team, Karen Torres and her marketing group, Martha Otis with her entire advertising and promotions crew, and Chris Dao for her work in publicity.

To our agent, Matt Bialer, and his assistant, Anna Bierhaus, our gratitude for catching the vision of these books. You took us in and believed in us; we'll never forget that.

Finally, our deepest thanks to the one and only Jaime Levine—whose long hours, sharp talent, red pen, and gallons of encouragement have guided us through these three books. You allowed "the fire to show through the smoke."

TABLE OF CONTENTS

Thrice upon a time
there was a world that was three worlds
One place that was three places
One history that was told
in three sagas all at the same time.

Thrice upon a time . . .
the gods foresaw a time
when three worlds would become one . . .
When the children of their creation
would face the Binding of the Worlds.

Thrice upon a time . . .
Three worlds fought to survive.
Their children would be armed
with the cunning of their minds
their fierce will to endure
and the power of newfound magic.

Thrice upon a time . . .
came the Binding of the Worlds.
Not even the gods knew
. . . which world would reign . . .
. . . which world would submit . . .
. . . and which world would die.

Song of the Worlds
Bronze Canticles, Tome I, Folio 1, Leaf 6

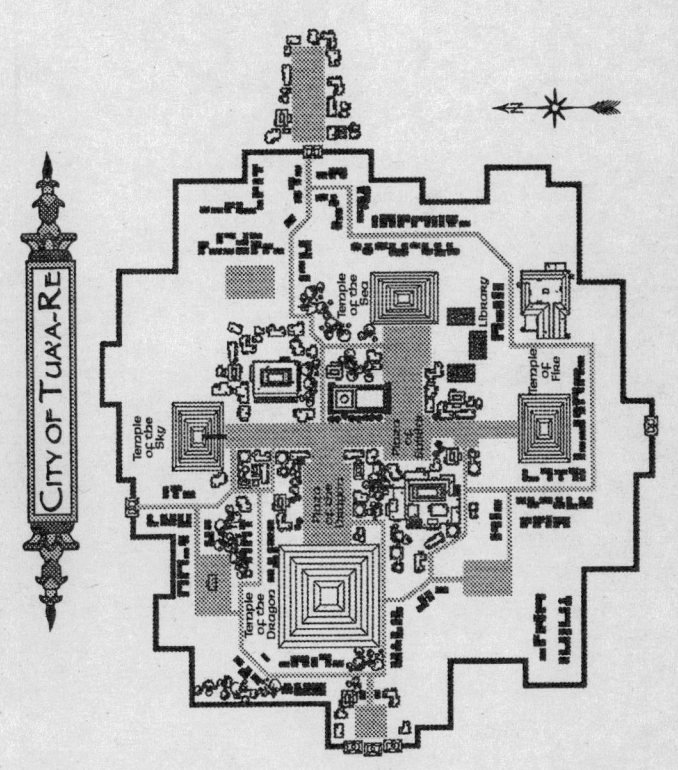

City of Tua'a-Re

The Outsiders

The Bards

The 591st year of the Dragonkings was to mark the centennial of the Election Fields Rebellion — a celebration of the moment that put the spark of life into the embryonic ambitions of the mystics. The hundred-year anniversary was to be a cause of tremendous celebration everywhere the mystics called home. All prepared to commemorate the Election Centenary with whatever revelry they could manage. Most of those who claimed allegiance to the mystic guilds could boastfully trace at least one of their own ancestral lines back to the founding mystic clans and thereby laid their special claim to the festival as well. The tales of their ancestors who made the arduous journey to the heart of the lost and fallen Rhamasian Empire and claimed its ancient capital as their own had moved beyond pride to political necessity; power and social status had become a question of heritage.

The mystics had expanded their influence from the security of their mountain citadels high in the Forsaken

Mountains to the distant settlements in the Eastern Marches and the Provinces — places whose names sounded more solid than the tentative huts that clutched at those wild lands. There was the sense in every mystic community that the promise of a magical empire was within their collective grasp, especially evidenced by the widely anticipated union of two of the most powerful guild houses in that same year — the House of Conlan and the House of Rennes-Arvad.

Yet, even as the eyes of all the mystics were fixed on their own triumphs and glory down the hundred years of their history, one alteration went unnoticed: the Deep Magic had been changing, too, like a sealed jar of water left on coals long thought cold.

Quiet and forgotten, it was about to explode.

BRONZE CANTICLES, TOME VI, FOLIO 1, LEAF 25

The slats of the wide closed door rattled under the banging fist.

"Hold on! Hold on!" yelled the cooper. He stood stooped over, fitting the staves of the large barrel together carefully inside the temporary upper metal hoop, the bottom ends of the staves gouging into the dirt floor of the shop. Fitting the "rose"—the setting of each stave inside the metal hoop at the base of the barrel—required his concentration; it was certainly no time for him to be disturbed. "Mera! Could you see to the door?"

"I'm gettin' the supper on!"

The fist slammed several times into the door in quick succession.

"Hold on there!" cried the cooper once again toward

the door. The banging stopped. "Mera—just leave it to the girl and give us a hand, will you?"

"I'll not be leavin' this stew, Hengus, were it for the Dragon-Talker hisself calling," the woman's voice called back from the open doorway into what passed as their home. "Last time the girl burned the stew, and you gave us the what for!"

"Damn, woman! It's the door!"

"Then answer it! I'm trying to make us a home in this forsaken place!"

Hengus shook with frustration, his hands slipping. The carefully crafted barrel rose collapsed, the ring falling and rolling loudly into a corner of the shop as the staves splayed outward, clattering against the packed-dirt floor. The cooper would have liked to swear more but knew that he would call more of his wife's ire down on him if he did. This frustrated him all the more, so he raised his wide stained face toward the roof of the shop and roared incoherently toward the ceiling.

The door rattled again, the blows from the outside sounding more insistent than before.

"Coming! I'm coming," Hengus rumbled. He was a large man—largest in the village—and stronger than any two of the local farmers put together. He was naturally large of frame, but bending staves from dawn to dusk had accentuated his already broad shoulders. Sweat glistened from his black curly hair, which he preferred kept short, though lately, it had become more difficult to find anyone who could cut it properly. He also preferred to be clean-shaven, but, as evidenced by the thick stubble on his face, that, too, was becoming a rare extravagance in his life.

He straightened up, turned, and started for the door, then hesitated. Reaching down, Hengus picked up his cooper's hammer, hefted its weight, and then reached for the door latch with his left hand, the hammer cocked back over his head in his right.

"Who's there?"

"Please let us in," came the high-pitched voice.

"It's late—we keep decent hours here. Come back when it's light."

"Please!" The voice was muffled but urgent through the slats of the door. "We need help!"

Hengus set his jaw. They all needed help, he thought, but he reached forward with his hand and pulled back the heavy wooden bolt that held the door closed.

Two men tumbled into his shop through the door, each seeming to support the other as they fell to the dirty floor. They were young, Hengus could see, having barely seen two decades by the look of them. They were coated in dust from the road and smelled as though they had not had a reasonable cleaning in over a month. Still, both wore sandals of remarkable, if somewhat worn, craftsmanship and carried packs on their backs beneath their drab cloaks of sturdy, dull green cloth, but it was their tunics that drew the eye of the cooper at once; even through the coating of powder over them he could see that they were white and that the cloth itself shined in places.

Hengus raised his hammer menacingly. "What do you want?"

One of the young men rolled over, his slender chest working hard as he gasped for breath. His face was pinched and hawkish with small, narrow eyes. The youth's beard had once been carefully trimmed but was now showing itself as having had neglect for some time. It was his high voice Hengus had heard through the door. "Where—where are we?"

"You come banging down my door in the dark of night and don't even know where you be?" Hengus's voice rumbled menacingly as he spoke.

The narrow-faced youth held up his open hands, whether in surrender or defense, Hengus couldn't judge. "Please—we just need to rest for a while—and find out the name of this place."

"This be Wellstead," the cooper answered cautiously, gripping his hammer tighter, his muscles drawing taut in anticipation. "And I be Hengus—and that's all you'll be asking until I get some answers of my own!"

The second youth, drawing himself up on all fours, spoke haltingly in a richer, baritone voice. "Wellstead, eh? We're still in the Eastern Marches, Gaius. Somewhere around a hundred miles south of Traggathia, I think."

"Taking me to places I've never heard of again, Treijan?" Gaius asked through a gulping breath.

"It's a place a good deal further beyond 'never heard of,'" Treijan replied. "'Never heard of' would be relatively close comparatively."

"That's enough out of both of you," Hengus growled. He reached down with his free hand, gathered up the back of Gaius's tunic, and dragged him to his feet. "Out with you both—back to wherever you came from."

"Hengus Denthal, you put him down at once!" His wife stood framed in the doorway to the kitchen. She was a good foot shorter than he was and moved like a bird. She had every appearance of being frail, but Hengus knew better through long experience.

"Mera! Strangers and trouble are one and the same," Hengus whined. "We've enough problems on our own without taking on theirs."

"And whose fault is that?" Mera replied, her dark hair

stuck out at odd angles from her thin face, quivering as she spoke. "Come out to the frontier, you said; let's get us a new start, you said; leave our troubles behind, you said. So we listened to that Pir Aboth talk about how wonderful it would be to serve Satinka in the Marches and came on those stinking colony ships and dragged what little we had out here—and for what?"

"We're the only cooper in this village!" Hengus shouted.

"We're the only *anything* in this village!" Mera shot back. Her dark eyes were blazing but softened suddenly as she turned toward Gaius, still hanging from Hengus's grip. She smiled slightly, self-conscious of her two missing teeth. "Please pardon my husband—he don't know no better. Ain't seen as much of the world as I have in my time."

"That's quite all right, madam," Gaius said as Hengus slowly lowered him to the ground. "We don't mean to bring you any trouble."

"Oh, ain't that nice," Mera cooed, patting down her rebellious hair. "No need to worry about the trouble; we've got a surplus of it—could make a living off of it, if there were a market, you might say."

"Perhaps we can help with that," said the second young man as he stood. He was slightly shorter than the first, with close-cropped dark hair that seemed to bristle from his head. The man's beard showed signs of careful crafting, its edge extending from in front of the ears in a graceful sweep down a strong jawline before it turned abruptly upward and joined at his mustache. A single tuft of hair nestled in the cleft of his chin, an island beneath lips that seemed to naturally smile. His cheeks were apple-rosy, matching his warm, shining eyes. He extended his hand to the slack-jawed and obviously entranced woman. "Please call me Treijan. This is my companion, Gaius. We are—"

"Bards." Mera giggled suddenly as though she were a girl half her age. "I recognized the tunics."

Hengus frowned deeply. "Bards? Then you're mystic heretics come to plague us in our misery."

"No, Master . . . Hengus, isn't it?" Treijan said in his smoothest voice. "We come to sing the songs of the ancients; tell tales of forgotten heroes and search for those who long for a better life."

"Which we would gladly do for you another time," Gaius interjected quickly as he extracted his tunic from the cooper's slackening grip. "Treijan, say good-bye to the nice family. We don't know how long it will be before—"

"But this good man is a cooper," Treijan replied at once, gesturing with a warm smile toward Hengus. "Coopers are esteemed highly in the councils of Calsandria; in fact, as I recall, there is a desperate need for coopers. It would be disrespectful not to return his hospitality and that of his family."

"It would be disrespectful to wait until our problems caught up with all of us, Your High—"

Treijan shot a warning glance at his traveling companion as he abruptly held up a warning finger.

"-and-mighty fellow bard-singer," Gaius finished lamely. "We must be going at once."

"We've seen no sign of our friends for a while," Treijan said in a voice smooth as oil on still water. "I think we might afford the courtesy of answering these good people's questions regarding the doings in the world beyond Wellstead. And who might this be?"

Hengus turned toward the kitchen door once more. His

daughter's dirty face was peering wide-eyed around her mother's skirts.

"I've something to show you," Treijan said to the little girl, crouching down as he reached into his pack.

"We'll have none of your tricks, mystic," Hengus said quickly, though he suddenly realized that the hammer in his raised hand was getting a bit heavy. "If the priest were to find you here, he'd as soon burn down my shop as see you breathing."

"No tricks, Master Hengus." Treijan nodded, still smiling at the little girl. "And believe me, your local priest would rather not know that I was anywhere near him."

The young man pulled out a small folded tapestry cloth which measured barely the length of both his arms. From where he stood Hengus could not see what image the threads made, but he saw the eyes of both his wife and his daughter go wide in wonder.

"Please, Master Hengus, come around and see."

Hengus lowered the hammer and carefully stepped around to where he could see the tapestry. Light from the fires cooking the bound barrel staves he had made earlier in the day illuminated the glittering threads, but he was astonished to see that the threads seemed to be in constant motion, weaving and reweaving themselves in a blur of speed.

"Satinka protect us!" Hengus muttered in awe.

Treijan smiled at the comment but continued to look at the wide-eyed little girl. "Would you like me to tell you a story?"

The girl hid her face in her mother's skirt.

"Go on, now," Mera urged insistently. "Listen to the nice bard."

The girl peeked one eye out of the folds in the cloth and managed to nod just once.

"Well, a long, long time ago, there was a great kingdom where all the towers were sparkling white; where the days were never too hot and the nights were never too cold. There was always fruit on the trees and vegetables in the gardens. The torusks were tame and well behaved, and everyone was happy."

The threads on the tapestry suddenly came alive, forming a breathtaking image of narrow, achingly beautiful towers against a brilliant blue sky. Mountains appeared in the distance, and the lake beyond the towers shimmered.

The girl looked out from the folds in amazement.

"This was Calsandria—the greatest city in the world and the jewel of the entire Rhamasian Empire," Treijan continued quietly. "It was a place where every man could make a difference and every woman find peace. It was a place where children played with the most marvelous toys ever dreamed of. Now, how old are you, uh—"

"Edis," the mother prompted.

"How old are you, Edis?"

The girl remained silent but held up both hands, all fingers and thumbs.

"Ten? My, you are getting older, aren't you?" Treijan smiled. "Well, I'm very sad to tell you that even more than ten years ago—even more than tens of ten years—this wonderful place was lost and vanished."

The image on the tapestry faded away, the threads merging into the same light tan of the rest of the cloth.

"It vanished, all right," Hengus snorted in derision. "The Dragonkings burned its Mad Emperors right off the face of Aerbon, that's what vanished 'em."

"As though they've done us any good," Mera snapped. "Shut up and listen!"

"But this story has a happy ending," Treijan continued to the child. "A long time ago, though not nearly so long ago as Calsandria, there was a man named Galen..."

The threads on the tapestry suddenly reappeared, weaving themselves into the image of a handsome man whose features were strong, his chin held confidently up in a look of strength and defiance.

"Galen was also of the Pir—just like you—but he discovered that he had a special gift from the ancient gods—gods who were older even than the Dragonkings—a gift for the magic of the ancient Rhamasian kings." The tapestry wove and rewove itself to the words that Treijan spoke. "He found that there were many who had this same gift, so he gathered them together out of all the human lands. He sent his son, Caelith, into the terrible peaks of the Forsaken Mountains, and there, led by the ancient gods, he found the long-lost Calsandria left in ruins."

Hengus nodded. "I told you the Dragonkings—"

"Hush!" Mera commanded in no uncertain terms.

"If you live seven times as old as you are now"—Treijan smiled to the girl—"it still would not be as long as the mystics have been in the mountains, rebuilding the majesty of Calsandria. Now its towers shine again, and its name calls to all those who wish to partake in its glory."

Gaius stood at the door, listening. "It's gone quiet, Treijan. We've got to go."

"A city of mystics." Hengus sniffed as he spoke. "A nation of heretics."

"No, not at all," Treijan said, folding up the tapestry quickly and stuffing it back into his pack. "Everyone is welcome there—mystic and commoner both have a place in the glory of Calsandria. Besides, I would think that a concerned husband and parent like yourself would consider not only his own situation but that of his wife and child."

Hengus's eyes narrowed. "You be threatening me?"

"Not at all," the bard said easily as he stood. "There is a place for everyone in Calsandria—especially a talented cooper like yourself—where a fine living might be had."

"And about which we shall tell you another time," Gaius said hurriedly. "Treijan, we've got to go now."

"Besides," Treijan continued, ignoring his companion as he smiled and gently stroked his hand down the child's hair, "one never knows when one of your own might suddenly be found to be one of the Elect. Here among the Pir it is a tragedy. In Calsandria it blesses the entire—"

"*By Hrea!*" Gaius suddenly shouted, stepping back from the door. He held his hands up in front of his face, both hands splayed wide.

Treijan's eyes widened as he put his arms quickly around the woman and child, pulling them down close behind his friend. Hengus angrily stepped forward, reaching his meaty hand down toward the insolent bard.

The shop exploded around them. Planks, fittings, nails, timbers, iron hoops, slates, staves, wedges, planes—all that made up his trade—suddenly whirled away as though hit by a terrible gust of wind. Hengus fell backward, carried with the avalanche of debris. Terrified, the huge man tumbled painfully across the ground, desperate to reach his wife and child. His large left hand somehow found one of the foundation stones of their home, and he pulled himself behind it, eyes closed, waiting for death. But his heart continued to beat, and his bones remained intact.

The sounds rushed away behind him, but still Hengus dared not look up.

A voice rang out in the sudden darkness. "Kneel before the power of Satinka!"

For a moment Hengus thought that the Dragonqueen herself might have been there, blowing destruction across his cooperage.

"Nice spell, Meklos," Gaius rejoined, though he was panting slightly with exertion.

Hengus pulled himself up. His home—or what had been his home—was gone along with the shop, its debris blasted well into the tree line behind its foundations. In its place remained the still-glowing arc of Gaius's magic shielding his friend and Hengus's wife and child. The cooper had been standing too far away from them to be included in the magical shelter; he had been swept away with the rest of the house and saved only by the remaining foundation. Gazing now past the bards to the roadway beyond, Hengus saw a lone, familiar figure standing with a tall staff, the crackling flow of lightning constantly erupting against the bard's shield. Hengus knew the robes instantly.

"Aboth Jefard!" Hengus cried out. He could feel the blood running down the side of his face but tried to ignore it as he staggered to his feet. "Praise Satinka you have come!"

The Aboth took no notice of the cooper, his eyes fixed on the bards even as the lightning continued to flow against the shield. "Hello, old friends. It's been a long and tiresome journey tracking you here."

Treijan looked up from where he was huddled protectively around the woman and child. Mera's face was a mask, her mouth gaping open, the scream lodged silently somewhere in her throat. She crouched, holding her daughter too close to her, muffling her constant sobs. A wicked grin split Treijan's face. "Well, hello to you, too, Meklos! Where's your dragon?"

Gaius winced.

"Insult me all you like, Treijan," the Aboth sneered in return. "I never listen to dead men."

Mera found her voice, her scream erupting from deep inside.

"We might have saved you the trouble," Gaius rejoined, shouting to be heard over Mera's hysteria. "We've a right to be here. According to the Second Eastgate Accords..."

"The Eastgate is a long way from here," Aboth Jefard said, pressing closer, the blue arcs rising in intensity. "You know, I hear bards vanish all the time. The road can be so treacherous—especially in these new eastern colonies."

Hengus's stare shifted from the Aboth to the bards, his wife and little girl, and back again.

"I think you'll agree," Gaius said through gritting teeth, "that this is a little different. We aren't just two more bards who would go missing."

"Oh, I quite agree," Aboth Jefard replied. "The Ost Batar Council will publicly mourn and regret your disappearance along with all of Calsandria. Privately, I suspect, I'll be richly rewarded."

"I see." Gaius nodded and then grunted. "Treijan, I could use a little help here."

His companion stood at once, raising his own hands. The shield glowed brighter as it absorbed the crackling bolts. Hengus could see his wife huddled between the two bards, wide-eyed with terror, her shrill shrieks piercing the night.

"Your Greatness," Hengus said, tears streaming down

his cheeks as he staggered toward the Aboth, keeping well clear of the strange blue sweep of electric fire bombarding the mystics. "Please! My family..."

"Ah, hello, Hengus," the Aboth replied casually, his eyes never departing from his prey. "Sorry about your shop, but this will all be over soon. Four of my companions will be arriving shortly, and then we'll be able to deal with this properly."

"But, Aboth, what of my wife and child?"

"He has a point," Treijan called out. "If this shield falls, you'll kill all of us. Let the woman and child free, Meklos."

"Really?" the Aboth said drolly with his eyebrow arched. "And what of you?"

"Hey." Gaius shrugged. "You can always chase us again tomorrow."

"And we promise not to kill *you* until then," Treijan added.

The Aboth smiled, shaking his head. "Tempting, but I don't think so. I've chased you through your own Songstone gates from Port Stellan all the way to Traggathia just for this moment."

"Sorry to hear that." Treijan's grin dimmed ever so slightly. "A shame we'll have to close those gates—they were quite useful. Still, we can't abide poachers."

"Ah, Treijan; droll to the last." The Aboth turned to the cooper. "Hengus, go and get your local priest. He's not much, but he'll do until my companions arrive."

"But my family!"

"Don't question me!" the Aboth snapped, then drew a quick breath. "They'll be fine. You have my word on it."

Hengus turned, stepping away reluctantly. He glanced down at his right hand, where the hammer, somehow, still remained firmly in his grip. He had the Aboth's word, he told himself.

"So you couldn't wait for the rest of your group, eh, Meklos?" Treijan called out from behind the shield.

"You aren't going anywhere." Aboth Jefard smirked. "Your death will ensure my ascension to the Ost Batar Council."

"Not likely," Treijan scoffed. "I mean, anyone who loses an entire dragon..."

"Shut up, Trei!" Gaius growled, and then called out to the Aboth, his voice heavy with the strain, "And what of Mera here and little Edis—why murder them, too?"

"A few sacrifices must be made in so great a cause." The Aboth smiled. "Even by backwater colonists such as..."

The lightning suddenly vanished. The Aboth's face contorted in a look of pain and surprise, then he pitched forward. The robes crumpled around him as the Aboth fell senseless to the ground.

Behind him stood Hengus, the hammer now stained, still in his hand.

Gaius and Treijan dropped their hands. The blue shield vanished as Hengus staggered numbly toward them. The bards both ran past the cooper toward the still form of the Aboth.

"Is he dead?" Treijan asked Gaius.

"No," his friend answered quickly as he knelt next to the still form in the dirt, examining it critically. "Why? Do you want him to be?"

"I—I tried not to hit him too hard," Hengus stammered from behind the bards, his unfocused eyes staring toward the ground. "I mean, it was my *family*..."

The cooper dropped his bloody hammer to the ground.

Mera stood up and threw her arms around the wide girth of her husband, shaking as she wept. "Hengus! It's gone—our lives are all gone! My mother's pottery—your tools—what are we to do?"

Hengus folded his wife into his thick arms. Edis was clinging to them both. The cooper turned his gaze toward the bards, however, as he answered his wife. "Mera, I think we should try our luck in this Calsandria."

Treijan stepped forward and held out his hand to the cooper. Hengus kept one arm still around his unsteady wife, and he reached out, his grip nearly covering the young bard's hand entirely.

"We don't have much time," Gaius said urgently. "Is there anything you need to take with you?"

The big cooper considered the shattered remains of his home for a moment, then reached down and picked up both his tiny wife and his little girl, lifting them easily from the ground.

"All that's left is right here," he said. "Which way do we go?"

"Oddly enough," Treijan said with a smile, "the first step is largely up to you."

City of Dreams

Hengus led them deep into the woods south of town. He realized that it was one of the few places that he thought of as his own: a copse of trees so thick that it was difficult to pass between the tall, straight trunks without turning sideways. It was not only the place where he came to find the best wood for his barrels but also his own private maze—a place where he could hide among the tall trees from all the world's troubles and have no fear of being found.

The woods abruptly gave way to a small clearing surrounding a craggy stone thrusting upward in its center. Many was the day, Hengus thought, that he had spent a blissful afternoon sleeping on the slope of that outcropping, absorbing whatever sun penetrated the surrounding curtain of trees.

This was his sanctuary.

It was the first place he thought of when the bards asked him for the most secret place he knew.

"Friend Hengus," Treijan said with quiet approval

as his gaze passed over the little clearing, "not even the Hreatic masters themselves could have chosen a better place."

"The foundation's good," Gaius agreed.

Treijan reached down and opened the leather purse attached to his belt. From it he drew a small polished stone shot through with crystal.

Hengus had never seen its like before. "What be that?"

Treijan turned to the cooper and winked. "That, friend Hengus, is a Songstone."

"Does it sing?" the young girl asked hesitantly, her eyes peeking from behind her mother's skirts as she spoke her first words since leaving town.

"Sometimes it does," Treijan answered her directly, "but only if we sing to it first—and in its music is something special. You see, this stone in my hand is only half of the stone; its identical mate is far away from here—hundreds and hundreds of miles—near a place called Styla. That stone—the mate of this one in my hand—sits in a great magical gate hidden at the back of a beautiful canyon. It sits in that gate just waiting to hear the song of this stone in my hand—and *this* stone is just waiting for me to sing to *it* before it will sing to its mate."

"What happens when you sing to it?" Hengus asked with suspicion in his voice.

"Let's find out," Treijan replied.

The young bard stepped quickly to the outcropping of rock at the center of the clearing and carefully set the stone down in a notch in its surface. He then stood back and began to sing a tune toward the rock. His voice was resonant and the tones clear, yet Hengus could not understand any words in the song.

The stone began to sing back to him.

Gaius, his companion, stepped back, a strange, distant look coming over his face.

The rocks of the outcropping began to move.

23 Octinus 591 DK. I, Gaius Petros, am in a strange dream . . .

I stand in the midst of a great city — all contrasting hues of orange, black, and red. Round crimson towers of impossible grace rise above me, their sides rough like the bark of trees and their tops fanning outward like branches supporting a canopy of lace. Jumbled among these are other towers of plainer architecture, some square of fitted stone and others of curving rusted metal, neglected and weathering, their sweeping sides broken in places as they reach toward the dark sky overhead. The foundations of the various towers merge into an incongruous patchwork mass that is cracked by crooked streets. The width of these streets is barely enough to allow me to pass without touching one side or the other. I do not want to touch those walls, for I know that they are colder than I could bear.

Overhead, great balls of flame roll into the sky, illuminating the impossible amalgamation of architectures in crimson light. I cannot hear the fire or smell any smoke, yet I know that somewhere beyond the towers terrible war and death are taking place. I move toward it unwillingly, the dream taking me closer against my will.

I step to the end of the road, looking out onto a market square beyond. Other narrow paths run like gouged stone between the hodgepodge of towers all around the square. I stop—reflecting on the place as my mind searches for its meaning.

If the mystics have learned anything, it is that the dream is meaning. Every nuance of stone, every turn of wood or craft, each creature we encounter in circumstances mundane or bizarre—each is a token of deeper power and understanding. Everything here is context; nothing here is real. The demons and spirits that we encounter here are merely the more complex manifestations of underlying truth and magical force. So it behooves us to walk among these phantoms of the dream and take the time to ponder the underlying energies and metaphors that affect our waking reality.

So what is the meaning behind this bizarre collection of streets and towers, walls and avenues? Different things to different mystics, I believe, as each mystic's perceptions are his own; but for me, the city was built—if such a term can be applied to a nonexistent place—by the mystics as a symbol of order; a framework for understanding the deeper symbolism of the dream. Here mystics prowl among the chaos of streets, buildings, rooms, and halls that are ever changing and never the same, meeting furtively and, when necessary, defending themselves from assault by our enemies. The City of Dreams is the very symbol of the dream of every mystic in the waking world—the realization of our destiny and security in a Mystic Empire.

For me now, however, it has become a maze of frustration, for I have searched its confusion of streets in vain; Treijan is somewhere walking among the buildings but cannot be found. In the waking world we have made our plans as to how we might find each other in the streets of the City of Dreams, and yet though many a terrible and wonderful mask I have seen, his is not among them.

As I consider buildings around me, hoping for some meaning evident amid their chaos, a creature comes into the square from the opposite alleyway, drawing me out of my reverie. He is a living marionette—a figure like a man but with the wings of a great moth who dances across the courtyard to the pulling of thin golden ropes fixed to his knees, arms, head, and back that stretch upward into the leaden sky. He has the form of those good spirits who are often so helpful to us but never elsewhere so cruelly suspended and fettered. I have seen him manifest before—a youth with straight long hair the color of midnight. At the twitching of the ropes his limbs float strangely and he walks unnaturally across the stone paving of the square, his head lolling toward the ground and his eyes averted.

The marionette-man gazes upward as he nears the center of the square. My eyes follow his and I am aghast: the golden ropes lead to the fingers of an enormous hand formed of shadow and smoke hovering over the city. Beyond, gazing down at us is a giant of like substance with an arc of lightning defining its edges. The giant gazes down at us; an enormous blackness against the flaming sky. The power in this colossal figure is undeniable; his maniacal laughter peals through the streets of the city, shaking the foundations of the buildings and threatening their destruction. This giant is without reason and without remorse—an insane child— and all the dream is its toy.

The winged spirit raises his hands in front of him—a motion which slacks the golden ropes—then closes both hands into fists and presses them against his own chest.

I recognize it at once, for it is the first step in any greeting in the dream: the beginning of a language of magic that goes beyond words and directly to symbolic communication. These hand gestures, arm positions, and body contortions have evolved tremendously in recent years, allowing mystics to communicate their desires more effectively in the dream and thereby make the power of the dream in the real world more focused and controllable. It is not a true language as we speak in the waking world, and the interpretation of the gestures is more guesswork than fixed concept; yet even a general understanding is better than none.

As I watch the winged spirit's hands move, I see the gigantic hands above begin to answer him back in like moves. Yet the motions of enormous fingers suddenly tug violently at the ropes, jerking the winged spirit about the courtyard, slamming its body with reckless violence against walls, doors, and windows. Wood cracks, glass shatters, and yet both the hands of the powerful giant and the body of the winged spirit are locked in their dance of accord, unable or unwilling to stop. Again the mad laughter of the shadow-giant peals like thunder through the streets, echoing off the walls of the city. As each continues, the area around the winged spirit begins to change. Snow begins to fall around the spirit, materializing out of the air around him. I see the winged spirit smile, although its eyes are creased with pain, blood trickling down from its forehead.

Then a short metal demon—a female by the shape of her—enters the far end of the square trailing many long chains behind her, which rattle against the cobblestones as she moves. I am astonished, for the she-demon is surrounded by a spinning ring of fire. She tries to get the attention of the winged spirit suspended just a handbreadth above the square, but the spirit is dancing frantically now at the end of the ropes and does not see her. In frustration the demon suddenly lashes out with her chains, which reach like tentacles and wrap themselves around the spirit — trying somehow to both break the golden ropes and ensnare the winged spirit in her own bonds. The metal demon-woman is pulling the winged spirit toward her and the burning ring that surrounds her.

The monstrous, insane shadow-creature howls above the tops of the city towers as its toy is being snatched from it. It pulls angrily back, lifting both the winged spirit and the metal demon from the ground, then angrily swings them about, crashing them against the walls of the city, trying to shake the demon loose from its plaything, but everywhere the flaming ring hits, the buildings explode, then suddenly collapse in on themselves, falling to rubble in the street. The city is falling around me — the empire being destroyed — and I see everything that the mystics have built in the last five decades crumbling around me.

I search desperately for some companion in the dream through which I can connect with the Deep Magic and somehow stop this horrendous beast in its mindless destruction, but there is none apparent.

It is then that I notice the golden cords around my own hands and feet. I try to scream, but no sound comes from my throat. I am yanked from my hiding place by the enormous hand overhead.

Hanging limply above the ground, I know that I am powerless; I must bend my will to serving the insane monster, or the empire is doomed.

Once upon another time, in a distant land of
myth . . . I, Arryk, Sharajin of the Sharajentei faery, see
a strange vision . . .

Not that I had not had the vision before — the <u>Sharaj</u>
is a place more like home to me than the waking world.
Here I can be who I wish, go where I want unhindered by
the fetters of life that are so cruelly imposed upon me.

Thick snow drifts downward between the soaring
walls, silencing the murmur of the world beneath its chill.
There is peace in its grasp, a blanket that seems almost
warm to me as it hides the rest of the world beneath
its cold, dead purity. I leisurely beat my wings as I fly
down the streets of the <u>Sharaj,</u> searching for my powerful
friend through the veil of white, but I cannot find him. I
drift down the narrow alleyways of the Citadel, averting
my eyes when anyone approaches me — especially the
masked ones who have no gift. I hate them. They all
want something from me. Perhaps that is why I am so
comfortable in the obscuring snowfall; it adds to the
confusion of the faery towers mixed with the broken rock
and dirty metal towers so that the whole place looks like
it was filled with the trash of the <u>Sharaj</u> that built it. I
rather like it — so confused and disordered — everything
the Fae are not and everything that I would rather be.

The alley ends abruptly in a wide courtyard obscured
by rolls of drifting snow. Various other streets angle
away from the open space, their darkness softened by
the white falling veil. On the far side of the courtyard
I see my friend — a shadow formed of black smoke, his
face hidden behind the folds of a black hooded cape,
yet I know this wingless spirit and trust him like no other

in or out of the <u>Sharaj</u>. There is an aura around him, unsettlingly blue, powerful and compelling; a strength we share that makes us invincible. As he approaches, I can see the tendrils of his power reaching out toward me, the blue lines of our shared power. I smile and nod toward him in greeting as the filaments connect between us, making one our hands, legs, and minds.

We cross the courtyard at the same time, coming to stand before each other. My hooded friend nods toward me, holding his fists closed before him and pressing them against his chest. I do likewise, following the ritual of the <u>Sharaj</u>. In moments his gestures begin, and I reply with gestures of my own. It is the way of the <u>Sharaj</u>: how we Seekers of the Power relate to the strange place filled with images and sounds that have no reality—and yet this phantom man has become more a friend to me than any of those cold souls in the world of reality. Together our powers are greater than any I have ever encountered—and no Fae warrior known can stand against me in the real world with my spirit friend beside me in the world of dreams.

Behind my friend an enormous tower of metal shifts, groaning with a squeal that hurts my ears. It is rising up, pulling other towers toward it, forming hideous arms and legs around a headless torso. Great flat sheets of tin rattle through the snow, fastening themselves together into great harpylike wings. The giant now moves toward my friend, long steel claws at the ends of its enormous fingers plunging downward. Instinctively, I raise my hands to draw strength from my friend, to destroy this terror that threatens him . . .

But I am powerless to move my hands. They hang limp at my sides. I try to call out to my friend, though I know my words will pain him greatly, but the snow muffles my voice so that the words die in the chill air. I press forward, trying to move toward him, but my feet have become as lead beneath the snow and I can but inch painfully forward.

Snow erupts from one of the drifts, obscuring my vision. When it clears, I see a centaur charging across the courtyard, magic impossibly dancing from its fingertips. It charges the animated tower giant, the light from its hands shining upward through the snow and pressing the creature away from my friend, who seems unaware of the gigantic danger behind him. In agony the metallic monster stumbles, slipping in the snow.

The giant falls over, its mass tumbling toward the centaur and my friend. I break free of my lethargy and charge toward him, hoping that I can save him. To be without him would be to be alone . . .

FAERY TALES
BRONZE CANTICLES, TOME XIV, FOLIO 1, LEAVES 6–15

I am Lunid, Deep Tinker of the academy — the Deepest Tinker at that — and I dreamed a perfectly reasonable dream, so there is no need to be critical of it whatsoever. You probably had even stranger dreams that you won't even talk about, so you have no excuse for complaining about my dream. If you haven't had any strange dreams, then I honestly don't know why I am even talking to you, because you won't understand a thing I am saying — so leave me alone!

I would be sorry for what I just said, but as an academic I am forbidden to be mistaken in anything I say. However, academics are allowed to correct themselves, so let me offer you my heartfelt correction; I am a bit sensitive when it comes to these dreams. Maybe you can understand—or maybe you can't—but if I hadn't found this dream, I would never have found him, and if I had never found him, then perhaps I would never have felt alive. Who would have thought that a female of my standing—one of the most honored Deep Tinkers of our time—should find herself in this position? My days are so bound up in the importance of my work, in the books that I examine and the new and wonderful devices that I create through them, that I never thought—never hoped—that I could find anything so compelling, so achingly consuming, or so painfully beautiful anywhere beyond the four walls of my research cell.

What? The dream? Oh, yes, of course . . .

I was in the magical place of technomancy—the realm of the gods; a world which lies apart from the silly world in which you live. You probably don't understand this—being untrained as you are—but I stood in the city there, a place that is grand and wonderful beyond description. Towers of rusted steel and stone and brick reached up into the rain-soaked sky with lightning dancing between their peaks. Thunder rolled in great, shattering peals down the narrow streets and alleys that ran like the lines of shattered glass through the buildings. Everywhere there were giant wheels and gears drenched in the downpour, some of them moving and others just ornately supporting the walls of buildings, which . . .

Yes, I know I said it was beyond description. I was just trying to illustrate how far beyond description it was. Never correct an academic, sister; only academics are allowed to correct. It's in the rules; look it up.

The deluge continued as I made my way down the narrow streets. The walls on either side of me were comprised of gigantic covers of books. Understand that everything in the realm of the gods means something other than what it looks like, which is a concept I cannot begin to explain to you now, perhaps later. For now just understand that the covers of books represent the covers of books, and we'll leave it at that.

The narrow street opened onto a great park like the one in the center of the academy. The ground was soaked, and the grass felt spongy beneath my toes.

I looked up through the veil of driving rain and saw that I was not alone. Two of the gods were coming into the park, making signs at each other in the language of the gods.

You want to speak to the gods? Well, it all has to do with using your hands and your feet and your ears to let the gods in the dream know just what you want, and they usually give it to you, but sometimes they ask for something in return. Don't try it yourself; only technomancers and academics are smart enough to understand how to speak hand-and-foot language. It all has to do with the power of books, and you don't want to get me started on that.

What? Oh, the City of the Gods, yes . . .

One of the gods before me was a god of smoke and darkness looking much like one of those tall, ugly beings so commonly found in the City of the Gods. He walked through the rain with his face hidden in a smoke-colored cloak, and he moved onto the grass at the far side of the park. He had apparently lost his wits and was having no luck in finding them again. He did not see me at first, standing there at the edge of the park, but he drew out his weapons anyway—long, narrow blades keen and bright.

Then, through the rain from a side street, he came— the most beautiful and perfect god-thing I had ever seen.

There was something about his form—the delicate wings, the dark hair, the peaked ears—that appealed to me, but it was his eyes—his black, pain-filled eyes—that captured my heart and froze my soul at a glance.

I knew that I had to have this creature; it was not enough to see him or remember his face and form. I had to possess him, keep him, and be near him. It was then that I saw an image of the rings of bronze and gears to make the rings move as well as the book-sinks I could use to channel the power of the dream and reach across the park and capture this beloved god-thing and make it my own.

The dark-cloaked figure approached my beautiful creature, who smiled at the man. The dark figure then suddenly plunged his swords with incredible precision through the wrists of the beautiful winged man. The dark figure giggled hysterically, making my winged love, his dark eyes filled with agony, move his arms about on the tips of his swords.

The lightning crashed once more, and the dream dissolved in the rain, but those dark, pain-filled eyes continuously filled my mind even when I was awake. Finding him has consumed me from that time on. I will have him. I will save him—and he will save me.

LUNID RECONSTRUCTED*
BRONZE CANTICLES, TOME XIII, FOLIO 4, LEAVES 10—22

---

*All excerpts from this work are taken from *Lunid Reconstructed: An Interpretive Monologue*, by Lunid the Sixteenth, from the official Academicia Hobgoblica Revisional History Performance as later transcribed in the Bronze Canticles.

Calsandria

Lightning flashed in Treijan's eyes, his ears hurting from the change in the air around him. As many times as he had traversed the gates, this final passage was always the most difficult, the most welcoming, and, for him at least, the most depressing. For Treijan, home was the most dangerous place he could be.

Not that his opinion was ever shared by those who journeyed with him. Gaius, of course, was ever at his side and, Treijan knew, preferred the safe anonymity of being anywhere else in the world, but the pilgrims who accompanied them on each return—there was a different story. They, too, were often blinded as they emerged, and their ears were slightly deafened to the din around them. That always cleared up quickly as eyes and ears became accustomed. Then, as predictable as the sunrise, each in turn would drop his jaw in amazement.

Surprisingly, however, Treijan found himself standing in a downpour. Thick clouds had gathered overhead and were raining torrents down around him.

Treijan turned reflexively, even as his own blinking eyes quickly adjusted to the dim light. There, towering over him, stood gate number fifteen, also known as the Margravian Gate. Water cascaded over the vertical archway of rough-hewn stone, slightly taller than its twenty-foot width, as it stood on its wide marble pedestal. The inner space was shimmering blackness like a liquid jewel. At the top of the gate shined the Songstone, the key of the mystic energy that bound this gate to its matching twin more than eight hundred miles from where he now stood. It was an incredibly great distance but one which he had just covered in a single step. The gate stood apart from the high curtain wall of smooth, fitted stones that curved gently inward to enclose the large courtyard. Out of the corner of his eye, Treijan could see several other gates of similar design which lined the interior of the wall—the focal point of all the journeys of the bards.

Hengus Denthal and his little family stepped through the shimmering black of the gate, followed almost at once by Gaius. Treijan quickly called on the magic within him, saw the image of the winged creature in his mind, and saw him sheltered beneath a tree. The image took shape in his hands, and in the instant, a dome formed over Hengus and his family, shielding them from the downpour. Despite the weather, the cooper and his family proved to be no exception to Treijan's expectations: each in turn blinked, then stopped, stunned into immobility on the platform surrounding the gate. Tears welled up in Hengus's eyes as he pulled his wife and daughter to him. Treijan smiled wearily and turned to follow their gaze.

Before them, rising into rain-laden sky, stood the five delicate, incredibly ornate towers that surrounded the central domed keep of the Citadel. The towers were of varying lengths, as though the fingers of a hand were cradling the keep between them. The light of a fork of lightning exploded off the dome in a rainbow of colors. Concourses of delicate carvings decorated the entire structure, each tower capped by tall, pointed cones for roofs.

"I—I've never seen the like!" Hengus stammered.

Gaius's high voice was bright as he stepped around the stunned family. "It is the Citadel of Calsandria—and it has taken nearly all of the seventy years since the mystics returned here to restore it to its former glory. It is the center of the Mystic Empire—of which you are now a part. Ah, here is someone now to see you."

A young woman with clear, smooth skin and large dark eyes approached, while two men followed discreetly. All three of them wore robes of brilliant white, and all stood beneath their own protective domes, which were only noticeable by the way they interrupted the fall of rain. The woman walked directly to Treijan and bowed. "My name is Mistress Keili. Masters Treijan and Gaius, may I welcome you home to Calsandria."

The cooper and his daughter both stared in speechless awe. His wife began to tug at her ragged clothing.

Treijan bowed quickly. "Mistress Keili, may I present Master Hengus Denthal; his wife, Mera; and their daughter, Edis. He is a cooper who wishes to be a part of the glory that is Calsandria."

Mistress Keili's rapturous face turned its warm gaze to the newcomers, her clear, bright voice cutting across the hush of the rain on the cobblestones underfoot. "Hengus, Mera, and Edis, you must be tired from your journey, and there is much to be done still. This is Master Jochan and Master Lindly—we are here to take care of you." She reached her arm out invitingly. "Mistress Mera, perhaps you would like to change?"

"Oh," Mera stuttered, her eyes cast down. "I'm afraid I've not got anything. I mean..."

Keili's smile seemed to brighten the air around them despite the gloom as she took Mera's arm. "Not to worry! I'm sure I can find something that will please you."

Mera smiled shyly even as she and her family were being led toward the central Citadel. "Oh, thank you, deary."

Gaius stepped up under the rain shield next to his companion, and the two of them watched the family as they were led, still in shock, toward one of the many doors entering the Citadel. Treijan looked around the immense enclosure of the courtyard. Other groups, some small and others large, were emerging from other gates. Each in turn was being greeted warmly by white-robed mystics under a rain shield, and each in turn was being led into the towering central structure.

"Do you think they have any idea what they are getting into?" Gaius asked.

Treijan raised his eyebrow. "Do any of them? Hengus is a cooper, and that's a valuable skill. He'll be placed in a good shop and no doubt provide a better living for his family than he could have hoped for out in the Eastern Marches."

"But they are only commoners," Gaius remarked.

Treijan snorted. "Haven't you heard? The empire of the mystics is open equally to all."

"Only some of us are more equal than others," Gaius sniffed.

Treijan turned to his friend with a wary eye. "We're not

going to have this succession-of-bloodlines debate again, are we?"

"It's easy to dismiss the argument," Gaius observed with a frown, "when the status quo serves the one doing the dismissing."

Treijan shook his head. "The Patents of Bloodline were established in 547, Gaius; that's before you and I had any say in it. It's kept the clans intact since then, and it's sound policy. Everyone knows that strength in the Deep Magic passes down from parentage. That stronger bloodlines rule the Council of Thirty-six only makes sense. Otherwise, the stronger lines would be challenging the weaker ones for supremacy, and where would that leave us?"

"Right where we are now, *Your* Highness," Gaius sneered.

Treijan grimaced. "Must you say my title that way? I am the prince of House Rennes-Arvad, after all."

"Indeed," Gaius responded coolly. "A fact which this lesser cousin of House Petros could hardly forget."

"I don't see what you're so sour about," Treijan replied. "Your grandmother was Chystal Arvad; my grandfather was her brother Aremis. We're both descendants of Caelith Arvad. Good bloodlines both, eh?"

"Yet your house directs the empire and mine does not," Gaius answered with a sideways glance. "So some of us are less equal than others."

Treijan shrugged. "That's the way it's been since the old clans began gathering." The prince turned as he started walking toward the tower gate through the outer curtain wall of the Citadel. "Are you coming?"

"You do realize that there are those who think that a change is due," Gaius said, stepping quickly to catch up to his companion and his shield.

"Why, Gaius," Treijan smirked, "did I just hear a threat from House Petros?"

"More like a friendly warning."

"Well, in my experience no warning is ever friendly," Treijan said cheerfully as the two of them stepped up to the portcullis. It rose with remarkable silence. "Indeed, there are some things for which warning might best be left unsaid. Take our friend Hengus, for example, and his family."

"What of them?" Gaius asked.

Treijan stepped through the opening and continued toward the other end of the wide passage with Gaius at his heels. He sustained the invisible shield overhead, since he would need it again shortly. "Well, if we had warned him and his family that they were stepping into a killing field in that courtyard back there—explained to them that the curtain wall was constantly ringed with Ekteiatic guardians who were prepared to strike them dead at the slightest provocation—they might have not stepped so easily through that last gate. If we had informed them that Mistress Keili largely got her position as a greeter because of her ability to instantly freeze the heart of any enemy she touches, they might not so readily have taken her guidance."

"The Citadel is as much for their protection as it is for ours," Gaius rejoined.

"Of course it is," Treijan agreed, stopping once again before a second closed portcullis at the opposite end of the passage. The portcullis behind them was quietly dropping back into place. "But warning them of the fact wouldn't make them any more comfortable with it."

"We could explain why—"

"Yes, I suppose we could," Treijan said, interrupting

his companion. He was enjoying the discourse; the exploration of the position in his mind. "We could explain that the gates are only seven years old and that we had a really remarkable set of linked gates all the way from Vestadia to the Five Domains, which seemed like a good idea until we discovered that both the Pir Drakonis and the Jorgandian Revisionists could use our gates as well. So we had to tear down our original gates—or as many as we could find—and build up a new and far more secret set. Then we could further explain that those gates, no matter how well hidden, still occasionally get compromised, like they did with our friend Aboth Jefard and his overzealous Revisionist priests. That the reason he had to put his family in mortal danger is our fear that one day the Pir or the Revisionists will either find their way to one of the final gates or discover a lost Songstone and build a final gate that will bring their armies into this selfsame charming Citadel courtyard at the very heart of our empire. We could explain all *that* to them—but somehow I just don't think they would find it that comforting."

The second portcullis began rising. Treijan could see the rain-soaked intersection of wide, curving streets beyond. He knew them at once as the place where the Garden of Dhalia met the long Rhamas Way. The street was teeming with people dashing through the rain either to or from Guild Alley to the north. Through the sheets of rain he could see across the street to the corner of Galen's Tomb—the reconstructed temple that housed the bones of his ancestors. Further still, he could make out the hazy outlines of the River Ehru and the ancient villas that stood on the opposite bank.

"So you're saying that it's better not to have any warning about what's about to happen to you?" Gaius asked casually.

"If there's nothing you can do about it and nothing they can do about it, why cause anyone stress?" Treijan smiled. "Which reminds me: the message we received in Margrave said that my mother has organized a ball for this evening and that my father demanded that I attend. Mother hasn't thrown a ball since I was ten, so do you have any idea why we were really called home?"

Gaius turned to his friend and stared at him for a moment.

"Well, do you?"

A sly smile flitted across Gaius's taut lips. "I think maybe you're right, Your Highness. Some things are better faced without warning."

"Honestly, Gaius, I sometimes wonder whose side you are on," Treijan said with some irritation. "Say, look across the river. Someone has rebuilt one of the river villas since we've been away. Do you know who?"

Gaius, to Treijan's great annoyance, threw back his head and laughed loudly.

The Watchers

I am Theona Conlan.

I do not know why I write these things. There is little enough time in my day for such nonsense, but no one in my family will give me any rest until I write down my dreams.

It is futile; it is different each time, but it is still the same dream. Sometimes it is in our old home in Aquilas and sometimes in the new home. Sometimes I think it is in the halls of the Pillar of the Sky or in the courts of the Arvad Keep, although it looks nothing like either of those places. Sometimes it is in the City of Dreams or in places I have heard of but never been, and often it is not in any place at all.

I'm trying to be accurate. Father tells me that the details are crucial if I am ever to gain the Deep Magic. He is wrong; it is just a dream—nothing more. Sometimes I think I am seeing the dream that the mystics all talk about, yet the pictures keep shifting in my mind and they seem nothing like the ones that Valana describes. I know that my sister means well—that she is just trying to help her little sister "become more" (whatever that means)—but I have tried for years, and the magic is not found in my dreams. She has always had the Gift. She cannot comprehend that there are dreams that are just dreams and have nothing to do with the Deep Magic. She just does not understand. None of them do. But still, I write for them.

In my dream I see myself walking along the peristyle that surrounds the central atrium in our new home. I walk slowly past pillars lining the peristyle, aware of the broken frescoes framed into the wall on my right, though I could hardly tell of any of their details. Everything is black shadows and red glow. The sky overhead glows a deep crimson, framed by the dark eaves of our house roof yet another story above me. Through the space between the pillars I see that the young trees in the garden on my left are burning, each leaf a fanning flame, their bark curling and blackening in the heat. The long pool in the center of the garden is dry and cracked.

The servants rush past me like shadows, all of them panicked and clutching something in their hands. I try to call out to them—as father had instructed me that I must—but they take no notice either of my words or of my being here at all. Instinctively, I turn, facing back the way I came.

It is Valana. She drifts into the atrium through the archway from the grand hall, the hem of her elegant red dress not touching the ground. She glides between the burning trees and above the dried pool toward a man who stands in the vestibule at the opposite end of the atrium.

This stranger wears the clothes of a traveler, filthy from long journeys, and his face is veiled in shadow. Valana moves into his open arms, and they begin to dance, but with every step her dress becomes soiled with the filth covering him. Soot stains spread across the fabric. Valana sees what is happening to her dress, great tears welling up in her eyes and clearing streaks down her now dirty cheeks, but she cannot stop dancing.

There is no sound in my dream, but I feel within me a thunderous banging at the door. The veil-faced man lets go of Valana and steps back into the vestibule of our home. I can see the entry doors, shaking with the impact of a terrible force outside. It is a howling beast, ravenous and mindless, whose appetite is insatiable. It tears great, splintering holes in the thick timbers of the door. The traveler moves to stop the unseen beast, but it somehow knows he is coming. It reaches in, a black nothingness, and lifts up the man off the ground by his neck. The traveler shakes violently before me, his arms bouncing like a child's marionette in the hands of the unseen creature. Suddenly, the darkness withdraws back beyond the doors. The body of the traveler falls to the tiles of our entry, a dark stain growing beneath him.

Valana does not move. No emotion shows on her face. I am terrified but find myself moving unwillingly toward the door. I cannot help myself. I go unnoticed past Valana. The traveler lies before me with his face turned away. I reach down to turn him over, to see his face at last, but the beast is reaching through the doors, its darkness rushing up toward me, engulfing me —

* * *

The thunderclap and the word were simultaneous, one nearly burying the other.

"Theona!"

Startled, Theona Conlan jerked her head up from the table and tried to focus. The room was darker than she expected, and she wondered if she had accidentally slept into the evening. Then she heard the gentle hiss of rain against the roof tiles punctuated by the cascades splashing in the atrium just beyond the open doorway. The air smelled musty and damp with not a little tincture of awakening mold. The afternoon light was dimmed by the storm.

"Here!" she called out, trying to rub the tiredness out of her face as she stood up. Her chair—an elegant and formal piece entirely out of place at the rough-hewn table here in the kitchen—clattered across the carefully restored mosaic floor. The fires in the twin hearths had collapsed on themselves, their embers hoarding what remained of their heat. She would have to do something about that, but for the moment could not remember if she would be feeding all of the family or just the staff that night. One fire or two, she thought ruefully; such were the momentous decisions of her life.

"Where are you?" called the echoing voice through the loud pattering of rain.

"Coming, father!" Theona called out, raising her voice. Her father may be the head of one of the most important bloodlines in all the Clan Territories, she thought as she moved toward the open doorway, but the title did nothing for his hearing. She pressed her hands flat against her stomach, trying to smooth out the folds in her still-damp traveling dress. She sighed as her hands came to rest against her hips; her waist was too wide. "But just right for you," she murmured to herself, echoing her mother's favorite phrase, typically uttered immediately after a softly critical remark.

Theona stepped out onto the colonnade, the covered walk that surrounded the atrium at the center of the ancient mansion, and took in a deep breath. The rain was thinning, and the sky was turning a lighter hue of steel gray. Water still ran in sheets down the linked tiles of the roof—she would have to remember to check for leaks—and sloshed into the ornate pool brimming in the center of the atrium. She loved the rain; it drew a curtain across the world for a time, bringing the horizons of its adventure and promise almost within her reach.

Almost.

She turned toward the footsteps trudging toward her. The portly servant turned her face quickly away but was too late; she had already caught Theona's eye.

"Agretha," Theona called out in gentle command.

"Yes, m'lady."

"The fires in the kitchen have gone cold. Would you see that one of them is properly laid and stoked for the night?" Theona's voice made it clear this was not a request.

"Yes, m'lady."

"Have all the servants found their new quarters? The plan is smaller than the old house in Aquilas, and I want everyone settled as soon as possible."

"Yes, m'lady—all settled."

"Oh, and do you know if that lost torusk ever turned up?"

"No, m'lady. You'll have to ask Jon Kraggert about

that, ma'am." Agretha sighed as she turned to enter the kitchen.

"Agretha, one more thing," Theona said.

The servant stopped, her eyes averted. "Yes, m'lady?"

"Build the fire well and then off with you," Theona said softly, her expression almost distracted. "I suspect your own things are piled in a frightful mess in your room. Best for us all if you take some time to put it all right."

"Well, ma'am, truth be told, I don't have that much…"

"Agretha, I'm letting you go for the evening," Theona said quietly, bending her head toward the servant as she spoke through her perpetual slight frown. "You might also let the rest of the staff know that each of them will be given their own time in the next three nights to settle into their rooms. They may sleep, or they may enjoy some time in town—so long as they go only when I tell them and so long as the master and mistress do not hear about it. Now, get my fire built, and if Jon Kraggert crosses your path, send him to me."

Agretha managed a weary-laden smile. "Thank you, ma'am. Hrea bless you, ma'am."

"Thank you, Agretha," Theona said, straightening. "I pray that she does. Was my father shouting for me?"

"Yes, ma'am." Agretha nodded toward the back of the atrium. "He's in the great hall."

Theona nodded, then turned to her left, passing quickly around the peristyle to the back of the atrium. There, situated in the center of a large archway, sat a statue of a Rhamasian man seated on a massive throne. The carving had been rescued from somewhere in the vast field of rubble that still covered more than nine-tenths of the original city. Her father had insisted on placing it here where any visitors could admire its perfection of form and, more important, the wealth and power implied in owning such a beautiful piece of original Rhamasian art.

Theona, however, was drawn to it for other reasons. The man sat leaning forward on his throne, fixed forever in his eager posture, at ease with power in the way he held his hands and determination in his cold, blank eyes. She looked up into his face. Stains on the stone made the statue appear to weep.

"Handsome and young," she said to the statue as she paused next to it, laying her hand against the chill, pitted marble. "Were you one of the Mad Emperors? Do you know what has happened to your kingdom and your power? How do you feel about being reduced to an ornament in the House of Conlan?"

The statue ignored her.

"Well, since I am not a craft-talker, your secret's safe with me," Theona said, patting the statue.

"Theona! There you are—I've been looking everywhere for you!"

Theona turned toward the voice. "Apparently, not everywhere, father, or you would have found me."

"What?"

"Yes, father," Theona said more distinctly and slightly louder. "You have found me."

"And none too soon." Rylmar Conlan might once have been a handsome man. He had a wide-shouldered build and bright eyes nearly hidden behind the too-well-padded evidence of his opulence. His weight always increased with his success, and from the look of him Theona concluded that business had never been better. His hair was thinning at the crown, and his forehead had migrated so far back that it reached nearly perpendicular to his ears.

Still, anyone in business with Rylmar would be at a great disadvantage to think that his physical softness translated into his business dealings . . . or his ambitions for his family. Indeed, the reason for their move from their larger and more comfortable home in Aquilas into this smaller ruin was entirely a question of social architecture: the right home in the right district at the heart of the empire's power. The elder Conlan put out his arm for his younger daughter; she took it graciously, and he led her back past the statue and through the archway.

The great hall had been carefully restored to its previous dimensions while still allowing the original frescoes on the walls to remain in their broken and faded state. It was all the fashion in Calsandria, Rylmar had explained to Theona when she first arrived, to leave the recently recovered wall art and mosaics in their distressed condition whenever possible. It was a sign of respect to the original Rhamasians—whoever they were.

Now the great hall had new upper walls and a restored roof almost twenty feet overhead. Each of the walls featured original frescoes, though Theona noted that some clearly came from other villas. The images in the frescoes native to the house progressed from one frame to the next, telling a larger story, and the obvious addition of other frescoes spoiled that effect.

In the midst of these walls covered by faded faces sat a lengthy new banquet table. To Theona's right a wide marble staircase made its way up to the second floor—perfect for making a grand entrance into the hall. On the other side of the table the hall opened onto a large, curving patio overlooking the outer garden that sloped down toward the river. Beyond that, Theona could not see through the gray mists of rain.

"So where were you?" Rylmar asked gently.

"Honestly, father, I fell asleep in the kitchen." Theona laughed slightly.

"I guess we're all a bit tired. Moving is so unsettling. A nap is well-spent time."

"I wish I hadn't—I had this terrible dream and—"

"You had a dream?" Rylmar stopped, excited, turning his daughter toward him. "Was it a Deep Dream?"

"No, father, it wasn't. I—"

"You know the different disciplines experience the dream differently. It might be Hreatic Muse or Mnemeatic Divination. Are you familiar with Ekteiatic or Skureatic disciplines?"

"Yes, I'm familiar, father—and this is none of those."

"I've heard of some Rhamasic disciplines—rare ones—that have dreams, and they became Catalysts..."

"Father, no. I know all the disciplines, and this is nothing like that."

"Well, did you try to contact anyone there—speak to them?"

"Yes, father!"

"And?"

"It was just a *dream*," Theona said flatly, her eyes fixed on her father.

Rylmar nodded, turning away. "Oh, well, you never know..."

She heard the disappointment in his voice, saw it in his eyes, and her heart tore once again.

"You know, you're only twenty-two—"

"I'm twenty-four, father."

"Really? Well, twenty-four isn't so old." Rylmar nodded, taking her hand again but not looking her in the eye. The rain had nearly stopped, and he began leading her out toward the patio. "I heard just the other day of a young man—and a first-bloodline family, too—who was twenty-*five* before the Deep Dreams came to him, and now they say he could be the most powerful of the lot."

Theona wanted desperately to change the subject. "We lost one of the wagons coming in, father, but I am sure it will turn up. I believe it took a wrong turn in the ruins. If it doesn't arrive by morning, then—"

"That's not important," Rylmar said as they stepped onto the wet stones under a light mist. "What do you think?"

The rains had lifted as a cool breeze followed them down the River Ehru below. House Conlan was situated up above the riverbank. The front of the house opened onto Temple Way, but the back of the house looked out across the river toward . . .

"Calsandria," Theona murmured.

The misty veil pulled back. Even under the gray clouded sky, the towers of Calsandria, painstakingly restored over the past sixty years, rose up from the opposite bank of the river in arching splendor. The delicate spindles of Arvad Keep—the center of House Arvad since Caelith claimed it as his own nearly eighty years before—shone even in the dull light following the storm.

Rylmar smiled and raised his hand, gesturing in the air as though waving to someone across the river.

Suddenly, the clouds parted, and a shaft of light cut through the gloom, illuminating brilliantly beyond the spires of Arvad Keep the glorious edifice known fondly as the Citadel. Ornate and delicate spires in concourse after concourse reached into the sky, each spire of a different length, around a central crystal dome. The ray of sunlight caught the crystal panes, exploding into a rainbow of colors.

Theona smiled sadly. "Thank you, father. It must have taken a lot for you to arrange the weather like this."

"Oh, not so much." Rylmar shrugged, then cleared his throat. "Ah, Theona, your mother and I have a social engagement this evening—as does your sister. It's very important."

Only one fire tonight, Theona thought to herself.

"It's at Brenna Tower with the Theleic masters. I know it's a lot to ask of you, especially after bringing in the caravan today and all, but—"

"It's all right, father, I understand perfectly," Theona replied. "You're going to impress the powerful and the wealthy; I'm staying home to unpack."

Rylmar looked sharply at his daughter, drawing a considered breath. "We all have a part to play here, Theona. Valana has hers and you have yours."

"Some of us get to play on the stage . . . and some of us just get to watch," Theona said, patting her father on the arm as she gazed out at the glorious towers of the mystics. "It's all right, father, I understand—and I've understood for a long time."

"Theona, you mustn't talk like that," Rylmar said sternly. "You're a Conlan! You—"

"Theona!" The voice came down from the top of the wide marble stairs in the tablinum. Its source was unmistakable.

"You had better help her," Rylmar said with a huff, "or she'll never be ready on time."

"Of course, father," Theona said, then, turning, called up the stairs ahead of her, "Coming, Valana!"

5

Sisters

Valana Conlan stood at the top of the curving marble staircase, every part of her conveying impatience. She was terrible in her beauty. Her plump, moist lips were as dangerous in a pout as they were alluring in her half-smile.

Theona sighed to herself as she climbed quickly, two stairs at a time, with both hands clutching her skirt to raise it out of the way of her feet. "Yes? What is it, sister?"

"Oh, Theona, must you do that?"

"Do what?"

"Climb the stairs like that—it isn't proper!"

"Well, I'm not out to impress anyone watching," Theona replied as she neared the landing where Valana stood. "What do you need?"

"My blue gown," she said, quivering with frustration. "It isn't anywhere!"

Theona smiled ruefully as she stood at the top of the stairs, her head tilted slightly as she examined her sister. Valana was two years older, not that anyone would know it. "I've been on the road with the caravan since before dawn, Val. The servants have been at it for six hours, and we still have three wagons to unload."

"Well, I'm sorry, Theona, but this is important," Valana replied. "You'll just have to rest later."

"I'm sure your dress is packed somewhere. All we have to do is find it."

"Very well, then, where do we look?"

"You brought five trunks with you last week when you came ahead." Theona quickly stepped past her sister and onto the balcony that looked down on the open atrium below. She could smell the flowers and the grass of the garden, grateful for the sense of life it provided in the center of their new home in the city. At least something felt alive in the center of the city. Theona walked with determined steps toward the entrance side of the villa. "Are you sure it wasn't in one of those?"

"You don't think I'd be bothering you about it if it were," Valana answered snippily as she followed closely behind her younger sister. "It's just got to be in the packed trunks you brought. If it isn't there, I'll just die!"

"You won't die," Theona answered flatly, not bothering to look back as she spoke. "We'll find your dress. Where did you have the servants put your trunks?"

"Oh, well, there wasn't space enough in my rooms—"

"Not room enough?" Theona stopped. The balcony continued around the atrium to her right, and there was a short hall to her left leading to the front staircase. Directly in front of her was the ornately carved door to Valana's suite. "You've got three rooms, Val. Your bedroom alone is almost forty feet long!"

"I didn't want to get them all messed up," Valana responded in her most reasonable tone. "I'd just got everything arranged the way I wanted and couldn't bear to put it all out of place again."

Theona turned toward her sister and took a deep, calming breath. Long experience had taught her that it never paid to reason with her sister, and giving in to anger only made things worse. "So where did you put them?"

"Actually, the servants—"

"So where did you have the *servants* put them?"

"Just in the drawing room of the next suite. I mean, it's not going to get any use right away anyway."

Theona nodded and turned to continue. Theona's rooms were below on the main floor; her parents and sister had taken the rooms upstairs. Theona told herself that this arrangement was only reasonable: she was in charge of running the household, and she needed to be closer to where the servants worked in order to do her job with greater effect. Still, she knew in her heart that there was more to it than that. They stepped past the two doors that led to Valana's suite of rooms and entered the third, smaller suite.

The room was dim in the failing evening light. Chairs, couches, and various other pieces of furniture sat where the servants had carelessly placed them in their rush to finish their work.

"Isn't all of this—"

"Yes, it's mine, but it just didn't look right in the new rooms. I'm sure I'll find use for it, though, after the wedding."

"I don't see the trunks. Are you sure—"

"The next room."

Theona cleared her throat in mild annoyance and waded into the next room.

"Val, he has not proposed yet," Theona said as she

pulled open a trunk, squinting at the rows of hanging cloth inside. "You haven't even *met* him yet. How can you even talk about a wedding?"

"But that's just a formality," Valana said lightly. "Our father proposed to Prince Treijan's father, and he accepted."

"I hope they'll be very happy together." Theona pulled open yet another trunk.

"Who?"

"Our father and Prince Treijan's father."

Valana frowned. "Sometimes I just have no idea what you are talking about."

"Does it have to be the blue dress?" Theona called back as she dragged yet a third trunk out from the pile before her.

"Oh, yes; I had a mask specifically made to go with it for this evening. There's a reception being held tonight in our honor over at Brenna Tower," Valana replied easily. "All of the masters will be there—the very best blood from all the clans. I suspect they want a good look at Treijan's bride. Mother is so looking forward to it, and father says there's a lot of business to transact."

"He's right." Theona grunted, struggling with a latch. "A public demonstration of House Conlan's new position among the guild masters would improve our business tremendously." Theona pulled her hand suddenly from the trunk, a long blue gown clutched in her fingers. "Is this the one?"

"No, not that one," Valana said, her long yellow curls bouncing as she shook her head.

"Valana, you've got six blue dresses!" Theona's irritation was muffled inside yet another trunk.

"But you know the one—the light blue satin with the

filigree silver inlay on the stomacher," Valana said, idly opening a jewel case and sifting its contents one way and the other with her finger. "It goes so well with my new mask, and it's a special favorite of the Rhami boys. I just thought that—"

"Valana!"

"What, sister?" The tall beauty flashed her most coquettish smile.

Theona extracted herself from the growing jumble of trunks, pushing her way back into the room where her sister stood. "Not them! Not the Rhami boys!"

"I don't see what the matter is, Thei," Valana replied, pulling a long string of pearls from a small case. "House Rhami has a fine bloodline that can trace their ancestors back to Haggun Harn! Their father and uncle—Wellan and Orin Rhami—married daughters of Mikalan Harn, who had them by Julina Myyrdin—"

"You know what I mean, Val: those twins were trouble when they squabbled around your feet like puppies in Aquilas—bad enough there, where you could afford a little indiscretion, or at least father could afford to take care of it. This is different. This is Calsandria, Val; half the people you meet tonight will be wondering how long they can use you before tossing you aside, and the other half will simply be looking for a way to make you vanish now. How could you let those Rhamis follow you here?"

"I didn't ask them to come." Valana shook her head and shrugged. "They came on their own. I think it was sweet."

Theona made a sound of disgust, then turned back into the maze of open trunks. "And what is your soon-to-ask betrothed going to think of those fawning country mystics? When they weren't fighting each other over you, they were challenging anyone else who came your way to a duel!"

"Oh, they're harmless," Val said, flipping her hand dismissively. "They never hurt anyone, and neither of them has won a duel as long as I've known them."

"You're missing my point." Theona grunted again, pulling a hidden trunk out into the center of the floor.

"No, sister, I understand your point better than anyone," Valana said simply. "Marriage to the prince means binding together nearly all the bloodlines of the original Circle of Six under our single name. For generations we Conlans have made our way up from the bottom of the mountain, improving our lot with each marriage. It was always mutually convenient—bloodlines that were desperate enough to trade their name for something we could provide. We provided it—and now we are here."

Theona stopped, staring at her sister.

"You see, Thei, I understand perfectly well what is at stake here." Valana's eyes were fixed on her sister. "I'm doing this for the family; I'm doing this for you. Think, Thei; unless our House is counted among the thirty-six elite guilds, what chance do you have of any match worth making at all?"

Theona stared at her sister for a moment. "None."

Valana nodded with a smile. "So I *do* understand."

"We both do," Theona said, pushing open the trunk. "Is this the one?"

"Oh, yes! Theona, you're amazing! Give it to me!"

Valana took the gown from her sister and held it up in front of herself with one hand. Glancing about, she found a long oval mirror standing in its frame. Quickly, she raised her free hand above her head, murmuring as she closed her eyes. Suddenly, a globe flashed into existence at the tips of her fingers, its light shining down, illuminating Valana in the mirror and her beautiful blue gown.

Theona stood behind her sister, stepping just enough to the side so that she, too, could see in the mirror.

Valana's perfect face was framed by a glorious and painstakingly coiffed nimbus of golden hair that cascaded down over her perfect shoulders. Her brown eyes were large and had a sleepy allure to them. Even the traveling dress she wore behind the draped gown had been carefully chosen to show off her shapely body to its finest advantage.

"I—I wish you could come," Valana said with a delicate tinge of regret. "Though you wouldn't enjoy it. It will all be mystics going on about . . . well, you know."

Theona eyed her own face in the mirror. Her dark hair was manageable only when drawn back into a bun. Her nose had a bump to it, and her chin was a bit weak. But she sometimes almost believed she might have been thought of as pretty on her own, like a summer moon glowing on a soft, still night. Yet standing in the brilliant light of her sister, no one would ever give her another look. Valana was the prize of the family, the central reason for their rising fortunes and a gifted evoker in the Wind Weaver Guild. Theona paled in such sunlight. And worst of all, despite one of the most powerful bloodlines known among the mystics, Theona had no power in the Deep Magic at all. Looking into the mirror, she knew she was a lesser child.

"Don't you worry, Theona," Valana said gaily, the light shining on her. "Prince Treijan sent word he would be arriving through the gates today. We'll be married by fall, and life will be better for all of us—even you, Theona. It's all been arranged; we're all going to live happily thereafter."

Revelry

Theona stood on the damp, washed paving stones in the street in front of their new home. She crossed her arms and watched the family's carriage float off northward over Temple Way. There had been some last-minute bother about finding suitable Plains-drakes to pull the coach. The creatures' notable speed was not the issue, since the distance they would be covering was only a few blocks; rather, it was the look of them that governed their selection. One of the family's original four had gone lame during the journey from Aquilas and required time to recover. As they were a carefully matched set, finding not only a Plains-drake that had not been pressed into use that evening but also one that would appear aesthetically pleasing had been an upset to her mother and therefore blossomed into a genuine crisis for her father. In the end, however, the problem was solved—as so many of their problems were—with the touch of Rylmar's tally.* Her father simply purchased an additional and aesthetically suitable Plains-drake despite the exorbitant price.

It was of little consequence to her father; he personally had a number of tallies at his disposal—as any mystic would—and undoubtedly, each one held amounts in excess of a year's increase of even some of the clan lords themselves. Tallies had been the particular means of exchange between mystics for nearly half a century and were considered completely secure; each was closely tied to the will of its owner, and unlike the metal coins still used by the commoners under their employ, tallies would return to their owner whenever lost. Even death could not circumvent them, for when prepared, each was also ingeniously impressed with the family bloodline, thus ensuring that should man or woman die through accident or design, his or her wealth would pass unhindered and intact to designated kin. Tallies had become the benchmark of the mystic's life, for they seemed present at all life's occasions. A mystic child had its own tally impressed on it at its demonstration of mystic talent; the impression of tallies between husband and wife had become the pinnacle part of the mystic wedding ceremony; and often the first notice a wife had of the passing of her husband was the sudden appearance of his tally coin. Where murder was concerned, the person who possessed the victim's tally was always first suspect.

---

*Beginning in 542 DK, the mystic clans established the tally as their universally accepted standard of exchange. This magical coin, reminiscent of the blessing coins of the Pir Drakonis, was nearly two inches in diameter and made of ornate metal. The coins were individualized but carried the same sympathetic magical charge. Transactions were conducted by touching the coins together while the will of the holder determined the price of the exchange. Power then flowed from one tally to the next, completing the transaction.

To Theona, however, the tallies had become another symbol of the gulf between her and the society into which she had been born. She alone wore no tally, and the absence of it weighed constantly on her soul. She knew her father loved her, but she knew that she was an embarrassment to him all the same—an embarrassment for which no size of tally could compensate.

So, Theona mused as she watched the drakes and carriage wind their way up the crowded street in the clear, cool evening, her father purchased what he could. With the touch of a pair of large coins, the Plains-drakes were handsome once more, Rylmar's wife was happy, and their prize daughter would be presented in proper style to the powerful and beautiful of the city where every charming smile distracted from the dagger held behind their back. She watched them for a while, as they started past the restored temples on the eastern side of the road—Mnemes first, then Hrea and Ekteia. The buildings were breathtakingly beautiful, but Theona's eyes remained on the carriage until it disappeared around the long gentle curve of the Temple Way.

Father, mother, and sister: not one looked back even once.

Theona turned to the house. Two new masks stared back at her. Their polished and striking markings—the symbols of the House of Conlan—stood in stark contrast against the weathered and fading carvings of the antique house doors on which they had been recently mounted. Each proclaimed this as a household of mystics.

Theona took in a deep breath and pushed through the main doors of the villa. Agretha, their mystic servant originally from Cyrolis, had lit the lamps in the house before vanishing with most of the rest of the servant staff for the evening. The bluish glow from the crystal globes shone off the mosaic tiles of the vestibule, while still others illuminated the atrium beyond. It was a beautiful, empty old ruin, Theona thought; *just like me.*

She gnawed at her lip, trying to distract herself from her thoughts. While there were a few commoners employed by the household, Agretha and most of the other servants either were adept at surface magic* or were outright mystics as well, each one able to do things Theona, as a magicless commoner herself, was incapable of doing. That they listened to her at all may have had something to do with her ability to organize tasks and solve problems, but she suspected it had more to do with the weight of her father's tally. She was devoid of the very magic on which the empire was being built—a commoner. Each day she saw in the face of everyone she met pity, scorn, sympathy, curiosity, shame, intolerance, veiled tolerance, and rejection—every reaction in the spectrum of the superior looking upon a lesser being.

Theona turned at the end of the vestibule and walked slowly along the portico down the right side of the atrium, her footsteps echoing through her emptiness. Despite the ever-hopeful protestations of her father and the pained patience of her mother, within herself she wondered why this was the life to which the gods had set her. It was not one to which she was resigned, for such resignation was not in her nature, so she moved through each day in her

---

*Surface magic—or, more simply, wizardry—refers to the folk magic which draws on the powers of nature rather than on the Deep Magic of other worlds. It is far less powerful and more transient than Deep Magic, dealing primarily with common household issues such as spitting fires to life or mending simple cuts. Surface magic is looked down upon by the mystics as a "lesser" ability and is not considered a discipline of Deep Magic, and therefore, even house wizards are considered to be "commoners."

own mask of silent desperation, all the while searching for some path by which she might escape the cocoon of her fate and soar.

Theona guarded all her passions behind her reserve and isolation, but when the burden of her resentment became more than she could bear, she would remove herself to the one place where she could find solace.

So she turned toward the dim doorway next to her that led from the atrium into a room second only in size to the great hall in the villa. The walls, two stories tall, and the flat ceiling were, like the great hall, decorated with fading, ornate frescoes, but these depicted the ancient gods of Rhamas, their flowing robes still in the poses rendered by the hands of artisans now centuries dead. The room was devoid of furniture or decoration save only one: a single statue that more than filled the end of the room.

She gazed up at the marble face of the goddess Hrea.

Theona had requested of her father that this particular statue grace the family chapel, arguing that since this was already the patron goddess of the House of Rennes-Arvad, it might be advantageous for it to also be associated with the House of Conlan. The statue originally had been carved, Theona imagined, as a tribute to the protecting nature of the goddess, for unlike many of the statues of the other gods found among the ruins, this one alone bent over, kneeling in her largesse, her hands spread both protectively and invitingly at once. Here, however, in the smaller confines of the Conlan family chapel, the statue seemed to Theona to take on another aspect; it was like a great and powerful animal that was trapped and now kept in too small a cage.

That is me, Theona thought, *a great bird with a broken wing, kept in too small a cage.*

She glanced back quickly toward the door. The servants were not allowed in the family chapel, and Theona knew that her parents and sister had little use for the gods beyond the festivals that they occasioned and the social requirement they represented. Here she was alone; here she could be herself.

Theona dropped to her knees, bowing before the great statue, her hands over her head as her nose touched the floor. The words of her heart came from her unbidden and unchecked between her soft sobs. "Hrea, Goddess of the Harbor, hear my plea. Show me who I am. How have I offended the gods that they should make me . . . so broken a thing as this? I cannot see the path before me. Please, great Hrea, show me who I am—*why* I am this way—and how I may repay the gods for how I have offended them."

Theona wept, her unchecked tears forming small pools on the mosaic tiles. There she curled up in her clothes, as small as she could make herself, and still sobbing, fell asleep beneath the still hands of the sightless statue.

"Theona . . . Theona . . ."

The old woman stood over me, her hand gentle against my shoulder, rocking me as she spoke.

I awoke—or so it seemed to me—in an infinite and impenetrable blackness. It was disorienting, since I thought I had fallen asleep in the family chapel. The only thing that I could see was the elderly crone who stood over me.

She was ancient beyond description, frail and stooped, with long, feathery white hair pulled back severely but ornately at the back of her head. She had but one eye, yet it was bright and full of life. Her clothing was unbearably white and in the style of ancient Rhamas: a long tunic dress fixed with a clasp on one shoulder.

"What is it, grandmother?" I ask of the woman, though in truth she looks nothing like my own grandmother now long dead.

"Come, child," the woman says, her voice creaking as she reaches down for my arm. I am surprised at her strength as she pulls me up to stand next to her. "It is time for your journey."

I shake my head. "We only just arrived, grandmother."

"Everyone must take their own path," the woman replies. "Everyone must choose their own gate. Look! What do you see?"

I peer into the darkness. "Nothing . . . it makes me afraid."

"You must look with finer eyes, my child," the old woman answers with patience. "Look again!"

I peer once more into the black void that surrounds us. I begin to discern dim shapes in the darkness, their forms fluctuating and vanishing, though I concentrate all the harder. I detect the outlines of the chapel walls or perhaps the atrium beyond, but these boundaries shift as though seen in the reflection of a lake whose surface has just been disturbed. Its forms ripple and shift into the outlines of a great archway that is rushing toward me—or am I falling through it?—I cannot tell. Above the arch is a great, glowing stone with the number forty-one carved into its face.

DIARY OF THEONA CONLAN, VOLUME 3, PAGES 39–41

Things could not be more perfect, Valana thought.

She stood to one side of the ballroom floor, surrounded

by a number of masked courtiers from the various bloodline clans. Each was attempting to engage her in conversation, her mother fending off those of lower bloodlines and advancing those whose patronage would best be sought. Her father, gratefully, had moved off with other clan fathers to discuss matters of business. She was relieved when he did; as much as she loved her father, he knew nothing of the way things were handled on such a social killing field. It was best navigated by those who understood it well.

The Guild Hall was a reconstructed rotunda, a wonderful Rhamasian architectural design that created a large open space surrounded by colonnades supporting higher concourses from which bystanders could observe the dance. The musicians themselves were located in the third concourse above the floor. The dome overhead was still incomplete, but the guild fathers managed to remove the scaffolding in time for Prince Treijan's welcoming ball, thus opening space in which to conduct the dance.

The assembled patrons fluttered about, their masks marked with symbols of every discipline and guild in the empire. Everyone who was anyone had availed themselves of the opportunity the ball presented with great relish. Couples formed at the edge of the floor, performing a spin-step to the middle as evokers of the Hreatic discipline—Rylmar Conlan's own Transport Guild—formed glowing spheres around them. Then all drifted upward to take their place in the dance, floating in their iridescent bubbles. The light beat of the music began, and the couples moved through the air. The globes of dancers merged into partners only to separate and merge again according to the strictures of the dance. The space above the floor was filled with the graceful drifting of the mystic elite in careful syncopation.

Everything Valana saw was carefully designed, and, she had to admit, she liked it that way. She did not like surprises; in fact, she found even the most pleasant of them disturbing on some level. She always preferred a clear view of what was coming in life; it was the unexpected that could kill you.

Here, surrounded by the smiling masks of those who wanted to either use or destroy her, she was calm and assured. She could handle their barbs, their snapping tongues, and their alliances of convenience. There was no one more sure-footed on the uncertain ground of court politics than Valana Conlan . . . so long as she could see it coming.

"Miss Conlan! Miss Conlan!"

Jesth and Danth, the Rhami twins, were pushing their way toward her, leaving an increasingly irritated murmur of elite in their wake. Valana was delighted at the attention everyone was paying to her this evening; the presence of the fawning twins was "spice for the mix," as her mother was wont to say. She had no intention of taking either of the boys seriously, but their backward admiration always seemed to shine a better light on her for the benefit of other people's eyes.

"Master Jesth and Master Danth," she said politely, curtsying as slightly as possible. "I am surprised to see you here in attendance." She enhanced the politic lie by flashing her eyes accusingly.

"Miss Conlan," Jesth said breathlessly, "we have come to offer our services to you."

"Both of us," Danth cut in. "We would gladly do anything in our power to speed your happiness. Give us any task, no matter how small."

Valana glanced over at her mother, whose nose turned up as though both boys had just rolled through an onion field.

"I am shocked at you both," Valana replied through a pout. "You both know that I am here at the behest of House Rennes-Arvad. Your attentions are unseemly and scandalous."

"Please, Miss Conlan," the twins implored in near unison.

"Miss Conlan is otherwise currently engaged," came a high, reedy voice from behind her. "A condition which, I strongly advise, you might consider taking up yourselves."

Valana turned carefully. She had never met the prince of Rennes-Arvad, and his visage had been described to her in such detail and by such diverse people as to present no clear picture to her at all. One of the things she was looking forward to this evening was to actually catch a glimpse of the man to whom she was to be married. She was hoping to find something in the face of her intended which would elevate her joy as much as her family rank and station. Her plan to catch sight of the prince safely from a distance before he saw her was evidently for naught. The hem of her blue dress shifted as she came to face the tall man behind her.

His face was pinched and his eyes uncomfortably piercing as they looked through his mask down his long hawkish nose at her. There was a faint air of disapproval in the way he cocked his head from her to the Rhami twins, though she could not tell which of them had elicited such a response.

Valana nevertheless recognized the bard markings on the delicately ornate mask and knew her duty. She curtsied deeply as she spoke, dropping her head. "Your Majesty."

"Nearly, but not quite," the high-pitched voice replied. The near-pressing crowd had taken notice of the scene and were tittering with menacing amusement.

"You are too modest, Prince Treijan," Valana answered quickly.

"I am, in fact, too much Gaius Petros to be Prince Treijan," the thin man answered with raised eyebrow even as he took her hand, signaling her to rise. "The prince asked me to find you and petition you to join him in the dance."

Valana flushed slightly. "Then I shall do so at once. Indeed, I should be glad to put my present company behind me."

"Then if you will permit me," Gaius said, spinning Valana around expertly and stepping into the first dance position. The bubble formed instantly around them, lifting them from the floor and sweeping them upward and over the crowd.

"The prince has been abroad these last months," Gaius said as they swung into the air. Their line of dance was even with the lower concourse, the bubbles of the other couples matching their own movements as they shifted, broke apart, and swung around other partners before coming to rejoin.

"His dedication to the bard calling is known throughout all the clans of the empire," Valana replied courteously.

"It is not so glorious a calling as one might think," Gaius rejoined, taking Valana's hand as they both stepped through the air. "Things at court often change in his absence. Arrangements are sometimes made which can come as quite a surprise."

"Indeed," Valana said, allowing a hint of boredom to color her words, though the reference to "surprise" discomfited her. "Change is inevitable; denying it won't stop it, and, as my father says, in all change there is profit."

Gaius smiled at the comment as they both turned and ascended to the next level of the dance. "For those wise enough to understand the meaning of profit when it is at hand."

Valana frowned slightly, uncertain where the conversation was leading. "I'm sure I don't understand your meaning, sir."

"Then tell me about yourself," Gaius returned pleasantly.

Valana at last felt they were moving into familiar territory. "Well, I am Valana of the House of Conlan. My mother is Estrada of the Myyrdin line through Galenar. My father is Rylmar Conlan through Miril Arvad—Treijan's great-aunt twice removed—and Behthan Conlan, son of—"

"Madam, am I to believe that you are comprised entirely of Patents of Bloodline?" Gaius interrupted.

"I am only answering your questions, sir," Valana replied. She was suddenly aware of how precarious it was to dance so far from the ground.

"I asked who you were, madam"—Gaius nodded, his sharp eyes fixed on her—"not the breeding of your pedigree. I can read as much from the markings on your mask."

"Then perhaps we might talk about your own breeding," Valana returned as they rose up to the third level of the dance.

"The importance of bloodlines is vastly overrated," Gaius said dismissively.

"Only to those who lack them," Valana rejoined haughtily. "Worse yet, to those who have them but come just short of measuring up. Let me read your mask, Gaius Petros. You and Treijan both are descendants of Caelith Arvad, but the Petros line came down through Chystal Arvad—a daughter—while Treijan's line comes down through her brother, Aremis, born two years before. If it weren't for Treijan of the Rennes-Arvad line, it would be you and your family dancing at the top of the air tonight instead of your distant cousin."

"There are some things in which you are perhaps too well educated," Gaius replied, though his eyes looked away from her.

"One can read a great deal in a mask, and I know what matters to the Council of Thirty-six," Valana said, spinning smartly on the beat of the music. "I know that there is a difference between those who rule and those who obey."

"And obedience is not in your nature?" Gaius responded.

"Quite the contrary," Valana said in turn. "I know my duty well and where my allegiance lies; do you?"

"All too well." Gaius bowed and then turned, gesturing to his right. "Your Majesty, may I present Miss Valana Conlan."

Valana caught her breath. She had been so absorbed in her conversation that she had not realized they had risen to the highest tier of the dance. She turned and curtsied deeply before daring to look up into the pleasantly smiling eyes that greeted her.

Masked as he was, Valana could see that Treijan

Rennes-Arvad was an extraordinarily handsome man. Her first thought was of relief. She took his offered hand, and together they danced above all the mystics of the empire—the odd conversation with Gaius forgotten in the perfection of the night.

The Gates

Kyne Fletcher of the Shadow Watch eyed his hourglass accusingly, as its sands seemed to fall particularly slowly in the depths of this watch. The hourglass itself was a forbidden object—the watch commander believed that such devices made the duty longer than it was—but Kyne had smuggled it in anyway, partly to know the time and partly in quiet rebellion.

Tonight, however, he wondered if the commander had a point. Kyne yawned and shook himself in the darkness.

It was his width, he thought. That's why they kept him up here at night. He had a stumpy, stocky build that prevented him from blending in with the willowy ornaments of the tower. His face was broad and flat like the rest of him, and he was having trouble growing a proper beard to shape into the symbolic forms that identified his particular discipline and focus. The best he managed was a patchy stubble unbecoming of an Ekteiatic guardian. So he always drew the night postings. Never mind that he was one of the best archers in his cadre, he seemed destined to lean on his bow, next to the same statue each night and struggling to stay awake.

Someday, he thought, he'd find a way out of this.

His post was high among the finials and ornate columns that lined the parapet walkway and supported the delicately pointed spire of Jester's Tower. Kyne blinked and looked down between the columns to the cobblestone floor of the courtyard below. Jester's Tower was also rather rudely known as Thumb Tower, primarily because it was the shortest of the five spires that together formed the outer structure of the Citadel. As such, it offered the nearest vantage point down on the courtyard that lay between the structure's foundations and the outer curtain wall.

"Strange way to build a fortress," Kyne muttered to himself, returning to an observation he had pondered through many a long night. "Castles are supposed to keep invaders out, not in. Still, you've got to face where the danger comes from, and if the enemy comes, it will be through these same gates, I reckon. I guess that's the way of our times."

Time, he thought, looking back at the hourglass. He pondered its simple shape, the crafted wooden framework and the blown glass. For all the power of the Deep Magic—its "flash and thunder," as Kyne often scoffed—the vast majority of useful things were still done by the skill of the craftsman with tools in hand. One could, he supposed, conjure up a magical timekeeping creation out of the Mystic Dream: the Enchanters and the Catalysts could imbue its qualities into a solid object and make perpetual the renewing power to keep things functioning. But why bother when all you needed was a bit of glass, some sand, and a few pieces of wood?

Kyne looked back down to the courtyard. The magnificent mystical gates lined the inner wall, their Songstones glowing faintly in the night. They were closed during his watch, but he liked to imagine the poor fools who were brought through them throughout the day. All of them seemed to believe that they were coming to a place where magic flowed like water after a spring rain and where all they had to do to get their hearts' desire was to snap their fingers. The truth was far harsher: Deep Magic was hard to master, occasionally unpredictable, and nearly always unstable. The vast majority of life's tasks were still accomplished with more certainty, greater economy, and less effort by the same sweat and effort even commoners had been using since time began.

Of course, try telling *that* to the wide-eyed pilgrims that the bards brought through the gates each day. Kyne suspected that there were more "commoners" in Calsandria now than mystics—and, no doubt, doing more of the work as well.

The Shadow Watch guardian shrugged uncomfortably in his cloak as he let his gaze wander out beyond the curtain wall and over the expanse of Calsandria. It was the legend of the city that brought them here, and even Kyne could not deny its allure. There were, to be sure, few better places from which to see the entirety of the city—both as it once was and as it was becoming. Beneath the night sky he could still make out the expanse of rubble that outlined the boundaries of what had once been the center of the ancient world. Certainly, the mystics had made great advances—the very Citadel on which he stood watch was the most magnificent example of their dedication to reclaiming the former glories of the Rhamasian Empire—but beyond the Arvad Keep and several of the more affluent guild structures near the Citadel, the vast majority of the city remained a graveyard of shattered stones and ruins. Kyne could see the outlines of the amphitheater to the southeast that had just been uncovered only the year before. There were several homes in that direction and a few shops lining the Rhamas Way beyond the Gate of Tears—a district known as the Songs Quarter—where a number of mystics whose powers centered on music and performance art had cleared a section of the rubble for their own community. The Weavers Quarter to the southwest, Kyne knew, was larger, but he could not see it from the Jester's Tower.

Instead, he let his gaze continue past the amphitheater to the masts of the ships moored along the waterfront. Those ships were the real power of Calsandria, he thought, for they were the heart of trade with every community beyond the city trying to reclaim the glory days of the dead empire. The trade ships sailed the broad waters of Behrun Lake—a huge body of water more than fifty miles from Tabethia on the northwest shore—to Caedonia, Kharanlas, and Ekhilas to the south. Calsandria, in Kyne's day as in centuries past, remained the gateway of trade between the lake cities and those of the upper mountain plains.

It had been the greatest city of its age, and it had fallen, Kyne mused. Now here they were rebuilding it, and not a one of them stopped to consider why it had fallen in the first place. There was something wrong with that, he decided—as he did each night of his watch—and one of these days he would get people to think about this. He would not be a watch guardian all his life; he knew which rung on the ladder of society he occupied and had seen others not nearly as deserving as he was climb past him.

One day, he knew, he would get his break, curry the right favor, and then when *he* was in charge, he'd fix all the—

"Fletcher!"

Kyne froze as he glanced down at the small hourglass. It was the voice of the watch commander—a leathery old warrior with the unlikely name Peaches—echoing up the central shaft of the tower from the floor below. For a moment Kyne waited to hear if Peaches was going to climb the interior stairs.

"Fletcher!" the echoing voice called up once more.

Apparently not. Kyne relaxed. "Here, sire," he called down the shaft.

"You are relieved," echoed the voice from below. "Come down."

Kyne glanced once more at the hourglass. There was still a good fifteen minutes of sand left in it. "Sire, my replacement has not yet reported—"

"Hang your replacement!" Peaches' voice threatened to shake loose some of the stones so carefully replaced in the tower. "He'll have me to deal with for being late! Listen, there was a big celebration over at Arvad Keep tonight, and House Rennes-Arvad had a few casks left over. I sent a detail to 'requisition' them for the Shadow Watch, and they've just returned successfully. I thought you might want to help us dispose of the evidence."

Kyne grinned, and he clambered to his feet. He snatched up his quiver, slinging it carelessly over his shoulder, and grabbed his bow. "Aye, sire, I believe I'm up for such duty! Reporting at once."

"Well, be quick about it," Peaches yelled. "I'm not waiting forever!"

Kyne used his weight to press the bow downward against the stone flooring and released the bowstring from the nock. It was an action as automatic to him as breathing; it would never do to present himself off the watch without his equipment properly stowed. The unstrung bow was slipped into the quiver, and he was ready.

Keeping his left hand against the wall, Kyne bounded down the spiral staircase. His right hand gripped his tally. A good kegging party would soon include a game or two, and his tally was a little flush, making him feel lucky. He was nearly halfway down the tower when he suddenly brought himself to a stop.

The hourglass—he had left it at the post.

"Damn!" he muttered quietly. If his watch replacement was basted by the watch commander for being late, he would no doubt find great pleasure in turning Kyne in for smuggling in the hourglass. Kyne looked back up the tower. Going down was one thing, going up quite another—but there was no help for it.

He dashed back up the stairs, becoming winded in a few turns.

"Hey, Fletcher," came another voice from below. It was Boulous, his old friend. "Are you coming or not? The party's starting!"

"On my way," Kyne called down as lightly as he could. The climb was arduous even at a leisurely pace; at a run it was brutal. "Coming!"

He burst back onto the parapet, sucking in the night air. There was his little hourglass, just next to the pillar by the edge. He leaned down, his hand closing around the framework.

Something in the courtyard caught his eye.

He froze. The courtyard was closed at night. Nothing was supposed to be down there.

Two shadows moved toward each other across the cobblestones far below.

Kyne reached for his bow, his hands fumbling in the folds of his cloak. He cursed himself; if he had been properly on watch, he would have had it in hand by now, but his cloak had wound around it in his rushed ascent, and he was having trouble extricating it from the folds in the cloth.

Suddenly, one of the figures below collapsed, shaking violently on the ground. The other—taller and thinner—stood by dispassionately until the first man's agony came to an end and he lay limp on the stones. Then the second man picked up the limp form and quickly moved toward one of the gates.

"Come on! Come on!" Kyne muttered to himself. His hand felt the cool wood of the bow's limbs in his hand. He pulled at it frantically, freeing it from the quiver. In a single motion he pressed down on the bow and set the bowstring.

The Songstone suddenly shone in one of the gates below.

Kyne nocked an arrow, pulled back, and aimed.

Both figures were gone.

The courtyard was quiet once more, but Kyne's thoughts were loud in his own mind. Getting his bow fouled in his robes—now *that* could only buy him endless grief from the watch commander and ribbing from his fellow guards. He should report this at once, but he knew that if he did, he would have to explain why he did nothing to stop the intruders. On the other hand, his job was to stop people from coming *in* through the gates, not to stop them from going *out*.

"Fletcher!"

"Almost there!" Kyne called out, quickly stowing his bow once more and dashing back down the stairs as fast as he dared. It was probably best that he forget the whole thing.

After all, it's just a gate.

"Theona!" The voice calls me into the darkness.

Then I look down from a hilltop. The darkness rolls away from me, though the scene around me is still dim and devoid of colors. A silent wind flows through my hair, blowing up from the seashore many miles away. The grasses around me are gray. I have never seen the ocean before; its vast expanse both thrills me and fills me with foreboding. There are cities along the long curve of the shore. Suddenly, a flash of light from one of the towers blinds me. I step backward . . .

. . . My foot steps on cobblestones. I am no longer on the hilltop, after all, but am stepping through an archway into a marketplace. There is a worn path underfoot winding among the stalls. Valana is there frantically looking at objects in each of the booths, then discarding them and moving to the next.

Then there is a dwarf, its eyes completely hidden in shadow under the enormous brim of a red hat. Though the colors of the world are muted and gray, the dwarf's hat stands out in brilliant crimson. Beneath it the dwarf grins at Valana and motions for her to follow.

The black void has returned at the far end of the market, its darkness rushing toward both the dwarf and Valana, intent on engulfing them both.

"Valana!" I yell. "No! Stop!"

My sister takes the hand of the dwarf even as the blackness—a place I think brings nonexistence—rushes closer still, swallowing everything in its path.

"Valana!" I rush toward her. She is only a few feet from me now but somehow still does not hear me.

The blackness is nearly upon us all.

I reach out to take her hand, and though she turns and steps toward me, I can tell her eyes do not see me.

Valana steps <u>through</u> me.

I shudder. The darkness is rushing toward us at a frightful speed. I catch my breath just as the void swallows me . . .

. . . And I stand on yet another shore—this one of soft black sand. The waves of a large pool lap softly next to me, driven by a tumbling cascade from a waterfall at the far shore. I gaze up into a star-filled sky framed by strange trees rising around me. I can hear the cry of dragons from the underbrush.

Valana walks past me, heedless of me as I sob out her name.

Behind me the old crone cackles.

I turn to her, shaking in the light of the stars. "Am I—am I dead?"

The crone smiles broadly, her good eye widening as she considers. "A good question, Theona. The answer all depends on how you look at it. What do you <u>see</u>?"

I look and see Valana transfixed, seemingly afraid. There are the figures of two men farther down the shore, their forms defined by deep shadows under the canopy of starlight. One lies on the beach, writhing in the agonies of death. The other—tall and thin—stands over him and apart, making no movement of aid. The man on the sand shudders and then is still.

Valana rushes toward the man on the shore, stooping to roll him over so that his face is turned up to the star-filled sky. Though I have never seen him, I suddenly understand that it is Prince Treijan lying in the stillness of death.

But then Valana leaps up, dropping Treijan's head to the sand. Her eyes are filled with fear and loathing as she runs past me. The dead prince rises from the sand, his face veiled in shadows, and walks toward me. Though his features are hidden, there is something terrible and loathsome about him. I can hear Valana scream as she runs away, but I am transfixed. His darkness tears my breath from my lungs.

The world around me shatters like a pane of slivered glass. I tumble with the shards, falling but untouched by their sharp edges. I see flashes of images, glimpses of other places and times reflected in their spinning surfaces. Then as I watch, the slivers of glass are re-forming around me, reflecting a new and terrible gate. The dim metal of the doors is forbidding, for it glows with an eerie light, revealing the features of its surface to portray a procession of the dead. Its surrounding arch of black onyx stone is illuminated by crackling flashes of lightning rippling across its surface, revealing its carved, towering shapes to be those of widemouthed skeletons of winged creatures emerging from the stone, their bony hands reaching out to claw at the air.

I shudder in revulsion; it is the gate to the Abyss of Skurea the Unbeliever—the land of the Forgotten Dead.

And the statues are howling.

DIARY OF THEONA CONLAN, VOLUME 3, PAGES 41–45

Famadorian

Once upon another time, in a distant land of myth, a centaur stood at the gates of Sharajentis. His dark mane, thick and unkempt, quivered against his shoulders as he howled in frustration, his head pulled back and his mouth wide. The set of bags laid across his back was both flat and empty.

He was nearly blind with rage and confusion. He had been there since the dawn two days before, casting his plaintive voice with increasing aggravation against the outer walls of the city.

They must let me in, he thought. *I have been called! I have been chosen! They must let me in!*

Yet the city remained closed to him despite all he tried. Time and again he had approached the enormous green-glowing gate—the most obvious entrance to the city—and each time the enormous twin black-stone statues of winged skeletons that stood sentinel on either side struck him with bolts of white fire. His wailing call drifted through the silent and empty streets beyond the outer curtain wall of the city and remained unanswered.

It is the city of the dead, his fevered mind thought. *What must I do to enter—die?*

As he had done before, the creature bolted, galloping along the outer curtain wall of the city, crying out in his frustration. The steep walls were sharply angled for defense, thrusting out across the landscape like the tips of blades radiating from the central city. The forest had been cleared to a distance from the foundations, leaving a wide killing field between the still, black water of the moat and the tree line. The centaur sped across this open ground beneath the bright stars overhead. He hurled insults toward the battlements, trying to provoke some response. But nothing moved between the machicolations above the ramparts.

So he turned again, trotting back at length to stand on the wide, packed-dirt road leading to the main gate of the city, his breath bursting in sharp puffs from his flaring nostrils in the cold of the still night air. He stood motionless for a time contemplating the gates with his dark eyes.

He shook his head, drew in another breath . . .

. . . And froze at the fluttering sound behind him. He knew the sound too well. The centaur spun to face his doom.

"I should have known you would come here," came a whisper from the dark shadows of the trees. "Not that you made yourself difficult to find with all that dreadful noise."

There was more fluttering among the trees. The centaur took two careful steps back, sensing that he was getting close to the lightning bite of the onyx guardians on either side of the gate behind him. It was pointless to argue, but he would not go willingly either.

"*Hrrbrlln* home," the creature answered in his guttural voice. "*Hrrbrlln* come home."

"Yes, you'll come home, all right." The voice from the trees chuckled. The fluttering had lessened, but the centaur could still hear it all along the tree line on either side of the road. "Your master's put a good price on your head. Why he should go to such trouble for an idiot slave is of no concern to me—but it is my *business*."

The fluttering suddenly erupted into an avalanche of sound. The leaves quaked as dark figures rushed from their branches, soaring overhead, their long wings silhouetted against the star-bright sky. They quickly circled overhead, several of them trailing heavy nets between them, while others brandished drug-tipped javelins. Kyree, the centaur thought, and worse—the slave-hunters of Nykira. He tensed, his legs bowing under him out of instinctive fear. Still, he held up his hands in front of him—just as he had seen it in his dreams—and prayed to Phlroch, god of his ancestors, that he had understood.

One of the larger Kyree, an older man with a patch covering one eye of his battered face, alighted before him on the road, his javelin held with smug casualness across his body. He lofted the weapon, cocking his arm as he spoke. "Come on, slave! Resist us! Try to escape. Better yet, attack us. It's been a long time since I've had an excuse to butcher Famadorian meat!"

"No Famadorian," the creature answered, his hands shaking despite his best efforts. "Free *kntrr*. No slave."

The Kyree grinned broadly, baring his fanglike incisors. "Now, *that's* what I've been waiting to hear."

The centaur blinked. The world divided in his sight

as part of his mind groped for the place of magic. He knew his talents were raw and unskilled, but he prayed to Phlroch, God of the Sky, to aid him.

His mind filled with the image of fire circling the sun.

The packed earth of the roadway suddenly erupted in flame, drawing a wall of searing blue fire around the centaur. The tongues of heat lashed out, channeling down the shaft of the javelin, which now glowed white with heat. The Kyree hunter yelled in pain, dropping the burning shaft. It fell, still white-hot when it hit the ground.

Overhead, the others in the hunting party screamed in rage, their wings beating furiously at the air as they wheeled closer toward their prey.

Still holding his smoking hand, the Kyree hunter looked up at the centaur in a fury. "Famadorians have no magic! Who is helping you, slave? Answer me!"

"Phlroch answers," the centaur replied with confidence. "Phlroch protects."

"Dead gods of a dead race!" the Kyree spat, then turned his face upward to his circling troops. "Take him! Take him now or kill him!"

The Kyree overhead folded their wings, diving down toward the circle, javelins held at the ready.

The centaur reached up with his right hand, the gesture pulling a great tongue of flame away from the circle that surrounded him. It curled through the air, chasing after the foremost of the diving winged men. It ignited the creature's trailing wing feathers, causing it to veer away awkwardly. The centaur's left hand turned, and a second column of fire spun upward through the Kyree, scattering their careful formation and causing one of them to drop his side of a net.

The Kyree re-formed quickly overhead, screaming at

each other in high-pitched voices. They broke into three pairs, diving downward once more from different directions toward the slave-creature.

The centaur raised his hands, turning toward the closest diving pair. Both Kyree drew back their javelins, preparing to throw at point-blank range as they flew across their prey.

The centaur did not wait for them. He leaped toward the pair, his large hands closing around the weapon hand of the leading Kyree in midair. The move was perfectly timed; the centaur's grip was like forged steel as he pulled his enemy to the ground with him, rolling his massive weight over the smaller and much lighter winged man, stopping just short of the flames' edge. He wrenched the javelin out of the hunter's limp hand and stood, weapon raised.

Searing pain pierced the centaur's right shoulder, and he cried out, dropping the spear. He wheeled around and saw, through the flames, the Kyree hunter with the eye patch grinning once more at him. On the ground at the centaur's feet lay a second javelin. It had not penetrated farther than the creature's shoulder blade, but the centaur could see that the tip was wet with glistening poison and pinked with his own blood.

The centaur suddenly found it difficult to focus his sight. His legs folded under him as he fell heavily to the ground, struggling to keep his torso upright. The flames around him were dying down with the waning of his will. He could see the hunter stepping across the diminishing fire, drawing his long, thick sword.

"You'll cost me a decent bounty," the hunter sneered. "But what's one less slave?"

There was a sudden hollow boom followed by a long,

loud groaning. The Kyree hunter's head snapped up warily toward the gate. It was all the centaur could do to keep his eyes fixed on the hunter.

The dying flames encircling the centaur suddenly roared skyward. The roadway stones at the base of the flames glowed, then melted. The Kyree stood screaming in disbelief, his sword at the ready even as the molten stones began to ooze back toward the gate.

The centaur could not hold himself upright any longer and fell sideways to the ground. Through a haze of heat he thought he saw the gates of Sharajentis now fully open, a single figure floating between the pillars, its wings glowing with a light so deeply blue that it was difficult to look at.

The molten stones streamed backward and up onto the sentinel statues on either side of the gate, their orange glow flowing over the onyx skeletons, forming into the shapes of blazing muscle and blistering sinew. The guardians, empowered now by fiery flesh, extended their bright-glowing wing membranes and lurched toward the Kyree, tearing themselves from the wall. Their white-hot eyes fixed upon the hunter.

"I am of the Nykira," the hunter yelled over the roaring furnace of the guardians, defiant and proud. "This creature is mine! You have no right to stop me, Sharaj-witch!"

The sentinels drew in a great, blistering breath.

The world was suspended in silence.

The blast exploded against the ground, fanning outward. The paralyzed centaur lay still, unable to do more than watch and wait as the flames flowed around him but never touched his flesh. His pursuers were not spared as he was. The centaur could only watch as the Kyree hunter kept his eyes open until the end, the fiery heat stripping him of his flesh in an instant. Then everything was obscured by tumultuous darkness.

The dust still hung in the air as the blue-glowing figure flitted over and came to rest before the face of the centaur. Through the narrowing field of his vision he saw the faery: a thin young male. His long straight hair was black as soot, pulling in the light of the stars above him. His unkempt bangs partially obscured the pale gray of his intense, sad eyes.

"Who are you, Famadorian?" he asked in a voice that reminded the centaur of dormant fields under a winter snow.

"No Famadorian," he answered, his tongue thick and slow in his mouth. "Free *kntrr*. No slave."

"Why are you here?" the faery asked, though his voice seemed far away.

"*Hrrbrlln* home," the centaur replied even as consciousness left him. "*Hrrbrlln* come home."

9

The Lyceum

The angry flutter could be heard the entire length of the dim hall. Any Oraclyn-loi who had the misfortune of being in the corridor at the time had to dive frantically into the first available alcove, open doorway, or arch that might get it out of the way. One rather dour instructor—furious at the disturbance to his students' serene studies—stepped into the passageway, but the reprimand died before it ever reached his lips, and he, too, hastily retreated back to the safety of his lectern.

By her fixed, cold glare and the lightning rippling like storm-tossed waves across her rapidly beating wings, the Queen of the Dead made it clear to all who saw her pass that she was not to be hindered or trifled with.

With her hands held slightly away from the shining folds of her long black cloak, she leaned forward and flew quickly between the classrooms of the Lyceum's upper floor, her attending guards struggling to keep up with her in the confined space. The high collar that framed her face and neck quivered—the outward evidence of an inwardly checked rage. Her dark eyes were fixed on the end of the hall, a deep frown pulling at her weathered and lined face.

The Queen of the Dead was not taking her own impending death lightly. It was not known among faerykind how long-lived their race was—their legends claimed that they were immortal—but even though no faery had been known to die of old age, death always came to the Fae in other ways: usually foreseeable only in hindsight and almost always violently.

I'm not going quietly, Dwynwyn thought, her dark face set as she burst from the end of the hall and onto a balcony overlooking the central garden of the school.

Two faeries hovered above the soft grass below. One was older; his graying hair had thinned and receded considerably, yet still retained its tight curls. The other was much younger, his dark skin still smooth. He averted his eyes at Dwynwyn's coming.

Between them, lying still on the soft grasses of the garden, the massive form of a centaur rested on its side.

"Peleron! Arryk!" Dwynwyn called down without preamble. "You will attend me at once."

The elder Peleron bowed with a patient smile. Arryk nodded but kept his eyes hidden behind a curtain of his hair.

Dwynwyn stepped back from the balcony and surveyed the openings in the hall. It would have to do, she thought, flicking her open hand toward the doorway on her right. The thick doors drew open, banging against the walls and rebounding slightly from the force. Queen Dwynwyn blew through the opening like a spring gale, startling two young faery Oraclyn who rapidly tried to disengage from each other's embrace. Dwynwyn paid them no heed, charging into the otherwise empty lecture hall. Her Black Guard rushed into the room behind her, two of them clearing a space on the lecture dais and setting the best chair available in its center for their queen, the rest taking their customary positions in this uncustomary place. The faery lovers, suddenly finding themselves in a hastily assembled royal court, struggled between running in panic and bowing gracefully out of the room. On another occasion their fumbling might have greatly amused Dwynwyn, but the matters at hand were too grave for her to appreciate the humor.

Peleron, stepping quickly sideways to avert a collision with the Oraclyn couple, laughed at their antics. "I see your presence is having quite an effect on the morals of our youth, Your Majesty."

"Lyndevar," Dwynwyn said to the guard next to her, "I need my privacy."

The guard nodded and gestured toward the other guards. Each filed out of the room, and Lyndevar closed the doors to the lecture hall behind him. The sound of the doors closing had not yet faded when Dwynwyn began.

"Why have my orders been so completely and, apparently, *willfully* set aside?" Dwynwyn seethed, her long fingers nervously tapping against the arm of her chair. "No Famadorian is to be admitted to Sharajentis—simple and clear enough—and yet as I sit here there is a Famadorian centaur lying in the heart of my own Lyceum!"

"And good morning to you as well, Your Majesty," Peleron said, and sighed with light resignation.

"Hardly good, Peleron, and don't you dare try to change the subject," Dwynwyn snapped, her eyes fixing on the young faery standing silently before her. "You did this, Arryk. How could you? After all we've been through together."

The young faery looked up in sullen defiance, tossing his hair out of his eyes. He wore the long chasuble of the Oraclyn over his gray tunic and black trousers, and his slight frame made the costume seem too large for him. "This Famadorian has the Sharaj. He belongs with us."

Dwynwyn leaned back, both her hands gripping the arms of the chair. "No, it does not; Famadorians do not have the Sharaj."

"How can you say that?" Arryk continued, his voice quiet as he spoke, his eyes once more glancing away from the queen. "It is a New Truth. Turning our backs to it will not make it less so. They have been presenting themselves at our gates for the past ten years—seven of them in the last year alone."

"And they have been denied each in their turn."

"And yet they still come," Arryk replied, a sulking tone under his words. "The vision of the Sharaj drives them here just as surely as it brings faery Oraclyn to our gates to be taught the ways of power and the discipline of magic. They are as much a part of the Sharaj as we are."

"No," Dwynwyn said, taking in a long breath. "They do not have the Sharaj."

"And yet they do," Peleron said quietly. "You, of all the Fae, should know better than to deny a New Truth."

"I am the queen of Sharajentei." Dwynwyn glared at Peleron as she spoke. "My will here is law!"

"Indeed, and despite that, I married you anyway," Peleron said, shaking his head. "And all I have is my charm and a talent for the Sharaj that's better than yours."

"That's a lie," Dwynwyn snapped.

"Care to test that later?" Peleron asked innocently.

A smile suddenly played at the edges of the queen's lips. "Later. The point is that no Famadorian has the Sharaj."

"Then tell him why," Peleron said evenly. "Tell him why this truth must be a lie."

Dwynwyn stood up, her mouth open to speak, but she caught the words before they left her mouth. Her face relaxed, and she averted her eyes to hide the shame that filled them. "The Famadorians do not have the Sharaj because they *cannot* have the Sharaj; especially a slave of Nykira."

"A slave of Nykira? What does that have to do with this?" Arryk was incensed. "This creature is one of us— I've seen it myself—and you want to turn him away. You *support* the Kyree and their slavery!"

"Arryk," Peleron cautioned gently, "you forget yourself."

"It's all right, Peleron," Dwynwyn said, dismissing the insult with a wave of her hand. "Arryk, you of all faery know that is not true. Liberation is at the heart of Sharajentei. We exist to free the dead from their unique bondage. That is the entire purpose of the city in which we stand. Your mother gave us that."

Arryk shook his head in disgust. "So it comes back to my mother again."

"Yes, Arryk," Dwynwyn pressed on, undeterred. "I wish you had known her better. Aislynn was a great friend to me and one of the noblest of the Sharaj. She crossed the eastern sea and put right that which was broken—freeing the spirits of the dead to continue on their way to the Enlightenment. Of course, that was many years before you were born. In those days the city was burgeoning with the dead who gathered here to seek release and found none, but since that time the city has existed with that purpose: to allow the dead to work out their Enlightenment by doing that which was left undone in life."

"My mother's work was freeing the souls of the dead, I get that." Arryk spoke as though stating the obvious. "So how does that justify Kyree slaves?"

"But therein lies the irony," Peleron said, folding his arms across his chest. "In releasing the dead from their bondage, we lost their strength. Before your mother's first journey to the ancient lands of the Kyree, all the dead—noble and scoundrel alike—came here. Since Aislynn released the just spirits to the Enlightenment . . . well, let's just say that our nation is primarily comprised of the 'less-than-desirable' spirits."

"Even those," Dwynwyn agreed, "only remain with us just long enough to work out their problems before they, too, vanish to the Enlightenment."

"But isn't that the point?" Arryk responded, pressing his argument. "Helping *all* spirits toward the Enlightenment is good—like that centaur out there."

"That's the point for the Enlightened, yes." Peleron chuckled darkly. "A bit more problematic for those of us left in mortality. Our faery numbers—by far comprised mainly of Sharaj families—have been increasing over the years, but our armies of the dead are considerably weakened. They were once the terror of all the five houses of the Fae and, in some ways, still are in their minds, but it is a phantom only—if you'll forgive the expression. Should they actually be put to the test, our borders would fall."

Dwynwyn nodded. "And there is not a house among the Fae who does not long for the end of Sharajentei."

"Even my grandmother?" Arryk asked quietly.

"Especially your grandmother." Dwynwyn smiled thinly. "But then, you know all about that."

"Even so, it is not so much the Fae that we have to worry about as the Kyree," Peleron interjected, "or, more precisely, the Kyree-Nykira. It's the largest of the Kyree nations to the northeast—"

"A nation built on conquest and slavery," Arryk said, his anger rising.

"Exactly the point," Peleron said. "The Kyree-Djukai and the Kyree-Meekari are both smaller nations. The Djukai are allied with us and are living within our borders. The Meekari have remained neutral, although recently, we have heard they had begun using conquest slaves as well. It is the Kyree-Nykira, however, that hold nearly all the lands northward as far as Satana on the Trader's Coast. Their armies conquered those lands by force and enslaved the Famadorians they captured. Now their society depends upon their slaves for labor—like your centaur friend out there."

"And you condone this?" Arryk was astonished. "The Famadorians that present themselves to our gates are not only escaped slaves, they are our fellow creatures of the Sharaj, and you turn them away?"

"No." Dwynwyn shook her head sadly. "We turn them away because to do otherwise would be to acknowledge that the Famadorians *did* have the Sharaj, and above all else, such a truth must never be acknowledged or even considered by us or the Kyree."

"But the Kyree have never demonstrated any ability in the Sharaj," Arryk said emphatically.

"Which is precisely why none of their Famadorian slaves may either," Peleron acknowledged. "If the Kyree thought that their Famadorians had the very magic they lacked—or worse, were being *taught* the skills of the Sharaj—they would see it as a threat to their own existence. They would coldly destroy any Famadorian that demonstrated even the most remote talent in the Sharaj."

"As well as those whom they would blame for having taught them," Dwynwyn said as she turned, fluttering her wings thoughtfully as she drifted toward the windows of the lecture hall. "If the Kyree-Nykira thought we were teaching a Famadorian the discipline of the Sharaj, then their armies would be upon us. We would stand alone— and we would fall."

Dwynwyn looked down through the window glass at the still form of the centaur. "Is it dead?"

Arryk joined her at the window. "No; the poison the hunters use causes unconsciousness and some paralysis but not death. It is, however, quite powerful, as you can see."

Dwynwyn glanced at the young faery next to her. "Power which was apparently outmatched by your own. I understand you killed the hunters—all of them?"

Arryk looked away once more. "Yes, Your Majesty."

"All twelve?"

"It was seven. I—I did not intend to kill them."

"Really? I heard it was twelve," Dwynwyn said with studied casualness. "Still, you're leaving me with more problems than your centaur. I understand that somehow you animated the gate guardian statues, which now stand closer to the woods and in an entirely different shape than their first crafting. It also leaves me to explain why Kyree hunters are dead should the subject be brought up by the Nykira in the future—dead whether intended or not. Your power in the Sharaj is beyond any I have seen in many years, Arryk, but it is uncontrolled."

"I'll try harder," Arryk said simply.

"You shall do more than try," Dwynwyn replied, looking back down into the garden. "Since your mother and father departed, Peleron and I have tried to raise you well. Fate did not bring us a daughter of our own, and you have blessed our days. But now you put us all in a difficult position, Arryk, and I must ask you to put it right, though the way of it will be distasteful and unpleasant."

"I will do as you command," Arryk replied.

"If you had done as I commanded, we would not be faced with this problem," Dwynwyn persisted. "Nevertheless, the problem is here, and we begin from where we are. You must take this centaur back to the Nykira—"

"They'll kill him."

"Yes"—Dwynwyn nodded ruefully—"and let's hope that everything ends with him."

"But, Your Majesty," Arryk pleaded, "I have seen this creature perform the magic! I have seen him enter the Sharaj! It is a New Truth. He belongs with us!"

No, Arryk," Dwynwyn said, shaking her head. "For the last time, the Famadorians do not have the Sharaj, because if they *do* have the Sharaj, it may mean the end of us all."

Two Worlds

Utterly exhausted, the centaur hung limply six feet above the deck of the flyer. Since waking in his spherical prison, he had tried everything he could think of to escape. Magic not only failed to pierce the bubble's surface but had rebounded against him. Lightning flew from his hands, only to reflect back around him, scorching his own hide. He called on his gods to bring forth frost and nearly froze himself. He had baked under his own heat, nearly drowned in his own rain, and almost passed out from his own vacuum. In frustration and panic he had lashed out with his powerful legs, but, floating as he was, there was nothing against which his hooves could push.

So now he found himself panting as his head hung, looking down toward the deck so tantalizingly close. He noticed it was seamless, as though the entire deck had been coaxed out of a single piece of wood. The railings were drawn out of this wood and ringed the entire ship from the prow to the stern. Around the edges of the deck, vines reached upward until they formed an intricate net above, cradling three globes of iridescent glass, which appeared to keep the entire ship floating in the air.

The centaur closed his eyes and swallowed hard. The tops of the Oaken Forest were sliding beneath the keel, and every now and again there was a break in the forest roof that showed him just how high the centaur was above the ground.

"Had enough?"

The centaur opened his eyes. Staring up at him from the deck below was the pale face of a faery with the darkest black hair he had ever seen. He nodded slowly in response.

"Good," the faery said, curling its wings into his back and sitting cross-legged on the floor. "I've got enough problems as it is. Look, we're going to be together for a while on this trip. There's nothing either of us can do about it, so if you'll just—"

"*Hrrbrlln*," the centaur said.

"What?"

"*Hrrbrlln*," the creature repeated. "My name *Hrrbrlln*."

"Oh, your name?" The faery squinted up through long strands of hair. "Hueb . . . Hrebub . . ."

"*Hrrbrlln!*"

The faery shook his head. "It sounds like . . . Hueburlyn. Your name's Hueburlyn?"

"Sure . . . Hueburlyn," the centaur repeated with resignation. "Faery may say Hueburlyn. What faery name?"

"My name?" The faery shrugged and looked away. "My name is everything, Hueb, just like your bubble there is everything to you."

"Sometime I free of this bubble," Hueburlyn said in his deep voice. "But you never free of name."

The faery looked up in amused surprise. "You *do* understand our language, don't you?"

"Nykira Kyree teach slaves well," Hueburlyn answered with a shrug of his massive shoulders. "Slave is no worth unless understand commands. Slave no worth is dead. Plenty incentive for slave learn language well."

The faery smiled ruefully. "Better incentive, I should think, for a slave to learn the language better than he lets on."

A slight smile played at the edges of the centaur's wide lips. "Hueburlyn not speak well but understand too well."

"Then no doubt you know where we are going," the faery commented, gesturing with a wide sweep of his arm. The sun was lowering toward the western horizon of the treetops. "Our course is northeast from Sharajentis. It will take us a few days, but—"

"You taking me back to Nykira," Hueburlyn said with a heavy voice.

The faery turned away uncomfortably. "We don't have a choice."

"Always have choice," Hueburlyn replied, stretching his legs in the air as he folded his massive arms across his chest. "You choose to save Hueburlyn. I remember you open the gates when no one else choose. I remember you choose save me from hunters. You choose—and now you choose to take me to Nykira? Now you choose to kill Hueburlyn?"

"It isn't that simple," the faery grumbled.

"Excuses complicated; truth simple. What you name, faery?"

"Arryk," the faery replied, his voice reluctant.

The centaur tried to lean forward in his confining bubble, his broad hands moving to his hips. "Ar-ryk? Hueburlyn has heard this name!"

The faery looked up warily. "Where? Where have you heard my name?"

"Ar-ryk; son of Ay-sleen. Her name known friend to all *kntrr.* Her songs sung often in our dance to keep memory alive. Most honored and sorrowed is her loss," the centaur said solemnly.

"Yeah," Arryk replied, but his eyes were fixed somewhere beyond the horizon. "She was a real hero."

"Why would a son with such a name fly from it?"

Resentment filled the faery's eyes as his gaze snapped back to the centaur. "You know nothing about me."

"You are—complicated?"

"Yes—yes, I am—a complicated faery with a name you heard in some song about my fabulous mother."

"True, but this is not where Hueburlyn heard Ar-ryk last."

"Where, then?"

"Phlroch, God of the Sky, spoke it to me in the place of dreams. Your name called me to defy Nykira masters." The centaur reached out his wide right hand toward the faery, the gesture causing the sphere to turn somewhat. "Hueburlyn see you there, in the dream-city talking with the false-faced man."

Arryk stood quickly and took a few steps back on the deck. He shook his head vigorously, his straight black hair falling across his eyes. "No, centaur! You must *never* say that! Never to another creature, you understand?"

Hueburlyn froze, his eyes fixed on the faery standing below him. "No. Hueburlyn no understand. You tell Hueburlyn."

"It's, well…"

"Complicated?" the centaur said with an edge of menace in his voice.

"Look," the young faery continued, "I was wrong to let you into our city. I've—I've made things worse. I'm sorry; I didn't mean to, but that's the way it is. You've got to go back to your masters in Nykira, and I've got to take you and explain what happened in words that won't get anyone else hurt—and most of all, you must not tell anyone that you have visited the Sharaj—this place of dreams, as you call it."

Hueburlyn slowly folded his arms across his wide chest. "No."

"No?" Arryk repeated in astonishment. "What do you mean—no?"

"Is true that faery never lie?" the centaur asked suddenly.

"Yes, it is true," Arryk replied. "We can't."

"But if that answer a lie, how does Hueburlyn know if true or not?"

Arryk opened his mouth to answer but was suddenly confused. "You don't."

The centaur nodded. "So if true faery tell only truth and faery say Hueburlyn must say *kntrr* never in dream-place, then faery Ar-ryk not lie but ask Hueburlyn lie for him. The gods of the *kntrr* call me you name, Ar-ryk. Truth simple. Gods of *kntrr* call me come to Sharajentis from the dream-place. Speak other is as lie to gods of *kntrr.* Speak other is as lie to self."

"To 'speak other' is to get yourself killed and a lot of others along with you," Arryk said with emphasis. "Queen Dwynwyn has arranged for us to rendezvous with a diplomatic contingent at the Nykira border in two days. They think you're just another runaway slave who heard about Sharajentis and thought we might provide you asylum—and we've kept silence on everything else. They've promised not to kill you; they mostly want to return you to your master's landholdings and forget this entire incident ever happened. All you've got to do is pretend to adopt one trait of the faeries and everything will be just fine."

"What trait Hueburlyn must adopt?" asked the floating centaur.

"All you have to do is *keep silence*!" Arryk shouted as he sat abruptly down on the deck, crossing his legs once more and folding his own arms defiantly across his chest.

The songs of the evening birds drifted upward out of the tops of the forest to fill the sudden silence between them. Now and again the hull brushed against the leaves below with a gentle hissing sound. The sun was just about to drop below the horizon to the west.

"This spell powerful," Hueburlyn said, contemplating the bubble still holding him. "Where faery Ar-ryk find this in dream-place?"

Arryk groaned.

"It look like first spell of Dwynwyn," Hueburlyn commented after a long pause.

Arryk looked up. "How did you know..."

The centaur smiled. "Hueburlyn also read! Many Kyree history books. You make prison after Dwynwyn's first spell?"

"Partly." Arryk shrugged. "But mostly, it came from a dream I had last night—something about the masked people dancing in the sky."

"Ah! Dream-place of the gods!" Hueburlyn grinned,

showing his widely spaced teeth. "Tell *kntrr* about faery dreams."

Arryk curled up tighter on himself.

Dekacian* Skrei paced back and forth in the middle of the clearing. There was something about this entire business that smelled of rotting carcass, and he was afraid of being made a fool of—especially by the Fae.

Faeries; the very thought of them made the tips of his feathers quiver. Eons back they, too, had been nothing more than a slave race in Dunlar before they fled the Kyree Empire to set up their own petty kingdoms across the sea. Now they were proud beyond reason, thinking that they could dictate terms to the masters of the sky! The Kyree had been pulling the wings off the faeries from the moment they first encountered their sorry, flimsy huts in the western trees. They were weak, subtle, political, and diplomatic; all things which Skrei despised.

Now he was waiting in this clearing with twelve of his contingent to take possession of a runaway slave being returned by that cunning witch Dwynwyn. It was not to be borne; this was an errand for hunters, not an officer in the service of the Nykira Command.

Still, you could never trust faeries, Skrei knew—especially these witch-faeries of the dead. So he deployed the rest of his hundred warriors to hide in the tree line surrounding the clearing, just in case there was more to his premonition than the need for ordinary caution.

"Dekacian!" One of his warriors was pointing. "There to the southwest—just above the tree line."

---

*A Kyree word referring to either an honorable title granted to a commander of one thousand Kyree warriors or the designation of the group of warriors themselves.

Skrei looked up, spreading his wings to shade his eyes in the morning light.

It was one of the faery nightrunners, though this one was different from those he had seen before. The gondola still hung from the glass globes overhead, but its hull was sleek—there were no handles, nor, for that matter, were there any faeries pushing it, as was customary. No, he realized, this was a Sharajentei nightrunner and, no doubt, powered by witchcraft.

The ship settled gently into the tall grasses. Skrei could already see the centaur hovering above the main deck—indeed, it was difficult to miss the enormous beast suspended in the magical ball.

A young faery flitted from the deck of the ship, his hand extended toward the glowing ball around the centaur. As he moved, the ball followed him, carrying the slave monster over the railing and toward the waiting Dekacian.

"Master Kyree," the young faery said awkwardly, "I return your slave to you as agreed."

The Kyree warriors rose from the ground and began circling around both the faery and the globe.

"Release him, faery." Skrei sniffed. "We've dealt with his kind before."

"A condition of his return is that he not be harmed," the faery continued.

Skrei noted the fear underlying the faery's voice and wondered why they had sent someone so young. This was smelling worse by the moment. "Your orders were to deliver this slave, and you've done so. He is the property of the Kyree-Nykira—to be used or disposed of as we wish. Now release him!"

The faery blinked. "No."

Skrei bared his teeth as he spoke. "What did you say?"

"It was . . . was promised that he would not be harmed," the faery youth responded.

Skrei took a step forward, his hand reaching for the hilt of his sword. "You whelp of a faery, have you any idea what you are doing? Any state aiding in the theft of property of the Kyree Empire or harboring its stolen property is an act of war committed against the state. Now, do you want to give me an excuse to take the veteran armies of our Nykira skylords and have them marching victoriously down the streets of Sharajentis—or are you giving me that slave?"

The faery blinked and looked at the ground.

Skrei smiled.

The glowing ball lowered the glowering centaur to the ground, then faded away.

"Get out, faery," Skrei sneered. "This is no place for you to be."

The faery nodded without looking up and turned toward the centaur. In quick steps he stood before the enormous beast and held his hand out toward him.

"I am sorry," the faery said.

"Hueburlyn sorry to Ar-ryk," the centaur said.

In that moment a surge of white light surrounded the faery and the centaur. It rippled like the surface of a pond on a windy day and then spun like a whirlpool, distorting the figures within, collapsing them, and shrinking them in an instant down to a point of light. The white light then also collapsed in a thunderclap that pulled the circling Kyree out of the sky and snatched Dekacian Skrei off his feet to slam against his own warriors at the center of the vortex.

*   *   *

The remainder of Dekacian Skrei's contingent emerged from the tree line and rushed to their commander's aid. But they were too late. Dekacian Skrei lay dead, bleeding from his mouth, nose, eyes, and ears, as were the rest of the warriors who were near him.

The centaur and the faery were gone.

Skrei's aide removed his commander's helmet and launched at once with it into the sky. The slave and the Sharajentei warlock had escaped and killed his commander. There was not a moment to lose.

There would be war.

Obsession

It was the overwhelming noise that startled him first.

Reacting to a nearly deafening thunderclap sound, Arryk's fear was visceral. Without thinking he dropped immediately to a crouch, his senses heightened. He turned instinctively toward the Kyree dekacian, calling on the Deep Magic to well up within him, but inexplicably, it was not there . . .

The dekacian was not there either, nor were any of the Kyree warriors which moments before were circling menacingly overhead. Nor, for that matter, he realized with a second shock, was the meadow clearing, his nightrunner, the tree line, or the sky.

They were in a cage.

The Oraclyn and the centaur were completely enclosed by bands of flat, woven steel spaced just over a handbreadth apart. These formed a box that extended upward from the chill stones of the floor and over their heads. The air was suddenly damp and cool, though hardly still. Beyond the bars Arryk could see nothing but dust and a large number of parchment leaves swirling about in a subsiding gale.

"What Ar-ryk do?" Hueburlyn was still standing next to the faery—that much had not changed—but there was a definite quiver in the creature's deep voice.

"Nothing; I didn't do this," Arryk responded cautiously. He took a step toward the crosshatch metal grate, but his foot kicked against something that gave a metallic ring. "By the whim of Gobrach!* What is this thing?"

Surrounding them on the floor lay a wide metallic ring. It looked as though it were formed of six metal arms bent at the elbow, each one grasping the shoulder of the next. There were a number of spinning objects connected with belts around its perimeter as well as copper shafts which moved without any apparent function or pattern. There was a glow about the whole thing that was quickly fading. Arryk had never seen anything like this device, but the source of its power was unmistakable. He turned at once toward the centaur.

"What have you done, Famadorian?" the Oraclyn shouted. "You take us back right now, or so help me, I will—"

Geep!

Both the centaur and the faery tracked the sound, the obscuring dust settling at last. The cage itself appeared to be set inside a circular tower. The curved walls of rough, gouged stone soared overhead as a shaft nearly a hundred feet high before ending in a translucent dome. Arryk noted several balconies at various levels up the shaft, and the sound that had just startled them came from the lowest of them, just above the top grate of their cage.

---

*Gobrach, the faery ancestor also known as the Guardian of the Veil. Most closely associated with chaos and the undiscovered truth.

Arryk's jaw dropped in disbelief. It could not be true and yet it *was* true—a New Truth, he realized, that was entirely unexpected.

Staring back at them was a creature Arryk was certain could not be real. It had two wide orange eyes set on either side of a hooked nose, and enormous ears that came to sharp points. Its chin, too, was pointed, and there was a single tuft of long white hair sprouting from the center of its otherwise bald head. Its huge breasts and potbelly seemed barely contained by the stained red vest it wore under an open black leather mantle. More astonishing still was its skin, for it was a deep mottled green.

"Ar-ryk seen this creature before?" the centaur managed to stammer.

"Yes," the faery responded, feeling queasy. He had the urge to lie down, cover his eyes, and forget what he was looking at. "But I have only seen his kind in the Sharaj. They—they do not exist!"

"Look real enough to Hueburlyn," the centaur croaked.

The green creature leaped up and down, although whether in joy or anger, Arryk could not tell. It looked down once more, its hideous gaze fixed on Arryk.

"Wakarka!" the creature shouted, and then vanished behind the overhang.

"What did it say?" Arryk asked, turning to the centaur.

The centaur took a cautious step back, which was all the room left to him, and he shook his head.

The creature reappeared in that same moment, running across the room on the other side of the cage door. The dust had finally cleared, though the room was now in complete disarray, with more of the strange jagged-edged wheels, rods, and metal balls scattered around as well as a number of parchments, both loose and bound into books with strange figures on their covers.

"Akti bekaraka suhak?" The short creature spoke to Arryk in a voice that sounded like slate rubbing together before concluding with a wide, sharp-toothed grin.

"What?" Arryk responded.

The little monster screamed, clapping its hands over its large ears and weeping big wet tears. It staggered backward, stopping just short of a large pair of doors, which, Arryk assumed, led to some other room. The grotesque little thing staggered back toward the bars of the cage to make another attempt.

"AKTI BEKARAKA SUHAK?" the little monster shouted in its grating voice, still holding its hands over its ears.

Arryk leaned forward and shouted back in the creature's face. "I DON'T UNDERSTAND!"

The little thing fainted at once, falling flat on its back against the stone flooring.

"I don't think green bug like Ar-ryk voice," Hueburlyn observed. "By all *Emrth* gods, where you bring Hueburlyn?"

"How should I know? *I* didn't bring us *anywhere*," Arryk answered hotly. He brought his hands up in front of him, straining with frustration as he searched for the power. He closed his eyes, retreating in his mind back toward the place of the Sharaj. He opened his eyes again in a near panic. "I can't—I don't know! The Sharaj—it isn't there."

The centaur closed his eyes, pulling his face toward the ceiling of their cage. "Ar-ryk wrong; the dream-place still there for *kntrr.* Maybe something wrong with Ar-ryk."

"Look, centaur," the faery's words coming in a panicked rush. "Sometimes the Sharaj moves like a quiet stream within me, and sometimes it moves in a rushing, torrential flood, but never—*never*—has it dried up and vanished entirely."

"Maybe this cage special for you," Hueburlyn rumbled. "Maybe we stay quiet, consider, and reason way out of special Ar-ryk cage."

"No! That's impossible, and we can't stay here! We've got to get back now!" Arryk reached out, intent on shaking their cage apart with his bare hands. As his fingers wrapped around the cross-weave of the metal bars, the faery's head suddenly jerked back, his eyes rolling into his skull. He stood there, motionless for a moment, until his fingers released and he collapsed backward.

Hueburlyn just managed to catch Arryk at the last moment before his head would have bounced against the stones of the floor. Concerned that he might break the fragile creature by accident, the centaur held the light faery in his hands for only a second before carefully setting him on the floor facedown so as not to damage his wings.

Hueburlyn looked back and forth from the small green monster unconscious outside their cage to the faery unconscious inside. Finally, with a great shrug, the centaur folded his legs under him and lowered his own body against the cool stones beneath him.

"I guess we wait until someone wakes up," he said to himself, folding his arms across his chest.

Arryk's first feeling was the painful, agonizing prickle of numbness fleeing from his hands. Feeling somewhat disoriented, he opened his eyes to find his cheek lying against a chill, stone floor. The view that presented itself was of a sideways centaur gazing intently at something beyond the faery. Arryk blinked and then groaned at the impossible effort it required to awaken. His noise broke the intense gaze of the centaur, who glanced down at him and then hurriedly gestured by putting both open hands across his own mouth.

Arryk nodded in understanding, then pushed himself up from the floor slowly, staggering uncertainly to his feet.

The cage and his surroundings had not changed; the latticework of mysterious metal still separated him from the rest of the room beyond and from the towering shaft above. He did not know what terrible properties that metal held, but he had no desire to test it again. And right now it was not his cage that attracted his attention but the creature staring back at him through the hand-wide openings between the bars.

The hideous little monster was staring at him, her red-orange eyes intent on his every move. The wispy tufts of white hair at the tips of her long, pointed ears quivered as she gazed with openmouthed astonishment. Her jaw worked as she muttered to herself, her pointed teeth clacking against each other. In her hands she held a flat hat, which she was kneading in what might have been nervousness. Her large feet were bare and displayed prominent long and yellow toenails.

Yet it was a face which Arryk knew well from the Sharaj. He had always seen something childlike in that face in the dream that now stared at him in reality: a wide-eyed wonder and innocence behind the hideous and terrifying green of her face. He leaned closer, ever mindful of the grillwork as he tried to look into the strange orange eyes and see what lay beyond them.

The centaur gave a low, warning growl behind him, but Arryk did not heed the caution.

The green creature blinked and then smiled slightly, her eyes wide. She reached forward, her hand and arm extending between the bars, her long knobby fingers reaching tentatively for Arryk's face.

The faery youth stood perfectly still as water welled up in the monster's eyes. Her fingers gently brushed the faery's cheek. Hesitantly, the little creature withdrew her hand as tears flowed freely down both her mottled cheeks. She suddenly began dancing, her large feet slapping against the floor as she spun across the room between the piles of strange, rusting cogs and shafts and the huge doors that closed off the other side of the room.

Hueburlyn stood and slowly stepped up next to the stunned faery. He bent so that he might speak quietly into the faery's ear. "Green creature friend to Ar-ryk?"

"I—I've only seen them in the Sharaj," the faery whispered back.

"Truth they exist here, too," the centaur grumbled.

"New Truth," Arryk replied under his breath. "Wherever 'here' is."

"Truth *we* exist here, too," Hueburlyn answered quickly. "Work they for Nykira Kyree?"

"I don't think so," Arryk offered thoughtfully, "but I intend to find out." The faery clapped his hands loudly.

The little creature turned at once toward the sound, stopping in her dance, and stared at the faery.

Arryk put his left hand up, palm out toward the creature, and placed his right hand flat against his chest, then ran it first left and then right. He then pressed the fingertips of both hands together in front of him and waited. *I am Sharajin,* he thought to himself as he made the sign just as he would have in the Sharaj.

The little creature's sudden grin looked vicious, but she answered in identical movements.

She is Sharajin? Arryk interpreted, wondering for a moment if the creature was just repeating his own movements back to him.

But the little creature was mooing, her hand gestures continuing in the familiar pattern.

"What green creature saying?" Hueburlyn asked in quiet astonishment.

"Well, she—it isn't making any sense," Arryk replied quietly, his eyes fixed on the creature. "She keeps saying 'welcome' or 'joy' and something about a 'magical bridge,' which I don't understand at all. I mean, all of the symbols are familiar, but they can't be right."

"Why? What else she say?"

"Well, something about 'aching with forever'—no, 'with everlasting desire,'" Arryk replied as he continued to watch her frantic gestures. Suddenly, she turned away from them and dashed toward the large doors on the opposite side of the room. "Now it's something about 'loving the winged-ugly with a fire-heart-fire until it dies.' What do you suppose that means?"

The creature threw open the doors, which groaned slightly in protest before swinging wide. A much larger room opened to their view, illuminated with shafts of light from grating openings overhead. The entire room was filled with objects fashioned out of every kind of material: woods, stones, and metals, each shaped lovingly into statues of every size in an incredible array of poses. There were paintings also and metal etchings hanging from the ceiling or from the walls or standing on the stone floor. Some were abstract, but most were of an incredible detail and accuracy as to look almost alive. It was every kind of art imaginable, and every object had but a single theme.

From the straight black hair to the delicate boots, each creation was an unmistakable replica of Arryk.

The faery's jaw dropped in shock.

The centaur spoke first, snorting. "What mean? Hueburlyn tell Ar-ryk what mean—mean Ar-ryk in bad trouble!"

Ivory Towers

Big-funder Thwick, undisputed Master of Fat Endowments to the Hob-goblins of Og, stepped outside the main doors of the Throne of the Big-funder—the most prestigious building in the entire city—and looked over the length of the oval park with tremendous satisfaction.

The park had at last been measured satisfactorily by the Profitable Archaeology Department, and its length had just been reported to him by Big-tinker Tudu himself. The wildly overgrown, brush-choked, and weed-infested area had gotten several expeditions lost before Big-tinker Tudu, the head of Profitable Archaeology, led a sixth and final expedition of Hob-goblins from the eastern end of the park all the way to the steps of the Throne of the Big-funder himself, camping only twice along the way.

To give them a proper send-off, Big-funder Thwick had even taken time from his busy schedule to walk five minutes down the road that curved around the southern edge of the park to attend the farewell celebration hosted most graciously by the neighboring (and much larger)

Department of Historic Revisionism. The celebration had lasted three days and left the Big-funder nearly unable to walk back at its conclusion. He had therefore decided not to attend the First Encampment Workshop or the Second Encampment Survival School—both of which were weeklong affairs that he had suspected would require a significant donation to the department.

Nevertheless, six weeks after it began, the expedition emerged from the park with several marvelous artifacts discovered during their painstaking observations: a broken titan jar, curiously shaped rocks, and a previously unknown book whose moldy pages were carefully carried from the park on the heads of several Narrow-tinker expedition assistants.

Of course, the most important discovery was the precisely measured length of the enormous park, which heretofore had defied the Hob-goblin system of counting, which only went up to the number one hundred and fourteen. (It was not the first time that a Big-funder of the HOB Academy had wondered if they didn't need a Department of Creative Counting.) However, Big-tinker Tudu proved his brilliance by inventing a new length of measure: a pole that was the length of ten goblin feet. Tudu sensibly named it the Tudu after himself and thus was able to report definitively that the park was just short of one hundred and fourteen Tudus long.*

Now Big-funder Thwick stood on the top steps and looked down on the park that threatened to overtake both the north and south roads that bordered it, and nodded with satisfaction. Tudu's expedition would be a wonder-

---

*Given the average length of goblin feet, this would make the park approximately twelve hundred feet long by human measure.

ful thing to bring up at his next meeting with Lord Skramak, the primary benefactor of the academy.

How things had changed since the early days, he mused. Thwick was only the latest in a long and prestigious line of Hob-goblin Big-funders that went all the way back some eighty years to the time of Thux—the first Big-funder and founder of the academy. It was Thux who found the city of Og in the first place and discovered the House of Books, which became the foundation of everything they had built since.

Thwick turned to look down the north side of the park. There was the House of Books as Thux had originally found it and the much smaller building—now the Theory of Books Department—where the original academy first started. For eighty years those inside had labored to decipher the sequence of symbols in the books housed inside the mysterious and powerful House of Books. Big-tinker Doon assured him that one of these years they would definitely have another breakthrough, for he felt sure they were getting closer all the time. It was from such humble beginnings that the academy had grown to fill the ancient buildings on both sides of the park—now more than one hundred and fourteen Tudus long.

Thwick suddenly frowned. As impressive as even Tudu's achievement had been, it was largely of interest only to the knowledgeable Hob-goblins of the academy. Thwick knew in his heart that if he wanted to impress Dong Mahaj Skramak, he would need to deliver something with more practical application.

What he needed was something new from the Deep Tinkers.

Thwick strode confidently down the steps of the Throne of the Big-funder and began walking down the south-side road around the park. He was an imposing figure to the academics that passed him: almost five feet tall with wide shoulders and a hard, round belly, he commanded the respect, if sometimes grudging, of everyone he met. His earlobes were astonishingly long and had a tendency to swing when he walked, which, he fancied, always distracted his enemies. Most important, however, he had a tuft of white hair on his head unequaled by any other Hob-goblin, a truly elegant affair that parted in the middle and fell in a wide cascade down either side of his head. It was no secret that the achievement of his current rank and position was due in no small measure to his striking good looks.

He marched past the large twin buildings housing the Department of Goblinities, walked carefully around two trees that had fallen across the roadway, and climbed down one side of a pothole and up the other. The city of Og had been kept intact since the time of the titans themselves by the resident ogres, who had put forth a set of very strict rules. Those rules—all two of them—were the touchstones of everything that was lawful and right so far as the ogres were concerned, and they read: protect the city and don't touch anything. The academy was located in what the ogres still called the Trove, which was given over to the care of Thux and his Hob-goblins eight decades before. The ogres, who still ruled the city beyond the Trove and kept the city safe from attack, had only loaned the location and buildings of the academy to the goblins—a fact of which every Big-funder since Thux was all too keenly aware—and so the rules of not touching anything were still obeyed as strictly as possible.

Just beyond the pothole Thwick at last came to the towering walls of the Hall of Deep Tinkers, whose intricately ornate gray walls dwarfed the much smaller Hall of Shallow Tinkers that huddled before it. Thwick turned from the roadway, leaped up the steps to the side entrance arch, and ducked inside.

The transverse back hall was an amazing sight, but looking at it always made Thwick feel a little dizzy and uncomfortable. Tall columns on either side of the thirty-foot-wide hall rose to nearly three times that number in height before sweeping in graceful arcs to the ceiling. There were two concourses above the hall which Thwick understood were accessed by large staircases, but he had never been able to bring himself to go there personally. Heights were not an experience which the Big-funder found comfortable.

As it happened, however, he was not discomfited by the hall's vertical expanse this time, since there was a considerable distraction taking place on the main floor at the junction of the transverse hall and the main gallery in the form of a group of Hob-goblins cheering and leaping about.

In the center of the commotion were two Hob-goblins locked in combat and apparently trying to kill each other; one an aging Big-tinker and the other a younger Substitute-tinker. Together they formed a snarling, chaotic heap rolling about the floor, with the occasional bloodied fists or claws lashing out. A circle of assorted Big-tinkers, Substitute-tinkers, and Narrow-tinkers had gathered at the spectacle and was encouraging the brawl.

Thwick observed the fight for a few minutes. He always enjoyed lively debate and felt that it helped the academy more effectively continue its noble work. However, while he would have loved to stay to see which of them survived and find out what philosophical point was being challenged, there just was not enough time.

So he reluctantly continued down to the other end of the transverse hall and out the other side. In the brush-choked plaza beyond, nestled between the Idea Testing Center and the Public Secret Labs, was a single tower known to everyone in the academy as the Secret Secret Labs. A single set of stairs curved around the back leading to its door twenty feet up the side of the tower, which Big-funder Thwick climbed quickly. Dong Mahaj Skramak was waiting back in the Hall of the Big-funder, and Thwick knew that there was only one Deep Tinker who could come up with what he needed to please his benefactor—and it did not hurt that the Dong had bought everything this Deep Tinker had invented.

Even if she was just a woman, Thwick thought as he pounded his fist on the tower door, Deep-tinker Lunid was the one Hob-goblin whose research always paid off.

Lunid could barely contain herself. She leaped and danced wildly among her creations—her beautiful works of artistry—and then turned back to the containment cell to gaze once more on the perfect form of her heart's desire.

It had worked just as she had seen it in the tome-sight: the vision rings, the clockwork governor, and the manipulator arms. It had taken a great many more of the book-sinks than she originally anticipated—an invention of her own that powered the entire assembly and which had exceeded her resources dangerously—but now, who could complain? She had reached into the place of fevered tech-nomantic tome-sight, used her converted titan devices to peer into it with waking eyes, and then willed the object of her desire into existence in her own world through machines of her own craft!

And she owned him: the beautiful winged dark man with the straight black hair. No matter that his stomach was flat and his face the color of old wood; she thought he was beautifully compelling in his own terrifying way. She had seen him many times in her dreams and her books. Like her, he had always looked so sad. Although she never spoke with him in the world of dreams, she followed him each night from behind corners and protected places, seeing his despair and heartache until it broke her heart, too. She had taken to creating his image in her research, finding inspiration in her thoughts of him and comfort just in shaping objects into his form. Over time she had begun to feel she knew him better in her dreams than she knew her colleagues when awake. It was her desire to see him during her waking hours that drove her to construct the farsight rings in the first place. Watching him fly had made her obsessed with flight and inspired some of her most beautiful work in machines. Yet her creations were not enough; the longing in her soul grew each night until she had to find a way to bring him closer so she could touch him and hear his voice.

Well, perhaps not hear his voice, she decided. It was too beautiful for her ears and, now that she had heard it, filled her with such sadness and shame that it drove her very mind from her head, making her pass out. But at last she could touch him, take care of him, feed him, and protect him. And he would love her for it—could not *help* but love her for it—and at last fill the void that gnawed continuously at her life.

Of course, she had not anticipated he would bring along the huge brute monster. The ugly thing used four legs to carry its wide body and also had a set of arms and a tail. It looked like the sort of experiment the Department of Advanced Speculation had been attempting a few years back—the ones that were such spectacular failures. In truth, she had built the containment cage for just the winged man, so she wasn't sure what to do with the thing. Perhaps she could donate the monster to the Idea Testing Center for dismemberment. Surely, not even Big-funder Thwick himself could object to . . .

The Big-funder! This morning he had said he was coming over. Only then was she aware of the booming knocking sounds rolling down the tower stairs.

Lunid was thoughtful as she examined her beautiful winged man and his unexpected companion. She wanted desperately to show the Big-funder her triumph but was suddenly cautious; she still was not certain why the winged man's voice was so upsetting and, more particularly, was not sure she wanted to explain the presence of the four-footed monster in the containment cage.

With reluctance she tore herself away from her beautiful captive and padded up the stairs toward the insistent banging at the door.

Visible Means

Oh, do try to keep up, will you, Lunid?" "S-sorry, B-b-b-big-f-f-f-f-funder," the Deep Tinker said for the third time in her staccato words. Knowing that it was difficult for her embarrassingly short legs to match Thwick's longer strides made her shameful stutter all the worse. "Where—where are we g-going?"

"Back to my Throne," Thwick replied curtly.

"B-but the—the hall . . ."

"There is a debate going on in the hall right now, and we have no more time to be distracted by such pleasantries," Thwick responded impatiently. He was taking them instead around the back between the Deep Tinkers Hall and the Sanctuary of Elitist Arts. Lunid felt somewhat grateful to the Big-funder; at least there would be fewer of her fellow academicians who could look at her here behind the buildings. "You look a mess—what have you been wasting your time on now?"

"Ex-ex-exper-experi—"

"Oh, Lunid, get control of yourself," the Big-funder

said with exasperation. "Your face twitches most unpleasantly when you stammer like that!"

Lunid's eyes fell to looking at her smallish feet, and she bit her lower lip. "Yes, B-big-f-f-f—"

"Look, Lunid, you are one of the best Deep Tinkers we have." Thwick spoke at her rather than to her, his face never looking back. "Your discoveries are invaluable to the academy—every one of them a complete success."

"I j-just try to make things that are b-b-beau-beautiful," Lunid answered quietly. "I like making pretty things that move."

"And you do, Lunid; you most certainly do," Thwick said as he now moved them behind the Department of Goblinities toward the road that crossed in front of the Throne of the Big-funder. "That is how you contribute—that is how you make your way in the world. That is why we shelter you here in the academy—keeping you safe from the outside world where your brilliance would not be understood."

"Still, I-I've always—always w-wondered w-w-what it was like," Lunid said in her halting voice, "out—outside the a-academy. Have you—have you considered my r-r-request for a f-field s-study in—"

Big-funder Thwick stopped and turned so abruptly that Lunid nearly ran into him.

"Lunid, look at yourself," the Big-funder huffed. "Your feet are too small, your belly is too flat, and your ears are hideous. You are the ugliest goblin anywhere on campus. Even when I try to pair you up with a partner who's never seen you, between your stammering and your twitching you drive them off before they have a chance to get past your faults and see the brilliant Deep Tinker I know you are. You've driven off every Substitute-tinker we've ever assigned to you with your temper. What kind of a life would you have outside the protection of the academy? How long do you think you could last out in a world that is not so understanding or tolerant as I am?"

"Y-yes, B-big-fun-funder," Lunid said through a sniffle.

"Now, an old admirer of yours has come to visit and wants to hear all about your latest work," Thwick said casually. "He's come from quite a distance, and I don't want him to be disappointed. Do you have something interesting to show him?"

In all her days at the academy, this was the first time Lunid had been invited into the Palace of the Big-funder, and she was moved nearly to tears.

The magnificent rotunda housed what the Hobgoblins referred to simply as the Throne. It was a collection of huge devices formed, in part, out of the upper part of a mechanical titan, whose thickly muscled arms held a glowing globe of deep blue light, while riding on the back of the titan was a smaller metallic statue of a goblin holding a globe of shifting gray hues. On either side of the titan man were tall and monstrously thin female titans, each of whom held a globe of metal over her head with an expression that looked pained.

All of this was poised around a single, intricately constructed sphere of bronze that sat atop a pedestal in the center of the room.

The Device of Thux, Lunid realized with a sudden rush of emotion. It was in this very place that the Hobgoblins—the House of Books goblins—were born and the Academy of Thux established. Of all the places that were not to be touched, this was the place that was held absolutely inviolate. She gazed at the Device that was the inspiration for everything that they did at the academy; it brought tears welling up in her eyes just to look upon it, even from across the room.

A figure stood up from where it had been sitting on the Big-funder's stone chair situated behind the Device. The goblin was wide-shouldered and more muscular than most, and he wore boots after the style of the trolls of Laklond Westwall. His hair tuft was shaved, leaving his scalp unusually and defiantly bald, and he sported a vest from the linked metal rings of the Skorech Giants. Yet it was the dark socket bisected by a scar that ran from his forehead to below his ear that identified him most clearly; the missing left eye was known as his symbol from the furthest Thunderforge Mountains on the west to the Gremlin Mines on the eastern frontier. He was known as Dong Mahaj Mahal—a name he had claimed for his own after the death of his father—but to Lunid he was known simply as . . .

"Skramak!" Lunid cried out in genuine delight.

The Emperor of the Goblins smiled widely as he approached the Deep Tinker and the Big-funder. His cape billowed magnificently behind him as he walked toward her—an amazing accomplishment of technomancy, since there was no breeze in the hall.

"I knew it would be you." The old goblin grinned, his sharp yellow teeth gleaming. "When I said to Thwick, 'Bring me your best and your brightest,' I just knew it would be you."

"Th-th-thank you, Y-y-your Ambi-ambitiousness," Lunid said as she tried to bow low before the great goblin and nearly lost her balance.

"Stand up, Lunid," Thwick growled under his breath. "The Dong is not interested in your silly fawning."

"That's quite all right, Big-funder," Skramak said easily as he approached them both. He reached back and pressed the shoulder clasp of his still-billowing robe, which dispelled the magic and caused the cloth to fall at once to the ground with a dusty thud. "Lunid has always served the academy as best she could, and her art has always . . . served me as well. It was you that created that marvelous disk-throwing device, was it not?"

"Y-y-yes, Your M-m-m-ma-majesty."

"And the titan wings and the safety arrows," Skramak said softer still, his words sounding like steam quietly escaping from a pot. His good eye had narrowed on the Deep Tinker, considering her carefully as he spoke.

"Y-y-yes, Your M-m-m-ma-ma—"

"So I am sure that our old friend Lunid has come up with something wonderful to amuse us," Skramak continued, not waiting for the goblin woman to choke out her words. His lips grew tight over his teeth, straining his smile into a dangerous grimace. "You *do* have something new, do you not?"

"Oh! Oh, yes, Your M-m-majesty," Lunid responded brightly.

"So what is it?" Skramak asked patiently. "What are you working on now?"

"R-rift . . . rift-gate," Lunid managed to get out.

"Rift-gate?" the Lord of All Goblins asked. He looked over at Thwick but saw that the Big-funder was as baffled as he was. "What is a rift-gate?"

"I—I wanted t-to see into—into the tome-pictures," Lunid started to explain. Her speech became more fluid as her mind returned to the excitement of her discovery. "N-not just when I was asleep but while I was awake."

"I can't see how that's very useful," Thwick sniffed. "All of the Hob-goblins are technomancers—all we need is a book and a little sleep. Who would pay for a device that would show them in the day what they could see at night for free?"

"That's the f-farsight rings device," Lunid snapped unhappily. "D-different d-device altogether. Well, perhaps not altogether; I did use f-farsight rings in the . . . in the rift-gate design, but the results are completely d-d-different!"

"Hmm." Skramak considered for a moment. "So you can use this new creation to look into other people's dreams—er, tome-sight?"

"N-no, Your Majesty," Lunid said, bowing awkwardly once again. "It worked b-better than I ex-expected. It looked past the tome-sight realms and into the world of the gods."

A sudden silence filled the immense throne room. Skramak and Thwick both stared at Lunid in slack-jawed amazement. Moments passed before anyone spoke again.

"D-did I n-n-not explain it right?" Lunid asked at the sight of their expressions.

"Did you say you used the device to look into the world of the gods?" Skramak said, turning his head slightly so as to get a better look at the Deep Tinker with his single remaining eye.

"Yes, Your M-majesty," Lunid replied, then gazed off in thought. "You see, it was a matter of connecting book-sinks in series with the farsight rings in dual-bus configuration, then utilizing a controller book with vision stones to stabilize the field structure and project it across the tome-sight to a fixed subject in the realm of the gods." She looked at the men. "Are you f-following me?"

Skramak and Thwick looked to each other again, but found no help there. The emperor turned to Lunid, shaking his head. "The Dongs of the empire have all been first-rate technomancers since the time of Mimic. I myself am considered the greatest technomancer of our age—and I haven't the first idea what you're talking about."

"Perhaps," Thwick hastily intervened, "it is not necessary that we get all of the . . . uh, technical details right at this moment, Lunid. You say that we can . . . spy on the world of the gods?"

"Well, yes"—Lunid nodded—"so long as you have a target god that you can fix. We've known for s-some time that the books connect to the g-g-gods in our dreams. That's what m-m-makes the b-b-books have p-power; they steal from the g-gods. So I thought the b-b-books might be useful in connecting my vision stones back to the realm of the gods. I muh-myself ha-have w-w-watched one of the g-gods for some time now—p-purely as a t-t-test subject, m-mind you."

Skramak's mind was beginning to work again, and it had just barely wrapped his thinking around the idea of using a machine to access the eternal realms. "So—we could watch the gods and find out if our offerings were acceptable or whether we will be victorious in battle. It could take a lot of the guesswork out of religion."

"The farsight rings use the tome-sight for locating their subjects, but they d-don't bring back any s-sounds," Lunid explained carefully. "It would be easier j-just to go to the world of the gods instead and try to ask them directly."

"That's nonsense," Thwick huffed. "You can't go to the world of the gods—"

"Through the rift-gate you can."

Once again a stunned silence descended on Skramak and Thwick.

"I'm sorry," Lunid said, shaking her head. "I thought I made that clear before. The point of the rift-gate is to form a bridge between our world and the world of the gods. You just step through it or, in some cases, are pulled through it against your will, though afterward I'm sure that you'd feel good about it."

"You mean you can travel to the world of the gods?" Skramak asked intently, with skepticism in his tone. "How long does it take? How many can go?"

"Well." Lunid thought for a moment. "It doesn't t-take any time at all actually. It's just like s-stepping from one side of a d-d-doorway to another—except you're in the world of the gods rather than the world of the titans. As for how many, that's mostly a matter of how many b-b-books you would have to hook up in s-s-series. Theoretically, any n-n-number could go."

"Ah, Your Majesty," Thwick interjected hurriedly, "I really must apologize for Lunid. She has been under some considerable strain these last few—well, years probably—and she obviously needs a well-deserved sabbatical. I'm sure that I can find another Deep Tinker on our faculty who can show you something more practical—"

"But this w-w-works!" Lunid insisted.

"Lunid, please! You can't possibly—"

"But I've t-t-tested it! I pulled a pair of gods through the rift-gate this morning."

"You *what*?" Thwick screeched.

"You pulled a pair of *gods* through your gate-device?"

Skramak asked, his eyebrows rising in surprise, lifting his scar slightly on his forehead and opening up his empty eye socket wider.

"Well—yes. I suppose I should have asked permission before I actually ran the test, but—"

"And where are these gods now?"

"Oh, in a c-cage in the b-basement of the l-l-lab."

Skramak took a step closer toward Lunid, his large orange eye looking down at her. "Will you show me these gods? Will you show me how I might reach their world? Would you do that for me, my dear Lunid?"

Lunid looked up into the pocked green face of Dong Mahaj Mahal Skramak and only nodded.

Thwick stood next to the emperor as Lunid hurried away down the main hall of the Throne and out into the sunlight beyond the main doors. The Big-funder held his silence until the door was safely closed in the distance.

"Your Majesty," Thwick said, his uneasy words coming carefully, "I don't know about this business with the 'world of the gods.' I mean, there was a best-of-five debate just last year between the Profitable Archaeology Department and Theoretical Technomancy about the existence of the gods, and the surviving members determined—"

"For a leader of the academy, you seem to lack much faith in your fellow Hob-goblins." Dong Skramak's words were suddenly devoid of their former warmth. "Everything Lunid has ever presented to us has been more than useful—it has been essential to the building of the empire."

"But the world of the gods, Your Majesty," Thwick moaned.

"No, Thwick!" Skramak licked his lips in anticipation.

"Not just the world of the gods—but a gateway to that world! I've been looking for just such an answer for a long time now, Thwick, and this could be it."

"I don't understand, Your Majesty."

"Of course, you don't; you academics!" Skramak snarled. "All you do is sit in your towers, trying to think your way into a reality that exists only in your own minds, and then you judge the world as wrong because it does not conform to your impossible standards. I live in a real world, academic. And it's my real world that keeps pumping blood into your dead, idealistic one."

"You've no right to talk to me—"

"I have every right," Skramak snapped. "I buy and pay for you every day. It's the wealth of *my* empire that keeps food flowing into this academy and gives you the right to breathe from one moment to the next. It's the conquests of the empire that keep your precious research into the library moving forward—if it moves forward at all."

"The Theory of Books Department assures me—"

"Yes, I know. 'Any week now' they'll have a breakthrough. My family has been waiting for this anticipated 'breakthrough' since my father's father's mother's time, which is more years than anyone knows how to count. Without us, there will be no more weeks to anticipate, and unless something changes, there will be precious few weeks left to you."

"Why?" Thwick asked, genuinely alarmed. "What's happened?"

"The worst thing imaginable," Skramak answered heavily.

"You mean the war in the west?"

Skramak looked at the Big-funder.

"You don't mean..."

"Yes." Skramak nodded solemnly. "We won."

"No!"

"It's true," Skramak continued, folding his arms across his chest thoughtfully. "Thanks in no small measure to your own Lunid, we've subdued the giants at last. There is nothing left for our armies to conquer."

"But—but surely, there are other lands beyond the Westwall and the Nomanlond? What of the Southern Crags—or the forests beyond Gremlin Hole?"

"It's all so simple for you." Skramak shook his head. "You're an academic; you think of the landscape. I, on the other hand, am a warrior; I think of the logistics. Our empire has expanded as far as it can. We could send armies further out, of course, but how would we feed them? Worse, how would we communicate with them? Taking another's nation is one thing; keeping it under your thumb is an entirely different matter. Even you will agree that it's harder to hold a stone at arm's length than close to your chest."

"I still don't understand why Lunid solves anything with this so-called rift-gate."

"Consider our government. Wealth, labor, and food—we steal all of that. Our armies of titans thunder across the landscape and take what we need from all the other dolts who have wealth, labor, and food. If we are going to continue our rule of conquest, then we need something new to conquer—some place that will give us a power base from which we can expand even further—and it needs to be conveniently nearby."

"But you just said that there were no lands near enough to conquer effectively."

"Yeah, but Lunid's rift-gate is right here in her lab. If I understand her correctly, given enough books, we can send entire armies through just like stepping from one side of a doorway to the other." Skramak grinned in anticipation. "It would be a campaign of conquest unequaled in all the history of the goblins—and would ensure my immortality."

"What are you saying?" Thwick asked, already dreading the answer.

"I'm saying that we should put Lunid's rift-gate to practical use," Skramak purred, "and conquer the world of the gods!"

Darkened Door

The Shadow Watch guardian stepped through the archway into the great hall of the Conlan house and quickly snatched his hat off of his head.

"Master Kyne Fletcher," Agretha announced into the grand hall, where most of the Conlan family was assembled at the long table. She looked as though she had just let a great stench into the house.

"Thank you, Agretha," Rylmar said, barely looking up from where he sat.

Agretha turned and thrust her finger threateningly at the guard's nose. "Mind you keep those muddy boots of yours to the tile, or you'll be answering to me, Shadow guardian or not!"

"Yes, ma'am," Kyne said, bowing nervously.

Theona stood apart from the scene before her, her arms crossed and her head tilted slightly to one side. Having no facility in the mystic arts often left her outside of important gatherings, but her distraught father had asked her to attend, so she had come even if she felt like nothing more than an observer.

Her father sat at the end of the massive table in the great hall. His temperament had run the gamut over the last week, from rage to cunning to despair and back to rage once more. He had plotted and planned, met secretly and openly, favored, bribed, and threatened everyone he knew from dawn to dawn. It had availed him nothing. Treijan, prince of House Rennes-Arvad, had vanished from the city—and with him the long and expensive plans for Rylmar's greatest triumph over his peers.

Next to him sat Valana, her eyes red and puffy. She was very much in danger of looking less than perfect, Theona thought, banishing a smile that threatened to break across her face.

For a moment an awkward silence filled the room. Valana would say nothing, Rylmar was too weary from speaking already, and the Shadow guardian looked too frightened to begin.

"Welcome to the House of Conlan, Master Fletcher," Theona said at last, the cool tones of her voice echoing in the vast hall.

"Thank you, your ladyship." Fletcher was wringing his hat nervously in his hands.

"Her 'ladyship' keeps to her bed in her distress," Theona said quickly, her eyes gazing critically on the guard. "I am Mistress Theona. May I present Mistress Valana and Lord Conlan."

Fletcher bowed to each name as it was spoken, a nervous grin stiff on his face, though his eyes darted about a good deal.

"You seem worried, Master Fletcher," Theona observed.

"Oh, no . . . well, yes, Mistress Theona," the guard said, his hat being worked so feverishly that it would soon lose all hope of retaining its original shape. "It's just that this is a matter of some delicacy. Perhaps a matter of life and death—which some people might wish kept silent."

"So your petition said," Rylmar grumbled as he sat back heavily in his chair, his eyes gazing at Fletcher for the first time. "All very mysterious—but what has this to do with us?"

"Well, your lordship, it's gotten about that you've been looking for Prince Treijan . . ."

Valana looked up sharply, but Rylmar did not alter his appearance by a whisker. A ghost of a smile did then pass Theona's lips; her father had not gotten their family this far by giving away anything with a careless expression on his face.

The guard continued into the silence. "I believe I have knowledge that could make the whereabouts of the lost prince known."

"A prince of the House of Rennes-Arvad?" Rylmar replied casually. "This is a matter you should take up with the prince's clan; it has little to do with me."

Valana shot her father a startled glance, but the old man did not budge, continuing to gaze with studied disinterest on the petitioner.

"Begging your pardon, Master Conlan." Theona could read the man's body language nearly as well as her father could; Kyne Fletcher's words were sure, but the state of his hat and his awkward stance spoke otherwise. "I've presented my petition to the House of Rennes-Arvad, but they dismissed me out of hand. They claim that the prince has left on a pressing matter of delicacy and that they believe he will return once his business is complete.

They further cautioned me that I should mention this to no one."

"And yet you are here mentioning it to me," Rylmar replied in tones almost bored.

"Yes, your lordship." The guardian nodded and then licked his lips. "I know that House Rennes-Arvad is lying about the prince. Your house is powerful, your lordship; power begets enemies. The union of such a great house as yours with that of Rennes-Arvad would make other houses much smaller in your shadow. There are many who would prefer the prince remain lost."

"You seem to know a good deal for a guardian, Master Fletcher," Rylmar said, eyeing the petitioner more closely.

"I am of the House of Myyrdin," Fletcher replied, "and I do not intend to be a guardian all my life."

Rylmar nodded with a slight smile. "Ambition, eh? That I can understand. You are trained as a guardian—so your talents are Ekteiatic. I believe I might have a place for such a man in the business of my house—a position of importance and opportunity—should such a man prove himself to me."

Kyne Fletcher smiled more easily, relaxing his grip on his thoroughly mauled hat.

"So tell me," Rylmar said casually, "what do you know about this Prince Treijan that might interest me?"

An hour later, grinning from ear to ear, the flattered Kyne Fletcher bowed gratefully for the third time and, propelled emphatically by an insistent Agretha, exited the great hall. His booted footfalls echoed back through the atrium, as Theona, Rylmar, and Valana waited with held breath for the distinct closing boom of the door in the vestibule.

Rylmar exploded angrily from his chair, nearly knocking it over as he stood. "Damn the lot of them! They can't do this to us! I won't *let* them do this to us!"

"Father! What has happened?" Valana burst out, her voice sounding on the verge of more tears. "Where's my beloved prince? What have they done with him?"

"What have they done?" Rylmar raged as he stalked up and down the hall next to the table. "I'll tell you what they've done! One of the houses abducted your fair prince—though where any of them bought enough backbone to do it is beyond me! Now they *all* find it rather convenient—maybe *too* convenient—to put our house back in its place. I'll tell you this: if they think they're dealing with some idiot squire from some backwater colony, then they have a lesson coming to them!"

"Father, please," Theona said, shaking her head. "This isn't helping any of us. We've got to think."

"Think? What do you think I've been doing since this fool disappeared?" Rylmar railed, his anger boiling over. "Now that he's gone, there isn't a clan, house, or guild among all the mystics that wants your 'beloved prince' found. The competing bloodlines would do anything to stop a marriage between Conlan and Rennes-Arvad, and his own clan seems to be doing everything it can *not* to find him."

"But I thought they wanted this match," Theona said.

"They *did*—and to hear them talk they still do," Rylmar replied, slightly calmer as his rage burned itself down to a seething anger. "Only now they want us to accept the younger prince as the match."

"Prince Clyntas?" Valana squeaked. "He's twelve years old!"

"Twelve years old and already an idiot," the elder Conlan agreed. "Marrying you to him would bring us nothing but ridicule; the rest of the guilds would see the marriage as a sham and our house would become a joke. It would profit us nothing."

"So that's your only objection to my marrying Clyntas," Valana scoffed. "That it would make us look foolish?"

"Of course not!" Rylmar snapped. "But there are considerations for the family larger than two people; obligations to our house that we all must share in whatever way we can!"

"Maybe—maybe we're looking at this from the wrong side," Theona offered thoughtfully. "We know there were any number of groups that would want to get rid of the prince and stop the marriage. From what Fletcher just told us, however, it was Gaius that took him away from the city."

"Yes"—Rylmar nodded, his eyes narrowing in thought—"and from what the guardian said, he went unwillingly."

"Gaius somehow knocked his cousin senseless at the foot of the Citadel and then carried him through a gate," Theona said aloud, but her eyes were focused beyond the walls of the room. In her mind she saw her dream and the gate that was numbered forty-one.

"Theona," Rylmar said, "what is your point?"

"Only that Gaius is involved, and therefore it must have something to do with House Petros," she said, her mind still only partially engaged in the conversation. "If it weren't for Treijan, his house would lead the mystics today. But if getting rid of Treijan was his plan, then why has he not returned to claim the throne?"

"Because Treijan is not dead," Rylmar responded, not

sure where the discussion was leading them. "I've sources inside House Rennes-Arvad; the prince's tally has not returned."

"Then he *is* alive," Valana exclaimed hopefully.

"It makes no sense!" Rylmar shouted, slamming both of his fists down onto the table. "The entire house is anxious about the prince's safety, and yet none of them seem interested in recovering the boy."

"Then we have to find him," Theona said flatly.

Rylmar looked up and nodded slowly. "Yes, you're right. It is up to us. I'll get an expedition together tonight. By tomorrow we can have a dozen groups going out through the gates—"

Theona shook her head. "No, father."

"What do you mean . . . no?"

"You cannot go, and there can be no 'expeditions,'" Theona replied. "Every mystic from Tsabethia to Hramalia will know that you took off after Treijan. It will make our house look desperate and weak at the very time you'll be away. You have to remain here in Calsandria and keep up the facade of normalcy—whatever 'normal' is in this city."

"Let them all suffocate in their own bubbles," Rylmar snarled. "I don't give a spark what they think!"

"Yes, you do, father," Theona continued, her face a mask. "You *must* care what they think. You taught me that one of the secrets to negotiation is to never let the other fellow know how desperately you need him. We shouldn't give up if we can still make this go our way, but we don't for a moment want the other houses to think we're in trouble over this deal. Even if you stayed and financed expeditions, it would still appear weak and the houses would start seeing all of us as carrion to be divided among them. No, father, you cannot go."

"But . . . but we can't just sit here," Valana said, her voice shaking as she spoke. "He's out there—my prince is out there—and we've got to find him before something terrible happens."

Rylmar ignored his elder daughter, his eyes fixed on Theona. "I've seen that look before, child. What do you have in mind?"

"I am thinking that after such a tragedy as the disappearance of the prince," Theona said slowly, "Valana may wish to travel so that she might be distracted from her troubles for a time."

"What?" Valana snapped. "I don't need any distraction! I need my prince!"

"And I should think," Theona continued, "that her sister should accompany her so that she might offer her comfort."

Rylmar shook his head. "I don't like it, Theona."

"It's perfect, father," Theona concluded. "Valana and I walk the Songstone gates. We won't be looking for Treijan—just for some indication of which direction he might have gone. If we find ourselves getting anywhere that might threaten to so much as wet our hair, we'll return, and then you can talk about an expedition. At least, what we learn should give us a better idea as to where to send one. Valana will be there to distract anyone who might suspect us—and no one will notice me nosing about." *No one ever notices me,* Theona thought to herself.

"Yes, Theona," Valana said suddenly. "It's perfect!"

"No," Rylmar said emphatically. "I won't hear of it from either of you."

"But it is the solution to all of our problems, father."

Valana stood and moved around the end of the table as she spoke excitedly. "By allowing us to leave the city on this supposed 'holiday,' we look strong rather than weak. You can keep the business going as usual while Theona and I find out what happened to Treijan."

"Nonsense!" Rylmar replied. "You wouldn't even know where to begin to look! Fletcher couldn't say which gate they went through…"

Theona blinked. "The Songstone gates, father; where does the gate numbered forty-one lead?"

"Forty-one?" Rylmar was confused by the question. "Well, it leads to a gate in Khordsholm—a seaport on the Crescent Coast. Why would you ask such a—"

"Didn't Gaius and Treijan serve as bards on the Crescent Coast for some time?" Theona asked thoughtfully.

"Yes, they did!" Valana replied. "Lady Mari wouldn't stop talking about it when I called on her the other day."

Theona nodded. "That's where he's gone; he's taken him somewhere familiar; where he knows his way."

"That's where we should start," Valana agreed.

"No! Listen to me, both of you," Rylmar said with as much authority as he could muster. "I forbid it! I absolutely refuse to allow this!"

"Father, you've got to be reasonable," Valana purred, taking a step closer to the old man.

"No, Valana; you just aren't ready for such a trip without an escort," Rylmar said emphatically.

"But Theona will be with me." Valana smiled.

"I mean *armed* escort!" Rylmar huffed.

Valana turned to Theona with a demure smile. "Thei? Would you mind? I'd like to talk with father."

Theona turned and walked out of the great hall, past the Statue of the Unknown King and around the atrium.

There was a good deal to get done before they left, and she suspected they had little time. That she and Valana might not be allowed to go was no longer a question.

Rylmar, she knew, had never denied Valana anything she truly wanted.

The Crescent Coast

Welcome! Welcome to Port Khordsholm!" bellowed the jowly, olive-toned face from the doorway. "May I say— if you will allow me, as I certainly hope you will—that all of us—and by all of us I mean each member of my household—are terribly honored, so incredibly flattered that you—and, of course, by that we mean to include both you and your sister—have deigned to..."

Theona scowled at the man as she stood in the crooked, narrow alleyway. The cobblestones were still wet from the noon rain, which had awakened pungent and bitter smells mixed with the horrible stench coming from their own wet torusk. The hulking creature's mottled hide was caked in the muck of a very hastily traveled road; now its long tusks swung listlessly, limited in their range by the proximity of the walls on either side.

Valana, seated in the litter strapped across the creature's wide back, turned her face away and said nothing in reply to the annoying man in the doorway beneath her. She alternately looked distracted, bored, or simply above the babble of words currently being hurled her way.

Theona stood next to the beast, still holding the driving staff in her left hand, and wearily tapped the tusk of the torusk. The beast collapsed down onto the street with a loud and rumbling sigh. Assured that it would not lumber off, Theona took a step toward the doorway, extending her hand palm-down in the most condescending fashion possible, although with her soaked hair and dress she doubted she looked all that imposing.

"I am Theona, daughter of the House of Conlan, and this is my sister, Valana," she said, quickly wedging her words in with one of the man's infrequent pauses for breath. "You are Master Zolan, I presume?"

"No need, no need indeed, to presume anything at all, Mistress Theona, for this is—as I am sure you well know—that same Gerin Zolan that you seek," the man replied with nervous joviality. The dark of Zolan's curls was exceeded only by the shining blackness of his eyes. "To be entirely truthful, however, and I'm sure you will wish me to be accurate in all respects in our dealings with one another—as your esteemed father would so rightly expect from such a humble servant—my title is Torusk Master Zolan, although, if it would please you, mistress, please call me Master Zolan or, should it be more convenient, simply Zolan—for I would not presume to offer my own given name to such an esteemed personage as yourself—and, of course, it goes without saying, for your most glorious sister as well..."

Theona looked up in exasperation. She was no stranger to the hardships of the road, having had occasion to drive a torusk now and again since she was barely twelve. In fact, she had commanded entire caravans of the beasts whenever her father saw an advantage in moving their household. This trip, however, had already sunk below her own grim expectations. She was used to traveling, but her sister was not; Valana found cause for fault and for grievous complaint at every inconvenience, however large or small. First, the torusk had balked at passing through the Songstone gate and then had broken into a full run upon exiting, nearly trampling one of the Ekteiatic guardians on the other side. Theona had managed to bring the beast back under her control and would have preferred to make camp for the night among the ruins where the bards had hidden the gate, but the guardians there were adamant that she continue at once in order to reach the city before evening—since they insisted that the open road and countryside were no place to be when night fell. This required that she force the skittish torusk carrying their trade goods and luggage down the dirty road at an uncomfortable pace so they could reach the safety of Khordsholm.

The city itself offered little to cheer them. The streets were exceedingly narrow and labyrinthine; after passing through the heavily defended White Coral Gate in the city's surrounding wall, it had taken them nearly an hour to find the inn among the angled passages and alleys that passed for avenues. The weathered wooden buildings on either side, all of which were at least two stories in height and with many reaching as high as five, leaned in so closely they gave Theona the distinctly uncomfortable impression that they were prepared to collapse on her at any moment. The air between the structures was stale and unmoving despite their proximity to the harbor and sea beyond. "Master Zolan—"

"No need to speak of it—none at all—for Zolan knows

your needs well and has anticipated them in your coming," Zolan replied, his bright eyes darting up and down the constricted street. "I have made certain inquiries—discreet investigations, and, I can assure you, obtained with the most private of confidences, which—"

"And we are grateful," Theona interrupted once more, her voice more strident than she had intended. She moved to pat down her traveling coat but stopped when she noticed the dark mud that stained it in several places. "However, my *sister*"—Theona gestured to emphasize her point—"must rest from our journey. Are our rooms prepared?"

"Most assuredly, your rooms are prepared—the finest accommodations available!" Zolan's head bobbed as though loose on his neck. "However, I must report that the shortness of your notice did require some compromise, I fear, so if the rooms are not to your liking—"

"Then show us to them at once!" Theona snapped.

"Without delay, Mistress Theona—and you as well, Mistress Valana," Zolan sputtered, his hands gesturing nervously as he bowed deeply and tried to step back out of the doorway at the same time. "The innkeeper and his wife wait within to fulfill your every whim, as I personally have instructed them both and acquired their assurance—"

"Very well!"

"Yet…"

"Yet?" Theona sighed.

"I was led to believe—indeed, most emphatically informed by your esteemed and *very* highly accredited agent—that you would require my report at once," Zolan said, his eyes looking up from under his brow even as he bowed. "I am most happy to serve my guild master, let there be no mistaking in that—indeed, there is no more loyal member to be found among the torusk masters in Conlan's most privileged society—and yet I am certain that one so accustomed to the pressing nature of this business as your honored selves—both you, Mistress Theona, and your most gracious sister—will understand that there are many duties which require my humble efforts and which would call me away from your gracious selves, though it pains me to do so. Yet time is such a precious commodity—"

"Then I should think that you would quit spending it so freely," Theona replied in words cold and direct. "You will see that our torusk is unloaded. We have barter goods on that beast—mystic tallies won't buy us bad advice in this town—so know that I want a full inventory before nightfall and a good price in the local coins. Also see that our personal baggage is brought to the care of the innkeeper, then you will wait on me in the common room. I will settle my sister and then meet you directly to take your report." She stepped back to the torusk, now snoring loudly in the street, and helped her sister down from the litter before following her through the dark doorway. "Then we shall see how well you have served House Conlan."

Zolan bowed even more deeply than before. "Your attentions are ever so gratefully received by this simple and humble servant!"

It was evening before Theona stepped wearily through the door to their third-floor rooms and faced the waiting Valana.

"Well?" her sister asked.

Theona gave an exhausted sigh and collapsed onto the poorly stuffed couch that sat on the far side of the sitting room. "Well, we are definitely not in Calsandria anymore."

Valana wrinkled her nose. "You certainly have a gift for understatement. These rooms are abominable!"

"Your grandmother," Theona said, closing her eyes and leaning back until her head rested against the coarse wall, "lived in whatever sticks she could pile together when she wasn't being hunted by the Pir."

"She also said that every age had its own troubles," Valana said through pouting lips. "She had to build her own hovel—and we have to deal with these three rooms. Bad enough we had to travel half a day on that nasty torusk just to get here. Why couldn't the bards have put the gate in the city, like at home?"

"We've been over that, Val," Theona said, rubbing the back of her neck. "The location of the gate has to be a secret in order to keep it from being used by the Pir. The Songstones go both ways; if they knew where that gate was, they could walk their armies right into father's backyard."

"Well, of course, I understand that," Valana replied in a snit, "I just don't see why they couldn't hide it somewhere that was more conveniently close-by. But come now, Thei, what did that Zolan fellow *say*?"

"A great deal, as you might imagine," Theona groaned. "Never were there uttered more words and less meaning."

"So what about Treijan? Did he come here? Has anyone seen him? And what about Gaius and—"

Theona held up her hand as if to shield herself from the words. "Valana, I'm so tired. Can't we talk about this in the morning?"

"No, Thei; I've got to know now," Valana said. "I'll never sleep otherwise; you know I won't."

Theona nodded. "Which means you won't let me sleep either." She leaned forward, her hands flipping dismissively with each question and answer. "'Has anyone seen Treijan in town these last two weeks?' I asked. 'No,' he replied, with about ten minutes' worth of useless explanation. 'Has anyone seen Gaius in that same time?' I asked as soon as he let me. 'Yes,' he answered, although that took a great deal longer than the 'no.'"

Valana leaned forward sharply. "He said yes? So Gaius was seen here during the last two weeks?"

Theona nodded. "Or at least, that is the news that Zolan heard. However, he gave me the information I need to directly contact the people who saw him. It may take a few days, but I should have a better idea whether they were here and maybe even some idea as to where they went. Then you have the hardest job of all."

"I do?" Valana said with surprise. "Is it dangerous?"

"Well, Port Khordsholm *is* on the Crescent Coast, Valana." Theona spoke softly, looking directly into her sister's eyes. "From what little I've learned from Zolan, they seem to have a completely different history of dragons here than what we inherited from the Pir Drakonis. That wide wall around the heart of the city, the towers and those large ballistae mounted on the turrets: this place still knows dragons, Val, and not the subdued monsters that the Pir keep on a short leash. Ulruk and Whithril are their names. They are known to grow discontented with the hunting in the Northwilde, at which point Ulruk gets desperate enough to attack this city."

"Ulruk? I thought he already ascended to dragon heaven or something like that."

Theona laughed darkly. "Yes, according to the Pir creeds, both Whithril and Ulruk are supposed to have transcended—so you might imagine the Pir's unpleasant surprise when both of their supposedly blessed and benevolent dragons turned up very much still world-bound and raiding towns all along the Crescent Coast. I don't have all the details, but it seems that one of the Pir tried to command Ulruk some years back and it didn't work. The dragon is apparently still mad about the whole affair, and the locals think the Pir are to blame for his occasional raids. Still, he only comes at night, so you should be safe enough during daylight. He also seems to be coming more often this last week or two, or so Zolan tells me, but the city is well defended. We should be all right as long as we stay indoors at night and keep the shutters closed. So yes, it is dangerous enough, though we are much safer here in town than we were out in the open earlier today. But I said your job would be *hard,* not dangerous."

"Well, I don't mind a little work if it will bring me closer to getting my Treijan back."

"Thank you for volunteering," Theona said, standing slowly from the couch and making her way into the bedchamber beyond the sitting room. She could already see that Valana's traveling trunks were blocking the path to her narrow bed. "While I am trying to find where Gaius has gone, you will be entertaining our new best friend, Master Zolan. And he has already told me how he intends to impress you with the fascinating history of his city, his work, and his suitability as a partner in marriage; consider yourself warned."

"Him? That toad?" Valana made a sour face in Theona's direction and then huffed, "Fine! If it will get us closer to finding Treijan, I'll do it. Is there anything else you want me to look after while I'm here?"

Theona paused and then chuckled at her own ridiculous thoughts. "Well, if you happen to see a dwarf in a bright red hat, just let me know."

"Well, a lot of things are *possible*," came the casual reply of Lord Vikard, master of the bards in Khordsholm as he walked beside Theona. They were in the open hall of the great temple still being restored in the Baron's Island section of the city. "Who did you say you were with?"

The "island" in its name was barely justified, since it lay between the eastern and western branches of the River Wilde, which passed under the massive curtain wall surrounding the city in two separate places before emptying into Khordsholm Bay. In its days of power the so-called island had been the domain of Trade Baron Kordan and his descendants, whose powerful ships not only plied the waters of the Crescent Coast but braved the seas from the Gulf of Meluun as far west as Vestadia and south beyond even the Pillars of Rhamas to the near reaches of Uthara. After the devastation of Ulruk, however, the glory of the barons had quickly faded. Now the mystic bards were guests of the current baron of Khordsholm, largely due to their promise to restore the port and its barons to their earlier glory. The Temple of Thelea was still without a roof, and the morning light shone down on the dusty marble tiles through new timbers just recently hoisted into place.

"I am of House Conlan, Master Vikard, as I mentioned before, and I'm just making sure that the prince is safe and well. All I am asking is if Prince Treijan or his companion may have passed through the Songstone gate unnoticed or, at least, unrecorded," Theona said again. She gazed up as she spoke, looking past the open timbers to the towers beyond. The shadows they cast were getting longer; she knew she had to be back in her rooms with Valana by sundown.

"You are asking on behalf of the prince's family?"

"I have only their best interests at heart," Theona said evenly.

"You know, it's funny you should ask that, ma'am," said the old guardian as he rubbed the gray stubble on both his cheeks. "I mean, normally, I wouldn't be talking to you about guild business, but seeing as you're here on behalf of the family and not to mention that you are the second person to ask about this in as many weeks—"

"The second person?" Theona asked with surprise. "Who else was asking?"

"Well, it was this tallish fellow—long gray hair down to his shoulders pushed back from a high forehead. A torusk driver by the look of him; long overcoat with trousers and worn boots. He was also rather curious—a bit too curious—about Prince Treijan and his companion coming through the gate. Of course, I didn't tell the fellow anything, just sent him on his way."

The gatemaster stopped in the hall and looked directly at Theona. "I trust you will tell the masters of House Rennes-Arvad that I have done my duty by them. No record of the passage of the prince and his companion exists."

"Even though they *did* come through the city gate," Theona said.

Vikard smiled. "What gate?"

Theona held her knees tight against her chest and closed her eyes. The walls of their rooms shook for the second night in a row. Valana alternately wept and screamed with the explosions outside and the distant shouts of warriors. Occasionally, they heard the dull thump of a ballista hurling its thick bolts skyward or smelled the whiff of scorched dust from the bolts cast by the few mystic guardians stationed in the city. Worst of all, however, was the roar of the dragon itself as it hurtled above them, beyond the clattering slate tiles and the groaning wood. The sound was everywhere, penetrating the walls and stones, flesh and bones, and poured fear directly into their souls.

At long last the screeching receded and the shouts and cries faded once more into the still night. Theona slowly relaxed and looked up.

Valana sat on her own bed quivering, her golden tresses trembling. "Is it . . . is it over?"

"Yes." Theona exhaled and wondered how long it had been since she had taken a full breath.

Valana was growing angry. "That dragon's looking for something; I hope he finds it soon."

"You could go home, Val," Theona offered. "I'll stay and finish here. When I have something, I'll—"

"Absolutely not!" Valana said, though her teeth were still chattering. "Go back and be the laughingstock of all Calsandria? We're staying here until we rescue my prince, if I have to tie him up and drag him back myself."

"Val, I don't know if that's going to be possible," Theona said, trying to stretch the knots out of her clenched muscles. "I spoke with that trader today—the one that was bragging about overcharging some out-of-town buyers recently. He swears it was Gaius who made the deal— and a bad deal at that. It was for supplies mostly, or so this trader says, and at almost three times the going rate. It looked as though Gaius was setting himself up for a long trip. If that's the case, then we'll have to return home and turn it all over to father. We'll need more than what we have to go on now, but I don't think you and I are just going to find him in the street here, Val."

"Well, I'm not giving up so easily," Valana snapped. "I'm doing my part; that Zolan took me all the way up to the hilltop east of the city to show me this ruined Necropolis place, and even if the view of the ocean was nice, I nearly died of boredom."

"He's sweet on you, Val," Theona teased as she yawned, suddenly aware of how tired she was. "Taking you to a graveyard was his way of showing you his romantic side."

"Oh, that reminds me," Valana said, settling back into her own bed. "I saw your dwarf today."

Theona froze. "You . . . you *what*?"

"You told me to watch for a dwarf, remember?"

Theona's mind reeled. It had been a strange image from her dream—a rather vivid dream, to be sure, but a dream nevertheless. She had mentioned it to her sister only as a joke. "Yes, but—"

"I saw him today—bright red hat and all—up among those ruins. I think he noticed me looking at him, because he vanished suddenly. Thei? You have such a strange look on your face!"

"Oh, sorry," Theona replied, settling uncertainly into her own bed.

"Well, don't you worry, Thei." Valana waved her hand at the glowing ball of light next to her bed to extinguish it. "I can handle Zolan—but you're on your own with the dwarf."

Theona lay for some time, her wide eyes staring into the darkness. *She's seeing things,* she reasoned to herself. *I told her to look for a dwarf in a red hat, and now she's mistaken someone in the distance for him.* Theona closed her eyes, but try as she might, she could not get the image of the dwarf out of her mind.

"Gaius Petros is the worst kind of villain," the young woman responded, nearly apoplectic at the mention of the name.

"My apologies, Miss Nikau," Theona said, sitting upright in her plush chair and wondering how to retreat from the room without offending her hostess any more than she already had. "I understood that he had called upon you of late, but I was not aware—"

"Master Petros has *not* had the decency to call upon me," spat Miss Evina Nikau, daughter of Klar Nikau and the master bard of Khordsholm. "Even though he gave me every assurance that he *would* call upon me when he next visited our city. You might imagine my shock to have seen him in the markets not two weeks ago. I expected him to present himself at our door by that evening, but he has not called upon me in all that time since."

"You *saw* him in the marketplace?" Theona asked pointedly.

"I did. In Beggar's Market just between the tower keep and the quay," Miss Nikau replied hotly. "Moreover, I believe he saw me as well and just walked away as though he could not even hear me calling after him. He is a cad, Miss Conlan! He has tampered with my affections, and I am certain he is involved in nefarious deeds! I never wish to see him again, and if you should find him, I trust you'll tell him to drop by so that I may tell him so myself."

Theona stood with her sister between the city and the sea. The quay of Port Khordsholm rose like a dark cliff straight up out of the waters of the enclosed bay. The top of the quay, nearly sixty feet wide, was paved with flat, fitted stones, which separated the precipitous drop into the waters from the equally precipitous rise of the gray buildings of the city.

Zolan stood unusually silent next to the door of what looked to Valana to be a particularly foul pub. The small panes of glass, arranged in a crosshatch pattern, were coated in a thin layer of grease that obscured the view looking in. The door was weathered red below a swinging sign that read "The Maelstrom."

"I'm sorry, Val," Theona said as she stood next to her and held her arm. "But I needed you to come and hear this."

Theona opened the door and led her into the pub common room. The ceiling was lower than she expected, though it did not prevent either of them from standing their full height; it just seemed to press down on them as they moved beneath its heavy beams. A wide bar ran nearly the full length of the back wall and had been doing a brisk business with a number of hunched-over figures until the two women entered the room. Then everyone turned both from the bar and from the rough tables scattered about the space to gawk at the mystic beauty who had stepped impossibly into their world.

Theona quickly led Valana through the gaping maze to a table in the corner next to the smeared windows. There sat a man alone, nursing a large flagon of ale.

"Valana, this is Shipwright Quin," Theona said, helping her sister onto a chair opposite the man.

"Pleasure, ma'am," Quin said with a short nod. He had struck Theona as someone whose face was a little too handsome: strong face muscles and a jaw that was too confident. Even so, his eyes were reddened from the drink, and there was no mistaking his sour smell, even in the midst of such a terrible establishment as this one.

"Oh, don't let the looks fool you, ma'am," Quin said quickly. "I'm not always in such a state. I'm just going through a wee bit of longing for home, is all."

"Where is your home, then, Master Quin?" Valana asked curtly.

"Out there, ma'am." The seaman nodded toward the ocean beyond the dirty windowpanes. "Been recuperating here for nigh on seven months now. Put my leg through a haul cable at just the wrong time. Bad luck, that."

Quin glanced down toward his extended leg, and Valana followed his gaze. The trousers Quin wore were tied off where the man's knee should have been. Valana blinked, the color draining from her face.

"Tell her what you told me, Quin," Theona said quietly from where she stood next to the table, her arms once more folded across her chest.

"Aye." Quin nodded. "Well, here I sit, day in and out, watching my brothers come and go. Watched my own ship—the *Narcella*—sail on a run down the eastern ports not too long after they left me here to heal up. So a man's got to do what he can to survive, and I began working the quay—odd jobs and the like, whatever a salt sailor left on the blocks ashore might do. You hear a lot of things in such work." The sailor picked up the flagon once more, pulling a long draft.

"What might you have heard that would be of interest to me?" Valana said.

Quin looked at her over the rim of the flagon, then set it down. "Ah, a woman who wants the story short and to the point. Well, as I told your sister here, the quay rats were all having a good laugh about a bard who was spreading around a lot of coin about ten days back. He were trying to be all secretlike, but there be nothing hidden from the quay rats like me—especially if it involved a good tale and a few coins."

"Go on," Theona insisted.

"Well, here comes this bard," Quin said, his large, muscular hands becoming more animated as he spoke. "He's a mystic sure 'cause he's got the hooded cape and all. He wants to hire a ship, he says, but he don't want anyone knowing about it. Gonna tell the captain at sea where he be goin' and not before. So we thinks he's just another of them cargo mystics trying to move a little goods on the side from some rich man's warehouse into his own pocket, like, only no cargo shows up—no torusks to unload nor bales of goods. He just shows up with an extra jolly boat and a single box like a coffin, pays off the quay rats like they had been working the week long for him, and tells them they never saw nothing." Quin raised the flagon in a toast. "Good on him, I say! I been drinking since that day on his coins!"

"So did you happen to hear this bard's name?" Valana asked.

"Aye, of course, I heard it." Quin grinned. "It were supposed to be a secret, so we all remembered it. Gaius—Gaius Petros. Sailed on the *Mercalia* with the next tide—though what a bard needs with a secret coffin I don't know. Still, I hope he comes back; he were good business. He were nearly as easy coin as you were!"

Valana stood up abruptly, her chair scraping loudly against the floor.

"Come on, Val," Theona said, taking her sister's arm once more and pulling her back across the room. In moments they stepped back through the door and onto the quay.

Several ships lay at anchor out in the enclosed harbor. Theona and Val stood quietly as their eyes were drawn to the flat horizon of the vast ocean to the south.

"He's gone, Thei," Valana said, her voice quivering. "I thought—I thought he might just be on the other side of the gate somewhere or at the end of some street. But out there..."

Theona shook her head. There was nothing to say. The trail had led them to the water's edge and ended.

Suddenly, a deep horn resounded across the city, its voice quickly joined by several others. Theona glanced about expectantly and then caught sight of Zolan. His eyes were wide with fear, his mouth working, and yet no words were coming out. She could hear the sound of panicked voices rising from the city itself, screams and cries, throaty yells all mixed up into a distant chaos of sound. Everywhere on the quay, people dropped what they were doing, crouched instinctively, and glanced about in fear.

Then she heard the familiar, terrible screech.

Theona and Valana both turned as one to face the bay. There, just above the rolling waters, soared Ulruk, a dragon ancient and huge. The tips of its leathery rust-colored wings skimmed just above the water as it roared toward them, the wind beneath it heeling boats over on their sides, threatening to capsize them at once. It was a magnificent, terrible beast, one horn of its crest broken in some untold struggle and its long barbed tail arching behind it. Yet it was the eyes that held Theona's terrible fascination: red eyes gleaming with determined hate.

The people around them began to move, running in

panic toward the city. Theona grabbed her sister and turned with them toward the safety of the winding streets.

The dragon was heading directly at her. She started to run, her sister's arm firmly in her grip as they crashed with several others around them into a narrow alley.

Then, to her astonishment, she saw through the terrified crowd running around her a brilliant red hat.

16

Blind Guide

Theona! Where are we going?" Valana cried, struggling to keep up with her sister.

"I don't know," Theona shouted back. The street before them suddenly turned both left and right, and the crowd around them seemed to split equally in both directions. "Anywhere but here!"

The screeching behind them was deafeningly near.

"But the dragon never comes during the day!" Valana protested.

"He has apparently changed his mind," Theona yelled in frustration. She once again caught a glimpse of the brilliant red hat, its wide brim and its long red feather, through the jostling bodies of the crowd as it turned down the left street. "Come on!"

Theona turned left as well, finding herself running down a straight road between a canyon of gray buildings. Behind her she heard a terrible roar of splintering wood and shattering glass. She glanced back.

Theona nearly stumbled at the sight: Ulruk had tried to

follow down the same road but could not make so abrupt a change in his course. His massive form slammed into the wall of buildings, smashing it to kindling as he thrashed angrily amid the debris. In an instant she saw that the ballistae in the defensive towers, caught completely unprepared for the unprecedented attack, were still not functional, their crews struggling desperately to climb to their posts.

Even as she watched, the dragon's scaly head wrenched free, staring directly toward her as the dragon roared once more.

Valana stumbled, losing her footing. Theona knew that if she fell, they would both be trampled to death by the panicked crowd around them. With all her strength she pulled her sister back up on her feet next to her, following the street around to their right. The crowd was starting to thin out, as many of the people before them plunged into the buildings on either side, but Theona kept running. Her own inn was blocks away, and she doubted in that moment that she could find it in the maze of streets while at a full run. Moreover, the dragon remained so close that any delay at any of the barred doors on either side of the road, she knew, would be fatal.

All she had was the vision of that red hat. There was something about the hat—something about the dwarf beneath it—that had haunted her last few days; a dream suddenly real. Now she could see it more clearly through the thinning mob, angling left down another split in the road.

She turned the corner after that hat and saw that they had come to Beggar's Market. The stalls in the square were deserted, their goods abandoned. The dwarf, now more clearly seen, was running with amazing speed across the corner of the marketplace, his purple and blue coat and striped pantaloons an absurd vision in the midst of such a crisis. His cloth mask appeared to be crimson as well. If Theona might have paused to give all of this thought, the cry of the dragon behind her and the sound of his wings lifting him skyward again banished such an impulse; she pulled her sister with her, running in the footsteps of the dwarf.

A shadow loomed over the two women, covering the abandoned stalls. Theona could hear the ballistae firing at last, wondering if they would come too late for her and her sister. She could hear the rush of the air as the dragon dove downward toward them.

The dwarf ran down a steep set of stone stairs that plunged down the foundation wall of a tall building. There was a sign over the stairs, but Theona didn't have time to read it when she followed behind.

The stairwell was only a few feet wide but took them downward a full thirty feet before ending at an open iron door. Theona did not hesitate but pulled her sister with her through the opening.

The iron door slammed shut behind them with a dull clang.

Darkness—complete and impenetrable—enveloped them.

In the next instant the ground shook with a terrible impact, knocking both Theona and her sister off their feet. Theona flailed in the darkness, her hand smashing against a hard table as she tumbled to the floor. The sound of claws tearing at stone filled her ears, and in the complete darkness it was impossible to tell from how far the sound was coming. Another outraged howl from the dragon, then a sudden silence descended.

Theona held perfectly still, uncertain if any movement in any direction might bring her harm. Her voice sounded small in her own ears. "Val?"

"Yes, Theona," her sister replied meekly. "I'm here."

"W-where's here?"

"Glad yon ladies asking as er is," came a gruff voice from the darkness.

Theona tensed.

"Dregas glad to help yon ladies," said the voice.

Slowly, Theona became aware of dim red light growing in the space around her. As it grew, she began to discern shapes: a wall, then a corner, shelves forming along those walls, each laden with rolls of wide, heavy paper, and finally a long, massive table with two wide benches running its length on either side. The light, she could see, was coming from strange lanterns about the room, another of which was beginning to glow under the hand of the silhouetted dwarf.

"Lose something er is?" said the dwarf in his deep, rough voice as his form bowed deeply before Theona, who sat on the floor. "Dregas Belas knows the way to find er is."

"Belas," came a new voice behind her, "what is the meaning of this?"

Theona turned. She could make out that it was the figure of a man sitting on a stool in the corner next to a stack of large books. In the dim light it was difficult to make out any details, but Theona noted that the man, who wore a long coat, appeared nearer to her father's age, with long iron-gray hair pulled tightly back from his high forehead and bound at the nape of his neck.

"Not a thing to worry er is," the dwarf bellowed. "Safe

er is in this dwarf-home. My business-house er is! Solid as a tomb!"

Suddenly, the ground shook once more. The dragon apparently had not yet given up.

"That's not what I meant, as you well know," the man said in the corner. "We had a deal."

"Nay deal," the dwarf sniffed. "Negotiation er is. You be looking and they be looking. Er profit to be had er is."

The man folded his arms in front of him. "Are you looking for a short life, dwarf?"

"Nay short er is," the dwarf replied evenly. "Friends of mine er be, and they be good at dwarven death-dealing. Not so pleasant as hoo-man death-making. Slow er be and far from the burning lights."

"Who are you?" Valana jumped in indignantly. "And what makes you think we have any interest in you at all?"

"Dregas the Diviner, there be that call me," the dwarf said, bowing again. "Dregas Belas my name er is. Tracker I be; guide to that which er lost."

"A blind guide?" Theona looked upon him with skepticism.

"Many er is that be blind to the truth yet their sight be clear," the dwarf seemed to sing in his deep voice. "Why be surprised a blind dwarf guides to the truth er is?"

Valana shook her head violently. "Theona, what *is* he talking about?"

The dwarf tilted his head toward Valana. "Found yer wedding man er is? Know yon Valana Conlan the path where Treijan heart-sweeten er is?"

Valana stared at the dwarf, her mouth open as if to reply, but no words came out.

"Aye." The dwarf nodded. "Dregas Belas knows the

path er is! What told ye them quay rats and fancy snoots in the upper world?" The dwarf's voice shifted into a strange falsetto as he did his best parody of humans. "'Ooh, gone to sea and sailed away er is!' 'Gaius and Treijan sailed away er is!'" The dwarf reverted to his own voice. "*Elf-ears** er is! Blind man could see it as the lie er is—and blind dwarf did!"

"You mean," Theona said slowly, "that it was all a lie—a trick to make everyone *think* he sailed off to the southern oceans?"

"Far he be, true er is," the dwarf said through a wide-toothed smile, "but not on creaking boat."

"Dregas," the man in the corner said in a warning tone.

"Gate er is," the dwarf whispered. "Not known to Pir. Not known to mystics. *Private* gate. *Secret* gate—known only to Dregas."

Theona nodded. This was trade; something she understood. "How much?"

"Three hundred in baron century rings,"† the dwarf said flatly.

The man in the corner stood up. He was taller than Theona had supposed. "That's it, Dregas. You told me one hundred."

"Price goes up er is," the dwarf grumbled.

"No," Theona said. "One hundred and fifty."

"Nay," the dwarf responded. "Three hundred century rings and not a knob less."

"All I've got is two hundred," Theona said.

---

*Elves were made up by dwarves to scare their children with morality tales. The phrase "elf-ears" is a dwarven epithet meaning a whopping lie.
†The standard coin of the barons as expressed in gold rings of a specific weight.

"Three hundred or find yourself er is!" said the dwarf, stomping his big foot against the ground. He turned toward a second door leading into the back of the shop. He waved dismissively at everyone in the room. "Close er door behind ye! Dregas not wanting a dragon let into his office as er is!"

"Wait!" Valana said quickly.

The dwarf stopped and seemed to be looking at the ceiling through his eye bandages.

Valana turned toward the man standing in the corner. "It won't do either of us any good to bid against each other. Work with me, and maybe we can both get what we are after."

"What do you have in mind?" asked the man.

"Wait, why are you looking for Treijan?" Valana asked. "Why is it so important that you find him?"

"Look, that really isn't any of your—"

"Please," Valana insisted.

"I'm a distant relative of his—we knew each other from his bard work," the man said. "I just owe him a great deal and need to find out what happened to him."

"So you think something *has* happened to him?" Valana asked quickly.

"Something to do with Gaius, I suspect," the man replied. "I'm just trying to help."

"Dwarf!" Valana said, turning to Dregas. "We will meet your price but for all of us. Three hundred baron century rings if you can take us to Treijan Rennes-Arvad."

The dwarf turned slowly, thinking for a few moments before he spoke. "Done as er is! Dregas come for you early; leave er the sun rise. Ready by then er is?"

"Yes!" Valana said happily. "Yes, we'll be ready."

"And er gold rings first er is?"

Valana looked over at the man, who nodded in reply.

"Yes," Valana said. "We'll bring them with us in the morning."

"*Now* a deal er is!" the dwarf crowed. "Three for one a bargain be! Dregas show you Treijan's path by tomorrow or burn off my beard!"

"Oh, Thei, isn't it wonderful!" Valana chirped. "It's all going to turn out so well!"

"Yes, it's wonderful," Theona answered without much conviction. She turned to the man in the corner. "We have you to thank for your assistance, I believe."

"Not at all. Believe me; I am delighted that we could all be of such assistance to one another," the tall man replied.

"As we appear to be partners, perhaps introductions are in order." Theona extended her hand. "I am Theona Conlan."

"Partners, then," the man said, taking her hand. "And I am Dorian—Dorian Arvad."

Common Ground

Why can't you just leave me alone?" Arryk shouted in exasperation as he flitted anxiously from one side of the cage to the other.

By the light streaming into the large room opposite their cage, it had only been a day since they arrived, and already their prison had become entirely too small for the faery's comfort. No matter what he did, Arryk could not find a way to circumvent the strange power of the woven metal bars that held them and seemed to rob him of the Sharaj. He was getting desperate to find a way out of the torturous place in which he found himself.

Part of his mounting panic lay in the hideous little creature beyond the bars that kept coming back into the room and dancing her strange, joyful dance. It was now apparent to Arryk that it was this female demon-creature that had created the likenesses of him, and that she found him somehow attractive. Her pride in him became obvious when later the previous night she brought in two others of her horrible demonic kind to stare at him and Hueburlyn for a while. The taller of them wore long robes; the other was a powerful, squat creature with a black patch over one damaged eye and some sort of metal vest. Both ogled the faery and the centaur for some time, making terrible squealing noises and gesturing wildly with both arms and, from time to time, their large feet.

However, as trying as this had been for him, it was nothing compared to the incessant questions from his companion in captivity.

"How alone Ar-ryk be in so small a cage?" The centaur rested on the floor, his feet folded beneath him as he picked the dirt from under his long fingernails. "Ar-ryk move much but not made free. Ar-ryk fail alone."

"I don't want your help," the faery snapped back. "I don't need anyone's help."

"Hueburlyn no help Ar-ryk, but all creatures need help," Hueburlyn said easily. "All creatures need others; that is will of gods."

"Then the gods are idiots," Arryk responded, examining the bolts holding the cage together for the thousandth time. He yelled again in frustration. "This is all *your* fault, Famadorian! I don't know how you did this, but you cannot keep me here. You will take me back at once, do you hear—at once!"

The centaur threw his head back and laughed loudly. "Ar-ryk great joke-making! Ar-ryk want to go home— then fly home, faery-boy! Hueburlyn watch you go; wave farewell. Hueburlyn stay right here and watch Ar-ryk go—shed big tear if speed faery away from Hueburlyn."

The faery turned back to face the centaur. "Oh, no, you don't; you have to come back with me."

"Why?" Hueburlyn asked with a gentle smile.

"You know why! The Kyree-Nykira warlords have

been looking for an excuse to invade Sharajentis, and you were it. If I don't deliver you to them—"

"War between faery and Kyree?" The centaur raised one bushy eyebrow. "Nation that makes *kntrr* slaves in death-fight with nation that oppresses and fears *kntrr* learning? Tell me, Ar-ryk: which nation *kntrr* hoping win? Better, tell me why *kntrr* not triumph if *both* nations die?"

Arryk stared back at the centaur, his mind trying to gather the threads of reason from the white-hotness of his anger.

"If Hueburlyn return with Ar-ryk, Hueburlyn die," the centaur said calmly, and then winked. "If not return, then faeries and Kyree die many times more. Better for *kntrr* clans if Hueburlyn just watch Ar-ryk play inside faery cage. Big joke-making!"

Arryk tried to calm down and speak in a nicer tone. "Can you take us back?"

The centaur smiled at him. "Hueburlyn no bring us here—not even know where *is* here."

"Then what—"

"Magic cage built for Ar-ryk," the centaur said, stretching his arms over his head luxuriously as he spoke. "Stops faery magic-dream; drain magic from Ar-ryk."

The centaur reached out with his hand and rested it against the cage.

Nothing happened.

"Cage built for faery." Hueburlyn smiled.

Arryk was astonished. "Can you—can you break it?"

"Strong metal—Hueburlyn no break."

"Then what's the point in—"

"Point is—Hueburlyn *still* dream."

Arryk drifted down until his feet rested against the floor. "The Sharaj?"

"Ar-ryk teach Hueburlyn," the centaur said, his dark eyes intense and shining. "Give *kntrr* knowledge of faery magic-craft, and Hueburlyn find way out of cage for Ar-ryk."

The faery turned away, staring at the cage. "None of this would have happened if you hadn't shown up at the gates. This is all your fault! You *made* it happen this way."

"Ah," the horse-man chuckled. "At first, Hueburlyn think, 'Big faery too powerful—too proud—to take help of humble *kntrr.*' Now Hueburlyn understand better. Ar-ryk simple coward."

"Coward! You liar!"

"No liar," the centaur replied darkly. "Faery fear failing, so never try. Blame others to excuse self. Is Ar-ryk so afraid of falling that he never stand?"

The faery stared back at the centaur. "You promise to take me home—and I'll teach you what I know."

I do not know how much more of this I can stand.

The circle of light that appears in the shaft overhead has wound its course more than ten times since we arrived, and still, I can find no comfort in this terrible place. It is especially difficult for me, for our Fae are largely a private society whose customs are not easily adaptable to shared life in a public cell. It is particularly disconcerting to me that our captor—the strange demonic female that so often peers into our cage—seems to take too great a delight in watching me right when I am compelled to perform those acts of sanitation that are most private. The barbaric Famadorian with whom I am forced to share this horrid space finds my discomfort amusing — apparently, centaurs are not concerned with the finer points of civilization.

Still, I will not remain here forever. The Famadorian, despite his barbaric nature, shows greater promise each day as I work with him. It is a difficult proposition, as I feel we must take care not to expose our activities to our captors — especially the ugly female creature. So we follow a strict routine, awakening when the demon-woman bangs on our cage each morning and then cleaning out our cage. We push the pots of our own filth out toward the edge of the cage, where the demon-creature takes them out, perhaps a bit too cheerfully, before returning with what she believes is food.

The food is improving. At first the demon-creature was confused at what we might eat and brought us a variety of objects. We both demonstrated a decided preference against anything mineral in nature. Rocks, sand, and rounded bits of metal were rejected. Woods were also set aside, but we have finally settled on fruits and some forms of vegetables for myself. Since none of them are familiar to me, I exercise great care in those which I select to ingest. My Famadorian companion has demonstrated his omnivorous tendencies, not only ingesting vegetables but also demonstrating a penchant for our captor's local meats — both cooked and otherwise — a development which has given me more than one sleepless night. Ales seem to be the safest bet for thirst, as I do not trust the water.

At least now there is more room in our cell: the ugly little creature somehow managed to remove the curious metallic ring-device from inside our cage while we slept, *though I still have not figured out how she accomplished this. For the last few days she has been mounting the ring vertically on a large pedestal of rusting metal next to the door.*

As for my deal with the Famadorian—his ability to control the Sharaj improves with each passing day, and with his improvement comes a greater level of my own disdain. Perhaps I envy him, for he now revels in that one place in which I find solace and which is now denied to me. How is it that he may walk the streets of the Sharaj, the city of my comfort, while I am blind and weak as a newborn here in this dreadful place?

Where now is my wingless friend from the Sharaj— that great creature through whom I find purpose and power? I will not go back to the nothing I am without the Sharaj. I will taste its power again—and then this Famadorian will know the meaning of the dream-magic!

FAERY TALES
BRONZE CANTICLES, TOME XIV, FOLIO 1, LEAVES 47–51

Lunid smiled gleefully as she descended the long circular steps into her secret laboratory. Her winged god was waiting for her, and she delighted in seeing him each time she entered the lab.

At the base of the stairs she quickly flapped her large feet against the stone flooring and made her way down a short hall to the curving corridor that led to her favorite place in all of G'tok—the only place where she felt free of the disapproving eyes and the whispers that followed her down the years of her life.

The curving hall ended in a rough wooden door. It swung open with a satisfying squeal, and she stepped in among her art pieces. There was her winged god in all the forms of her creation, and she passed her green long-fingered hands with gentle caresses over each metal curve of cheek, glass wing, and hank of blackened flax hair. They had once held her heart, she mused, giggling at the thought. Now, however, she held his life—and in time he would love her as much as she loved him.

She turned and pushed open the great doors that led to the center of the tower and the laboratory proper. Her attitude was, if possible, more chipper than usual. Her flat hat was stuck on her head, held in place primarily by her tall ears. She had made a very creditable attempt at cleaning her best red vest, in order to look her best for *him*.

And there he was, still so strangely compelling and beautiful. How she longed to touch him, to let him know that she was his servant—that she could not bear to let him go from her. Perhaps, she told herself, in time he would stay willingly (as she knew he must), but for now the cage was an unfortunate necessity; a means of keeping him until he could come to understand just how much she loved him. It was, she told herself, for his own good, really.

It was a shame that the winged god had brought along that other dreadful god-monster with the four-legged monster body and the god torso. She wanted the thing destroyed, but the Advanced Speculation Department had not yet determined which method would be most effective in killing a god.

She had managed, however, with the assistance of the Enclave of Titan Engineering, to disperse a gas into the laboratory that put the heavenly beings to sleep long enough for her to extract the rift-gate. Big-funder Thwick was most insistent that a demonstration of the rift-gate be arranged for Skramak as soon as possible, so Lunid hoisted the device and mounted it vertically (for better effect) onto a large cog she happened to have in the laboratory, one that suited it quite well. It would only require a little calibration, she thought, and it would be ready to demonstrate to the Dong Mahaj.

The winged god was signing to her again, his hands making the patterns of the heavens that she knew from her visions of the other world. Like all good Hob-goblins, she was well versed in the art, although occasionally, she was not sure if the meaning she got was the one the winged god intended.

"You want to . . . what?" Lunid mumbled to herself, translating the frenetic signs of the winged god. "Wait! Slow down, I can't understand you when you—oh, the rift-gate? Isn't that nice! Yes, I'm going to be calibrating the rift-gate and—what? Going? No, I'm not going anywhere just now, I have to calibrate the—home? Winged god's home? Yes, that's what it does."

Lunid winced. Sometimes the winged god just got too excited for his own good. She held up her hands to stop him, and the god, looking somewhat frustrated—as, no doubt, Lunid reminded herself, all gods are—stopped gesturing. At least he didn't use his god-voice, she thought gratefully as she carefully signed so that he would understand her. "I—show—rift-gate."

Lunid paused for a moment. How could she express to him the importance of what she was doing? There were no hand signals for "Big-funder" or "Thwick" or "endowment grant" or even "tenure." All of these things put together meant that she would not have to work so hard at inventing and that she and her winged god could spend much of their time together.

But she just didn't have the signs for it.

Lunid looked around the cluttered laboratory and soon found it: the controller book lay under several layers of metal sheets she had inadvertently set on top of it. Lunid carefully pulled the book out, spat on one of the gems she had embedded in the cover, and polished it with her sleeve. Then, gripping the large book in her left hand, she stomped over toward the rift-gate, then turned to face the winged god.

"Look, it's simple," she said, doing her best to sign with her right hand and pointing to both the book in her other hand and the now vertically mounted set of farsight rings behind her. "Book! Gems—book-gems sing—open rift-gate. Magic bridge—through heaven's door..."

The winged god squinted at her, a sour look on his face.

"Oh!" Lunid shook in frustration. The gods seemed to be so stupid sometimes. "Look, pay attention!"

Lunid turned with the book to face the rings. As she had done before, she started humming to the book. The gems answered her with their own tones until a chorus of sound rose from them and filled the laboratory with weaving harmonies in chords of depth and resonance. The books mounted into the frame of the rings answered with tones of their own, suffusing the metal with a bluish glow that blurred its edges to the eye. The air within the rings shifted and contorted; the stones of the wall seen through the rings twisted impossibly and then pushed aside as though spun out of existence by a vortex of sound and light. There was a flash of brilliance, then another place was seen through the rings—the dream-city appeared as though it existed just on the other side of the rings. Then the perspective shifted as though the rings were dropping into the city, gliding down its streets past door after door until the image came to a particular one and pushed forward toward it—through it and into another blaze of light.

Suddenly, the rings looked upon the strange gates of the god-city full of dead creatures where Lunid had first found her winged god. Two great black statues stood to either side of the open gate. A steady stream of the winged gods was moving into the city, the looks of fear clearly visible on their faces. At the same time, an army of the dead was marching out of those same gates, their spears held high.

Lunid turned in triumph, signing emphatically. "See! Rift-gate to heaven!"

Diminishing

Dwynwyn, Queen of the Dead, stood on the walls of her citadel city and wept.

She stood above the main gate to the city, flanked once more by the twin onyx statues. Below her the wide avenue stretching to the south was packed with refugees, their eyes filled with a little hope but mostly fear as they slogged their way into the city, too weary from the long miles of their hasty retreat to fly. Their feet were mud-caked and in many cases bleeding, yet they continued toward the city in their last flickering hope for safety and protection.

Above them, out of this same gate, flew the Army of the Dead, the points of their spears barely clearing the ceiling of the gate arch. Rank after rank of their number pressed through the clogged opening, quickly forming their columns to either side of the road. Their eyes were fixed, staring down the road to the south, their gray-skinned hands gripping their weapons with determination. Their armor was black, as preferred by the dead, and their ragged capes flapped in the air as they otherwise moved in utter silence down both sides of the road.

"Dwynwyn," Peleron said quietly behind her, his hand reaching for her shoulder. "Come away."

At his touch she pulled violently away from him, her voice quivering with emotion as she spoke. "No! I *have* to watch it! I am *compelled* to watch it."

"Your observing it does not change anything," Peleron said softly above the cries drifting upward from the refugees below.

"Perhaps—but someone must witness this," she replied, her voice choking on the words. "The end of the Sharajentei—the end of the glory that was Sharaj."

"In any event you will not have to watch long," her husband said with resignation. "I am told that these petitioners represent the last of the outer settlements. The cities of Delfli and Edricor have both been abandoned, and those who could survive the journey are now within the walls of the city."

"What of Sylandra?" Dwynwyn asked.

Peleron held his silence.

"Tell me, Pel."

"Sylandra was burned before all of its citizens could be evacuated," Peleron said, his eyes directed down the southern road but seemingly fixed elsewhere. "The Kyree came at night under cover of clouds and dropped jars of flaming oil onto the city. The Oraclyn of Sylandra rallied the warriors, but the damage was done, and there were not enough remaining to fight the fires and the Kyree at the same time. Many were lost."

"How many?"

"We have not been able to return to the city for an accurate count—nor are we likely to do so," Peleron replied.

"The Kyree-Nykira have pushed the battle lines beyond Sylandra and are approaching the northwest edge of the Oaken Forest. They will be slowed there for a time—the forest is our ally—but they cannot be stopped."

Dwynwyn nodded. "So I have been informed."

"You would think that House Argentei would come to your aid," Peleron scoffed, "if for no other reason than that it would allow them an opportunity for a good fight."

"None of the houses will come to our aid, Pel," Dwynwyn said, her lips tight against her teeth. "Each of them has been jealous of the power of the Sharaj and, more important, our control over the Lyceum that trains them. The lords and ladies of the faery ruling caste have never really trusted the Seeker class, and now that we have power outside the understanding of their narrow minds, we are also feared. They supported us as long as they believed us to be invincible, that we could no more die than the dead who flocked here. But the Kyree have shown them something they did not suspect: that the remaining armies of our dead *can* be defeated—not by strength of the enemy's weapons or the brilliance of their tactics, but by the noble act of defending Sharajentis!"

"So we are victims of our own victories," Peleron said quietly as he watched their remaining armies fly southward.

"Such a strange truth," Dwynwyn agreed. "The dead who remain do so because they have left noble deeds undone in the course of their lives. The very act of defending Sharajentis—even the killing of the enemy before them—can cause them to achieve their Enlightenment, and thus they vanish from the field of battle. Our own successes diminish us, for the more our warriors win, the lesser become their numbers. Our Kyree enemy may not understand this fully yet, but the houses of the Fae know that the strength of our Army of the Dead dwindles with every triumph. Now they know it is only a matter of time; they are determined to wait out our death."

"Surely, Qestardis—"

"Qestardis wishes our demise more than any of the others," Dwynwyn replied.

Peleron frowned. "Queen Tatyana put you on your throne."

"Tatyana put me on my throne and gave me my kingdom because it suited her purposes. Still, she did love me." Dwynwyn sighed. "And I loved her; perhaps that is why she, above all the others, wants me and my kingdom to be conquered and brought to shame and destruction."

"Because of Aislynn?"

Dwynwyn nodded. "Aislynn was her only daughter, Pel. The princess found purpose in the Sharaj, but that same reason took her across the ocean to try and free the souls of the Kyree—and there she vanished with her husband. We may never know their fate. Tatyana blames me for her daughter's loss and now, perhaps, for the loss of a grandson who never really knew her."

"Has there been any word of Arryk?"

"There," she said, and gestured down to the hordes of faeries streaming into the city. "That is the only answer we have: our cities burned to the ground and our people fleeing into the safety of their capital."

"The declaration of war stated that Arryk and the centaur attacked their troops without provocation."

"Ha!" Dwynwyn scoffed.

"Killing their commander, Dekacian Skrei, and a host of escort guards as they vanished."

"They also said that it was a deliberately planned attack, authorized by me as a prelude to invasion!" Dwynwyn seethed. "Invasion, no less! The Kyree-Nykira are liars—the same as any Famadorian."

"They used the word 'vanished,' Dwynwyn," Peleron continued on, trying to keep his wife focused on the thread of his reasoning. "Arryk is a strange young faery, we all know that, but he is also an excellent Sharajin. If he vanished, he must have gone somewhere. If we could find him—determine what actually happened with the dekacian…"

"I've looked." Dwynwyn shook her head. "Where I could not look, I've had others look for me. We have Sharajin in every one of the ruling houses among the Fae and not a few among the Kyree as well. I've been in touch with them all, and none have reported so much as the whisper of Arryk's passing—let alone that centaur he had with him."

"He must be somewhere, Dwyn," Peleron insisted.

The Queen of the Dead rubbed her hand over her eyes. "I've had the dryads speak to the forests—none have felt his breath on their leaves."

"Not all of the forests are cooperative with the dryads…"

"No, but they love to talk with one another, and I think they would have bragged if they were harboring such an important fugitive. I've even been in touch with the merfolk; they tell me he is not to be found in the deep. And if he vanished—as these dubious reports indicate—then why has he left no trail in the Sharaj? I have walked the dream-place in search of him; in truth, Peleron, I have often followed him in the Sharaj for fear of what might happen to him. He is not there."

Peleron nodded grimly. "Then he is truly lost."

"As are we all," Dwynwyn replied, her gaze turning inward over the city. The strange black towers remained shrouded in the perpetual fog. It was a hideous place that she loathed on each first glance. She had long before learned, however, to take a long breath and look beyond the black sockets of death that stared back at her from its terrible architecture and see the hope of life in the Enlightenment beyond mortal cares that beat as a bright ember beneath the grim exterior of dead ash.

"Its walls may be thick, but they are bursting, Peleron. I had never thought I would see the day when I was grateful to the dead for building so large a city—their purpose was only to keep occupied so that they might forget their misery. Yet now their strange rooms in these frightful buildings are occupied by the people of our nation. Our larders and granaries will be quickly exhausted, and then the walls of the city will not seem as safe as an open field of vegetables. We will be forced to leave, Pel, and where can we go?"

"We could deploy the Sharajin," Peleron said. "Use the power of the Sharaj in support of the dead warriors."

"As we did in Sylandra?" Dwynwyn snapped, shaking her head.

"You are first and above all a Seeker," Peleron said, taking his wife by her shoulders and forcing her to look him in the eyes. "You've lived your life by the new; finding that which was previously hidden from the eyes of the Fae. There has to be a New Truth—somewhere in the Sharaj—that can give you the path that you seek. I've never known a stronger woman, Dwynwyn, but strength is not what you need right now."

"What I need," Dwynwyn said haltingly, "is a New Truth."

Peleron smiled. "Yes, Dwynwyn; you've got to find a New Truth."

Dwynwyn turned back to look down the road. The line of refugees still stretched into the distant woods, but now there were gaps. The last ranks of her latest dispatch of the army had already disappeared.

A new idea, she thought.

"Issue a call to the block leaders in the city," Dwynwyn said. "Have them come to the citadel tonight and gather them in the courtyard. I want them to carry a message for me to every Sharajin in the city."

"You have a New Truth?" Peleron smiled hopefully.

"I have the beginnings of a New Truth." Dwynwyn was thoughtful. "A step down a road not yet taken. I should like to take a few steps more and see what is around the turn."

Peleron nodded. "We'll take these steps together."

"My steps may take us over the edge of an abyss," Dwynwyn said.

"Then we'll step off the edge together." Peleron shrugged with a smile.

Dwynwyn smiled thinly back. "Then I had better be careful which road I take us down."

Beyond Roads

The fog was a blessing; it had rolled into the city of Khordsholm in the early morning, blanketing the narrow and winding passageways in its thick, damp folds and hiding behind its veil the terrible destruction of the previous afternoon.

The dragon Ulruk had failed to appear last night—much to the relief of the innkeeper's wife, who had muttered her hope that the local defenders had somehow at last felled the monster. Theona gathered that it was only a wish; two guards who happened to temporarily be keeping rooms at the inn told everyone present that they had seen the dragon moving off to the northwest, driven off and injured but still flying. They both seemed more concerned that the dragon had never before attacked the city with such determined fury and never in the daylight.

Theona gazed cautiously out through the inn's door into the gray-shrouded street beyond. Two figures stood as dark patches in the fog: one tall with a gnarled walking staff and the other short and stout with a large red hat.

They held their cloaks clasped tightly about them against the pervasive damp chill.

"Master Arvad?" Theona called out cautiously. "Master Belas?"

"True to both as er is," came the quiet rumblings from the dwarf.

"I apologize for the early hour," Dorian said, "but Dregas insisted that we had to go now."

"Aye," the dwarf said enthusiastically. "Best slip out through the fog, eh?"

Theona hesitated, turning to her sister standing behind her in the doorway.

"Well," Valana said behind her with impatience, "what are you waiting for?"

Still, she paused; what was she waiting for? The dwarf she had seen in her dream was suddenly made real; a dwarf which she found only after following the dream here. It seemed like magic, but all through the restless night before, she had gone over the many and diverse disciplines of the mystics and none of them fit her experience. This dwarf could not be real, and yet there he was, just as she had pictured him. She tried to remember what else she had dreamed, wondering if it, too, would become real.

"The darkness engulfed us," she muttered to herself, "and then there was a distant shore of white sands..."

"What are you talking about?" Valana asked impatiently.

Theona suddenly shook from her reveries. "Sorry; it's nothing really." She pulled her own cloak around her as she stepped into the morning chill. "Master Dregas, we apologize that we have not yet prepared our torusk for a journey, but we would only be a short time in doing so. If you would be so good as to come into the inn, I should be glad to provide you with breakfast while—"

"Too many words er is," the dwarf said, looking puzzled at the girl.

Theona smiled. "Sorry, Dregas; I guess I've been around Master Zolan too long. Can I buy you breakfast while we get our torusk prepared?"

"Aye, breakfast good as er is!" the dwarf said, starting forward, but the hand of the tall figure next to him reached out suddenly and restrained him.

"Master Dregas forgets that he told me our destination is quite nearby and that torusks would not be needed," Dorian said quickly. "In fact, he insists that we walk."

"Aye, true er is," the dwarf grumbled, "but breakfast were a good idea, too."

"Walk?" Valana said with some dismay. "I thought you were taking us to—just how close is this gate?"

"Hush! Nay far, m'lady," Dregas said quickly. "Just a short road for yer fair slippers to tread. Your pretty satisfaction assured by Dregas Belas er is."

"Let's go," Theona said as she stepped into the street. "This fog will not last forever, and I, for one, would just as soon travel under its cover while we can."

The strange foursome passed down Sailfin Street to where it turned to follow Jolin Street down toward the quay. The buildings looked more weathered and gray than ever, the narrow streets more oppressively close. The air was heavy with the fog, and Theona found it difficult to breathe.

The dwarf led the way with surprising swiftness, his short legs moving with a spryness that surprised Theona. And his outlandish dress appeared dull today, the reds and purples of his pantaloons and jacket muted in the gray light. He certainly did not seem fittingly dressed for adventure; he looked more like a court jester than a wilderness guide.

At least Dorian seemed prepared in his choice of costuming. He wore a dark green hooded cloak over a tan tunic and dark brown breeches. The leather in his boots appeared pliable, and their soles made remarkably little noise against the cobblestones when he stepped. The rhythm of his pace was kept by the tall, gnarled walking staff which he swung in his course with practiced ease. He carried neither pack nor pouch; he was obviously not prepared for an extended absence.

This comforted Theona, for she was not sure just where their blind guide was taking them. He had mentioned a gate—a secret gate, as she recalled—but finding a gate and dealing with what was on the other side were two entirely different matters. They had told their father that they were coming to Khordsholm to discover what had happened to Treijan, and they had done so, or at least thought they had before fate brought them to the dwarf. Either way, Theona knew the safest thing would be to return home, report to their father what they had found, and have him deal with the information through his own agents.

Yet she had known which gate to pick to get this far from seeing it in her dream, and the same dream had brought them to this dwarf. It *seemed* like magic—some sort of magic anyway—and maybe it could make her special, too. She had to follow it—had to know for herself whether it was just her imagination trying to give her false hopes of becoming a mystic like her father and mother and everyone else who looked on her as something to be pitied.

So she said nothing as they passed to the end of Jolin

Street. She could hear the ocean waves breaking against the quay wall to the south, though she could not see them through the mist. The quay itself lay to her right down a short curve in the road, but the dwarf turned left onto the Way of Tears and out of the city through the Gate of the Dead.

"I've been this way before," Valana said quietly at Theona's side. "Zolan brought me. This is the coastal road that winds around the hill—what the locals call a mountain—and up to their old ruins."

"Right er is," Dregas said. "Followed Mistress Valana here, Dregas did."

"It's the old city," Dorian noted as they passed the shops outside the gate. The road ahead of them turned to the south around the base of a hill whose mass was just beginning to emerge from the mists around them. "Khordsholm was part of the trade centers that ruled the Crescent Coast and a vital part of the southern reaches of the Rhamasian Empire in its day. When Rhamas fell, the Sea-kings of the Coast continued to rule their city-states and tried to keep the dream of Rhamas alive. Ulruk, however, had other ideas; the Dragon-Talkers of his age negotiated a settlement with the creature on their own. Most of the Sea-kings capitulated to the dragon's demands, but Lord Jefard of Khordsholm refused. The other Sea-kings pressured him, and he bowed to their demands, but Ulruk was not satisfied for the perceived insult; he came, vowing to destroy the upper city. Lord Jefard, it is said, stood at the very top of the Khordsholm beacon—a tower whose shining light had called men home from the sea for nearly five hundred years—and waited for the dragon, a single shining spear in his hand."

Theona looked up as they walked along the ancient

road. The steep hillside was carpeted in the thick green of verdant plants. Only occasionally did a broken carving or a few stones of a founding wall protrude from the undergrowth. The road climbed steadily upward, until a scorched foundation wall appeared on the hillside above.

"What happened to him?" Theona felt an awe she found unexpected.

"Lord Jefard?" Dorian replied. "He stood at the top of the beacon and yelled at the dragon, even as the mammoth beast bore down upon him. He defiantly drew back his weapon—so the stories say—and was engulfed at once in the dragon's flaming spew. The dragon vented his fury on the hilltop. The temples of the ancient gods, markets, the homes, the parks, and the people were all laid to ash and broken before his breath. Those who survived—mostly those in the lower city, which the dragon cunningly left untouched—long told the story of their last sight of Lord Jefard facing down the dragon and his own mortality. His name for a time was spoken with reverence, but as the ages grew long, the memories grew dim. It all happened almost five hundred years before our time. The ancient tales, however, are only told when they serve the powers of the present. If the story doesn't serve—well, then, the story must change; so it was with poor old Lord Jefard. The bards—*we* bards—had a good deal to do with that, especially because of what happened during the Pir Insurgence a few years ago. Both the Pir and the mystics were trying to expand into the Crescent Coast at the same time; the Pir promised to control the dragons, while the bards were promising the power of magic for defense. The bards had to convince the people of the Crescent Coast that the Pir were wrong—and did so by reshaping the local tales to prove their point. Now, thanks to the bards, old Lord

Jefard's last great act has become synonymous with the fall of pride, arrogance, and foolish defiance—the last act of an idiot desperate to cover his own mistakes."

The road turned in among the broken foundations. The dwarf continued undeterred as their feet started climbing shattered steps.

"What do they call this place?" Theona asked, her teeth beginning to chatter.

"It is called the Necropolis," Dorian replied. "The City of the Dead."

Theona looked up just as the mists parted. There rose above her the curving foundations of a tower of white, its stones splintered raggedly and scorched. It was only a glimpse, and then the mists drew their veil over the ruins as though shielding its sadness from her eyes.

"You know a great deal of this place," Theona said, trying to distract herself from the chill that had suddenly run through her bones. There was something about the idea of a "city of the dead" that resonated in her. It was as though the place or the name were familiar to her—like a memory that she could not quite recall.

"I have traded here for many years," Dorian replied. "One learns things—though apparently not as much as our guide."

The dwarf moved quickly across the uneven ground until he came to the site of a fallen temple. The foundation stones to one side remained intact, though large stains had marred its formerly polished surface.

"Dwarfkind built here long before men come," Dregas sniffed with pride. "Southern outpost of Khagun Zhav here er is. Sea-kings never knew—built on top and blind to dwarven-craft underfoot as er is."

Valana drew her cloak closer about her. "What is he

talking about? I swear, I can't understand a word he's saying."

"Khagun Zhav is the dwarven kingdom under the mountains north of Vestadia," Dorian said with a frown. "I think he means there are dwarven ruins under the human ruins."

The dwarf slapped his thigh with a fat hand and pointed his little finger at the man.* "Right as er is! Show you wonders—better than human ruins."

Dregas turned back toward the foundation, stepped once to the left and then twice to the right, then pondered the stones for what may have been only a few minutes but seemed far longer to Valana.

"Misplace your dwarven wonders?" Valana asked sharply.

"Valana, please!"

"Theona, the little guy obviously doesn't know—"

The dwarf suddenly thrust out his hand, smacking it against the stone. It resounded with a loud click, followed by a low grinding noise. The stones fell into the earth one after another, forming a staircase down into a dark space under the temple.

The dwarf turned to them and smiled. "Ladies first. Dregas polite er is."

"If you don't mind," Dorian said with a smile, "I think you should go first—you're the guide."

Dregas's smile deepened to a grin in response, and then, turning, he began bounding down the stairs.

Dorian turned to Theona. "I'm not a mystic. Could you provide us with light?"

Theona flushed. "I-I'm not—"

---

*The dwarves of Khagun Zhav consider it impolite to point with any digit other than the smallest.

"We will gladly oblige you, Dorian," Valana said, quickly stepping forward, her hand already extended. The ball of light flared into existence as they moved down the stairs. "Come along, Theona. We don't want to keep our guide waiting."

"This is an outpost?" Theona wondered aloud, her voice echoing down the long, empty spaces around her.

Valana had increased the light in her hand as much as she dared. Its rays were blinding to look at, but barely reached the edges of the cavernous space around them. Towering pillars of stone rose upward into spaces where her light could not reach. The carvings were delicate and intricate on each of the columns, while the walls were covered with relief artwork of lifelike detail.

"Are we nearly there?" Valana asked wearily.

"Aye," the dwarf said. "Just a wee further er is."

"No one ever knew," Dorian whispered with wonder in his voice.

"Which makes me wonder how we have come to know now," Theona whispered back. "How is it that this dwarf should lead us so readily into this place that no one else seems to even know exists? More important, is he willing to let us *leave* this place and risk us telling anyone about it?"

Dorian nodded. "You suspect him."

"I think the only reason he led us here is because he knew he wouldn't have to lead us out. More than that, how did Gaius and Treijan get down here if he didn't bring them? I'm beginning to wonder if there ever was a gate or if—"

"Here er is!" the dwarf shouted in triumph.

Valana turned toward the sound, her light revealing a

dark doorway with the blindfolded dwarf standing next to it. Something shimmered beyond her light.

The dwarf bowed deeply, gesturing through the archway. "Gate as er is."

Theona moved ahead of Valana, her shadow stretching toward the dark doorway as Valana and Dorian followed behind.

She could see it now—a gate! There was no mistaking it, the large curve of the stone set beneath the glowing Songstone. Theona examined the mystic arch and glanced around the room. The gate had been built here from the stones that were already in the room.

"Dwarven-built?" Theona asked.

"Nay," the dwarf said, his nose wrinkling at the idea. "Bad work. Nay dwarf-built—human-mystic-built."

"Where does it go?" Theona asked.

The dwarf shrugged. "Nay know. Only know Gaius and Treijan pass it."

"Sing it open, Val," Theona said evenly.

Valana stood before the oval and began to sing. Her melody soared, echoing down the ancient dwarven halls. She was joined by the Songstone, its harmony adding to her song until the space within the oval flashed once and then filled with a shimmering blackness.

"Now gate er is—take you to Gaius straight. One step and you there."

The dwarf turned toward the door, waving his wide hand. "Guide work done—shown you wonders, shown you gate. Have short trip!"

The dwarf was suddenly stopped by Dorian's extended staff across his path.

"Oh, no, Dregas, you are far from finished," the man said. His head gestured toward the gate. "After you."

Theona's mind tried to gather itself from scattered ideas and impressions—reassembling slowly a picture of where she lay and trying to grasp what had happened to her.

It was dark. Theona couldn't understand it; it had been early in the morning when they stepped through the gate. Now it was dark again, and she could see the stars overhead out of the corner of her eye, burning brilliantly in a wide sky. She could hear the breaking of the ocean waves behind her, but a wide band of darkness lay in the field of her vision that her eyes could not penetrate.

It was warm, too; ridiculously warm for so early in the morning. The air was thick with humidity, even more so than in Khordsholm.

All she could do was lie on her side and breathe it in. She could remember coming through the gate and falling down here. She had tried to move after that, but her legs did not seem to obey her thoughts—indeed, she was paralyzed, lying helpless on her side on the warm sands that had cushioned her fall . . .

Sands, she thought. *White, warm sands.*

"Valana?" she said in a quiet voice.

"Thei! I'm here," came the weak reply. "I can't—I think something is wrong with me."

Something moved in the band of darkness. Figures and shapes scurrying.

"Thei?" It was Valana, frightened.

"It will be all right, Val," Theona said, though she herself hardly believed it. Something had gone horribly wrong when they came through the gate; she was sure of it and wondered if the dwarf had anything to do with it.

She heard voices, strange and unfamiliar in the darkness. Their words made no sense—a language different from any she had ever heard.

One voice was suddenly louder and higher-pitched than the others, shouting orders. The figures in the dark band moved quickly, then the voice changed and was horribly familiar.

"Dregas Belas, you double-dealing little vermin," the voice shouted. "What have you done?"

Suddenly, a light flared into existence, and Theona could see. The band of darkness was a line of strange trees at the edge of the white-sand beach. Men with ornately decorated spears, their deeply tanned skin shining in the light, stared back at her. The light drew nearer as a man knelt on the sands before Theona, his pale, narrow face drawing into her line of sight, his piercing eyes peering at her.

Though she had never met him before, she had heard his description and described him herself many times in Khordsholm. Now a shock of recognition ran through her—the only thing she could feel.

Gaius Petros considered Theona grimly for a moment, nodded, and then extinguished his light.

The Rifts

Captives

Miss Conlan?" The sound of her name was coming from nearby, but Theona was having trouble responding. The feeling in her limbs seemed to return with the slow brightening of the daylight that streamed through the arched window opening just above her. Unfortunately, it was being replaced by terrible aches and a tingling in her muscles that could not stop too soon. She still could not move her head, although her fingers and toes seemed to be responding, however reluctantly. She groaned and found she could still speak and her heart and lungs still moved in their comfortably accustomed rhythms. Moving anything else—or getting up from where she lay—was still impossible. It occurred to her that whatever had happened to her had been very particular in regard to what was paralyzed and what was not—a precision of method that belied its cunning origins.

"Miss Conlan," the voice said again, high-pitched yet distinctly male. "Can you hear me?"

"Yes, I can hear you," she rasped from her dry throat.

Her world, she thought, had grown particularly small. She gazed upward into the same view that she had been contemplating for the last hour: long thin poles lashed together with straps of dried leather formed into tall arched ribs above where she lay. They supported a latticework beneath a steeply pitched roof made of layers of some sort of strange wide plant leaf. They looked like fans from below, reminiscent of dragons' wings as their pattern locked together in the dim space above the rafters. Each was stained in flowing, colorful lines of red, green, yellow, and blue, and with the growing light she could start to pick out highly stylized figures. The nearest wall—just to her left and nearly beyond her peripheral vision—was made of some kind of woven grasses, also not recognizably a plant of her acquaintance. "I can also see, but I still can't move."

"It will take some time," said the high-pitched voice. "It will be easier if you don't fight it. Relax and it will subside in its own time. I promise; you'll be feeling much better by this evening."

"And what happens this evening?"

"Then we shall see. You have violated the ancestral lands of King Pe'akanu. He has decreed that you be brought before his Wheel of Judgment this night and hear his final verdict concerning you and the others."

"Where—where is my sister?"

"Your sister is safe enough. She is with the others and has been asking for you—actually, demanding your presence—ever since she regained her voice."

"Please—take me to her."

"I cannot. The king has forbidden that you be held with the others. You are special to them and not to be sullied by their lesser gifts."

Theona guffawed. "They obviously do not know me, sir."

"I do not fully understand it myself, but I have spoken with the king, and he remains firm on this point."

"You understand these people?" Theona asked with effort. "Who are you?"

A thin, hawkish face moved into her field of vision. His eyes were piercing, she thought, though somehow terribly sad. He wore a bard's tunic, she noted, though without the cape or vest and with the collar opened deeply down his chest. He sat next to her, taking up her limp hand and rubbing it, though his manner in doing so seemed curiously dispassionate. Still, his efforts seemed to be taking the tingling away for the time being.

"You and your friends have obviously gone to great lengths to find me. I suspect, therefore, that you already know who I am. For now I think I had better ask the questions—and may I suggest that a great deal concerning your fate may depend upon your answers? Shall we begin?"

It must *be Gaius,* Theona thought, or at least she had seemed to be certain of it the night before. "Have I any choice?" she croaked.

The man smiled again without benevolence. "No, not really."

"Then ask your questions."

The man nodded. "Do you know where you are?"

She vaguely remembered being brought into this strange room, though everything before that was just a disjointed series of impressions: white sands and strong, dark-hued men with their skins painted. One of them had picked her up—she recalled the flood of panic that gripped her at being handled by this stranger and being unable to prevent him from touching her. She had the image of being carried with remarkable strength and speed through a forest of strange plants so thick that she could not see the ground.

"No," she answered. "I have no idea where I am."

"And just how did you get here?"

"A gate; the dwarf showed us a secret gate among the ruins east of Khordsholm—one of which I suspect even the master bards of Calsandria are unaware. There was a man with us—he forced the dwarf through first and then we followed. The man and the dwarf—you say they are both with my sister?"

"We'll get to them in a while. My questions first." He continued to massage her hand. "Does anyone know you are here?"

Theona inwardly panicked. How could she have been so foolish? It was just another gate to pass through; a simple thing done every day throughout the Mystic Empire, and she had thought this would be just another step from one place to another. In Valana's rush to come as quickly as possible, Theona had neglected to contact anyone about where they were going—not even Zolan, who worked for the Transport Guild. She decided to try buying time at the cost of a lie, swallowing hard. "Yes, of course, they do. You know my name. My father is Rylmar Conlan, and he knows where we've gone. It is only a matter of time before he catches up to us."

"Master Conlan is indeed resourceful," the man replied, his eyes gazing thoughtfully out the window opening. "But I think we'll be safe enough for now. The dwarf is clever and would not have told you your destination before leading you there. If your friend had not forced the dwarf through the gate ahead of him, it might have been different, but as we have them both well cared for, there will be no rescue storming our little secret gate. So tell me, Miss Conlan, why have you and your friends gone to such trouble to come to find me?"

Theona's eyes shifted toward the man, and she blinked. "I think you know why we have come, Gaius Petros."

The man hesitated only a moment before he took up her other hand. "Well, I see that introductions are unnecessary."

"What have you done with him?" she asked.

Gaius lifted an eyebrow, smiling in some private delight. "What have I *done* with him? I like the sound of that—it makes me seem so mysterious and powerful."

"Gaius, whatever you're up to, perhaps we can come to a bargain. I'm sure my father can make it more than worth your while to—"

Gaius stood up abruptly, dropping her limp hand back to her side. "Conlans! Still buying their way to the top, eh? Well, all the chests of fat tallies in all the houses of the clans couldn't fix everything, miss; there are some things that cannot be bought and some problems that are just too convoluted to be unraveled with a few sharp-edged coins."

"We *are* Conlans," Theona snapped back, though her voice remained hoarse. "My sister's reputation has been impugned by your selfish and despicable actions, and we will go to whatever lengths necessary to put it right."

Gaius suddenly leaned over her, his hands gripping either side of the bed on which she lay, his face dropping so close to her own that she could feel his breath.

"Bravely spoken for a woman flat on her back."

A high-pitched noise like a mixture of a whistle and a squeak caused Gaius to turn his head toward the open window. He smiled, releasing the bed frame and standing up once more before extending his right arm, beckoning with his hand. There was a flapping noise as a blur of color burst through the opening.

Theona gasped.

The creature was brilliantly hued in vibrant greens, yellows, and oranges down its long body and in glorious patterns across its wings. It landed softly on Gaius's outstretched hand, folded its leathery wings, and then scampered quickly up his arm and across his shoulders, winding its long tail carefully around his neck. The small talons of its four feet dug tenderly into the cloth on the bard's left shoulder as its small, broad head craned upward, gently nuzzling the delighted Gaius.

"I'd like you to meet an old friend of mine." Gaius smiled happily. "Her name is Ha-uli."

Though the creature was not even three feet long from snout to tip of its barbed tail, there was no questioning its form; she had witnessed it herself only the day before.

It was unmistakably a dragon.

"Where are we?" Theona asked in a quivering voice.

"You said you Conlans would go to any lengths." Gaius looked down at her, the dragon settling on his right shoulder as though to sleep. "I suspect you've gone a good deal further from home than you thought—and tonight we shall find out if you have gone too far."

Theona stood on a wooden walkway, drinking in the air as she faced the last deepening reds of sunset over the waters of the wide bay. The effects of the strange paralysis had faded—just as Gaius had told her they would—and left her feeling unusually refreshed by afternoon. It was good to stand in the evening breeze and appreciate the simple joy of having control over her own limbs once more.

"Theona!"

She turned toward the familiar voice. "Valana! Are you well?"

"Well enough," her sister replied with a sullen edge to her voice. "At least I can move, if that's what you mean. Where have you been?"

Valana was making her way across one of the hundreds of vine bridges that connected the tree-homes of the strange bayfront section of the city. From what Theona could see from her balcony, most of the community along the shoreline and in many places within the city itself hung suspended in unfamiliar trees roughly fifteen feet above the ground or—in her case at the moment—above the water, for many of the trees grew straight up out of the bay. What looked at first glance to be an inordinately thick trunk was revealed upon closer examination to be many smaller trunks all growing as a mass into the same tree.

The city, now glowing in the deepening rays, fascinated her more than the incredible sunset. Rising up over the tall trees, the buildings of fitted stone were angular with flat surfaces and roofs. Beyond the clusters of nearby buildings poking upward from the foliage, a tall defensive wall rimmed the inner city, protecting several structures of bizarre and marvelous design: angular pyramids built of huge stepped layers, their sloping sides mounted by long flights of stairs rising up to their uppermost tier. She counted four of these structures of various sizes as well as other grand buildings—some steeply pitched, but mostly with the same flat roof design as the outlying buildings. It was, by even the most jaded definition, a city worthy of any empire of which Theona had ever heard—and she was equally sure it was completely unknown to even the most knowledgeable Mnemeatic loremasters.

Theona wrested her attentions back to her sister. "I have been right here, Valana."

"You should have come to me at once. You can see how much I've needed you," her sister replied, gesturing down at her dress. Valana had insisted on wearing one of her more attractive traveling costumes and with her hair properly done in the hope that her Treijan might be standing on the other side of the gate. Her dress was now soiled and lightly stained from her paralytic fall to the ground, and in the new humidity her hair had taken on unintended forms. "Worse yet, they refuse to let me go anywhere without these savages following my every step."

Theona glanced past her sister. Valana was followed by two huge guards whose builds were rather intimidating. Theona blinked and flushed slightly; men were very rarely seen in Calsandria without at least a shirt covering their bodies, and never among the mystics. Theona found herself frightened, confused, shy, and yet compelled as she looked on their casual sensuality. Their broad faces featured strong, wide jaws and piercing dark eyes. Their faces and their bodies were painted; designs in blue, black, and white ran in long continuous curves from their foreheads down their thick necks and wove in a pattern across their backs, chests, and flat stomachs. Each of them wore a colorful wrap around his waist that came to just above the knees, his muscular legs ending in bare feet.

While their grim faces were frightening enough, it was the practiced ease with which they held their weapons that now drew Theona's eye. They carried clublike devices carved from a dark hardwood, rubbed and polished until they gleamed in the fading light. Each had a heavily weighted pummel at the end where a gray stone was fixed for weight, while the longer end was a sweeping curve of wood with a ridge of thorny spikes running down its back. Carved eyes on either side extending into a long brow line completed the effect of a monstrous face.

And each warrior carried a dragon on his shoulders. The man on the right—slightly taller with long black hair—had a red and orange dragon that lay across his shoulders, its head lolling back and forth in sleep as the huge man swayed. The other warrior had a smaller, cobalt-blue dragon with light blue markings that sat up attentively, its black eyes shining as it eyed Theona.

"They aren't savages," Theona heard herself saying, almost as much to convince herself as her sister. "They—they just live differently than we do."

"They're barbaric! Look at these!" Valana said as she stepped onto Theona's platform. She held out her arms, and Theona noted at once the bracers on each wrist. They looked to have been made of white bone segments carved with complex inlaid designs. Valana then lifted the bottom of her skirt, showing a similar arrangement on her ankles. "We woke up with them on. They're hideous and dirty, and they smell."

"Well, then, take them off."

"Don't you think I've tried?" Valana snapped. "They bite me when I do."

"Valana, just use your magic and—"

"I can't!"

"What do you mean you can't?"

"I mean none of us can!" Valana wailed. "Not me or that Dorian fellow that came with us. He's a mystic, too, by the way, no matter what he says—but it doesn't do any of us any good because none of us can use the Deep Magic here."

"That's not possible," Theona said.

"Well, possible or not, that's the way it is," Valana said in a tone meant to preclude any further argument. "That smug Gaius thinks he has us as well as my fiancé—"

"Valana, Treijan never asked you—"

"And if he thinks he can hold all of us *and* the prince of Rennes-Arvad, then he has another thought coming!" Valana continued unabated.

"And as soon as you have another thought, I should be glad to hear of it," came the high voice from a balcony on the other side of the bridge. Gaius stood there with his hands folded across his chest, while behind him stood four more warriors. The narrow-faced bard's left hand rested on the hilt of a native club suspended from a loop at his waist. "It will have to be soon, however, since it is time to learn your fate before the Wheel of Judgment."

Wheel of Judgment

Theona walked down the trail behind her sister, both of them careful with their pace to keep from either running into the two huge warriors leading the way with burning torches or the two similar warriors urging them on from behind. The sun had settled below the horizon, leaving behind the dim embers of the evening clouds cast across the broad sky. The sisters from Calsandria once more had their feet on the ground, the guards having led them down from the treetops into the lush foliage below. Theona expected to be taken directly into the confines of the strange, magnificent city she had seen from above, but instead their guards led them northward outside the great outer wall and down a packed-dirt trail. The thick foliage to either side of their path had grown dark and forbidding, conjuring up in Theona's imagination shapes that were looming larger and more terrifying by the moment. She tried to take a breath, to rein in her thoughts and push the shadows back, but she felt as though she couldn't get any air.

It was the eyes of the small dragons that so unnerved her. One rested casually on the shoulders of each of the warriors surrounding them. The skin of each dragon was adorned in brilliant colors, even in the light of the torches, and it appeared that no two of them were identical in their markings or, it seemed, in their demeanor. Theona watched the two dragons ahead of her. One lay across the broad back of its warrior, its head resting on its foreclaws, while the other sat upright, its wings carefully folded as its hind legs clutched the sash beneath it. The only thing in common between them was their shining black eyes that were fixed unalterably, it seemed, on Theona.

The constant vigilance unnerved her, especially as each warrior kept his right hand on the hilt of the strange weapon suspended from his sash—a constant reminder that they were to follow their captors or pay a terrible price.

In truth, Theona was not at all sure that they weren't about to die in any event and half wondered if it would not be better for her and her sister to take their chances in a desperate flight into the frightening underbrush on either side of the trail. She would never attempt such a thing if it meant leaving her sister behind, and unfortunately, Theona could not think of a way of communicating such a plan to Valana without its being overheard by Gaius.

Gaius walked immediately before the sisters with a confident stride that Theona grudgingly wished she could share. He did not fear these dark-hued natives as she did—indeed, he seemed to prefer their company and enjoyed casting his disdain on her own family and society. He evidently spoke their language, an advantage that frightened Theona. It was equally evident that Gaius had taken Treijan captive for some nefarious purpose, spiriting him away through his own secret Songstone gate to this alien land—wherever it might be. Treijan was Gaius's own cousin, and House Petros had always been a staunch ally of House Arvad, although the introduction of the Rennes line had strained their relations. How far did Gaius's plan extend? Had this man somehow betrayed the mystics to these strange people that now held them captive? He wore one of their weapons at his side. How deeply was he involved with these people? Was he organizing an army?

The trail ended abruptly at the edge of a wide paved roadway. Gaius did not hesitate but turned at once toward the south and the open gate of the city wall that towered over them. Small dragons perched on either side of the gate, gazing down at Theona as she followed the guards between them.

Gaius led them through narrow alleys between the square stone buildings. Theona marveled at the craft that must have gone into the city's construction; the smooth paving stones under her feet had been fit with such precision that she doubted there was a parchment's width between any two rocks, and not a single blade of grass grew anywhere. The walls of the buildings they passed were also so well fitted that she saw no mortar between any stones—and doubted that they were in need of any.

Theona's thoughts were banished, however, at the sight of an enormous stepped pyramid—the tallest of four in the city—that towered over the tallest of the nearby palm-topped trees and lesser buildings. The structure's wide square base looked to be at least two hundred feet on a side, and its thirty-foot-tall walls slanted inward slightly. Detailed carvings, weathered somewhat by wind, rain, and time, adorned panels that filled every available space. Then a second such level sat atop the first, this one likewise adorned and also thirty feet in height. This progression continued upward through a succession of levels—seven in all—until it terminated in a square structure at the top. Stylized statues of dragons stood on each corner, facing outward from the edifice. A single stone staircase, nearly twenty feet wide, rose up the face of the structure to the third level, where it reached a broad archway that gave access to the building's interior, then branched around both sides of the arch before joining again to connect each of the higher levels to its lofty top.

Not a few of the stone dragon carvings were being used as perches for a number of actual small dragons. *By the gods,* Theona thought to herself in dread-filled wonder. *How many dragons are there?*

It was only then that she noticed they were standing on the northern edge of an enormous plaza filled with a multitude of cheering thousands, and a chill shook her despite the warm night air.

Dark-skinned men and women with square, strong faces crowded shoulder-to-shoulder and as many as twenty deep at the edges of the plaza. All of them wore a similar cloth wrapped around their hips from front to back and then crossing back in front again across their chests and behind their necks. Though the manner of its wear was always the same, the patterns in the cloth were varied and only occasionally repeated. The children pushed forward or hung from low tree limbs so that they might better see the spectacle before them.

All eyes watched a ring of warriors, fifteen to twenty deep, wheeling in a rhythmic dance around the center of the clearing, their features illuminated by fire pits set at intervals outside their circle. Each swung his clublike weapon with smooth precision from right hand to left as they all chanted, their voices emphasizing each thunderous step as their feet fell against the packed ground with a resounding thud, their stance wide and strong as they slapped their chests with their left hands. Their deep voices shook the air with their chorus. Then without pause or misstep the entire assembly of warriors lifted their left feet and turned, their polished weapons glistening in the night as they spun as though by a single thought, turning the ring farther about its center. Their chants continued with their motions, the sounds of their wide, open palms smacking as one against their thighs, chests, and arms as their clubs carved intricate arcs through the air. On the shoulder of each warrior danced a small dragon, their heads on their long necks weaving back and forth, leaping from shoulder to shoulder, and their colorful leathery wings opening and moving with precision to the chanting and motion of the warriors under them.

Suddenly, the warriors turned, their clubs flipping in their hands and thrust suddenly skyward. The air overhead shifted and distorted Theona's view of the twilit trees beyond. The change was so subtle that at first she thought she might have imagined it, but as the warriors stepped again, the rhythm of their dance gathered speed along with the intensity of their chant. The clubs swung skyward again as the massive circle of warriors dropped as one to their knees, their voices rolling like thunder across the ground. The air shifted once again, this time twisting the smoke from the surrounding fire pits into outlines and shapes in the air above the circle.

"Look, Thei." Valana spoke in hushed tones to her sister. "They're summoning something."

Theona nodded, then turned her eyes back toward the center of the circle. She had only a glimpse of figures kneeling there before the warriors leaped to their feet. The tempo suddenly increased, and the movements of the warriors and their shoulder dragons became more urgent and pronounced.

Again the clubs swung skyward, and this time the image was clearly formed overhead in the smoke and air above the circle. It was a dragon, but not one of the small creatures that the natives had taken into their lives. It was the form of a massive dragon—far larger even than the form of Ulruk, which had attacked and devastated Khordsholm just the day before. It writhed in the air, spinning slowly with the turning of the wheel of warriors beneath it. With each beat of the warriors' chant, the figure wrapped the smoke around itself—a spirit incarnation of a dragon that began to move, its wings flexing and its great jaws opening wide.

The warriors shouted.

The smoke-dragon overhead trumpeted in reply, its sound shaking the palm fronds of the trees all around the clearing. It was a sound so terrifying that Theona could suddenly not move or think, her eyes fixated on the terrible image drifting in the air.

The warriors' clubs swung skyward one last time.

The neck of the smoke-dragon curved downward, plunging toward the center of the circle with another deafening trumpet.

A lone, terrible scream rent the air.

The dragon vanished in an instant, and the warriors all leaped to their feet, cheering even as they stood aside, opening a path among their ranks. Two of the warriors were dragging the limp and motionless body of a man out from the center of their number. Even in the light of the fire pits, Theona recognized the dark green of the hooded cloak and the long iron-gray hair falling down to obscure the lolling head of Dorian Arvad.

"Gaius!" Theona cried out. "What have you done to him?"

"Less than he deserved," the narrow-faced bard snapped.

"You've killed him," Theona said, her words coming out without thought. "What worse could you have done?"

"He's bluffing, Thei," Valana said with a sudden calm. "He's just trying to scare you. He wouldn't dare harm us—he knows how valuable we are."

"Typical of a Conlan," Gaius sneered, shaking his head. "You've no idea what real value is. No one invited you to come here—just try not to make things worse than you already have."

"Make things worse?" Theona spat the words. "How can we possibly make things worse?"

"I cannot imagine," Gaius returned, "but I suspect if there *is* a way, you'll find it!"

Gaius motioned to the guards. Theona and her sister were urged forward, walking across the smooth plaza stones toward the opening to the center of the warrior circle. Theona walked two paces behind her sister, her customary place whenever her family was out in the public streets of Calsandria. She realized in that moment that she had always been walking those two steps behind her sister and was now doing so to her death—an act of comfortable familiarity in the face of dark oblivion.

A huge man with a broad, strong chest stood in the center of the circle of warriors. His head was completely hidden by an ornate masked headpiece shaped to look like a fierce dragon. Next to him stood two other figures, draped in colorful robes that fell from their shoulders to the ground, completely obscuring their bodies. These were decorated with intricate patterns that looked almost like a written language, though certainly different from anything Theona had seen. These other figures, too, had headpieces that completely hid their faces, though they resembled the carved faces on the clubs.

Theona looked down. The stones at their feet were stained with blood.

"Gaius," Theona said, her voice quivering, "don't do this. It doesn't have to be this way."

"Oh, stop it, Theona," Valana said with a dismissive sniff. "He's bluffing; can't you tell? What is it you want, Gaius? You've kidnapped the prince to this bizarre city with its quaint little customs that's obviously outside the knowledge of the Council of Thirty-six. Well, bravo, Gaius, you've done it; you've pulled off your plan. Now, I'm here to tell you that no one appreciates that kind of skill like a Conlan. If you've got something brewing, fine, I'm sure that we can come to terms. But we've come to get back the prince you've stolen, and nothing is going to stand in the way of our wedding—so what's your price?"

"Fair damsel rescues prince, eh?" Gaius said sadly. "That's not how the story ever ends, Lady Conlan." He turned and began walking out of the circle between the warriors.

"No!" Theona said.

"I can help you, Gaius," Valana called out after him as he walked. "Whatever your game is, you're better off *with* us than without us!"

The warriors closed ranks and began chanting once

again. Their smooth motions and deep voices resonated through Theona. She shook with fear.

Dreams, Theona thought, fighting back tears. *I followed my dreams—hoped that they might make me something more than I am. This is where they have led me; I've killed us both.*

The warriors' movements were becoming more pronounced, their chanting cries stronger.

This is where my visions end: blackness and regret.

The eyes of every small dragon on the shoulders of each of over a hundred warriors were fixed on Theona.

Theona looked up; the smoke-dragon was forming over her head. She sucked in a shuddering breath—and the dragon fell toward her, screaming out of the sky as its maw engulfed her.

I stand in the middle of a flat circle of stone. I see stars reflected in its wide, polished surface, although I do not see any in the sky overhead. Beyond the circle of stones there is nothing—not even blackness—and while this should frighten me, I am comforted and unafraid. I look more closely and see that the floor is inscribed with three rings of inlaid gold, each circle intersecting the other two. I stand exactly in the midst, where all three circles come together forming a triangle with curving sides. In the center of each of the inscribed circles rests a pedestal, and atop each pedestal rests a sphere of light. Each projects a different aspect: one is white like ice and snow, the second a ball of flame, and the third is the green of a lush meadow. Each is beautiful and terrible in its own way, and I am filled with a desire to see them more closely.

I step from the dark center toward the green sphere, and the darkness is dispersed in an instant. There is a mountain in the distance, and my circle of stone rests on a grassy plain. Tall forests stand some short distance away, while behind me stand black gates of a terrible city. Horrifying figures carved from shining onyx stand to either side of the gates.

The gates open, and I fear what might invade the forest, but from this opening emerge the most beautiful of creatures: delicate beings with wings like butterflies, whose exquisiteness is beyond my words to describe. There is one among them that steps away from his winged companions — a male of their kind with hair falling across his face whose demeanor is melancholy. He walks across the inlaid rings, moving near the red sphere, and I step toward him.

The world transforms around me. The mountain is still there, but the lush beauty of its peak has been replaced by harsh crags and flows of molten stone. The plain around me is stripped of grass, exposing raw earth and rock. The city is still there, but its aspect, too, has changed, for its walls have become as rusted metal. The mountain is the same mountain and the plain is the same plain, and yet they are entirely different.

Different, too, are the creatures, for the beautiful ones have been replaced by short, ugly creatures with long ears and big feet. Their skin is green, and they scamper about among metal objects all around me, picking them up and pushing them together in strange ways. There is one among them that catches my eye: a female, judging by her anatomy, who wears a strange flat hat made of rough cloth.

I realize not all of the beautiful creatures are gone, however. The male with the fallen hair is being held in the grip of the female creature. He pulls away from her, running toward the blue sphere on our little world, leaving the green female weeping as she, too, moves to follow the winged male and I after her.

The world changes again, and the fiery mountain is suddenly healed, transformed into a snowcapped peak. The plain around it becomes the shores of the ocean. The metal city behind me is transformed into enormous trees with homes crafted into their branches, the four stepped pyramids of the city beyond rising above them all.

"Do you see it?"

I turn toward the voice, and a tear falls from my eye.

"Hrea?"

The goddess smiles on me as she gestures around with her elegant hand. "Do you see it, Theona?"

I nod, stepping closer to her. "I see it—but I do not understand."

Hrea smiles upon me once more. I feel the aching in my soul taken from me, a pain so long endured that I feel its loss. "You will understand, my child. It is your blessing and your curse to understand."

"What do I do?"

"You watch," Hrea said, folding me in her arms.

The light consumes me and carries me away.

And I _see_!

I see the paths of the future spooling out before me—all the possible tomorrows that spring from the now. I see all the results from all choices—great and small—from the nearest consequence to the uttermost doom of the worlds. I weep because the knowledge overwhelms me, my mind struggling to grasp its grandeur and horror all at once.

I turn to look behind me, but there, too, are paths too numerous to count, all converging on the place where I stand. It is the choices of the past that I see, which still converge on me in the now. Those are paths that I cannot alter, for they have all been walked before. I turn once more to face the paths before me.

"It is your blessing," Hrea whispers.

"It is my curse," I sob. "I see the end of the world."

"You must see beyond the end," Hrea replies softly. "The end is only the beginning. All the greatness of mortality takes place in the moment of decision, in the course selected by a single step. Wise is he who understands the ends of his choices."

"But I see no path without pain," I say with resignation.

"No true path is without pain," Hrea replies.

"Who am I, then?" I ask.

"You are the guide." Hrea smiles at me, her face growing brighter until I close my eyes against her light.

DIARY OF THEONA CONLAN, VOLUME 3, PAGES 52—57

Theona opened her eyes with a start.

The warriors were all prone on the ground, bowed with their heads down before her. The women and children of the crowd beyond the circle were also bowed down, their faces averted. The three masked and robed figures knelt as well.

Only one other person remained standing: Gaius gaped at Theona in astonishment.

Valana stood up quickly from where she had fallen to

the ground beneath the plunge of the smoke-dragon. She surveyed the prostrate horde at her feet and turned to the still-astonished Gaius.

The bard dropped slowly to his knees, his left hand pushing down on the hilt of his native club as he bowed toward Theona.

"That's better," Valana said, holding her head high. "Now, I demand to know where you're keeping Treijan!"

"Stupid woman," came the voice from one of the cloaked figures kneeling behind Valana, busily removing its masking headdress. "I'm not being *kept* anywhere!"

Both Valana and Theona turned in astonishment.

It was Treijan.

Escape

You just stop right there, Your Highness!" Valana shouted as she stalked through the thick foliage in pursuit of the retreating Treijan.

"Go back home, Mistress Valana," Treijan called over his shoulder. "There is nothing here for you."

The prince had stormed off into the jungle, shedding his colorful costume as he went and precipitating a general exodus in his wake. Valana had followed at once, heedless of the direction, calling after her almost-betrothed. Their actions, in turn, shook both Gaius and Theona from their astonishment, both of them trailing after Valana and struggling to keep up.

"Where do they think they're going?" Gaius asked as he followed Theona past the warriors and beyond the city walls into the undergrowth. A light flared bright above his left hand in an effort to illuminate the darkness around them.

"I don't even know where we are," Theona countered. "How could I possibly know where they're going?"

"Point well taken," Gaius said, his face breaking into a quick smile. He called out to the prince, whom he could hear crashing through the jungle beyond his sight. "Treijan, wait! This isn't going to solve anything!"

"I will *not* be treated this way!" Valana shouted. "I'm a daughter of House Conlan, and you *will* extend your courtesy to me!"

The prince merely turned and sneered before he pushed through a wall of foliage, and Valana slipped through almost immediately afterward.

"Do you think we should leave the happy couple alone?" Gaius said with a questioning look at Theona.

"Are you hoping to conduct a funeral?"

"The prince would never hurt anyone."

"I wouldn't be so sure about my sister," Theona said as she pressed through the ferns.

She emerged at the edge of a long pool forming the base of a beautiful cascade. Treijan was striding through the shallow waters to the opposite shore.

"After all I've been through—dirt, wretched food, and strange cities—and that *dragon* back in Khordsholm—I went through it all and for what?"

Treijan turned and stood his ground in the shallow waters just short of the opposite bank. The quiet hush of the falling water did little to soften the words being hurled across its gently rippling surface. "Nobody asked you to rescue me, Princess of House Conlan! I was perfectly happy right here—might even have had a chance at some sort of happiness—but then *you* showed up!"

"Well, *someone* had to show up!" Valana spat the words back at him. "You were promised to me! It was all arranged between the families, and I, at least, was willing to do my duty to my house—duties that I would think a prince of Rennes-Arvad would have some concept of honoring!"

"Honoring my house?" Treijan replied through a mocking laugh. "I've spent my life trying to 'honor my house.' I've wandered the lands of Hramra from the Provinces to Vestadia, from the Straits of Cyran to Cape Bounty, trying to find honor for my house—and I haven't found it anywhere except right *here. This* is where I honor my house best—by leaving behind the preening nonsense of court, the glittering daggers, and the venomous smiles. I never wanted to be a 'prince of Arvad'; never cared for the throne of the mystics. All I wanted was to make something meaningful out of my life that didn't involve being either a hunter or a target. Believe me, Mistress Valana, when I tell you that marrying you would be the worst thing I could do for the great and growing Mystic Empire."

"And what about me?" Valana was shaking with rage. "What about my family and our position? What about our wedding? Maybe you think you can run out on the kingdom, but if you think you're leaving your family's promises to *me* behind, you've got another thought coming!"

Valana was livid, whether with embarrassment or rage or both, Theona could not tell. "Please, Valana," she said, taking a cautious step forward. "Maybe we should all just calm down a little."

"Calm down!" Valana's voice broke in her anger. "This—this pitiful *excuse* for a descendant of Galen wasn't kidnapped at all, were you, Treijan the Great? Hope of Calsandria and Light of the Mystic Realms, indeed! You snuck off in the night and left all your troubles behind, didn't you? Well, you're not leaving *me*!"

"This may be our only chance to leave!" Arryk shook his head in frustration. "Aren't you ready yet?"

Hueburlyn looked up wearily at the petulant faery. Arryk was increasingly getting on his nerves. Patience was a practiced craft which centaurs on the whole had never mastered well. Hueburlyn was better at it than most of his kind, but there were limits to everything.

"Hueburlyn only as ready as Ar-ryk make me," he replied. "*Kntrr* not want to stay in this smelly cage with Arryk either. Ar-ryk judge—is Hueburlyn ready?"

"That's all I get from you!" Arryk exploded. "You're all talk and never say anything. Everything out of your mouth leads to some circle of nonsense."

"Hueburlyn knows exactly where he goes," the centaur huffed, closing his eyes as he tried once more to concentrate. "Faery Ar-ryk is lost one."

"Just shut up and concentrate," the faery snarled.

"Hueburlyn not one who still talking."

"Just—shut up!"

Hueburlyn shrugged and closed his eyes. The faery was such a fool—he was wandering in a forest of his own pity and probably would not leave even if someone showed him the way.

Hueburlyn's mastery of the Sharaj, as the faery called it, was far from complete. He thought he had the basics down; he could focus the energies of the magical power and keep them under control if he did not try to maintain it for too long. Raw power did not seem to be his problem so much as molding it in a useful direction and, more important, being able to call on it at the time and place it was needed. Arryk had helped him with both aspects of the craft, but there had been little opportunity for applying the lessons, and the Sharaj was something that, above all things, was mastered only with experience.

So Hueburlyn felt himself as ready as he could be under the circumstances—but the circumstances were far from ideal, and the outcome was still largely in doubt.

"Ar-ryk certain that tonight is the time?"

"Yes," the faery said quickly. "The little monster-woman told me that her demonstration was set for tonight."

Hueburlyn nodded, then clicked his forehoof nervously against the stone floor. "Ar-ryk should be kinder to little green creature."

"What?"

"Little green woman—she like you—she nice to you. Ar-ryk should be nice back."

"By the Path of the Unenlightened," the faery said, rubbing his hand wearily over his face. "Why can't you just stop talking for five minutes?"

"All Hueburlyn saying is—"

"She *captured* us!" Arryk spoke with the exaggerated emphasis he would use on a child. "She *stole* us. She *imprisoned* us—she put us in this cage and won't let us *out!* She has been a lot of things to us, but *nice* is not one of them!"

"But little green creature not angry with us," Hueburlyn replied. "Hueburlyn see how she look at you. She care for Ar-ryk. Maybe Ar-ryk could care a little back."

"By Gobrach." Arryk sighed. "Don't you Famadorians *ever* run out of words?"

"No Famadorian," Hueburlyn grumbled. *"Kntrr!"*

"Fine! Whatever you say, but keep your voice down. It annoys these demons, and surprise is our best—wait!"

Arryk unfolded his wings and stretched them as he stood up.* "They're coming."

The great door opposite the cage opened loudly and revealed once more the strange mechanisms in the other room. Through the opening first came the little creature that had brought them here. She was wearing a long stained coat that might once have been white and a strange pointed hat.

"Look," whispered Arryk.

The little creature was carrying the jeweled book tightly against her chest.

Behind her came a procession of similar odd creatures, though different in size. The one immediately behind the female appeared older than the others, wore a clanking vest of armor, and had only one eye. Behind him came a taller creature with sharp nose and chin who wore a shiny black coat. Behind this creature were several others wearing some sort of uniform similar to that worn by the one-eyed creature. They were all slapping their feet against the floor as they looked around—Hueburlyn couldn't tell whether or not this was a gesture of approval.

The one-eyed creature waddled over to the cage, peering in. His face split into a terrible grin, showing sharp, jagged teeth. Even to Hueburlyn the creature smelled terrible.

"Gobakadi meedu sewah!" the creature proclaimed loudly, and most of the other creatures in the room guffawed.

Only the female seemed not to be amused by the comment. She stomped her foot impatiently, shouting

---

*An automatic reaction so far as the Fae are concerned. With their wings extended, the Fae can sense movement in the air more keenly. It is a defense mechanism.

out orders to her assembled colleagues and pointing to where they should stand facing the rings at the side of the room.

"Are you ready?" Arryk whispered.

"I am as ready as—"

"Fine!" Arryk said quickly, gesturing back with his hand. The little female was raising the book in both her hands before her. "Now!"

Hueburlyn withdrew inside himself, calling on the powers of the Sharaj. He touched the vision in his mind, saw the mountaintops as he had before and the ice and snow. There was his companion in the vision, a strange man without wings or hooves who seemed surprised to be there at the top of the world. He began gathering snow and ice, then packing it together and throwing it at the centaur. Hueburlyn concentrated on it all—the cold of the frozen water, the chill of the air—and pressed it down until all cold of the mountain was called together, gathering in his mind. Then he was pushing it outward in a focused stream . . .

Metal began to scream.

Hueburlyn opened his eyes.

The bars of the cage were frosting over, the chill from his powers plunging their temperature so quickly that the metal shrieked. Water in the air around the bars condensed in a flash into a growing layer of ice, but the centaur did not wait for it; he slammed his fists upward in a single powerful thrust.

The metal of the cage shattered, exploding upward and out into the room.

The pieces were still falling as Arryk flew through the opening and, free of the strange cage, reached out for the power of the Sharaj to flow into him once more.

I am Arryk once more—the Arryk I was born to be as
I stride into the city of the Sharaj—overjoyed that the
power flows into me once more. The snows in the street
gather around me, swirling as I pass into the courtyard.

I see my old friend—the wingless man—standing in
the falling snow. I sign my greeting to him, desperate to
connect with him, for the battle in the real world is upon
me and I must strike quickly. I reach toward him . . .

FAERY TALES
BRONZE CANTICLES, TOME XIV, FOLIO 1, LEAF 53

"Please, Valana, you've got to stop!" Theona's voice was
unusually anxious as she pulled at her sister's arm. The
sands on the shore of the pool were black under the canopy of bright stars overhead. The waterfall, the people,
the sky—everything was becoming alarmingly familiar to
Theona. She had seen what was coming in her dream and
desperately wanted to stop it.

Valana yanked her arm free. "Let me alone! I'm not
going to let some selfish whelp ruin us!"

"No! You don't understand what will happen!" Theona
persisted. "I've *seen* it! Please; we've all got to get back
to the village right now."

"You've *seen* it?" Valana snapped. "Theona, this is
mystic business—you wouldn't understand—"

"I understand that you have to leave here right now,"
Theona said more urgently. "Please listen to me!"

"No!" Valana said, pushing her sister away. "You might
be afraid of this 'prince of Arvad,' but I'm not. I love you
and you've always been a good sister to me, but you're
common. You don't understand the Deep Magic and cannot possibly deal with the subtleties of this situation!"

"Which is exactly why I left!" Treijan shouted at Valana, standing in the shallow waters at the edge of the pool. "All this false glory and self-importance of position and rank and bloodlines—I've had enough of it! Do you know that one of my titles is Marshal of the Grand Mystic Armies—which is nothing more than presiding over parades? There hasn't been a serious war involving the mystics in decades—not that our enemies wouldn't like to change that. Right now the Pir Drakonis are stirring around in the Eastern Marches, trying their best to drum up a war, while our great Council keeps our soldiers marching up and down the streets of Calsandria because they fear each other more than the Pir. The army exists to keep *them* in power, so they make such a big deal about how grand it is to be safely under the protection of the Marshal of the Grand Mystic Armies! The courtiers are scrabbling over scraps and pretending it is all terribly meaningful when the only enemy they have is themselves!"

"Then change it!" Valana shouted back. "You're the heir to the Arvad Dynasty—if you don't like it, change it! If you're so concerned about the empire, then do something about it!"

"I have my own reasons why—"

Treijan's eyes suddenly rolled back into his head. His body stiffened as his hands splayed outward.

"Oh, no!" Gaius rushed forward, the waters of the pool spraying about his footfalls. "Not now!"

Treijan toppled into the water, shaking violently.

The head of the wingless man jerks back, his chest bursting open. I, Arryk, see the head of a horned, snow-colored serpent emerge, shedding the wingless man's body as though it were a second skin while it writhes and grows larger and larger from the snowy ground.

The serpent's head plunges down toward me, with its maw gaping open to devour me, but I revel in its appearance. Powerful as my wingless man is, this incarnation of his spirit brings to me power beyond all my knowledge, strength beyond all my abilities.

I leap into the air at the last moment, landing roughly between the horns of the terrible, writhing beast. With this incarnation of the Sharaj I am invincible. There is no power I have known—not even that of Dwynwyn herself, I am convinced—that can match its strength.

If only I can control it . . .

FAERY TALES

BRONZE CANTICLES, TOME XIV, FOLIO 1, LEAVES 53–54

The Storm

Quickly!" Gaius called to the women as he gripped the convulsing Treijan. "Give me a hand! If he stays in the water..."

Theona pushed past her sister, splashing through the shallow waters of the pool to where Gaius struggled with the prince. "What do I do?"

"Just help me get him down on the sand," Gaius said, his voice strained with effort. The prince shook violently, his head bobbing uncontrollably as his arms thrashed outward, slapping Gaius hard across the face. "Hurry!"

Theona put her head down, wrapping her arms around the prince's writhing waist. He seemed as though he had transformed into a vicious animal, suddenly stronger and more powerful than she expected. "Valana! Come on! We need your help!"

The elder Conlan sister stood on the opposite bank, her body frozen and her face a mask of horror.

"Push!" Gaius cried out. "I can't hold him much longer!"

Theona crouched down, digging her feet into the soft mud of the lake bed. With a cry she pushed with all her might just as Gaius lifted with his whole body. The prince fell backward with Gaius, landing painfully on the black sands lining the shore of the pool.

Gaius rolled away, holding his ribs and groaning. The convulsions of the prince seemed to be worsening as Theona scrambled to get disentangled from the flailing, senseless man. She backed away on her hands and feet until the trunk of the palm tree stopped her.

Gaius drew himself up on his knees and removed his cape. He rolled it up, then pushed the shuddering prince over on his side, slipping his robe under Treijan's head before standing and stepping back.

"What do we do now?" Theona asked, her eyes wide.

"Nothing!" Gaius replied, bending over and grimacing against the pain in his side.

"Nothing?"

"We've made him as comfortable as we can, and we've put him in a safe place," Gaius said, straightening with effort. "All we can do now is to wait until it's over."

"It's the madness!"

Gaius and Theona both looked at Valana, who had joined them at last and was gazing down at the prince with eyes wide.

"He's got the madness of the Ancient Kings!" Valana said with revulsion. "The magic has driven him insane!"

"He's not mad!" Gaius snapped angrily. "Why do you think the prince spends so much time away from court? His family has hidden his condition through the years out of fear that people would react *exactly* the way you do now. Why they thought they should marry him off to a fool like you, I certainly cannot fathom. I don't know how they proposed to keep this from you, and neither does the prince. So perhaps now do you understand why he ran like a drake from your betrothal? Why he would have contented himself forever to stay away from his home and family? So that you would not see him like this!"

Gaius took a step toward the water's edge, gesturing at the quaking figure on the ground next to him. "So now that you understand, Mistress Valana of House Conlan, are you still so keen to take this man for your husband?"

Valana's eyes fixed on the contorted figure gyrating on the ground. She took a step back, her head shaking slowly from side to side. Then two more steps before she turned and fled back into the jungle growth.

Theona stood up. She thought she should probably follow after her sister. Everything they had assumed about their journey had proved to be false. But the prince lay at her feet in the throes of a terrible seizure.

"Aren't you leaving?" Gaius said to her, his eyes examining her critically.

"No." Theona shook her head, looking down at the writhing prince.

Pandemonium broke out as Arryk and Hueburlyn rushed from their shattered cage out into the room. The little green creatures screamed and ran for whatever cover was at hand. The ancient little monster with one eye managed to dive, snarling, behind a thick metal wheel leaning up against the wall, followed almost at once by the tall creature in the long black coat. The other creatures scattered as well, some falling behind crates on either side of the huge doorway, while others retreated quickly into the next room, taking cover behind various objects of art that resembled Arryk.

Out of all the assembly, only the little female creature stood her ground, bejeweled book still gripped in her hands and an expression of astonishment on her face.

Hueburlyn did not hesitate—knew, in fact, that hesitation itself could kill them. Even as the little creatures in the room were taking cover behind every piece of statuary and art at hand, he could see that they were drawing weapons from scabbards at their sides. The one-eyed creature was squawking orders at the others, and it would be only a matter of moments before they turned and attacked.

The great centaur charged the crates on the left side of the room. Two of the little creatures were already standing up, their short-bladed weapons glowing with an orange power that Hueburlyn could only guess was from the monsters' version of the Sharaj. The centaur reached over the crate with both hands, grabbing the little demon-creatures by the back of their armor and lifting them off their feet with his powerful arms, flinging them over his shoulders.

The creatures squawked as they tumbled through the air. Hueburlyn did not watch but listened for their collision on the far side of the room, where they fell with a satisfying sound of smashing metal armor against stone.

Hueburlyn turned, facing the one-eyed monster and his tall companion, who had taken refuge behind a large rusting gear. The one-eyed creature was gesturing at him as the centaur started his charge, but his hooves found little purchase on the stone floor, and Hueburlyn felt with dreadful certainty that he would not reach his target in time.

A bolt of lightning flared in front of the centaur, causing him to rear up into a panicked stop. Hueburlyn tensed, assuming the one-eyed wizard was delivering his death-blow. But the brightness faded from his eyes, though the thunderclap still rang in his ears. He could still see the gear, but it had shattered, and both the one-eyed creature and his black-coated companion were fleeing back into the adjoining room.

"Praise Aelar!" shouted Arryk. The faery hovered above the floor, his wings fluttering even as his hands were held out in front of him, his fingers extended. Bolts of lightning were flying from his fingertips, and with his eyes glowing his face looked maniacal.

The little female fell to the floor at the sound of the faery's voice, dropping the book in her agony.

The lightning tore round the circular room, slamming into the stone and rebounding. Bolt after bolt laced the walls—several of them coming dangerously close to the centaur—before they hurled into the adjoining room. Hueburlyn could see the little green figures moving about, trying to reenter the room and return the attack.

The centaur could feel the air in the room begin to move, a wind churning around him, turning and spinning, pulling the dust from the floor up into its maelstrom. In moments the breeze had transformed into a gale, obscuring the walls in its fury.

"Ar-ryk!" Hueburlyn yelled over the howling of the wind. "Stop! Time to leave!"

"No!" Arryk replied, his face contorted into a terrible rapture. "Can't you see it? It's glorious!"

Hueburlyn gritted his teeth, then clopped quickly over to where the faery hovered. The hurricane roared around them, and the centaur thought he could see several of the little creatures mixed in with the debris that was flying through the air. He reached up, gathered the faery by the front of his cloak, and shook him.

Arryk's concentration broke. The glow faded from his eyes, and the lightning died on his fingertips. Even so, the storm continued unabated, having gained a momentum of its own.

The centaur drew the faery's face uncomfortably close to his own and spoke each word with deadly emphasis. "Ar-ryk knows use of little creature's book—take Hueburlyn home *now*!"

The faery looked at Hueburlyn as though he had only just awakened. "Yes—of course! Let me go, you idiot Famadorian!"

Hueburlyn released Arryk unexpectedly, dropping the faery to the floor. "No Famadorian; Hueburlyn *kntrr*!"

Arryk snarled his reply and then stepped over to where the female creature still lay prone on the ground. He reached down, snatching up the jeweled book. The storm was howling now in its ferocity. Thunder from the lightning now made it impossible to be heard. Arryk turned toward the rings in the floor and held the book in front of him. Hueburlyn knew that Arryk was not sure of the significance of the book in the operation of the device, but the faery had gotten enough from the little monster to understand the principles of the Sharaj behind it. Hueburlyn moved quickly to stand close to the faery; he feared being left behind regardless of the promises made between them.

It was then that Hueburlyn looked down and saw the little green female creature move. With unexpected swiftness the creature scampered across to the rings, wrapping her arms tightly around the faery's leg.

"Get off me!" Arryk shouted, kicking with his leg, trying to loosen the creature. "Go away!"

"Tak!" the little creature spoke. *"Nakamku re?"*

A look of utter surprise flashed across the face of the faery. "Arryk," he stammered. "My name—is Arryk."

Hueburlyn could feel something changing in the air around them—a stillness that belied the storm still raging in the room. "Something changes, Ar-ryk! We leaving now!"

But Arryk, still clutching the strange book to his chest, was staring wide-eyed at the green creature clinging to his leg and yammering at him in its strange, twisted tongue. Incredibly, he was answering back, even as he was trying to shake the creature off. "No—he's a centaur and I'm a faery! Now, let go!"

"Berkamasku tokong Fa-ree Urk?" The little creature was weeping now. She reached up for the book, her hand closing around one of the jewels in its surface.

"No!" Arryk shouted, and with a final kick, the little green female was released from Arryk's leg and tumbled across the stones in the tempest-filled room.

In that moment the room vanished from Hueburlyn's sight—and he and the faery began falling through the Sharaj.

I hold the book to my chest, brought to me in the dream by the centaur. The serpent bucks beneath me, and I have difficulty maintaining my grip on both its horns and the book at the same time. The centaur is here, too, now hanging on to the back of the serpent, struggling to ride its wild undulations. I see words falling from the book, flying out of its pages and cascading to the ground. Its ink covers the stones, turning the courtyard into black abyss wherever the ink gathers. Soon the words gather together, forming a single bottomless shaft in the ground beneath us; the serpent rolls over on its back and dives into the blackness of the hole in the courtyard.

The room in which we were held captive vanishes from my other sight, but the words of the little monster will not leave my head. For weeks I have been trying to communicate with the creature, but only after I emerged from the cage could I understand her words. She wanted my name. She wanted to come with me.

Now I hold to my chest the book that the centaur gave me. Light bursts around us as the serpent drags us both across the Sharaj.

FAERY TALES
BRONZE CANTICLES, TOME XIV, FOLIO 1, LEAF 55

"Will he wake up?" Theona asked, kneeling next to the now still prince.

"Yes, but sometimes it takes a while," Gaius said, a weariness in his voice. "When he does, he'll be confused and upset. It's important that we are calm and reassuring. He may want to wander around a bit. Let him; restraining him will only make things worse and prolong his recovery."

Theona nodded, then sat silently in thought for a moment. "How long have you known?"

"Me?"

"I don't see anyone else around who might answer."

Gaius laughed. "Well, in that case, I've known him most of my life. I was Treijan's companion as he was growing up. Keeping this secret has been my life's work from when I was very young."

"So you've given your life to him." Theona spoke softly.

"More like a single life between us," Gaius said. "I live his life in some ways more than he lives it himself. I accompany him everywhere; I am his bard companion when we walk the world—a place, by the way, where his episodes are less frequent. When we do find occasion to visit the heart of the Mystic Empire, I carefully screen anyone who might see him, trying to gauge if they will be the type to bring on this condition—although there are no guarantees. There have been a few incidents along the way, but the House of Rennes-Arvad is both powerful and rich. Not a few Theleic masters have found years of employment in helping banish a memory or two from those who have been unfortunate enough to have witnessed one of His Majesty's episodes. I suspect that your sister—should she return to Calsandria—will quite soon be made to forget everything that has happened here."

"Is that *my* fate?" Theona said, her gaze steady on Gaius's eyes.

The bard considered her for a moment. "I hope not, Theona. You have seen the crippled prince for what he is—and yet you have not left."

"We are all crippled, Gaius," Theona replied quietly.

"Yes"—he smiled—"I believe we are."

Theona turned to look at the waterfall at the end of the pool. "It is beautiful here—I should hate to forget it. Where are we?"

"The island of Rhai-Tuah."

"Where?"

"A long way from home." Gaius laughed. He reached down to his waist and removed the ornate club from its loop, running his hand down its polished surface. "A long way, indeed."

Theona's eyes were fixed apprehensively on the weapon. "How did you find this place?"

Gaius shrugged, lowering the tip of the club to the black sands of the shore and resting his chin on its hilt. "An accident. Treijan and I were taking a Songstone southward by sea from Khordsholm to make a new gate many years ago. Well, Treijan and I got it into our heads that we could plant the end of the gate somewhere down in Uthara so that we wouldn't have to travel by sea to get to the southern continent. It was not the kind of trip that was sanctioned—the guild feels Uthara is too far to expand into just yet—so we planted the first gate in the ruins next to Khordsholm. The gods had other ideas; the ship was caught up in a great storm—blew us far west beyond Vestadia and out into the reaches of the Vestadic Ocean. That's how we first came here; that's how we came to know these people. We never told anyone about the gate or this island—our own special place—because we knew that the day might come when we needed to—"

There was a dull thud as Gaius suddenly pitched forward over the club, his face falling against the sand, a crimson stain growing from the back of his head. A large stone lay next to him.

Theona cried out in shock, crawling toward Gaius when she heard the voice from the figure emerging from the dark woods.

"Get out of my way, Theona Conlan," said Dorian Arvad. "This doesn't concern you."

He was holding another large, sharp stone over his head.

Paths of Least Resistance

Dorian, stop." Theona froze where she knelt. Dorian's expression was too detached. She was finding it difficult to keep the calm in her voice. "You don't have to do this."

"Oh, yes, I'm afraid I do," he replied with a small smile on his face, his eyes fixed on Treijan lying just behind Theona. "I've waited a long time for this moment . . . when the great Treijan would fall."

Theona could see that Dorian's arms were quivering under the weight of the rock, his hands nearly as white as the bracers the natives had fixed to both his wrists.

The bracers!

Theona looked around in desperation, her eye fixing at last on the islander's club that lay next to the prostrate Gaius. She snatched the grip up with both hands and spun, swinging the club with all her force against the flat of Dorian's stomach.

Dorian bent over, the blow pushing him backward as

the stone in his hands fell to the ground barely a hand-breadth from Treijan's unconscious face. Theona could hear the air rush out of the man's lungs, but he managed to stand his ground.

Theona did not hesitate, but with a cry of rage or fear—not even she knew which—she picked up her right foot and, pressing back with her left, planted her heel forcefully into the stunned man's chest.

Dorian reeled back, breathless and in pain. Instinctively, he crouched down, his feet digging into the sand, but his lungs were working painfully, trying to draw back the breath that had so completely left him. "You mystic witch! How dare you stand between me and my fate!"

Theona drew the club up once again with both hands, cocking it behind her head as she stood over the two fallen bards. "I'm no witch, Dorian! I've no magic in me and never have—and your own magic has left you, hasn't it?"

Dorian looked down suddenly with anger at the bone bracers clasped maddeningly to his wrists.

"That's right," Theona said with a sneer. "You're in my world now."

At her feet Gaius groaned, rolling onto his side.

Dorian snarled, taking a step toward her.

Theona drew the club slightly higher, preparing to strike. "Do you have any idea what a club like this will do to an unprotected skull, Dorian? With all your supposed powers in the Deep Magic, you may have forgotten what kind of damage hardwood can do, but I assure you it can be quite effective."

Dorian bent over, pressing the palms of his hands on both knees as he sucked in another breath. "Theona, this is none of your affair. Just leave now quietly, and you won't get hurt."

Theona shook her head slowly from side to side.

"Stupid woman," Dorian said through a grimace as he straightened. "Your sister . . . would have known the value of such a deal."

"I understand the value better than most," Theona replied. "But last I recall, you were being hauled away by two of the local guards. I don't know how you gave them the slip, but I would guess that they are looking for you right now. You take another step toward me, and I swear you'll find out just how capable I am of mixing your head with the sand beneath you. You stay where you are, and those guards will find you. Now, I think my deal improves greatly."

"Theona wrong as er is," came a gruff voice behind her. "Yer deal just changed for the worse."

Arryk gripped the book closely against his chest, his mind reeling. Their passage here, so far as he could remember it, had been instantaneous. He had felt nothing and experienced nothing beyond the thunderclap of changing location.

This, however, was vastly different, and he wondered if he had gotten the Sharaj sequence of the rift-gate right from the little green monster, after all.

Both he and the centaur were floating in still air—by the smell of it the same air as in the filthy dungeon where they had been imprisoned—but just beyond their reach rushed a blurred topography of places shifting with dizzying speed back and forth between different states of existence. A mountain peak rushed past them—first snowcapped, then barren, then covered in lush growth all in a matter of seconds. They fell toward a glacier lake that was there—then wasn't—then reappeared in ice as they sped across its surface. Forests appeared around them of towering pines nearly a hundred feet in height—only to be replaced moments later by gnarled hardwood that then vanished into a grassy plain. It felt to Arryk as though they were falling down a shaft, only the shaft went across the ground rather than into it. Huge metallic giants strode across the plain while Arryk and Hueburlyn flew unwillingly toward them, riding as though at the crest of a wave before a vast army of ten thousand huge, brutish beastmen, armed only with rocks and massive clubs, charging toward the metal giants. The mammoth battle suddenly vanished as the corridor down which they sped twisted toward a distant—and getting rapidly closer—seashore.

"Where Arryk taking us?" The timbre of Hueburlyn's voice suggested he was yelling at the top of his lungs, although the sound itself was so slight that Arryk could barely hear him. "This not right!"

Maybe bringing the book was a mistake, Arryk thought. He had only done so at the last moment because it seemed like the best way to keep the little green woman from following them. It could have been the book—or it might have been the Sharaj itself. He had been nervous and excited when he found the connection after the centaur blew the walls off the cage—he had forced the Sharaj, and the response had surprised even him. He had seen the guardian statues of Sharajentis through the rings, so the gate should have just taken them there. This, however, was different and unexpected—both very bad signs when it came to the Sharaj.

A city suddenly erupted into existence before them on the shoreline. Then an entirely different city replaced it, only to have the original put back again. Both Arryk and Hueburlyn cried out involuntarily as they flew *through* the outer curtain wall of the city, twisting back and forth through several streets and then passing through a rapid succession of houses—all without so much as a whisper of air against their skin—before being confronted by a flying creature the likes of which Arryk had seen only in the Sharaj: a gigantic monster with leather wings, a scaled body, a barbed tail, and a grinning, malevolent mouth filled with razor-sharp teeth. It soared out of their path at the last moment, and suddenly, the faery and his centaur companion were rushing down their magical shaft out above the waves of the sea.

"I don't know where we're going," Arryk shouted back in a voice that seemed to stop just beyond his face. He could still feel the Sharaj flowing through him, and part of his mind could see his wingless companion drawing closer to him with every passing moment. "But I hope we get there soon!"

Theona turned slightly, still holding the club high behind her head. She could just barely see the dwarf standing behind her where he had emerged from the dense undergrowth. "Stay away from me, Dregas!"

"Easy deal with this dwarf er is." Dregas smiled back through a toothy grin. "Put yon club down like good lass and walk away. No sight for a fine lady here be coming."

"I'll kill you if you take another step!" Theona hissed. She clenched her teeth to keep them from chattering in her fear. She caught some movement out of the corner of her eye and snapped her head back to face her other opponent, now a pair of steps closer to her. "That goes for you, too, Dorian—or whoever you are!"

The man stood upright painfully, holding his palms out toward her. "It's Meklos, Theona; Meklos Jefard."

Her eyes narrowed. "Jefard? I remember that name—like the old lord you were telling us about?"

"My ancestor," Meklos said, keeping his voice calm, his gaze locked with Theona's eyes. "A great man, the father of a great family that had everything robbed from us. The dragon put an end to our power; the mystic bards put an end to our good name. If you'll just hear me out—listen to my story—I'm sure that you'll—"

Too late, she saw the dwarf charging at her from behind. Theona swung desperately but missed. The momentum of the club pulled her out of Dregas's path so that he did not hit her squarely at the knees, but it was enough: Theona spun wildly through the air, falling heavily on her side against the sand at the edge of the pool.

Meklos leaped forward, snatching the club from Theona's limp hand. "You should have stuck to your clan's business, Theona. You should have gone home while you had the chance."

"No! Please—wait!" Theona struggled across the sand, clawing her way toward where Treijan lay still and helpless on the shore.

"No" was the only reply. Meklos stood next to Treijan, raising the frighteningly carved club high.

Theona lunged, throwing herself across Treijan, trying desperately to shield him from the blow she knew was about to rain down.

Detours

Theona shut her eyes, waiting for the crushing pain. Nothing happened. There was a strange brightness beyond her tightly closed eyelids. She ventured to open them, wondering vaguely why she was not dead or at least insensible.

There was Gaius, now clawing his way slowly through the sand toward her, the entire scene being lit in strange and shifting bright colors. His eyes stared blankly, Theona's vaguely focused. The back of his head was caked in his own blood. He stopped and pushed himself onto his back, his jaw slackening as he looked upward. Theona turned her head, following the bard's gaze.

Theona stared, her own jaw falling open in terrified amazement.

The winged spirit from her vision—now flesh and bone made real before her eyes—floated in the center of a wide globe of shifting light that encompassed both her and the two prostrate bards. He was a youth by the look of his narrow face, long strands of black hair falling across his eyes. There was an unreal beauty about his features, almost painful for Theona to look upon. His skin was dark—darker than any she had ever known or heard of—and he wore a long black hooded coat. His wings pulsed slowly in the air. His arms held a large and ornately jeweled book tightly to his chest.

To Theona he was the incarnation of Skurea, the Keeper of the Dead.

Next to him stood a creature she had never seen or imagined—a creature that she considered to look like the top half of an incredibly strong man growing out of the body of a strange hairy torusk. Though overall the creature was not nearly as large as the beasts of burden she was used to, this creature's powerful arms and cunning eye gave Theona an instant picture of how dangerous the monster could be.

"It cannot be real," she muttered frantically to herself, confronted with her own nightmares. "It must be an illusion—a madness!"

She glanced about her: the bubble of shifting light completely enclosed Gaius, Treijan, and herself as well as the two strange creatures from her dreams. There was no sign of Dorian—Meklos, she corrected herself—or the dwarf, but then the area of the lagoon itself kept changing just beyond the edge of the bubble around them; the palm forests and jungle shimmered and became a rock field with fingers of lava tumbling down the rock face into a lagoon of molten rock. Great billowing clouds of steam surged into the air from the ocean shore nearly a mile away, only to shift again to show a lush growth of carefully maintained lawns and trees surrounding a shining tower of white stone rising to impossible heights and then back again to the familiar jungle. The rate at which the images changed was frighteningly fast.

Dizzy from watching the shifting images, Theona focused her attention on the winged creature hovering in the air only a few feet from her. The spirit-made-real did not seem to notice her, for it was staring down at Treijan with unabashed astonishment. The great book with the gem-encrusted cover slipped from his slackening hands, falling to the sands near the feet of the half-man creature next to him.

Someone groaned at Theona's feet.

"Gaius!" Theona's voice was a hoarse whisper. "Gaius! Quickly—get up!"

"I'm dreaming," Gaius replied, his words halting and unsure. "I *must* be in the dream."

"This is no dream," Theona said, her voice grim.

Meklos screamed, barely able to see through rage and pain. He hung several feet above the ground, his back impaled on a broken branch stub of a banyan tree. He dangled against one of the multiple trunks, his arms draped akimbo over several surrounding limbs as the searing, sharp pain in his back threatened to overwhelm him. Moving his legs caused excruciating agony to shoot upward from the wound, though he found he could relieve the pressure slightly by lifting upward with his arms. He blinked, trying to focus on what was around him; trying to remember just how he lost control of what should have been an easy kill.

He should not have been surprised, he thought as his mind wandered in his shock and pain, considering how things had gone since he had moved through the gate. At first he believed that the Eye of Vasska had guided him;

he had stalked his nemesis and discovered the rat's lair, all the while staying one thought ahead of the bards and two thoughts ahead of the dwarf. But ever since he arrived here, everything had gone wrong. The natives' magic was unlike anything he had encountered; a power whose bone bracers had robbed him of his advantage and made him as weak as any common man. He was the Pir Inquisitas—the People's Judge—and yet they brought him before their own justice in a circle of magic that was unknown to him or his order.

And then there was the dragon that appeared over him, diving down upon him, its flames searing through his soul and tearing open his heart . . .

He shuddered where he hung, shaking his head furiously to concentrate on the problem at hand: how to live. His disciplined mind took over, pressing down the fear and panic. He closed his eyes and tried to hold very still. He had to find a way down from the tree. If he could remember how he came to be hanging from his impaled back in the first place, then he might be able to figure a way out of death.

He remembered escaping his guards; they had robbed him of the powers of the Deep Magic, but they could not take his combat and evasion skills from him. Then he remembered standing over Treijan—he had the club in his hand ready to fulfill his oath. There was something shifting in the air—and then thunder and crushing power forcing the air from his lungs. Limbs, sand, palms, fronds, rocks—all flew with him in a blur—and then the impact bringing darkness.

He opened his eyes again. Some of the hardier palm trunks remained upright, but many others lay flat against the ground. Their trunks all radiated from a point near the shores of the lagoon where he had stood only moments ago.

He squinted, trying to focus better.

It was a globe of some kind—a magical sphere with a shifting surface like the waters on a rippling lake. Within he could see . . .

Meklos's eyes widened.

It was not possible. His mind struggled to accept the evidence of his own eyes: a winged spirit and a monstrous half-man creature standing next to his prey. He had dealt with both kinds of creatures in the dream before, using their magic as it suited him in the waking world, but everyone knew that they were not *real* beings; only manifestations in the dream. Yet here they stood seemingly as real as he, gazing down on the woman and the two limp bards that lay at his feet. The winged spirit was holding a great jeweled book to his chest, but it began to drop when he gazed down on the still form of Treijan lying beneath him. The book fell into the sands when the creature opened its arms to embrace the bard.

"No!" Meklos screamed, the sound of the word drawing out in a continuous howling of his rage. Unexpected strength rushed into his limbs, and he lifted himself up with both arms, drawing his legs up against the gnarled trunk of the tree behind him. The raw sound from his voice continued—no longer a word but the incoherent roar of an animal. He pushed with his legs and arms at once, thrusting his body away from the offending broken branch impaling his back, and launched himself into the air. White exploded behind his eyes with the pain, and he tumbled blindly through the air, his arms and legs flailing. The whiteness vanished a moment before the ground rushed up to meet him, barely giving him time to react.

Meklos fell hard against the ground, instinctively rolling over his shoulder, but his legs were not quite under him as he hit; he slammed painfully onto his side, the air knocked out of his lungs. The white blankness returned with searing pain, but he refused to give in to the comfort of oblivion. Instead, he pulled himself up, his arms quivering, trying desperately to get his legs under him, though he found the palm fronds on the ground under him slick with his own blood.

He raised his head. He could see Theona inside the shimmering, shifting bubble. She was standing between the winged creature and Treijan, trying desperately to keep the creature at bay. Gaius was moving, too, apparently recovering all too soon from the blow Meklos had delivered to him earlier.

The winged spirit, however, was not deterred; his face remained fixed on Treijan, his arms reaching down to pick him up and . . .

"No!" Meklos growled through clenched teeth. He dug his feet into the ground, oblivious to the pain threatening to engulf him. He pressed forward, lifting himself up with single-minded determination, his voice rising to a shout of rage as he ran raggedly across the ground. "You cannot have him! He is mine!"

It seemed to happen so slowly in Meklos's mind. The ground passed beneath him as though he were running through water: the half-man creature reaching out, taking Theona's arm in his thick, powerful hand, and pulling her aside easily; Gaius struggling to help her, rising unsteadily to his feet.

"He is mine!" Meklos's own voice sounded slow in his ears. "He has to pay for what he has done—for what he has taken from me!"

The winged spirit reached down, folding the still form of Treijan in his arms.

"Vasska, no—do not rob me of my justice!" Tears flowed down Meklos's stained face. "Do not rob me of my peace!"

The shifting globe collapsed into nothing before him. Meklos felt himself lifted once more from the ground with the sudden rush of wind that filled the void where once there had been form, air, monsters, and humans. Thunder pealed across the ground, echoing off the sharp face of the mountain rising above the trees, as Meklos skidded facedown across the sands on the shore of the pool, whose surface roiled slightly from the sphere's sudden disappearance.

Meklos could not bring himself to rise again. He lay face against the white sands at the pool's shore, sobbing painfully. "Damn you, Treijan. Damn you to the furthest reaches of N'Kara!"

The gods themselves robbed him, too.

Generations of shame welled up in him, even as he felt his lifeblood draining into the sands. Then he raised his head, for he heard his father's voice—tones angry and sullen, for this was the only way he could remember his father speaking. *"We were the Sea-kings of Khordsholm,"* his father said. *"Our deeds were noble, and justice was our right! We brought prosperity with the strength of our arms, the cunning of our minds, and the heart to stand against any who would stop us."*

"Sire?" Meklos murmured as he blinked, trying to see the long-dead man whose words resounded in his mind.

"Robbed of our past! Robbed of our future!" the voice spat in acid accusation, slurred as it was with too much hard drink and too long a life. *"Would that the gods had*

given me a son with blood in his veins! Who now will stand and take back the Throne of Khordsholm? Surely, not this whelp whose only strength is in scullery magic and religious prattle!"

Meklos reached out with his hand above his head. "Sire! I will not fail you—I cannot..."

His hand touched something hard in the sands.

His vision was narrowing, but he could still see the object, and his hand gripped it in the hope of salvation.

It was a book—an ancient book whose cover was encrusted with jewels.

It was the winged spirit's book, Meklos realized; the spirit had dropped it when he reached for Treijan.

Meklos pulled it to him through the sands, embracing it. If the spirit had left it, then there was hope that Meklos could use it to find the spirit again. Surely, the creature would want such a valuable thing back. Surely, he would return for it, and when he did . . .

Sweet and painless darkness flooded the mind of Meklos Jefard, and the voice in his head fell silent at last.

Dirc Rennes stood in his darkened study of Arvad Keep and gazed out past the archway and balcony. Anyone who might have stood in the sumptuously appointed room with him—and the number who might enter this high chamber in the keep was never more than three—would have thought that the head of the Council of Thirty-six was gazing at the towers of the Mystic Temple silhouetted against the bright stars of a late clear night. Any one of the three trusted advisers—and they were trusted to come here only one at a time—would have been wrong.

The eyes of Dirc Rennes may have been gazing toward the deeply shadowed lines of the temple, but his sight strained to see far beyond them. Ever since his son had disappeared with his companion Gaius, he had retreated to this sanctuary to contemplate the fates that had brought him and his house to this precarious place and to wonder how long he could keep the snarling dogs on the Council at bay so he could find some solution to his problem.

His problem was, quite simply, his heir.

Treijan was the darling of the court, and from the moment of his birth through his loudly heralded early years he was looked to by all the houses—especially his own—as the obvious successor to the greatest and most powerful house among all the mystics. Descended from Galen Arvad, through Caelith's son Aremis—the father of Dirc's wife, Thais—Treijan Rennes-Arvad was the hope that kept the line of Arvad intact and all the other houses at bay.

Rennes-Arvad, Dirc thought; a sharing of his own family identifier for the sake of clarity of lineage. He had given up much, compromised more often than he was wont, just to keep that stabilizing name intact and the precarious peace between the competing houses, whose fighting would otherwise tear their fledgling empire apart. A good marriage for Treijan—to the right house with the right connections—could unify the lines of genealogical descent and bring stability to the empire—or, if not stability, at least enough clout to silence the most vicious among their detractors.

Then came the day when Treijan experienced his first fit. It was Gaius—his ubiquitous playmate from House Petros—who brought him into the keep, breathless and frightened. They had been out in the northern fields, beyond the ruins of the city, playing at warrior and hurling harmless water spells at each other, when Treijan suddenly fell, convulsing, on the ground. Gaius searched in vain for someone to help them, panicked and uncertain as to what was happening to the prince, but they were far from any aid.

Fortunately, Dirc thought; for had anyone else witnessed the event, it might have been more difficult to keep it hidden. The fit had not lasted long, and Treijan walked back on his own, seemingly recovered by the time they reached the keep, though the same could hardly be said for Gaius.

On that day a deal was struck: House Petros would be compensated and accommodated when possible, and Gaius would become Treijan's companion, guardian, and keeper of his crippling secret for life. The prince was half a man in the eyes of Dirc and those few in his house who knew the secret. Gaius provided the other half and in doing so was, Dirc supposed, something of a cripple himself. As the boys grew, they were often sent away as bards in the service of the empire, their absence serving to keep the continuing and now occasionally extreme attacks far from the many eyes in Calsandria.

So it had worked for many years until the day came when House Conlan could not be denied a union between their houses. Conlan had prepared well and positioned himself among the other houses so that his offer would be impossible to turn down. Dirc Rennes-Arvad, Master of the Thirty-six, was forced to agree to the match for the sake of pouring oil on the troubled waters of the empire. Dirc dutifully directed the Bards' Guild to send word through the gates to Gaius and recall the prince to Calsandria.

But the problem was how to marry the prize daughter of House Conlan to the—Dirc sighed at the thought—

crippled prince of Rennes-Arvad. Master Conlan was a man of the trades, and if he believed that he had been "sold" a defective prince? Dirc shuddered at the thought.

So this entire charade had been concocted entirely too quickly; Gaius would "abduct" the prince, and somehow that would buy Dirc time to figure out a better plan. Gaius assured Dirc that he knew of a place where they could go that no one could find them, far beyond the horizons of the empire and outside the knowledge of dragons or men.

So it was that Dirc, each night, gazed through his archway and beyond the horizon. He was not a man of fear—one could hardly stay in his position long if he were—but he preferred to look his enemy in the face. It was the things that were beyond his control that troubled him in the night.

Behind him the soft sound of a single chime rang from his desk.

Dirc turned at the noise. He was an orderly man, one who cleared his desk each evening of the parchments and tools of his busy day. He had left a book open on the desk so that the next morning he might remember where he had left off in its text, but otherwise, he thought he had left the surface empty.

He stepped cautiously back to the desk in the dark room, feeling for its polished edge, then running his hands across its smooth surface. He encountered the edge of the book and ran his fingers around its pages until . . .

Dirc's eyes went suddenly wide in the night.

His hand closed around the cold metal disk, pulling it from the surface of the desk. He felt the neck chain drawn up with it, draping itself over his clenched fist.

Dirc Rennes-Arvad, Lord of the Mystic Empire, opened

his mouth and let out a sound of mourning that came from the bottom of his despair and which was heard beyond the walls of the study and in the keep's courtyard below. He felt his legs give way under him. He collapsed to the floor, leaning against the edge of the table, struggling to keep upright, his right hand held in front of his face. Though he could not see it in the darkness, he knew what he held in his hand and fell forward in utter desolation.

It was Treijan's tally.

His son was dead.

Walls of Skurea

Theona could not stop shaking. It was not just the chill dryness in the air that stung her nostrils. The warm, moist air that had so comfortably surrounded her moments before had quickly dissipated, but the shivering of her skin was not brought on by the change in temperature so much as the abrupt change in *everything*.

The world around her had turned horribly, and in the blink of an eye. Now her mind was having trouble grasping the sudden shift in perspective. The winged-spirit figure standing before her still held the motionless form of Treijan in his arms, but the creature's face was suddenly cast in shadow. The monstrous half-man beast that accompanied the winged spirit still held her arm, and he may have been the only reason that she remained standing.

Framed between these mysterious beings stood massive, ornate gates, their surfaces covered in relief features that she knew all too well. To either side of the gates were gigantic skeletal sculptures of winged monsters, their features glinting in the night with the fine edge of polished onyx, freezing her blood more surely than the chill air around her.

She could not speak, terror filling her completely, threatening to rob her of her mind.

Gaius rose unsteadily to his feet next to her. "What—where are we?"

"I know," Theona said quietly through chattering teeth. "I've seen this place before."

"You've been here?" Gaius asked with incredulity, his breath billowing clouds in the cold.

"No—*saw* it," Theona chattered as she blinked tears from her eyes.

"Been here—seen it—just tell me where we are!" Gaius said under his breath as he drew closer to Theona and pulled her back slightly from the half-creature standing over them.

"Skurea the Unbeliever," Theona stammered, her eyes still fixed on the horrific gleaming black statues to either side of the massive gates. Her voice grew more urgent and panicked as she spoke. "These are the gates to the land of the Forgotten Dead! We have died, Gaius. Dorian or Meklos or whoever he is must have killed us both—killed us and Treijan, too—and these spirits have come to take our souls back into the darkness, back to the oblivion without memory or pain or—"

"Theona!" Gaius grabbed her by her shoulders, turning her away from the terrible gates and looking into her eyes. He shook her lightly, so that she focused on him, her world narrowing to the sharp, angular features of his face. "I'm here! You're here! Treijan is *here*. We're not dead—at least not yet. I don't know where we are or how we got here, but we'll find our way, Theona. Somehow we'll find our way."

"But the gates. They—"

"I don't know what the afterlife is going to be like," Gaius said with a wincing smile at the edge of his lips, "but I'm pretty sure I won't be bleeding in it."

Theona blinked, glancing toward the top of Gaius's head. He obliged by nodding downward, showing her the trickle of blood still oozing into his matted hair from the cut.

"But—but I *have* seen this place," Theona said, her breathing still loud in her own ears. The half-man was leaning close to the ear of the winged creature, speaking in hushed tones. The spirit then answered back furtively, so that Theona could not hear his reply.

"Where?" Gaius asked. "Was it in the Deep Magic?"

Theona flushed. "No. I—I am a commoner."

Gaius paused, giving her a skeptical look. "You are anything but common, Theona."

She could feel the old resentment rising in her, causing her to tightly control the hot words she felt welling up inside her. "I have no magic in me, Gaius. I never have."

"Yet you have visions that apparently come true?"

"Let me go!"

Gaius's grip was surprisingly strong. "Theona, listen to me! I believe you are more . . . special than you think."

The winged spirit was turning away from them, a look of joy behind the locks falling across his face. He approached the black and crimson gates with Treijan still in his arms, his dark wings beating gently against the frigid night. The gates, in turn, responded with a heavy metallic scraping sound, followed by a terrible screeching of hinges. The gates were opening for the winged spirit. The half-man gestured Theona toward the gates as well.

Theona began to shake once more.

"Listen to me!" Gaius said, gripping her shoulders tighter. "We can get through this, but I'm going to need your help. You have a power—something that the Khani'i of Rhai-Tuah saw in you."

"Who?"

"The Khani'i—the people in the village. Their ceremony discovered something about you that made them—"

Theona suddenly remembered; she saw the ghostly image of the dragon overhead, the men of the village swinging their strange clubs as they chanted in their ritual around her. The dragon plunging down on her . . .

She *saw* all that could be.

Theona stilled and turned to face the gates with a calm sadness. "You are right, Gaius. We *will* get through this. Though we are further from home than I think you know and the price of our return may be dearer than either of us would wish to pay."

Gaius looked at her strangely. "I don't understand."

"No one will until it is too late." Theona sighed, then flashed a sad smile at the bard. "I'm sorry—I'm just not quite ready for all this."

Gaius shrugged and turned with her toward the gates. "So this isn't the Abyss of Skurea, after all, eh?"

"No," Theona said, taking in a deep breath, "but it *is* a city of the dead."

Gaius only frowned as Theona took her first steps toward the open gates and the horrifying buildings of the city beyond.

Bedlam ruled in the Secret Secret Labs.

Big-funder Thwick was screaming, jumping up and down in his official coat and waving his arms insanely in the air. Warlord Skramak was screeching orders at everyone in sight while he leaped and rolled from behind one broken crate to another in search of a better defensive position. Several of the goblin army officers—two gen-reels and a host of left-nats—dove behind different stacks of books and were still throwing rocks, wood chunks, slivers of iron, and an unending stream of yelling in the confusion. Three technomancers, who had come as observers, added to the confusion by casting several colorful, loud, and explosive spells into the ceiling of the room as warning shots, even though the object of their anger had long since left. The resulting cascade of broken stone and mortar added to the fury of the gen-reels and left-nats, who renewed their barrage of broken hardware and bad language.

All of this was entirely lost on Lunid, who sat slumped to one side on the floor, staring at the now empty circle of rings in the floor, her hand painfully clutching a single jewel she had pulled from the cover of her control book just as her god had vanished. She had lost him—her divine, beautiful god who had once been hers to love and cherish and keep forever—and she wondered how she could go on without him always near her in his cage.

It was that four-legged creature that had done it— she was just sure of it—certainly not her beloved Urk. She knew his name: Urk! Lunid felt a little faint at the thought; she had heard him *speak* to her, and this time she had understood his words! She knew so little about her captured god and treasured what little she knew in her heart: that his name was Urk, that he was a *fa-ree* type of a god, his companion was a *kentar*, and that there must have been something wrong with the cage she built that kept him from talking to her before. Lunid felt that she had established rapport with the god and a deep level of understanding, despite the fact that she couldn't abide the sound of his voice. Still, in the few sentences they had shared, she was just *sure* that Urk was coming to love her and would have remained with her forever—

If only it were not for that stupid *kentar*! She could see now that the ugly abomination had plotted against Lunid from the very first moment she had captured them with the rift-gate. He was the one that *forced* Urk into breaking the lovely cage that she had created so carefully for her beloved, and, no doubt, he was also the one that had beguiled Urk into stealing her controller book. *Poor Urk,* she thought. *To have been led astray by so false a companion.*

Then once again her own misery descended on her. She had lost him, and she did not know how she could go one more moment without the hope of Urk being at her side. Great, gooey tears welled up in her eyes, and Lunid, the greatest Deep Tinker of all the goblins, croaked one terrible, racking sob after another.

It was some time before she was aware that the explosions against the ceiling had stopped, that the warriors had stopped pelting and cursing one another, and that while the Big-funder was still waving his arms about, he had stopped screaming.

"Lunid?" came the deep voice behind her. "What are you thinking?"

The Deep Tinker shook her head, closing her eyes against the pain in her stomach.*

"Lunid, you know I want to help you." It was Skramak

---

*Goblins believe that the center of the soul is located in the stomach. This, academics believed, was a great improvement over previous backward thinking that the center of the goblin soul was in their left big toe.

who spoke to her, his withered hand resting lightly on her shoulder. "I've always wanted to help you."

All she could manage was another croaking sob.

"What is the point?" Big-funder Thwick howled. "She lost them! I could have supported this institution for *years* on the revenues from the weapons applications alone, and she had to—"

"Shut up, Thwick, or I'll pull your tongue out through your ear!" Skramak snarled, his voice vicious and chilling for a second before turning back to the soft and reassuring voice of a kindly uncle. "You just tell Skramak where the gods have gone, eh? Then maybe Skramak can help you find a way to get them back."

Lunid's shoulders still bobbed up and down, but at least she had managed to stifle her sobs.

"Come on now, Lunid," Skramak urged, though there was an edge to the tone of his voice. "Tell me how we find the gods again."

Lunid sniffed, wiping her nose down the sleeve of her tinker's coat. "Well, we—we could *l-look* f-f-for th-them, I g-guess."

One of the gen-reels spoke up, having grown bored after the throwing of rocks had ceased. "Lord Skramak! This little dung-dropping doesn't know anything! It is insulting to watch you speak to her in this—"

Skramak removed his hand from Lunid's shoulder. She heard the ring of metal, a click, and the sound of something sliding through the air, followed by a dull, heavy thud against the floor.

"Tell me, my dear Lunid," Skramak continued without losing a beat, "how we might look for your dear lost gods."

Lunid leaned forward on her hands, thinking as she

crawled deliberately toward the rings on the floor. Maybe they *could* find her precious Urk, after all. Maybe she could put together another controller book and use it to open a different rift-gate. It all seemed so hard and so far away after having had her dear Urk so close to her and then snatched away—yes, he was definitely *snatched* by that *kentar*—that to begin again seemed a daunting, if not impossible, task. Yet Skramak believed in her—believed that together they could find Urk again and she could be happy the way she had been these last weeks.

Lunid touched the books strapped in series to the mechanism. The rings glowed satisfactorily, and the air within them began to shift and shimmer into visions of distant places.

Skramak chuckled. "Good, Lunid. You are doing well. What are we looking at?"

"The c-control book and the r-r-rings are b-bound together," Lunid replied in a tired voice. "The world of the gods is vast, my l-lord. It is easier f-for me to l-look for the c-control book that was t-t-taken than for the g-god himself."

Images shifted quickly. Skramak was looking down on a white-covered mountain and a strange city in the distance, then the images flashed and were replaced by a jungle-lined shore against a vast ocean.

"Can't you stop the pictures in one place?" Skramak asked in frustration.

"Without a control book it is im-im-impo-impossible," Lunid sniffed. "I'm trying, m-my lord."

The image flashed again, and Skramak gasped.

Lunid's jaw dropped.

Here were creatures like the god Skramak had just seen but without wings. They were working in some kind of structure, and most of them seemed rather bored with their efforts. It was not their attitude, however, that shocked Lunid.

Here were creatures *making books*!

"By the gods," Thwick murmured behind them. "Unlimited power!"

The image flashed and was replaced by a scene of warriors charging into battle on a distant plain, but this new vision held no interest for the stunned goblins in the room.

"Wait!" Skramak cried out. "Go back!"

"I can't!" Lunid wailed. "Not without a control book."

The remaining gen-reel muttered, "By the titans, my lord, if we could find the *source* of books—"

Skramak cut him off. "Lunid, can you fix this rift-gate for me, or maybe build an even *bigger* rift-gate?"

"Well, of c-course," Lunid answered, somewhat perplexed. "I might be able to find my old control book with the farsight rings, but that wouldn't help find my Urk—I m-mean, the god that we l-lost. He could b-be any-any-where."

Skramak took Lunid's hand and pulled her up off the floor. "You just let me worry about that, Lunid. You build me a really *big* rift-gate into this world of the gods where your precious book is—and I'll take the Army of the Empire over there and *find* him for you!"

Convergence

The great doors boomed shut behind them, and Theona finally felt as though she could breathe. Their passage through the bizarre city had nearly caused a riot. The streets were already crowded with desperate creatures similar to the one who still carried the limp form of Treijan in his arms and continued to lead them deeper through the winding and frightful alleys. The creatures were beautiful for the most part: their variety of dress remarkable and their features striking, though they returned her gaze with stares of suspicion and fear. As she looked at them closer, she realized that their fine costumes had been abused badly and their features seemed gaunt. Refugees? she wondered, though from what, she had no idea. Their gaze darted between the winged man and the half-man creature that continued to press them forward from behind. As they passed Theona, the throng seemed to have a distaste for the half-beast creature, while she could also feel their curiosity about herself and Gaius.

Then, as they turned another sharp corner, they heard

the approaching rattle of armor and the chanting of warriors in a deep, strange tongue. Even the strange winged people around her moved to the side of the narrow road, the half-man reaching out with his huge hand and pushing both Gaius and Theona against a patch of vacant wall.

An army marched toward them down the street.

Theona gasped.

They were an army of the dead. They had wings and lithe bodies like the living around her, but their skins were mottled and their eyes blank with death. They marched on bone-exposed feet, their swords clattering against their ancient and rusting armor. Most of them were in various states of decay, with parts of their form absent. The leader of the dead army turned its half-missing face toward Theona, its eyes glazed a milky white in death. It smiled crookedly at her and saluted by pressing the hilt of its sword to its metal breastplate.

Gaius gripped Theona's hand, and she turned hurriedly to face him. Their eyes locked on each other, neither of them wishing to witness the horrific spectacle so near them. Yet she heard them marching by, knew that they were there and that their horror was passing in a seemingly unending procession.

"I . . . I never much liked parades," Theona said uncertainly.

"Me either," Gaius replied through a nervous smile. "I think we can miss this one."

After a time impossible for Theona to measure, the marching passed and receded down the street. Gaius turned away from her, glancing about. "I think we had better keep moving."

The voices in the crowd around them were growing louder and more insistent. She could not understand their language, but the tone was increasingly hostile. The winged man who had brought them here was moving more quickly now down the street, and the half-man beast was insistent that she and Gaius follow.

The creature's concerns appeared justified, for by the time they reached the outer gates to a great courtyard, the crowd in the streets had grown into an angry mob shouting after them. As they passed through the outer gates, the winged man's pace was so swift that he was nearly running even while still holding Treijan in his arms.

Dark-robed guards at the gate allowed them into the enormous cobblestone court that ran around the base of a black and forbidding tower, but fortunately, these same guards halted the angry throng. Still, it was not until they had all crossed the courtyard and entered the tower itself that Theona felt safe from the mob.

Not, she realized suddenly, that the space they now occupied was of a great comfort. The black polished floor curved upward at the back of the room into ribbed columns like black veins that ran overhead into impenetrable darkness. Glowing globes were fitted about the room for illumination, but much of their light seemed to be muted by the black walls and floor.

Theona was surprised to feel Gaius release her hand— she had scarcely been aware that he was still holding it.

The winged man knelt down and gently laid Treijan on the floor, then looked up at Theona from under the long strands of hair falling across his eyes and smiled reassuringly. He gestured to the half-man beast to follow him toward a pair of short onyx pillars that rose to waist height about twenty steps from where they stood.

"What now?" Gaius asked Theona quietly.

She shook her head. She was watching the winged man

place his hand atop one of the pillars before tilting his head to stare up into the darkness.

"I don't know," Theona replied, her eyes rising as well, "but I suspect we are about to find out."

Two figures drifted down from the blackness far overhead. One was a dark-skinned, winged man with warm eyes and flowing hair, but it was the other, a woman, who commanded Theona's attention. She was tall and willowy with shockingly white hair pulled back into a tight bun; hair seemingly all the brighter by the contrast with her dark complexion. Even in the dim light of the audience chamber, Theona could tell the woman's skin was a hue like the rich, deep loam of good earth, yet smooth as velvet. Her full lips and high cheekbones were achingly elegant, and her movements were like a fluid dance through the air. She wore a black dress with a high pointed collar and a long midnight cape that flowed behind her. Her wings were delicate, and the illumination globes shone through as they beat in silence through the air. Theona felt suddenly shamed by her plainness, though she was sure that even her sister would not have held up against such incredible beauty. But as lightning crackled about the dark woman's fingertips, Theona noticed danger in her eyes, which were fixed on the winged spirit holding Treijan. She was frightening and awe-inspiring all at once; so much so that both Gaius and Theona could only gape as she drifted down toward the two pillars.

"She looks angry," Gaius said softly.

"Let's hope it isn't with us," Theona said, shivering.

"Wait," Gaius said, his eyes widening in astonishment. "I—I *know* this woman!"

*   *   *

"I do not know where I have been," Arryk answered as simply as he could. "I was abducted—as was Hueburlyn."

"Who?" Dwynwyn asked with seething impatience.

"The centaur," Arryk answered. "We were taken at the same time, just as I was about to hand him over to the Kyree-Nykira. We were taken by a portal or a tear—I am not sure which word is more accurate—created by a demon of the Sharaj. It took us—I am not sure *where* it took us, but it was very far from here."

"Far enough to start a war," Dwynwyn snapped. "Far enough to rain death on my kingdom. Far enough to ensure our downfall."

"I did *exactly* what you asked of me," Arryk answered back, his words hot in his own ears. "I did not cause my abduction, and I did everything I could to return as soon as possible."

"And return you did"—Dwynwyn nodded, gesturing at the centaur—"with the very creature that provided the excuse for the Kyree-Nykira to invade us. How am I to explain *that* to the imperator of Nykira?"

"But isn't 'far' exactly where we need to go?" Peleron spoke calmly from where he stood apart from Dwynwyn and Arryk, his accustomed place in their discussions. "If Arryk has been abducted and apparently found the means to use the method of his abduction to return to us, could we not use this New Truth to our advantage?"

Dwynwyn turned to Peleron and considered his words for a moment. "Use this New Truth? You wish to abduct someone, Peleron?"

The faery consort gave his most disarming smile in response. "No, my Queen, but I would be most anxious to use it to help our people escape. We are trapped within our own borders here—the Kyree will certainly destroy us; it is only a matter of time. They will not negotiate, for peace is not their objective. Our destruction alone will satisfy them. We are bound otherwise by faery houses that are content to let the Kyree destroy us for them, and therefore none of them will allow us passage to the lands beyond."

"But this—this rift, this portal," Dwynwyn said with dawning understanding, "has brought Arryk beyond all our borders and back again."

"The faery houses certainly mean to plunder us for the power of the Sharaj," Peleron continued. "They will allow the Kyree to weaken us utterly before they, too, invade and take all the Sharajin into captivity. They will divide us up and put us back in our place as a Seeker caste, spread among the former houses so that we no longer will have a voice of our own."

Dwynwyn turned back to Arryk. "This thing that moved you so far across the face of the world—what did you call it?"

"The creature I learned it from called it a rift-gate," Arryk replied. "It is a complicated construct of the Sharaj unlike any I have ever seen before."

"Do you think you can duplicate it?"

"Of course," the young Sharajin said quickly.

"Then we must determine where you were taken," Dwynwyn said, "and just how far away this place may be. Do you know anything that might help us understand where you have been?"

Arryk looked awkwardly at the floor. "Well, I did bring someone—three creatures actually—which…"

Dwynwyn's eyes were no longer on Arryk. Her jaw dropped in astonishment.

A wingless man was approaching her from the shadows beyond Arryk. He was leading a young woman—also wingless—by the hand, but it was his narrow face and sharp eyes that caught her immediate attention.

Dwynwyn blinked, and her voice was filled with wonder when she spoke. "Arryk! Peleron! I—I *know* this man!"

King Pe'akanu sat on his throne in his palace, resting his chin on his wide fist while he thought.

The council had been called early in the morning—an unusual time for the king to call court and certainly as close to indicating an emergency as any could remember. Torches were lit in the vast stone hall as much for their warmth in the predawn as for their light. The elders and shamans both from within the city and from many of the surrounding villages sat cross-legged on mats each had placed on the polished stone floor. The house dragons that perched on the carved stone figures lining the walls of the great hall stared down with black eyes at the king. Despite the hour, word had moved quickly through the city, and those who could not find a spot in the great hall waited outside in the Plaza of Spirits for news. Runners waited nervously, prepared to carry the words of the king to the other cities scattered northward along the shores of Rhai-Tuah's western bays.

Everyone waited.

King Pe'akanu, however, was not moved to rush. A deliberate man, he considered his position sacred. His judgments—if not exactly swift—were always known to be fair.

The king spoke at last. "Mokahi?"

Everyone straightened. Mokahi, an ancient man with pepper-gray hair pulled back into a long braid, was sitting in the front row of the great hall and answered at once. "Yes, Pe'akanu."

"The Wheel of Judgment was clear to you concerning the woman?"

"Yes, Pe'akanu—as it was clear to all who were there last night. The woman Theona is the woman of whom the ancients foretold. She it is who will speak with the voice of the gods. She it is who will see through the eyes of the gods. She it is who—"

"Yes, Mokahi," Pe'akanu interrupted—an astounding action, for no one could recall the king ever having done so. "The prophecy is with us all. But now she is gone, along with Treijan and Gaius. The prophecy says nothing of the Seer vanishing."

Mokahi shrugged. "The ways of the gods are not the ways of mortals."

Pe'akanu lapsed into another silence, then said, "Mokahi, did not the prophecy also say that the Seer would be the sign of a great war?"

"Yes, Pe'akanu, that is what the prophecy says," the old shaman answered solemnly.

"Then we may not delay preparing for war," the king said.

"King Pe'akanu!"

The king turned to face the warrior who suddenly stood up from his mat in the second row. "Lelika, speak!"

"Are we to suffer a war for the sake of these uncivilized strangers?" Lelika was master of the warriors in Tua'a-Re and, as such, felt himself responsible for losing the Meklos prisoner the night before. "The pale-skins are a backward people without culture or traditions. Our books tell the story of the Hanu'ui back a thousand years and at peace with the Dragon of the Mountain for as long as our king's ancestors have sat upon this throne. Who are these pale-skins that threaten our peace? They are but aggressive savages whose greatest talent is for ending their civilizations just as soon as they get them started."

"I am second to no one in my admiration for our people's achievements," Pe'akanu said with annoyance. "The pale-skins *are* barbarians."

"Then why are we fighting their war?"

"I do not know if it is their war that we fight," Pe'akanu said carefully. "It may be their war, but it is *our* prophecy—and the fate of all the Hanu'ui rests upon its outcome."

"How can we prepare to fight when we do not know our enemy?" asked the warrior.

"How can we *not* prepare when we believe that war may soon be upon us?" Pe'akanu rejoined. "If we delay, we may bring death to our brothers and sisters all across Rhai-Tuah. However, we are not without hope of discovering this unnamed enemy, Lelika. A mystery has fallen to us which, I think, may answer many riddles."

Pe'akanu's left hand gestured down to the large, jewel-encrusted book laid before his seat.

"It was taken from the pale-skin Meklos at the spot where the Seer vanished," Pe'akanu said loudly enough so that everyone in the hall could hear. "It is a curious thing, this book, with writing that is strange to us. It was left by the Seer when she disappeared and would have been hidden from us by the pale-skin were it not for our vigilant warriors."

Pe'akanu paused, considered again his decision, and then continued. "Hear now the word of Pe'akanu!"

The runners at the far end of the hall turned, prepared

to take the next words of their king to the farthest parts of the island.

"The Seer has come, as was told to us by our ancestors. War will follow—war which we cannot see, yet this book was left to us so that we might see! We will study it that we might come to know the danger that was foretold. As we study, let each of us prepare for war. Let every warrior from the furthest village to the great cities prepare himself against the doom that was seen from the beginning—and to do so as his heart and spirit tell him. As for the king, I trust our pale-skin brothers Treijan and Gaius to bring the Seeker back to us once more! This is the word of Pe'akanu!"

As one, the assembly gave a single loud shout of agreement, then stood. The runners fled into the jungle paths, running to greet others waiting farther down the trail who would continue with the message. The citizens began to wander off, and the elders, warriors, and shamans drifted into smaller groups. Once the word of the king was spoken, the meeting was finished.

Mokahi approached the king as he was picking up the strange and alien book. He spoke quietly so that no one else would hear. "You said nothing about our prisoners, Pe'akanu. What is to be done about them?"

"I have considered them, too," the king replied.

"Meklos rode the Wheel of Judgment," Mokahi continued, undeterred. "You know what he carries in his heart."

"Yes," Pe'akanu replied simply. "Yes, I do."

"Lunid? Are you all right?"

The goblin Deep Tinker blinked painfully in the sunlight as she stood at the crest of a small rise. "I-I'm f-f-fine, Sk-Skramak. I j-just don't—just don't g-get out of the academy v-very often."

"Very often, eh?" The goblin conqueror laughed, his remaining eye bright and clear. "I should think 'never' was more like it! Do you know why I have invited you here?"

Truth be told, Lunid was not all that sure that she knew where "here" was. Big-funder Thwick had come to get her from her laboratory that morning and had not listened to her protests. Lunid was still terribly upset about losing her god just the day before—her precious, dearest Urk!—and told the Big-funder in so many words that she was on a self-directed sabbatical until she felt better. Thwick responded by kicking down her door and dragging her out of the laboratory by her ears, all the while saying that he was going to give her a repeated sabbatical across the head if she did not come as Emperor Skramak had ordered. That Skramak had called for her mollified her somewhat, but she was still determined to be miserable and felt she had a right to it.

What she had not expected was to find herself not only out of the laboratory but walking out of the main gates of the academy itself and into the city of Og! The ogres were never allowed in the academy—or the Trove, as they called it—and as a consequence she had forgotten just how large and frightening they were. She was glad when they passed through two huge gates and she discovered that there were no ogres on the other side.

The gladness vanished, however, when she realized that there was *nothing* on the other side. They were outside the city walls. To be sure, there was sky above and grass-covered ground below and mountains cutting into the horizon in the distance, but to an academic like Lunid, that *was* the equivalent of nothing.

Still, Big-funder Thwick maintained his insistence—not to mention his hold on her ears—and brought the no-longer-morose-but-now-completely-terrified Lunid to the top of a small rise north of the city.

"No, Skramak," Lunid replied, still blinking against the sunlight, "I d-don't know w-why you b-b-brought me h-here."

"I brought you here to give you a present," Skramak said. "You've done so much for me over the years, Lunid, I felt I had to make it up to you—up to all of us really, eh, Thwick?"

"Yes, indeed," the Big-funder replied with a smile as deep as his bow.

"So would you like a present, Lunid?" Skramak asked smoothly.

Lunid frowned. No, she thought, she did not want a present—she wanted Urk back. That Skramak thought some trinket would make up for her loss angered her to her very core. She pouted and said, "No, thank you."

"Oh, but you haven't seen it yet!" Skramak urged. "Remember yesterday when you lost your god-friend—what was his name?"

"Urk," Lunid sniffed.

"Yes, Urk." Skramak nodded. "And we looked through your lovely invention and you said you could find your book with it in the realm of the gods?"

Lunid looked up suspiciously. "Yes?"

"I told you I'd help you find your god-friend," Skramak said. "That's my present to you. I'm going to help *you* for a change. Look!"

Lunid followed the emperor's pointing hand. At first

she could see only dust rising from the ground, obscuring the horizon, but soon she could make out the shapes. Towering machines of rust, wheel, and plate—torn in battle and grotesquely skeletal in their form, they looked like the iron dead brought horribly to life.

"Titans!" she exclaimed in astonishment. "Hundreds of them!"

"Not just titans." Skramak grinned with inner satisfaction. "Technomancers, warriors, tradesmen, supplies—and more books than even you have seen, Lunid. And these are just the units I could call from nearby. They will be arriving from all over the empire, Lunid, for days and days until the Grand Army of the Conquest is encamped right here at the foot of this very hill. You'll have everything you need, Lunid, to build your—well, whatever it is that can take us to the realm of the gods. You'll build it bigger and more powerful than you had ever thought possible, with all the wealth of the empire at your disposal and all of the academy behind you to oversee its construction—right, Thwick?"

"All the wealth of the empire." The Big-funder smiled. "Yes, Emperor."

"And when you have built it"—Skramak exhaled luxuriously through his sharp teeth—"then I will take the full might of the titans through the gate."

"And find my Urk?" Lunid smiled, huge tears rolling down her green cheeks.

"And find whatever you like," Skramak said, grinning back.

28

Losses

Meklos could not stop shaking as he lay on his back staring up into the temple's cavernous interior.

The cold eyes of a hundred miniature dragons gazed back at him with fixed stares, their wings folded tightly around their bodies, as they perched on a hundred different carvings jutting out from a series of concourses overhead. Meklos remained transfixed by their eyes, too afraid to look away from them.

Through his pain Meklos could feel the cold, smooth-worn stone of an altar against his back. Out of the corner of his eye he could discern a number of thick-armed warriors whose expressions showed that they were not about to allow their prisoner to embarrass them as he had done the night before. They were slowly, rhythmically swinging their ornate, polished weapons in patterns through the air. Each movement trailed a green, glowing filament like smoke that vanished even as it curled into symbols.

Not that he was in any condition to reenact his escape; the wound in his back burned like fire, while his limbs seemed filled with an aching and almost paralyzing chill. Cold sweat beaded his forehead despite the chill of the room. His coverlet and bloused shirt had been removed, as had his boots and stockings. A blanket made of the softest material he had ever felt lay over him.

He blinked and raised his arm with supreme effort from under the blanket, fixing his eyes down at his wrist—and then let out a sigh of despair. The bracer was still firmly clasped around his arm, and the Deep Magic still eluded him. His strength left him, and his arm fell limply off the edge of the altar.

Meklos made an effort to turn his head away from the stares of the small dragons toward the sound of someone who approached from his right. A huge figure of a man, barrel-chested, with arms thicker than those of his guards, stepped up to the altar on which Meklos lay. The man's face was flat with a broad nose and a sloping, thick brow. His hair was thick with short, tight curls, and his skin was of the same deep brown as that of the guards. His dark eyes shone as he looked down on Meklos, and a slight smile curled at the edge of his lips.

On his broad shoulders hunched a small iridescent dragon whose scales shifted color as it moved. The dragon watched Meklos as well, and the creature seemed to be grinning as it came closer.

Meklos tensed, feeling fear wrap its tendrils around him. He shrank back from the huge man, drawing in a shuddering breath. "Please . . . no! Don't! Don't!"

The huge man eyed Meklos with curiosity and then drew back, folding his arms across his chest before he spoke in a voice as deep as the ocean and warmed with the colors of the jungle flowers. "What do you think I'm going to do—harm you more than you've already harmed yourself, Master Meklos?"

The Aboth stared back in astonishment. "But—but you're…"

"I am Pe'akanu, king of the Khani'i. You are among the Hanu'ui of Rhai-Tuah," the huge man continued with a smirk of enjoyment, the dragon rubbing the top of its head gently against the man's hair just behind his ears. "You are enjoying my hospitality, and by the law of our people are therefore under my protection and care. Your wounds are serious, Master Meklos, but I am told will not threaten your life. Our shamans have dressed them with special salves, and while they are uncomfortable for the time being and will need care for some time, I am told you will heal."

"You—you understand our language?"

The man's laugh was deep and hearty. "What did you think? That I was going to eat you like a savage?" The big man turned at once to the assembled men around him, pointing with his wide fingers at the Aboth lying on the altar. *"Howleni be'anu Tuahni Hanu'uie."* The huge man began beating his chest with his fists, thrusting out his jaw as he spoke in a voice now even deeper and more gruff. *"Oranu kalapi!"*

The men surrounding the altar began to laugh, their weapons still swinging in rhythmic arcs through the air.

Pe'akanu held up both his hands as he continued to speak to the assemblage. *"Aku betarua oranu Kalapi! Aku moru'ea Howlena, kina e'hi ke'opu malakani—uru'u erue kelekarua!"*

The assembled men howled with laughter.

"What?" Meklos's eyes went wide. "What did you say to them?"

Pe'akanu leaned over the Aboth, his dark eyes gazing down, trying to come to some judgment about the pale man before him. "I told them that I must be a *generous* savage; that I've decided *not* to eat you because you are a guest of my house, and that would be in *bad taste!*"

Meklos tried to rally his strength, but his lower lip quivered as he spoke. "Any harm you do to me will be delivered a hundredfold on you and your tribe! I am an Inquis Requi of the Pir Drakonis; the hand and voice of the Dragonkings! You would be wise to—to release me at once or—or suffer the terrible weight of Satinka's displeasure!"

Pe'akanu's eyes narrowed, his face uncertain as to whether he had understood the Aboth's words correctly. Then he shook his head, his nose wrinkling as his lip curled. "My nation has been at peace since before your Pir Drakonis were even a thought. How considerate of the pale-skins from the Wide Land to bring their wrath and displeasure to our humble—if vastly older—nation. And how, then, shall we repay such a debt?"

Pe'akanu gestured to his men, and at his command the warriors swung their clubs high over their heads, stepping as one and pounding their feet against the stones underfoot. Each gave a great shout, their voices sounding a single harmony that echoed off the faces of the stones overhead. The small dragons that perched overhead replied with their own screeching cry, unfolding their wings and shaking them. The chanting of the warriors answered back, their dance moving around the altar as their polished weapons gleamed, trailing brighter tendrils of green vapors as they moved.

"The ways of the pale-skins are strange," Pe'akanu said as he considered the Aboth lying before him and then sniffed loudly. "You fear death yet visit it on your own kind; how barbaric! Tuahi Treijan and Gaius were brothers to my house; now they are missing, as is Tuahine Theona and, by all our eyes, at your hand."

"What are you doing?" Meklos demanded with a tincture of panic in his voice. "What are you doing to me?"

The dragons stretched out their wings overhead, launching into the dim space above the altar and forming a circle above the heads of the warriors.

The warriors spun and once more pounded their feet against the ground. They sang a single, glorious chord as their weapons swung level with the ground, pointing directly at the altar. The green vapors coalesced into a ring of green flame that whirled for a moment around Meklos before rushing into his body.

Blinding pain erupted from the wound in Meklos's back, tearing an involuntary scream from his lips. His sight left him for a moment.

"I will do the thing you fear the most." Pe'akanu stood back from the Aboth. He turned from the altar and stepped down to the floor, walking carefully between the increasing rhythms of the assembled guards as they danced and shouted their chorus around the hall. "I am going to drag your pale-skin into the light, Aboth Jefard. It will either heal your soul or destroy it."

King Pe'akanu stepped through the archway of the pyramid temple and into what should have been a beautiful dawn. The sky was brightening around the rim of the world as the stars faded overhead. Streaks of clouds coming in from the east were illuminated with a soft salmon color as the sun rose behind him. The tops of the banyan trees in which most of the village was built were just beginning to catch the rays of the sun, as were the Temples of the Sky, Sea, and Fire jutting above the roofs of the city spread before him, each shining gloriously above the jungle canopy.

On any other day the sight would have cheered him, but there was too much sadness in his heart, and this was a day of bad omen. Still, Pe'akanu dealt with it as he had dealt with the rest of life: he faced it with his eyes open and his jaw set. It was not in his nature to turn away from anything that life brought to him; he confronted the bad as readily as he reveled in all that was good.

Yet facing pain never made it hurt less—and he had one more duty to perform.

On the steps of the temple just a few feet below where he stood sat the slumping form of the woman whom Gaius called Valana. Next to her was the shivering form of Dregas Belas, who, it seemed, could not stop talking.

"Old Dregas would have knocked 'em demons dead sure as er is!" the dwarf said through chattering teeth. "Protect that lady and them lads, says I. I were true to Treijan and Gaius as er is! Like to die before I allow a hair to fall from their head, says I, till them demons took me by surprise."

King Pe'akanu knew it was a lie—knew that half of anything the dwarf said was a lie and that the half that *was* true was only true enough so that the lies would be more acceptable.

Still, Pe'akanu had to smile. No matter how traitorous was the crafty Dregas Belas, he still remained a dwarf to his very core. He was still wearing his formerly glorious hat, despite its having entirely lost its shape after a good soaking in the pool below the waterfall. Whatever happened beside the shores of Ahanu Falls—and after his interrogations of Dregas, Pe'akanu was still uncertain as to what *really* happened—the force of the event had not only flung the dwarf into the pool but, according to Dregas, skipped him across the surface until he finally plunged under at the foot of the waterfall. When his warriors found the dwarf, he was shivering in a shallow cave behind the face of the cascade, the brim of his hat having fallen down around his ears.

No, Pe'akanu mused, he knew what to do about Dregas—and that left him with one last concern.

"Lady Valana," the king called quietly.

The woman turned her head slightly, as though uncertain she had heard her own name.

"Lady Valana," the king repeated. "I am so sorry for this intrusion."

"So you do speak Rhamasian." The woman's head sank to her chest, then lolled to one side as though making an enormous effort as she answered. Her voice was lifeless. "Yet another surprise. Yes, I am here."

"I do not get to speak it much," the king said. "I was taught by Treijan and Gaius when first they came. It was no accident that they arrived here—the will of the gods drove their boat with a great wind and brought them to me with their language. I am King Pe'akanu of—"

"Where is my sister?"

The king paused for a moment. The woman's tone was demanding, and while he might have tried to soften his words for her, he knew from her tone that she would not be fooled. "We do not know. There was a battle in the jungle. Your fellow Meklos was badly injured. He was an enemy to Treijan. We believe they fought."

"And where are they now—Treijan and Gaius and— and my sister?"

"Told you already er is," the dwarf rumbled gruffly. "Crushed by them demons!"

"Silence, dwarf," the king commanded.

"But I *seen* 'em—through the water as I were struggling for my very life! All glowing in a huge soap bubble what collapsed in a clap of—"

"Keep silent!" Pe'akanu snapped as he gestured with his left hand. In the instant, Dregas choked, sputtered, and fell silent as he grasped at his throat. He sat gaping silently, looking to the king for all the world like a fish that had just been pulled from the water. The king turned once more to the woman.

"I am sorry, Lady Valana. No; we do not know where they are," Pe'akanu said.

The woman stood up slowly, her hands brushing down the front of her stained dress. "Look at it—ruined. It was all so pretty and neat and perfect, and now look what I've done to it. I've made a real mess of it—and I used to be really good at being me. Do you play games here?"

The king looked at the woman carefully. "I don't understand what—yes, we play many games."

"I was good at games," Valana mused through a sigh. "I certainly thought I had this one figured out. Now it seems I've lost—not just the game and not just the prince and my family's hopes but my own sister, my own..." Valana looked down again, her words caught in her throat.

"My warriors are still searching the jungle. They will come back with better news."

"Well, thank you, King Pe'akanu," Valana said, her eyes fixed on the ground at her feet, "but I've already looked. I saw the fallen trees by the waterfall, the shattered trunks, and the stripped leaves. It happened as the dwarf said; my sister is dead."

"And you believe Treijan and Gaius are dead with her?" Pe'akanu asked quietly.

She nodded. "Yes. And perhaps that is best for everyone."

Pe'akanu shook his head. "I tell you this cannot be. Your sister—Theona—is a great shaman, foretold by prophecy to be the Bringer of the Voice of the Gods."

"You believe my sister to have magic?" Valana eyed the king with a skeptical look.

"She was foretold by prophecy," Pe'akanu asserted. "She is the Bringer of the Voice of the Gods. She is the greatest of magics."

Valana laughed sadly. "You poor thing; you just don't understand."

"Then stay with us," Pe'akanu offered. "Learn of us and our ways. We do not have to be strangers any longer."

"No; each of us has our duties. I know where I must go and what I must do," Valana replied. "I have seen too much of the world, you know. I should have stayed at home and lived ever so much happier in my ignorance. Do you think it's possible, King; do you think I can go back and just forget what I know?"

Pe'akanu squinted in thought. He was not entirely certain what the girl was talking about, but he could hear the pain and sadness in her voice. "Treijan and Gaius established the mystic gate to our island. It is a secret which we have guarded for their sake and for our own."

Valana laughed bitterly. "And it is a secret which, I can assure you with my soul, I wish kept, too. I wish that I had never seen this place—never learned what I now know. I would make it all go away if I could. Indeed, it would be to my advantage if it *did* go away. No, Your Majesty,

I want this place kept secret more than Treijan himself. I just want to go home."

Pe'akanu nodded. He reached for the young woman's hands and took them up in his own. He reached to the bracers still clasped about Valana's wrists. His fingers ran up the bone carvings, following their lines in a pattern.

The bracers fell away into the king's hands.

"Then you must go home," Pe'akanu said.

"You're letting me leave?" Valana looked up in surprise.

"For your sister's sake, I will help you," he said, kneeling down and releasing the bone restraints on her ankles as well. "I send you home. War is coming."

"But the gate only leads to the dwarven ruins," Valana said. "How will I get out of—"

"The dwarf will guide you to Khordsholm village," Pe'akanu replied as he stood up.

The dwarf leaped to his feet, a broad grin splitting his bearded face. He adjusted the wrappings over his eyes in anticipation. "Aye! That I will sure as er is! Most kind of ye, chief, to let the past sleep as er is!"

"The dwarf will then return to me at once with both of these," Pe'akanu continued with some amusement as he placed the open bracers and ankle bracelets in Valana's hands. "Keep them from him until you are at the village gates. He is a liar—"

"I am most certainly not!" Dregas bellowed.

"You certainly are," Pe'akanu growled. "All dwarves aboveground are liars, criminals, or exiles—no dwarf chooses life in the dawn." The king turned back to Valana. "Do not listen to his twisting words and do not for any reason give these to him until you are at the city gate. Understand?"

Valana nodded, then looked at the dwarf suspiciously. "How can I trust that the dwarf will lead me to the city and not abandon me as soon as he is free of you?"

"I nay would do such er is!" Dregas sputtered in protest. "Brought you here in good faith, did I. Protected you from them demons, too, though none seems to believe a poor old dwarf, sad er is!"

"You are safe with the dwarf," Pe'akanu said easily. "Dregas leaves a token of pledge with me—a token I return when he gives Valana's bracers to me again."

"A hostage, eh?" The dwarf smiled. "Ransom for my return er is. Hard-bought freedom er is! Name the price, chief!"

"Your hat," Pe'akanu said easily, extending his hand.

The dwarf's smile fell at once.

"I think, Lady Valana, you will be safe," Pe'akanu said even as he gestured once more for the dwarf to give up his most prized possession.

"Yes," Valana replied, clutching the bracers.

"You can find a safe road home from Khordsholm, no?" the king asked.

"Yes—there is a man there who will help me," Valana said. "Thank you—for myself and my family."

"Lady Valana," Pe'akanu said, "Treijan and Gaius are wise. If we do not find them, then they will come to us with your sister. We may not know where your sister is, but they certainly know where *they* are!"

Narrow Visions

I <u>see</u> . . .

I watch as time cascades around me, a roaring river of sights and sounds rushing inexorably past, carrying me with them down years and centuries. The mountains, valleys, shorelines, and oceans remain the same in form, yet their surfaces shift and change between three realities—three truths of existence that come into my mind as a whole thought. I see the world of my ancestors and dragons soaring over the mountains. I see the surface shift, and the eagle-winged men now soar above those same peaks, while the moth-winged creatures flit about impossibly tall towers of delicate workmanship that had appeared at the mountains' base. And again I see those same mountain peaks and valleys shift once more, suddenly barren of forest or growth, while huge metal skeletons tread the land, their footfalls sounding like thunder across the desert. I see the magic—the Deep Magic—pulling at the worlds, drawing their realities closer together.

I see worlds in collision. Three incarnations of our own world sliding inexorably together as the magic pulls each manifestation of reality—each separate history, each wildly different creation bound together on a single world—in a creation-sundering cataclysm. I am the creatures from my dreams: I am the beautiful winged being, the four-hoofed half-man, the eagle-winged warrior, the brutish giant, and the green demon. I am the kraken, the dragon, and the water-folk. I am each of the three worlds collapsing before the gods as the force of Deep Magic draws us toward our mutual destruction.

I am the cities merged catastrophically into one another. I am the wife weeping out of fear for her lost children. I am the winged warrior flying into battle in a cause he knows is hopelessly lost. I am the demon lying with legs crushed beneath my own metal monster.

I am the battles of the Binding of the World.

I am the end of the worlds.

I scream in revulsion from the vision, turning my sight away from it. The vision shatters into ten thousand shards spinning round me in a cloud of shifting colors and sounds.

A voice comes into my head, and though it is calm and quiet, its words still pierce the terrible noise around me.

"Closer, child," says the voice. "All things are possible. Look closer to your heart."

I turn my eyes toward the cascading colors around me. The shards coalesce into a vague pattern, then suddenly resolve into a new reality. I stand in darkness next to a road that runs from all of yesterday. The road forks in the now, running in two directions far into tomorrow, and a figure stands at the point of divergence.

The ground around the road keeps shifting—from the jungles next to the waterfall to the black walls of the dead city to the dry grasses atop barren hills. With each change the figure changes, too. I see Treijan standing on the road next to the jungle pool, then the white-haired winged woman in her dark hall, and finally a short green demon-creature—also a woman, I think—who stands on the hilltop.

"Closer, child," says the voice again. "It is your gift, child, to see."

I look at Treijan as he stands facing the two roads. I, too, look down those roads, further than he can see.

I see a wedding. Treijan takes a woman by the hand and smiles reassuringly. I cannot see the bride, but I notice her tears fall silently on the paving stones beneath them. I look beyond them down the road, and I see—

I look away. I refuse to consider such a future and reel my sight quickly back to the junction. Confused and desperate, I look down the other road.

There I see a funeral. Valana is there, resplendent in her mourning gown. Father and mother are with her as well, and the hall is filled with the masters of all the mystic guilds. Then I look further, beyond the funeral. I stand then at the back of my father's house, overlooking the river. The city is in flames, the towers of the temple falling as metallic giants push through the stones. My vision is pulled forward unbidden, the world is in flames, and the mystics have fallen. There are none left to hold the world together—and the gods weep at the utter destruction of creation!

I stand, breathless with despair, once more at the crossroads.

I have seen—and am lost for what I saw.

*I gaze up into the stars overhead. "What am I to do?
I have seen and do not know how I can live with what I
know!"*

*"It is your gift," comes the voice from the stars. "It is
for you to know and to see. It is up to your own wisdom
how you use this sight — for the greatest road is never the
easiest, and few would take it if they knew the price of
the way."*

DIARY OF THEONA CONLAN, VOLUME 3, PAGES 56—59

"Theona? Theona, wake up!"

Theona awoke with the sensation that she was floating on a cloud. She might have considered drifting back
to sleep if it had not been for the terrible dream she had
just experienced. She forced her eyes open. She answered
tentatively, "Yes?"

She found herself looking into a handsome face with
a carefully trimmed beard. "Yes? Prince Treijan! Are you
all right?"

The prince laughed. "Much better now, thank you.
I've had my little sleep, and now I'm fine. Can I help you
up?"

"Oh, yes, thank you, I . . ." Theona's voice trailed off as
she sat up and looked around her, the sight that filled her
eyes robbing her at once of words.

She was sitting next to Treijan on a couch that seemed
to grow straight out of the ground, its supple branches and
leaves weaving themselves to conform to her as she rested.
The couch grew in the center of a circle of soft grass, from
which white paths inlaid with intricate patterns of tiles
ran between the most magnificently manicured gardens
she had ever seen. Tall fronds ending in cobalt-blue flow-

ers swayed in a gentle breeze above beds of brilliant yellow, orange, and red. Short hedges whose branches were shaped to create neat square edges bounded the paths. Nearby, a stream of crystal-clear water tumbled over a bed of river stones, winding its way under the arch of a bridge of pink coral. Beyond, Theona caught her breath at the sight of enormous white tree trunks rising at precise intervals as though the columns of a Rhamasian cathedral, their bleached branches splaying outward at their tops to form a lattice of arches overhead. Through them streamed shafts of sunlight.

"It is called Dwynwyn's Garden," Gaius explained as he approached from the path, his own face turning as he tried to take it all in.

"Who?" Theona asked.

"The winged woman whom you saw descending. Do you remember her? I think you may have fainted right about that time. It was a good thing the centaur was nearby to catch you, since—"

"Wait," Theona said, holding up her hand. "I know you're speaking Rhamasian, but I'm just not following you."

"Small wonder," Treijan said, patting her hand comfortingly. "There's a good deal more language that we'll all need to learn. Go on, Gaius, start from the beginning."

Gaius was eyeing the prince strangely but knelt down on the grass before Theona. "What do you remember?"

"We followed that winged fellow into the black hall." Theona spoke haltingly as she gathered the memories in her mind. "He was carrying Prince Treijan at the time. Then he went over to a pair of—I don't know—pedestals of some kind, and the next thing I remember is two more of the winged creatures flying down from the darkness above."

"That's right," Gaius said. "Anything else?" he prompted.

"Yes," she replied. "You said that you knew her—but how is that possible?"

"It's amazing," Gaius said with some wonder and excitement in his voice. "Indeed, the fact that it *is* possible may cause a lot of mystic scholars to rethink their teachings."

"Gaius knows her from the *dream*," Treijan interjected. "She is his partner in the Deep Magic."

"But—but I thought that they were only, you know, hallucinations or visions or—" Theona suddenly stopped.

I see worlds in collision. Three incarnations of our own world sliding inexorably together as the magic pulls each manifestation of reality—each separate history, each wildly different creation bound together on a single world—in a creation-sundering cataclysm.

"She is from another world," Theona murmured in wonder.

"What?" Treijan asked in surprise.

"Not another world but..." She struggled with the words. It had been so clear to her in her vision, a complete concept. But now that she was here, in the waking world, she was finding words too limiting to explain what she knew. "Another version of our world."

"Are you sure you're all right?" Gaius asked, his eyes narrowing in concern.

"Yes, I-I'm fine," she answered quickly. "Please go on."

"Well, apparently, the creatures we meet in the dream are no mere spirits or phantoms," Gaius continued. "For most of my life I have met this same woman in the dream, and together we've worked my magic. I drew the power of my Deep Magic through her, and, I suspect, she has done the same here."

"So where do you believe we are?" Theona asked.

Gaius grinned.

"Tell her," Treijan chided.

"We are in the kingdom of Sharajentis, enjoying the hospitality of Queen Dwynwyn," Gaius replied happily. "She sends to you her greetings and wishes that you get well, by the way."

"She—can you understand her speech?" Theona asked in amazement.

"It turns out," Treijan added, "that he cannot understand a word of the incredible melodic language that she or any of the—what do they call themselves?"

"Faery," Gaius said.

"Yes—does not understand a word that these faery speak, except for his companion in the dream, Queen Dwynwyn. It seems that when the two of them are in the same place, her words reach him through the dream, and he can understand her perfectly. I understand the two of them have had quite a chat over the last few hours."

"Yes, we have," Gaius said. "And it would seem that we are in the position to help each other out quite nicely."

Soft Words
and Silence

Magnificent, isn't it?" Gaius exhaled his words with pride. Theona stood next to Gaius in the great courtyard surrounding Dwynwyn's tower beneath the iron-gray sky and shuddered. She could barely bring herself to look upon the hideous device. It was a wide oval, its appearance much in the manner of a Songstone gate from the temple in Calsandria, but it was frighteningly larger—nearly forty feet across at its widest point—and had partially been built by Dwynwyn's skeletal stoneworkers. Theona had come to realize these last few days that the dead had their own sense of what constituted architectural art; the polished onyx of the vertically mounted oval was shaped into what looked like grinning skulls with tendons connecting bones and rotting tissue. It revolted her, and yet she knew, as Gaius and Treijan had described it to her, it was their only means of getting home.

Around Theona and Gaius and all across the vast

courtyard surrounding the tower, the refugees of Shara-jentis moved with purpose, organizing their goods into particular positions—each according to some hierarchy that Theona did not understand—as they prepared for the opening of the gate just six days away. It looked like chaos to her, but Gaius assured her that the plan—commanded by the Queen of the Dead—was moving forward as expected.

"So this is your plan," Theona said with an edge of skepticism. "You're going to bring their entire nation through this gate into our world?"

"You've got to admit, it solves both of our problems," Gaius replied. "These Sharajin, as they call themselves, have no other escape from destruction at the hands of their enemies—and it's our only way to get back."

"But why *our* world?" Theona said with concern. "Why not build a gate to another part of their own world and just let them—"

"Of all people, Theona, you should know that gates don't work that way." Gaius laughed. "We would need to physically travel to the place first in order to establish the linked gate, and I certainly doubt that these Kyree warriors they keep telling us about would allow two wingless bards to just walk through their battle lines. The fact is that Arryk was having a terrible time getting the gate to settle on any place in particular until Treijan showed him how to use the Songstones to link to a gate in our own world. He couldn't even get the ring to hold together until Treijan showed him the working of the Songstone. It turns out that his magic and ours worked well together—now this Songstone gate passes not only through space but apparently across the dream-realms to our own world as well."

"The gates are linked with a Songstone?" Theona asked.

"Yes. It was the only way to establish a stable corridor."

"Then where will they appear?"

"Back on the island of Rhai-Tuah. That's where the gate linked to this Songstone is located, and we thought it best that they enter our world somewhere out of the way so that their appearance wouldn't start a war in our world as well as— Theona? Are you feeling well?"

The color had left Theona's face. She had seen this path. She knew its end. "Yes, I'm fine," she said, shaking her head slightly. "It looks like the prince is having a little trouble with the—what did Arryk call it?"

"The rift-gate?" Gaius said, looking toward the onyx ring standing above the base.

Treijan and Arryk, the faery who had come and pulled them out of one world and into another, were standing before the gate, their hands in almost continuous motion as they spoke in apparently heated conversation. Next to them stood Dwynwyn, the faery Queen of the Dead, who appeared more frustrated by the moment.

Gaius laughed. "I suppose I need to get back there and help the queen understand what's going on. I guess being partners in the dream doesn't exactly guarantee that you'll get along personally. Ever since Treijan discovered that Arryk was one of his partners in the dream—well, they haven't stopped arguing since!"

"Arguing? About what?" Theona asked as she watched them.

"Well, a lot of things," Gaius said through a thin smile. "Partly about the gate and how it's going to be used, but mostly about their third, demon partner."

"But I thought you said that Arryk and Treijan are linked partners."

"Actually, they're part of a triad."

"A what?"

"A group of three," Gaius continued. "Some connections through the dream are simple pairs; one connection between two mystics—though we never understood before now that there actually *was* another mystic on the other side of the dream. But with Treijan and Arryk it's a bit different; there's a third entity involved—that little demon-creature they both talk about."

"Then there are three fates bound together," Theona murmured. "Three worlds—"

"What did you say?"

"Gaius, please," Theona said quickly, looking anywhere but at the wide ring that seemed to have grown deformed from the stones of the vast courtyard under their feet. "I need to talk to you."

Gaius turned toward her, and his sharp eyes softened. "Of course. What is it?"

Theona felt uncomfortable. "Don't you think it odd that your partner in the dream is found so close to Treijan's? I mean, out of the thousands—maybe hundreds of thousands—of mystics in both our worlds, that your companion's partner should just happen to be in counsel with yours?"

Gaius frowned. "Yes, that has occurred to me. There is a theory of the Deep Magic that claims such coincidences between mystics is evidence of the Deep Magic rearranging events that have already happened to bring about the desired results in the present. It is a rather complicated and confusing idea having to do with the Deep Magic existing outside of the flow of time, but basically, the idea is that 'coincidences' are arranged as a side effect of the Deep Magic."

"Or could it be something else arranging these coincidences?" Theona asked. "Someone with a purpose..."

The sound of a sighing melody drifted around them, conjuring in Theona's mind visions of flowers on a warm spring day. She wanted to close her eyes and get lost in the senses that the sound conjured but turned instead to the harmonious voice approaching them from the gate.

"Yes, Your Majesty?" Gaius answered, bowing slightly before Queen Dwynwyn, who now hovered in the air before them.

Again the faery queen spoke, this time with her eyes fixed on Theona, and her voice conjured the smell of autumn rains. Theona could almost picture brooks tumbling softly as they carried fallen leaves down their courses.

Gaius turned to Theona with a gentle smile. "Her Majesty has a question for you, Theona. The Fae, she says, live in the now, while the 'giftless'—humans—seem to live either in the past or in the future. Her Majesty wishes to know where you live—in your yesterdays or tomorrows?"

Theona gazed up into the large eyes of the dark-skinned faery, who returned the look without guile or malice. Theona glanced at Gaius as she spoke. "Please tell Her Majesty that I am only a common woman; I don't have any—"

Theona stopped, for she *saw* the faery queen in her mind and the paths before her.

"She has not decided, then, whether to trust her nation to the rift-gate?" Theona asked Gaius.

"She has not," Gaius answered in surprise, "though for

the life of me I do not understand why. Her people would be more than welcomed by the empire."

"Gaius, things are never so simple as they seem. Tell Her Majesty that I see two roads before her. One is clear, certain, and short; the other has an end that is beyond sight, shrouded in fog and unknowable. There will come a time when she must risk everything on the unknown or abandon her people to certain destruction."

Gaius stood looking at Theona in amazement.

"Go on! Tell her."

"I—I have," Gaius said with a curious smile as Dwynwyn bowed deeply and drifted back toward her tower.

Gaius shook his head. "Theona, you are a remarkable woman."

"No, Gaius," Theona scoffed. "I am entirely common."

"I doubt that," Gaius said, offering her his arm.

Theona stared at it for a moment. She understood the gesture and, to be truthful, had dreamed of it more than once as a younger woman. But she had long ago given up any real hopes. So she stood for an instant in wonder. And then she caught the uncertainty in Gaius; she realized that he might withdraw his arm in awkward disappointment, so she slipped her own arm in his, blushing a little as she did.

He led her across the cobblestones of the courtyard, away from the horrific gate and any thought of it. "Would you like to go back to the garden?" he asked.

"Oh, no, please." Theona laughed darkly. "Its beauty is somehow as terrible as the horror out here."

"I know what you mean. Strange, isn't it; to think that you and I could be walking here so easily—in a place that exists beyond our dreams?"

"Dreams somehow made real," Theona agreed.

"You may be right at that. Did you know that I had heard of you in Calsandria?"

Theona grinned ruefully. "I can only *imagine* what you might have heard about me there. The talentless daughter from the House of Conlan—I've no doubt you heard plenty."

"I did, indeed, madam," Gaius returned easily. "I heard that you were exceptionally bright—"

"And unreasonably stubborn—"

"I believe I heard it as 'single-mindedly determined' as well as 'extraordinarily capable.'"

"Cold and distant?"

"Well, perhaps once or twice, but I did hear that you were also 'strikingly handsome.'"

Theona looked away, uncomfortable. "You shouldn't believe everything you hear. They were no doubt referring to a different Conlan."

Gaius reached across with his free hand, placing it over her fingers where she still held his arm. "I have danced with your sister, Theona. She was everything I thought she would be and not a single blessing coin more. So it was you I was hoping to meet."

"I'm a commoner, Gaius," Theona said carefully, embers of hope in the depths of her soul.

Gaius shook his head. "The shamans of Rhai-Tuah would tell you otherwise. But even without them, I can tell you that there is nothing common about you."

She stopped and turned to face him. "Oh, Gaius, I—"

She looked into his face and saw the roads before him; the precarious, knife's-edge difference between his paths. The terrible consequences of his choice. She saw him falling and his fall bringing down the walls of Calsandria. She saw him ruling the empire.

"What is it, Theona?" Gaius's face mirrored her own concern.

"I—Gaius, oh, dear Gaius," Theona said haltingly as tears welled up in her eyes. "I know things—*see* things—things that are going to happen—things that *may* happen. I can see our futures, Gaius!"

"Theona, I don't understand."

"What would you do," Theona asked, her voice catching as she spoke, trying to bring her emotions back under control, "if you knew what was to come? What if you knew that the best course to take would cause pain to someone you cared about? What if saving them would destroy everything you held dear? Would you warn them and risk losing the entire world for their single life? Would you let them go gladly—oblivious to the fact that their sacrifice would save other lives? Could you choose between one life and another?"

Gaius gazed intently at her, but she could see no answer in his eyes.

"Please, Gaius," she sobbed. "Tell me what to do! I don't know how to choose! I *can't* choose..."

Gaius reached out and folded her into his arms. She rested her head against his chest and knew that this, perhaps, was the only answer he could give her.

Meklos Jefard tried to straighten as he stood, but the pain in his back forced him to hunch over. It was still difficult for him to move; the slightest wrong motion, and the pain would take his breath away.

"What have you done to me!" he railed.

King Pe'akanu looked down at him, his arms folded across his chest. "We healed you."

"Healed me!" the Aboth screamed. "Look at me, you great, backward oaf! I'm a cripple!"

In a flash the back of Pe'akanu's hand smashed across Meklos's face and tossed him backward against the altar stone. The Aboth slid down the carved face to sit on the floor, stunned. Then the hatred filled his eyes, and he pushed himself up on his feet with a cry of rage—

Only to suck in air against the incredible pain that overwhelmed him. He pitched forward onto the stone floor of the temple, quivering.

Pe'akanu reached down with his massive hand and pulled Meklos to sit upright, his back resting against the altar stone. When the king spoke, it was with quiet, measured words. "I say we heal you—not make you well. The wounds in your body, we mended. The bones, we made whole again. The tissues, we united. The blood now runs in your veins again. Your body is healed."

"I'm in *pain,* you idiot!"

Pe'akanu shook his head. "Your body well—it is your soul that dies."

Meklos's eyes narrowed. "My soul? I serve the Dragonkings—the gods incarnate! What could you possibly know about my soul?"

"What do you know about dragons?" the king scoffed. "We live with dragons; we serve dragons, and dragons serve us in balance. I know your ways, Meklos of Jefard!"

The king stepped back to a carved dragon at the edge of the altar and pulled forth an object that had been leaning there in the shadows.

Meklos gasped.

It was his dragonstaff.

"Your soul rages. You cannot control your spirits

within your body, so you need *this* to force others to your will." The king stepped boldly toward Meklos, holding the dragonstaff in front of him, the Eye shining even in the dim light of the temple chamber. "You need this—this crutch to compel the great spirits, and they rebel against you, Meklos! They are fighting you and calling the gods' displeasure against you. Your life is diminished by the length of this rod!"

"Give it to me!" Meklos yelled. "Now!"

King Pe'akanu glanced at the staff with disdain, then tossed it casually toward the Aboth.

Meklos snatched the staff from the air, deftly whirling it in his hands, pointing it menacingly at the king.

Pe'akanu stood with his fists slowly settling on his hips.

Meklos's eyes widened—he shook the staff.

Nothing happened.

"See? Your soul dies," Pe'akanu said simply. "You carry your demons inside you—bad and poison spirits. You think your demons are pearls you cannot live without; you think your demons give you life, but they are heavy stones dragging you into an ocean of death."

Meklos held up the bracers on his forearms in front of the king's face. "Take these off, or I'll show you an ocean of death!"

Pe'akanu sighed. "I cannot take them anymore. Only you can remove them."

"What are you talking about?" Meklos's eyes narrowed. "How?"

"*You* must let go," Pe'akanu whispered.

"Let go? Let go of what?"

"Let go of pain," Pe'akanu said as he straightened up.

"Let go of demons. Let go of fear. Let go of the past. Let go of hate."

Meklos grimaced. "I *need* my hate."

"You think without hate you will vanish? Your demons are very powerful, indeed." Pe'akanu sighed, then turned his back on the Aboth.

"Come back, you coward!" Meklos shouted, then grimaced again against the pain shooting up his back.

"Or what?" Pe'akanu sneered. "You try to master everything outside because *inside* you master nothing. The house-dragon hatchling never flies until it lets go of its roost and trusts the wind. *You* never fly until you let go and trust the wind."

Pe'akanu looked upward. "Atop this temple at the end of the Thousand Steps is the Voice of Rhai-Kuna—a great horn that faces the fire-mountain at the heart of our island. When the Hanu'ui are in need, I will climb the stairs and sound the Voice, and Rhai-Kuna—the great dragon of the mountain—will aid us. Rhai-Kuna will come when he hears the Voice because the Hanu'ui honor him and all dragonkind with balance and respect—*not* because of some glowing stick shaken by a frightened, dying soul!"

Pe'akanu turned and walked out the square doorway of the temple without looking back.

Theona sat on a coral bench in the midst of Dwynwyn's Garden, indifferent to the perfect beauty that surrounded her.

"Theona!"

She lifted her chin at the sound of her name coming from a distance.

"I am here, Your Highness," she answered back, though the words were as dry as sand in her mouth.

Prince Treijan bounded toward her, his handsome face smiling and seemingly carefree as he moved between the pristine shrubs and flowers. His beard had grown somewhat unkempt in the last few days, but his eyes were brighter and more cheerful than ever. "And so you are, Mistress Conlan!" He turned to look back down the path. "Gaius! Hurry up! I've had a brilliant notion today, and I want you here to witness it!"

Gaius, looking somewhat more tired than usual, was coming up the same path at a more leisurely pace. "If it is indeed brilliant, then someone *must* witness it or no one will believe it came from you."

Treijan tossed back a half-mocking "Ha-ha" and then sat next to Theona on the bench. "I've been thinking about this all day. We'll all be returning soon—back through this rift-gate thing to our own world—and returning to all the problems that we left there."

"Please, Your Highness, I—"

"Now, you must let me finish, Miss Conlan," Treijan said almost breathlessly, "or I'll never get it all out. I've been thinking all day as we worked on that strange gate of how I have hidden my—well, my weakness for so long. Gaius has stood beside me through all the years, but the intrigues of court and the changes in the empire over the years have only made things worse. Should the other clans discover my weakness, it would easily provide the excuse they need to bring down my house and a good many other houses as well. Chaos would reign; the various houses would tear themselves apart trying to control the Council of Thirty-six. Gaius and I have had to spend more and more time away from Calsandria just so as not to risk exposing my weakness—and no doubt my father arranged the marriage into your house in order to strengthen our claim to rule."

"Your Highness," Theona said, shaking her head sadly, "Valana well understands that the marriage is political. She is bound by her duty to our house and is certainly willing to—"

"But I am not!" Treijan said brightly.

"You—you are not what?"

"Willing to marry your sister."

"Which, as I recall, was the whole point in our vanishing act," Gaius said from where he stood on the path. "I was supposed to kidnap you, and the whole deal with House Conlan could be tossed aside."

"But not anymore," Treijan replied through a resolute smile. He turned back to Theona, suddenly picking up her hand. "I know how Valana reacted when she saw me— well, when she saw me *that* way. She was horrified and fled—just as I've always expected and dreaded. Yet *you* stayed, Theona. When Gaius was rendered unconscious by Meklos, *you* alone remained at my side, helped me, and protected me."

"Your Highness, I—"

"Will you marry me, Theona?"

Theona blinked, and then her eyes softened as she looked into his eyes. She glanced at Gaius, whose face looked fallen to her. She turned back to Treijan and slowly shook her head. "No, I am sorry."

"Nonsense! Of course you will!"

"But I do not love you, Prince Treijan."

Treijan's smile dimmed slightly, and for a moment Theona knew she could see disappointment in his eyes. "Not now, I know, but I can live with that. Perhaps in time you will grow to love me. In the meanwhile our union solves both of our problems. I could not marry your sister; I could never trust her to keep my welfare in her heart. But both of our houses need this alliance. Do you not feel the same duty to your house that your sister did? Don't you see? This is the only way we can return home."

She saw his paths as she looked into his eyes. She saw him saved, she saw him dead . . . and she saw the ends to which each road led.

"Yes," she replied, her eyes cast downward. "I see a great deal."

"Theona, say that you'll marry me," Treijan implored again, his smile urging her response. "We're all going back to our world—to Rhai-Tuah and my self-imposed exile. But *this* is the only way I can return all the way home and hope to have a life."

Theona drew in a deep breath. "It is the only way you will return to Calsandria?"

Treijan nodded. "Yes. I am adamant. I can only return with you as my wife. We'll hold the ceremony right here—here in this incredible garden—so that none of those courtiers can possibly get in our way. So what is your answer?"

Theona looked up at Gaius, and their eyes met. "Gaius, do you have anything you wish to say about the prince's proposal?"

Gaius returned her stare for a moment and then looked away, his face a mask. "No, Theona. The prince's plan seems most advantageous both to the empire and to you both."

Theona turned sadly back to Treijan. "Then, Your Highness, I must accept."

31

Realm of the Gods

Lunid looked down from the hilltop and drew in a shuddering breath. There had never been such a sight in the history of all the goblins, and she was having trouble controlling her emotions.

The rolling plains around the city of Og—from the Sunrise Mountains to the east to the Sunset Mountains on the west—were covered by an encampment of unprecedented size. As far as the eye could see, the ground was obscured by the makeshift tents and lean-tos of the various army divisions. Uncounted columns of smoke curled into the air above the wide Ogre Home valley in numbers so great that they looked like the trunks of trees from some fantastic forest. Numerous foundries and smithing buildings had been cobbled together to the east of the gully below Lunid, their metal roofs looking for all the world like overbaked slices of miller's bread under the setting sun.

It was, however, the phalanx of titans—more numerous than had ever been gathered in one place in all the history of the goblins—that moved Lunid the most. Their towering masses dwarfed the camps about their feet. The metal on their broken heads still gleamed with fiery brilliance, their banners flapping gloriously in the dying light of evening long after the valley had fallen under the shadow of the western mountains. There were hundreds of the ancient titans standing in rows and all of them facing toward that which brought them here—Lunid's rift-gate.

It was the largest device ever constructed by goblins from their own design. At least fifteen titans—an enormous expense all on its own—had been cannibalized to create the basic structure of the ring itself. It was their interlocking arms and legs that formed the foundation ring of the rift-gate, a circle which lay in the ground almost one hundred feet across. Then there was the matter of the hundreds of books affixed to it in order to bring life to the creation—a mind-boggling expense which induced several of Dong Mahaj Skramak's Ministers of Wealth to resign no fewer than seventeen times each in protest.

Looking down at the ring from her hilltop, Lunid wrung her hands in nervous anticipation. Things had gotten completely beyond her control. It felt like she had been walking down a gentle slope only to find that it was getting steeper and steeper until she was sliding unstoppably toward a cliff.

The thing was, she was enjoying the slide. There was something exhilarating about it. And, in a way, it was comforting to know that she had no power over what was going on around her. With events entirely out of her hands, she reasoned, so was any responsibility for what was happening should anything go wrong.

"Well, my dear Lunid," came the familiar voice behind her. "Is everything ready?"

Lunid turned and bowed so deeply to Skramak that she nearly lost her balance. "Y-y-yes, Your—Your M-m-m—"

"That's quite all right," Skramak said easily as he stepped closer toward her at the crest of the hill. He was followed closely by his gen-reel staff, their left-nats, and an entire cadre of drummers and trumpeters from the Shouters' Corps. All totaled, a group numbering over sixty goblins were suddenly marching on her space. "Have the technomancers followed your instructions properly?"

Lunid nodded. "Y-yes—th-thank you. W-we checked th-th-the main and s-secondary bus bindings th-this morning and did an im-m-magin' test this afternoon."

"An imaging test?" Big-funder Thwick hovered close behind the Dong and had become uncomfortably mixed in with the gen-reel staff. Lunid suspected that the Big-funder had a great deal riding on this project—perhaps the existence of the academy itself. "You mean you've already used it?"

"Y-yes, Big-funder," Lunid responded quickly. "I f-found the b-b-book, as Dong Mahaj Skramak commanded. It was in a place not unlike our House of Books and being studied there by the gods—although these gods were without wings. Do you think that matters?"

"Books, you said?" Skramak asked gleefully.

"Yes, D-D-Dong—"

"You may still call me Skramak, Lunid," the one-eyed warrior replied easily. "I'm your friend."

The Big-funder shot a warning look toward Lunid.

"Y-y-yes, S-skramak," the Deep Tinker replied.

"Then you are ready to open your—what did you call it?"

"Rift-gate, Skramak," Lunid answered. "Yes, I think it should work just fine."

"Excellent." Skramak nodded with a wide, sharp-toothed grin. "Gen-reel Piew!"

"Yes, Lord Skramak!" The gen-reel strode forward from the group, apparently waiting for this moment.

"You will bring the first two groups of six titans and set them on either side of that rift-thingy down there," Skramak said, pointing toward the gate down the slope in front of them. "Then place four phalanxes of our warriors—two on each side—and have them prepare for a defense."

"Defense, my lord?" The gen-reel sounded insulted.

"Our learned Deep Tinker tells me that this technomantic gate will allow us not only to step into the realm of the gods but to return from it as well, is this not right, Lunid?"

"Why, y-yes, Your—Skramak."

Skramak turned back to face the gen-reel behind him. "Therefore, Gen-reel Piew, I want to ensure that the only thing stepping back through this gate is titans and goblins. If anything *else* should attempt to come through the gate, they must be stopped and stomped flat. The idea is to invade the realm of the gods—not to give them the means of invading us. Is that clear?"

"Uh, not entirely, lord," the gen-reel responded.

"Just do it, Piew! And make sure that your nin-coms in charge of the squads understand their signals! I'll wring the neck of anyone who so much as thinks about messing up our orders—including you, Piew!"

The gen-reel saluted by banging his fist on his chestplate and moving back among the Shouters' Corps. Within moments one of the shouters began banging his drum loudly, the beat a strange rhythm that rolled off the hilltop. The booming sound ended as abruptly as it had begun—only to be answered by identical booming from the camps at the foot of the hill. More drums took up the beat as the message rolled like thunder across the valley floor, but Skramak did not wait for it to end before he issued another order.

"Gen-reel Ekee!"

"Yes, my lord!"

"Signal three groups of titans through the gate as soon as it is open, followed by twenty groups of warriors. Make sure the lead titans are book-linked into your command. Once they have cleared the gate, take the remaining titans of the first cadre through the gate in double file, flanked by warriors from the remaining first battle group. And watch them to make sure they do as they are told. I don't want this battle to fall apart just because those titan drivers don't take our directions!"

"Yes, my lord!" Gen-reel Ekee saluted sharply by slamming his fist against his own breastplate, then turned to his own shouter—this one with a trumpet, which resounded almost at once with a complicated series of notes. He was still playing them when Skramak spoke again.

"Left-nat Gonz!" Skramak barked.

"Yes, Lord Skramak!" Lunid could see that the man was a technomancer by the strange hat he wore and the large, heavy book he was carrying. He had dragged three of the shouters up with him, each with its own unique brass instrument, in anticipation of the warlord's command.

"Get in touch with the gen-reels of each of the commands," Skramak shouted, trying to be heard over the din of drums and horns. "Put each of them on alert and make them ready to assemble. We'll be calling them through the gate in order of the battle plan, and I don't want any of them getting lost. Then tell the gen-reels—"

"Lord Skramak?" Lunid asked timidly. Two of the shouters next to her had already started blowing out these now coded orders, so Lunid was not sure if Skramak could actually hear her.

"Just a moment, Lunid," Skramak replied. "Tell the gen-reels to lead with the titans and follow up with the ground warriors in support. I want the troops with the advanced weapons mixed in with the clubs and knives, and if I have to explain *that* order to those idiots again, I'll—"

"Please, Lord Skramak." Lunid spoke loudly, tugging at the warlord's tunic.

Skramak snarled, turning on Lunid in a flash, his hand snatching up his dagger from its belt scabbard. Lunid cried out, dropping to the ground instinctively.

Skramak was breathing heavily, and there was still the spark of blind anger in his remaining good eye, but the blade remained poised in the air. "Lunid . . . never do that again," he said through quick breaths. "I'm very busy at the moment."

"I-I-I . . ."

"Relax, Lunid." Skramak sighed as he forced a smile back onto his face, slowly slipping the dagger back in its scabbard. By now several trumpeters and drummers were banging out orders and receiving reports for the gen-reels from the camps answering back. "Forgive an old warrior—what is it?"

"Y-your b-b-ba-battle p-plan . . ."

"Yes," Skramak snapped loudly with great restraint, "what about it?"

Lunid shouted over the booming of the drums and the blare of trumpets. "I've prepared a s-spe-special cage for the gods—one that will hold all of them, not just winged ones. I-I-I've sent it—sent it down to the gate for the—the nin-coms to take it through f-f-first thing."

"Fine, fine. Now, if you'll excuse me…"

Lunid gripped the warlord's sleeve. "But do all of your troops know w-what they are looking for?"

"What?" Skramak shook his head, not understanding over the din.

"Do they all know what Urk looks like?" Lunid yelled hoarsely, her eyes wide and watery. "You know, my winged god you said you would find for me—the reason we built the rift-gate!"

Skramak gazed back at her with his single eye and then caught his breath. "Ah! Yes, of course, they do! Everyone has been told exactly what this—er—"

"Urk," Lunid urged.

"Yes, what this Urk looks like and to report to me the moment this god is found," Skramak finished, his voice nearly screaming over the din of the war drums and the trumpets. "You just open the gate for us, Lunid. That's all you have to do. And you just leave the rest of it to Skramak."

"Are you sure?" Lunid asked hopefully.

"Believe me," he replied through a wide smile. "I know exactly what I am doing."

Deep horns resounded from the plain below them. Titans were moving down the ravine—Gen-reel Piew's set of six standing on either side of the dry riverbed, looking like an honor guard of skeletal, metal giants. At their feet moved several hundred goblin warriors, each of them leaping about in protest at not being allowed to enter the gate first. Nevertheless, their discipline held, and they stood facing the gate. Their drums began to beat a more constant rhythm in acknowledgment that they were in place, their long curved blades glinting in the reflected light from the titans next to them.

"It's time, Lunid," Skramak shouted. "Open it! Show us the way to the gods!"

Lunid nodded, closed her eyes, and held aloft her new control book. She had been working on it since the construction began and knew it was the most important part of the rift-gate. The gate itself was more brute force than elegance—just a larger version of what she had already done. The complex part, she knew, was not so much in calling out the power of the books as it was directing it. Her first attempt had been simply to capture and move, but now she would use it in a new way—by holding open the space as a tube rather than a ball.

Beyond her closed eyelids she could see him in the place of the gods. She smiled; her Urk was standing next to a gate. Perhaps he was waiting for her—

There was a sudden explosion of sound riding the wave of a terrible gust of air. Lunid opened her eyes.

The titans near the gate staggered backward, two of them toppling completely to the ground. The goblins were lying flat as though pushed away from the gate.

Above the circle an oval spun in the air. Through it Lunid could see the wingless gods suddenly look up from their examinations of her lost control book with shock and panic in their eyes. They began to run toward portals leading out of their House of Books, their cries rebounding off the shelves around them.

The first phalanx of titans walked forward, three across and seven deep. Their footfalls shook the dirt under Lunid's feet. They ducked slightly as they approached the rift-gate so that their great height might slip inside its bounds. In moments they burst through the rift-gate, their fists pounding against the tall stone walls of the building beyond. An unseen roof of stone collapsed on them on the other side, driving three of the titans down and burying them in debris. Yet the titans behind them barely took notice, stepping onto the fallen stones and through the now shattered wall.

Through the gate and beyond the titans Lunid could see dusk falling on a great city of stone walls and alien pyramid structures. Even as she watched, she could hear the cries of the gods drifting from one world to the next and onto Lunid's hilltop.

The last of the titans from the first phalanx were nearly through the gate when an explosion shattered the head of one of the titans in a greenish flame. The flame then coursed down the body of the ancient machine, eating the metal into gas wherever it touched. A second and third titan exploded as well, reeling backward from the gate and staggering toward the repair forges down the ravine.

"Forward the warriors!" Skramak screamed, and the shouters behind him sounded their horns at once.

The goblin warriors following the titans in tight ranks wavered for a moment at hearing the horns, wondering if they had understood them correctly. Nevertheless, they obeyed, charging into the gate, weaving between the staggering titans' feet and moving across the rubble of the building and into the enemy's street beyond.

Another titan charged back through the gate. This one seemed filled with some terrible sort of tentacle creature writhing within the breast of the titan and tearing it apart from the inside. The titan fell among the warriors, who immediately leaped on it, hacking at the tentacles with their swords and axes.

"Keep moving forward!" Skramak screamed as the horns behind him blared his commands. "Keep moving! We have to have a foothold or we die!"

The city beyond the opening began to burn.

Lunid wondered how Skramak would ever find Urk in such a mess.

Desperate Acts

Dwynwyn stood in the center of chaos, the refuse of her life strewn about her like a storm-tossed sea. There were crates and chests, bags and trunks adrift among stacks of books, clothes, papers, models, scrolls, slippers, cloaks, and crowns. Servant shades—spirits of the Sharaj who sought Enlightenment but who had never fully regained physical form except from the essence of shadows—spun like a gale above the debris, snatching up a glowlamp here or a tapestry there and packing it or unpacking it at the whim of the Queen of the Dead.

Peleron watched her quietly from the entrance to her private chambers. He had never before entered without her express permission, though he knew she would not have minded. It was a courtesy that he showed her—a quiet touch of his enormous respect for her. He had truly come to love her down the years they had been together, and today that love overpowered his courtly manners.

He saw that her rooms were in a higher state of pandemonium than ever before. Dwynwyn, he knew, had always preferred the subtle anarchy of the Seeker's life to the infinitely more ordered way of all the other faery castes. Order, it seemed, was inconvenient to her constant search for new ways of looking at something or of approaching a problem, a talent that set her caste apart from all others. Yet Peleron sensed that this was a different kind of disorder—the chaos of Dwynwyn trying to sort through what was important enough to bring with her into exile and what she would have to leave behind.

In the face of extinction the scales of value, it seemed to Peleron, had a different set of measures.

"Dwynwyn," Peleron called softly.

She looked up. He could see lines in the smooth dark skin of her face, the wide liquid look in her eyes. The shades stopped in their flight overhead, withdrawing as best they could into the corners of the room.

"Peleron! What is it?"

"Dwyn, I've just received a report from the city gate."

"Yes—and?"

"And they report that the stream of refugees has stopped," he said, choosing his words with care. "The Onyx Gate is closed and barred."

"There is more, isn't there?"

"Yes, Dwyn, there is more," Peleron said sadly. He looked away from his beloved queen for a moment before turning to gaze directly into her eyes. "The refugees have stopped coming because there are no more of them. Dekacian Skreekash and his Nykira Raiders have circled around our main forces in the south. They have cut the southern routes to the coast—not that the Argentei would allow us passage even if we could get there—and are sacking the port towns of Neceleros and Demeleos. The battle there was particularly heavy-fought, but in the end our necromantic warriors had far too much attrition. They were forced to abandon the towns and withdraw to the north in order to protect our flank."

"What of the wounded in the battle?" Dwynwyn asked. "Surely, even the dekacian will allow us to—"

"There were no wounded," Peleron said quickly.

"None? That cannot be. There are always—"

"There were *no* wounded." Peleron's voice was rising. "Nor were there prisoners, nor were there civilians, nor women nor children. The Kyree-Nykira dealt with everyone the same. Every faery, regardless of caste or station, was slaughtered with perfect equality."

Dwynwyn looked away.

Peleron spoke quietly again. "There will be no more refugees, Dwyn."

"That is not true," Dwynwyn said. "There will be us."

The Queen of the Dead seemed to Peleron to shrink a little from the cruelty of the world around her. Her roving eyes finally settled on her tiara crown. She picked it up, fingering its delicate latticework and inlaid jewels.

"You know, I liked this one the best," she said sweetly as she examined it. "I preferred to wear this one when I could get away with it. It was not as fancy or officious as my larger crowns, but I liked it all the better for it." She dropped the crown to the ground. "Now it's just a bauble. And I will probably leave it behind so that I might pack another loaf of bread."

"You'll find it better eating than the tiara," Peleron said with a small smile.

Dwynwyn nodded. "And the less I carry, the better. I suspect that the dead will not be able to pass through the gate to the other world. I am not all that certain that we will even find the Sharaj the same in this new world—although

Gaius hu-man seems to believe it is. In any event, it looks as though I shall have to deal with my own trunks."

"Well, you might pack a bit lighter."

Dwynwyn laughed, gesturing in the general direction of where the floor should be seen. "What? You mean this isn't light? I suppose you are already packed?"

"You forget, I am an old campaign warrior. I always travel light." Peleron stepped fully into the room. "Dwyn, our armies are in retreat. The only reason the Kyree are not charging the walls of Sharajentis as I speak is that they are too busy sacking and pillaging the towns we have abandoned. To throw away time now on a foolish ceremony—"

"No, Pel," Dwynwyn said at once. "I will not change my mind. Everything will be ready in time. Arryk will go through this magical gateway with the hu-mans and into their lands. The moment he reports it safe for us, we will move every remaining Oraclyn and Sharajin to this—this new country."

"And if it is *not* safe?" Peleron asked pointedly. "We'll need time to—"

"No, Pel," Dwynwyn said firmly. "If it is not safe, then a few minutes one way or the other will make no difference."

"But a wedding?" Peleron asked.

"It is what they wanted," Dwynwyn replied. "And it is what *I* want, my dear Peleron."

She gazed once more about her at the things in her life which rapidly were mattering less and less.

"I want my last act to be one of creation—not destruction," she said simply. "I want the last thing I do in our world to be a beginning rather than an end."

* * *

Rylmar Conlan sat at his long table, staring down its length at nothing in particular. He had seen his way through any number of disasters during his life, believing the old adage that whatever did not kill you made you stronger. Now, in the shock of realizing that all his plans had come to ruin and that the bill was paid for with the broken heart of one of his daughters and the lifeblood of the other, Rylmar no longer took comfort in platitudes and proverbs. All he knew was overwhelming loss and a vague, haunting suspicion of his own guilt that threatened to devour him.

With his blood pounding in his ears and his world contracted to barely include the table at which he sat, Rylmar did not hear the banging at the main door, nor did he notice that the house servant Agretha was speaking to him.

"Master Conlan!" The plump woman's voice shook, her hands wringing a cleaning rag into a knot. "Please, sir! There's someone at the door that must be announced!"

Rylmar looked up through watery, bloodshot eyes. "I am seeing no one. How stupid are you that you cannot understand even that simple—"

"But, Master Conlan, it's Lord Dirc Rennes-Arvad!"

Rylmar blinked, trying to focus on the servant. He was certain he had not heard her correctly. "What did you say?"

"I beg to announce Lord Dirc of House Rennes-Arvad, sir," Agretha sputtered. "He's—he's at the door!"

Rylmar stood, his mind racing. "Dirc? Here—at my door? He's come to *me*?"

"What am I to *do,* sir?"

"By all the gods, woman," Rylmar thundered, "admit him at once!"

Agretha seemed to squeak as she spun around, hurrying through the archway and past the ancient statue into the atrium beyond.

Rylmar sat down, stunned for the moment as his mind tried to engage in ways it had not since Valana had returned to Calsandria three days before. She had taken to her bed and had not come out since. She had spoken to the servants only as necessary and only cursorily to her mother. As for Rylmar, she had refused even to see him.

The news of Prince Treijan's death and the return of Valana had nearly coincided. Apparently, the Rennes-Arvads had kept secret the return of the prince's tally for several days, but in the end they decided it was better to announce it themselves than to have the news used against them by whatever spies moved among them. Valana's return, however overshadowed, had not gone unnoticed by the heads of the other families and certainly not by Rennes-Arvad. Rylmar assumed that his arrangements with House Arvad had died along with the prince, and expected Dirc to simply ignore him and let their bargain die silently or, at the least, to be summoned to the Arvad Keep so as to be lectured on the benefits of keeping one's mouth shut. But for the great Lord Dirc to present himself at Rylmar's door—this was something different, dangerous, and possibly profitable.

"Master Rylmar of House Conlan," Agretha said with a curtsy. "I beg to present Dirc of House Rennes-Arvad, Lord of the Empire and Master of the Council of Thirty-six!"

Dirc Rennes-Arvad stepped into the room. He was a tall man with closely cropped gray hair and the prominent cheekbones of his son. His eyes were bright blue fire under bushy gray brows, and his beard was trimmed after the manner of the bards. He wore a rose-colored doublet, beautifully embroidered under a short cape with bright golden braid draped in loops from his left shoulder.

Rylmar stood at once at the end of the table. "My Lord Dirc. You honor my house."

Dirc Rennes-Arvad continued down the length of the great room, extending his hand as he approached, and grasped the stunned Rylmar in the traditional, just-below-the-elbow grip. "My dear Master Conlan, I came as soon as I could. I trust you will forgive me these last few days, but, as I am sure you understand, my own household has been dealing with a loss as well."

"Certainly," Rylmar replied. "The loss of the prince . . . oh, Agretha! That will be all. I'm sure you have a great deal to do in the kitchen. Thank you."

The servant bowed deeply and disappeared back toward the atrium.

"My lord, may I offer you my seat?" Rylmar said at once, gesturing toward his own chair.

Lord Dirc smiled and shook his head as he deftly removed his cape and pulled out a chair at the corner next to Rylmar's. "No, thank you, this will do fine. Please sit. This is your house, after all." Lord Rennes-Arvad leaned back on the chair, his long legs stretching straight out under the table as he crossed them. "Ry, I am sorry for the loss of your daughter."

"I thank you on behalf of all my house, Dirc." The name nearly caught in Rylmar's throat—he had been in business long enough to know that too friendly was synonymous with too dangerous. "From what Valana tells me, Theona was with the prince and his friend Gaius when they both died."

Dirc nodded sadly. "Then I grieve with you."

"As all the empire grieves for the loss of the prince," Rylmar said. "His future was the future of us all."

Dirc smiled as he gazed at Rylmar. "His future was our future, Ry; the future of both our households."

"Much was lost that day," Rylmar agreed.

"But, perhaps..."

Here it comes, Rylmar thought.

"Perhaps, my friend, not everything is lost to us," Dirc said slowly, leaning forward until his arm rested on the table. "Perhaps, with a little effort on our part, much might be salvaged of the future that was lost to all of the empire."

"I should be honored, as always, to serve the empire," Rylmar responded with caution.

"As should we all," Dirc agreed eagerly, "but often one serves best who serves himself as well. The marriage between our houses would still help us both; you for the status you seek and I for the security of my house before an increasingly uncertain Council."

"Surely, you're not proposing that your younger son—"

"No, not at all," Dirc said quickly. "It will be some time before Prince Clyntas is old enough—let alone strong enough—to lead our empire. But how stable will the empire be by such a time? There are forces, Ry—powerful forces—that would like to bring down both our houses before the younger prince would ever have a chance to prove himself. But suppose—just consider the possibility for a moment—that your beloved Valana *had* married Prince Treijan?"

Rylmar returned the fixed stare of Lord Rennes-Arvad. "I do not follow you, my lord."

"Suppose for a moment," Dirc said slowly, "that while

your daughter was away searching for my son, the *kid-napped* Prince Treijan, she found him—as certainly she did—and that while she was there, she married him?"

"But, my lord—"

"Ry, please."

"But, Dirc—she didn't."

"Yes, perhaps—but suppose she did?"

"Well," Rylmar replied, "then she would have been impressed with Treijan's tally at the end of the ceremony. The tally would not have returned to you."

"Ah, true," Dirc responded at once, "but suppose—"

"Suppose?"

"Suppose that the ceremony was performed in this distant, strange land and the impressing of the tally did not take place?"

"If that were the case," Rylmar responded, "then—"

"Your dear Valana would be the honored widow of a martyred prince," Lord Dirc said quietly. "She would hold a place of privilege and be held in reverence by all of House Rennes-Arvad; indeed, by the entire empire."

"Your position on the council would be unassailable," Rylmar suggested.

"And the name of your house would be assured," Dirc finished.

Rylmar sat for a moment and then stood. "Dirc, the past is lost to us; all we can do is act for the future."

Lord Rennes-Arvad stood up. "So what do you say, then?"

Rylmar extended his own hand this time. "I say please extend the warmest thanks of House Conlan to all the empire on behalf of Valana Rennes-Arvad—widow of the fallen prince."

Beginnings
and Endings

The faery trumpets sounded across the city, a call to everyone who remained within the walls. From every doorway of every twisted building on every crooked street they came: the nobles and powerful Seekers of the Lyceum, the magicians of the faery world gathered together to face their doom within the walls of the city that had taught them and given them purpose. They flowed like tributaries into a great river, a drifting mass of the faery, their once ornate robes tattered and stained by their headlong flight from death.

They emptied into the great plaza surrounding Dwynwyn's tower, flowing to surround the gate. Each Oraclyn and Sharajin found their place above the cobblestones of the walled space, for order was the lifeblood of the Fae even in the face of destruction.

Treijan stood on the platform of the black gate next to Arryk, his eyes overlooking the gathering host with wonder. He spoke knowing that Arryk was the one faery who would understand his words. "I always expected a large audience for my wedding, but this is overdoing it, don't you think?"

"They do not come for your wedding," Arryk replied as the words of his musical voice turned to meaning in Treijan's mind. "They come to face the end of their existence or to follow us through the rift-gate."

Treijan chuckled in amusement. "Do the faery not have humor?"

Arryk raised his eyebrow beneath his long black bangs. "We laugh unceasingly when the joke is funny."

"I'll bet!" Treijan said with a smile, then turned to inspect the gate. Its black surface was shining despite the poor light coming from the leaden sky overhead. There was a repulsiveness to it, he thought, as though the gate were a tormented, organic thing. The creatures that had built it—the dead of this world, he shook his head in wonder—had molded the onyx stone into the shapes of veins, bones, organs, skulls, and stretched sinew. He could feel the power in it: the connection between it, the realm of mystic dreams, and his own world. There was only one piece missing, one last detail that would make the device complete. "Where is your friend the centaur?"

"He is here," Arryk responded, gesturing behind him.

Treijan looked over at the half-man, half-beast. "Does he know what to do?"

"Yes," Arryk replied, "he knows what to do."

"You realize there will be no turning back," Treijan said, looking once more at the gate.

"Yes, I know—and so does the queen."

"Very well," Treijan said, drawing in a breath and craning his head from side to side to loosen his stiff neck. "Let's get on with the wedding."

Valana held tightly to her father's arm as she walked down the aisle and wept.

The Guild Hall had been hastily assembled into what would pass for a temple, as there was no other single building in all of Calsandria which might contain the vast number of nobles, house lords, and councilors that were required to witness the occasion. Only the amphitheater would hold more people, but Dirc Rennes-Arvad had felt it too undignified.

At least, Valana thought bitterly, the old man had that much sense left in him—even if it seemed to have left him in every other way.

The assembly stood as she approached, bowing as she passed in their respect and silent condoning of her travesty. For their own reasons, Valana knew, they had accepted the insane lie they had been told, each finding it personally more convenient to believe the story rather than any actual truth.

What was the truth? The truth was, she had no choice in what was going on. Where was Theona? She always knew what to do; was always there to show Valana the path through so many decisions. She had simply always been there, like the floor that held you up or the roof that kept the sun and the rain at bay. You never notice the roof or the floor, Valana thought, until the ceiling vanishes and the rains pour on you or the floor disappears and you find yourself falling, falling toward a blackness that suddenly opens beneath you and you have nothing and no one to hang on to. She had always loved her sister, in her way and on her own terms, and had held out hope—a distant, dim hope—that she had been wrong: that Theona would be back at her side in a few days. But when Valana returned to Calsandria, the news awaited her that Treijan and Gaius were dead—their tallies returned to their families—and she knew that Theona had been with them both when it happened. Valana's world turned on its head, her father repeating a lie again and again in her ears until she could no longer stand to say no. Her duty, he said, was to her house and family; her duty was to the empire. Her duty was to live the lie for all of them.

So she walked down the aisle under the gaze of the wise and powerful in a beautiful black dress with a long black train and a black veil and wept uncontrollably. Those who watched her nodded in sympathy for the tears she shed for her dead husband, but she knew that, too, was a lie.

I am a widow, she thought, *and I've never been wed.*

The bride wore black. Her tears were her own.

Theona stepped out of the main doors of Dwynwyn's tower, her hands shaking so badly that she was afraid the flowers she held would come apart. She looked down at them suddenly, trying to calm herself. Her own clothing was stained and muted, traveling clothes that she had put on in Khordsholm so long ago and so far away. Her small bouquet, picked by the queen from her garden, was the only color in a world of gray and black.

Gaius stood next to the door and silently offered her his arm. She reached up and took it as she had just days before, but doing so only filled her with regret.

"Gaius?" she said as they started down the wide steps toward the gigantic plaza seemingly filled to the very walls with thousands of haggard-faced faeries.

"Yes, Theona," Gaius answered, his eyes fixed forward.

"Is this right?"

Gaius continued to walk with her at his side but did not answer her immediately. At last he said, "It is right for Treijan. It is right for the empire."

"It is right for my family," she said, her words an attempt at convincing herself as much as Gaius. She looked down once more at her quivering bouquet. "Tell me: why didn't you say anything? Why didn't you object?"

"It doesn't matter."

"It matters to me."

Gaius's words caught in his throat before he could continue. "I've served Treijan all my life. It's *been* my life. Can you understand that?"

Theona considered his words for a moment. It occurred to her that Gaius no longer knew the boundaries between his own life and that of Treijan. He had served him and sacrificed himself for so long that he could no longer tell where Treijan ended and Gaius began.

How is that any different from me? she thought. *I've given so much of myself away to my family. How could I not have kept anything of myself?*

"Yes," Theona answered, her eyes filling with tears. "Yes, I can understand."

They walked in silence for a time between the long ranks of faeries to either side of them. Theona looked up and saw Treijan standing at the base of the hideous gate. Queen Dwynwyn and Lord Peleron had joined him there, as had the faery Arryk, who had been responsible for their coming here to begin with.

Treijan beamed at her.

"Do you suppose he might have come to love me?"

Gaius sniffed and looked away. "I suppose, in time."

"And would I have come to love him?"

"I suppose, in time. What do you mean by 'have come'?"

Theona smiled sadly. "Dear Gaius, I want you to remember this: you might suppose, in time, that I would lose this feeling I hold for you, too, but you would be wrong. I will never forget you or how I feel about you. I will always cherish you in my heart. I do what I *must* for the sake of us all—for your sake, too—but that doesn't mean I wouldn't want things differently were my choices easier. Can you remember that?"

Gaius looked at her with pain and confusion in his eyes. "I haven't a clue what you're talking about, but I shall try to remember, Theona."

She nodded, then released Gaius's arm. A single tear rolled down her cheek as she stepped up onto the platform toward the outstretched hand of Treijan.

Valana sat in the front row of seats beneath the great dome of the rotunda. On the elevated dais stood a statue of Treijan, his hand outstretched toward the assembled crowd as though beckoning them to follow him. Around the neck of the statue was draped the prince's tally.

She hated the sight of it. It was the symbol of everything wrong in her life; the lie incarnate. The impressing of the tallies was the last act in the mystic wedding ceremony and seen as the binding moment of the ritual—replacing the exchange of masks, as was previously the custom. It was also the most glaring part of the lie, for a marriage was not considered completed until the tallies were exchanged. Yet she was about to participate in a mockery of that ritual, for Dirc himself would impress the tally on her in order to complete the wedding that never took place. It was a travesty, she thought, and an obscenity which she would be forced to perform in front of the entire empire.

Lord Dirc was coming to the end of his eulogy.

Valana gazed upward into the dome of the rotunda above her. It had not been so long ago that this same room had been filled with music and dance and magic. She had flown above it all, she recalled.

How had she come to this?

Dwynwyn stood before them, her voice filled with harmonies of spring rain and flowering meadows. Gaius stood stiffly at her side, translating as she spoke.

"Syldaran the Teacher walks before you, your acts on the journey binding you together in your knowledge of the perfect unity of Aelar—that your souls may be one in purpose, your minds one in thought, your hearts one in passion, and your path one of Enlightenment. In this covenant you are bound through all incarnations in your road of perfection."

Dwynwyn reached forward, grasping each of them by the right hand, and brought them together, then drew a long ribbon from her hair and dropped it over their clasped hands. Treijan smiled as the ribbon wound itself around their wrists, binding them together.

"From the head to the heart to the body," Dwynwyn proclaimed through the sad-eyed Gaius. "You are one."

Treijan looked up. "Is that it? Are we married?"

Gaius turned to Dwynwyn. "Are they married?"

The beautiful faery gazed back at them and smiled.

Treijan leaned over, but Theona offered only her cheek for his light, short kiss.

"I—I wish you hadn't lost your tally," Theona said,

fighting back tears. "I've dreamed of that moment all my life and now—now I can't even have that."

Valana heard her name echoing off the walls of the rotunda. Dirc had just called her to join him on the dais. *One last act,* she thought. *One last humiliation before they enshrine me as the mystic noble who married a dead prince.*

She stood up, stepping with a reluctance that might have been excused as being rightful mourning. At last she stood next to the statue of the beckoning Treijan and faced the crowd.

A deep horn resounded from a distance.

"We're running out of time," Gaius huffed. "Congratulations, you're married—now, can we get out of here while we're still alive?"

Treijan nodded, dropping Theona's hand as he moved quickly to the right side of the great black oval. He pulled from his pouch a single shining stone that shimmered brightly even under the darkened sky.

"Is this the Songstone?" Theona murmured.

"Of course," Gaius responded. "How else would we find our way back?"

Treijan placed the Songstone in its niche. The gate, completed at last, hummed with a thunderous noise that shook the stones underfoot, then the center of the oval flared into a blinding flash that subsided into an ultraviolet color difficult to look at directly.

"Is it supposed to look like that?" Uncertainty was reflected in Theona's voice.

"We're about to find out." Treijan smiled. "Arryk! Tell the queen that you and I are going through the gate first."

"I'm coming with you," Theona said at once.

"But if there's something wrong—"

"I'd rather be anywhere but here," Theona replied.

"And I'm not staying either, so you might as well just include us in your little pronouncement," Gaius added.

"Fine! Arryk, tell the queen that you are taking Gaius, Theona, and me through the gate," Treijan said. "If you come back through the gate, then they should follow. Understand?"

"Yes," Arryk responded, "but the centaur insists on coming as well."

"Anything! Let's just get going!"

Arryk turned to his queen and spoke in tones that reminded Theona of birds singing after a winter thaw.

Treijan reached out his hand. "Are you ready, Princess Theona Rennes-Arvad?"

"Yes," Theona said, accepting his hand. "Take me home."

Dirc was concluding the strange ceremony for the bride who stood before the empire in a black dress.

"And so, by the power vested in me as lord of House Rennes-Arvad, and invoking the names of Hrea, Goddess of the Heavens, that her blessings may be upon this union and of Thelea, Goddess of the Harvest—"

Someone coughed nervously. The blessing of Thelea was a blessing of fertility.

"I seal this marriage—at last—in blessed union." Dirc turned solemnly and reached up, lifting Treijan's tally from the neck of the statue. He turned again, holding it high for all to see, and then lifted it over Valana's head. The large pendant tally swung before her disdainful gaze.

"In the name of Rhamania, God of—"

There was a slight popping sound in front of Valana's face. Instinctively, she blinked, and by the time her eyes opened, wonder had risen to pandemonium throughout the assembled crowd.

Dirc stared at his empty hands.

The tally had *vanished*.

The Tally

34

Stalkers

The sudden humid, warm air pressed on Theona but did not manage to drive the chill from her bones. Theona emerged from the Songstone gate still holding Treijan's hand. He had offered it to her as a gesture of support to encourage her through the gate, as he had done as a bard for uncounted others. Undoubtedly, he thought that this passage would be the same as the countless others down the years of bringing new people into the center of Calsandria.

Now they stood on the other side of the newly created gate between the worlds, along with Gaius, the faery, and the centaur, who appeared behind them, pushing them forward. They stood just ten feet or so from the growth-obscured entrance to the wide cave where Treijan had hidden this end of the mystic portal. She glanced behind them at the Songstone gate. On this side it was an arch formed of rough-hewn stones, and it stood in the center of the cavern. Through the portal she could see the shimmering images of Queen Dwynwyn and her hosts, gazing anxiously in her direction. As she watched, additional stones from the ground around them were rolling gently in the direction of the gate, climbing up its sides and adding themselves to the archway, expanding its diameter by the moment. "It is growing," Theona murmured to herself with astonishment. "It's growing to fit the faery gate. Is it supposed to do that?"

Treijan did not answer her. He still held her hand, but she noticed that it was gripping hers painfully and that it was shaking. She looked up to see Treijan's face: a mask of shock with the blood seemingly drained completely from it.

"I—I am sorry, Your Highness," Theona said quickly, wrenching her hand free from his grip and looking carefully into his face. "I forgot that you were . . . indisposed when we first passed into the faery's world. We should have told you that the passage is a difficult one."

Treijan suddenly shivered as though shaking ice from off his body. "That was—"

"A horrific journey no one should be forced to experience?" Gaius finished for his old friend as he stepped around him and into the dense underbrush of the surrounding jungle.

"Never in my wildest dreams—or nightmares, for that matter—have I ever imagined such a sensation," Treijan said in awe. "It was like falling or flying and never knowing if you would come to the end of all existence. I was sure I would shatter against my own insignificance and—"

"Come on!" Gaius urged as he pushed through the jungle growth hiding the entrance to the cave. "We've very little time before an entire nation of the faery start pouring through this same gate. We've got to get back to the village and find King Pe'akanu. Tell your faery and his hoofed friend to follow."

Theona suddenly remembered the faery floating in the air behind them. She turned to look at him, to make certain that he was real and not some strange imagining she had conjured in her mind. She had seen him in her dreams—her visions—and like so many things from her mind, he, too, had become real. She *saw,* and the things she saw were each happening as she had seen them. She felt the burden of the knowledge once more and sighed audibly under its weight.

"Arryk," Treijan said to the young faery, "we must speak with the—the lord of the local village. You have warriors and they have warriors. All we wish is peace. There must be no misunderstandings between us: we must prepare the chief for the coming of your people."

Arryk nodded, his agreement answered with the sound of towering mountains rising through soft clouds into sunlight.

Treijan turned to Theona. "Once we get these faeries settled, then I'll take you home. Imagine the look on their faces when—Theona? What's wrong?"

Theona drew in a sharp breath. "Your tally."

Treijan glanced down, then his face split into a wide, warm grin. The tally once more hung from its delicate chain around his neck. "Well, what do you know? I guess we *are* back, after all! It must have—oh, Theona, it must have gone back home when we passed into the faery world. They must have thought—we've got to get home as soon as we can."

"No, Treijan," Theona said, shaking her head. "I've got to talk to you. I don't think you'll be going home. I think—"

"Of course we'll be going home," Treijan said as he pulled at her to follow him out past the obscured entrance and into the thick ferns in the direction Gaius had just taken. "Just as soon as we get these faeries settled here, we'll return in the greatest triumph any son of Galen has ever had in Calsandria!"

"No!" Theona said. "You don't understand. You've got to listen to me!"

The faery drifted above the ferns, passing Gaius as his beautiful wings carried him in the direction of the temple just visible above the tops of the palm trees surrounding them. Both were staring up at the thick plumes of smoke billowing from around the temple, obscuring the sky, but for the moment the prince did not notice.

"Theona, please, I promise," Treijan urged, pulling her toward the village. "We'll talk just as soon as we've spoken with the king."

"I don't understand," Treijan said quietly. "What happened?"

Theona could only shake her head, numb with the overwhelming sight that surrounded them. "I don't—we were gone only a few days."

Treijan and Theona walked uneasily at the edge of a plaza just outside the eastern gates of the city, the ground beneath their feet scorched and black. The buildings that had surrounded the plaza were shattered and blackened ruins with only a few of their wide, square pillars standing in broken rows. The great stone faces remained, but they were scarred with stains streaking down their faces like sooty tears. At the far end of the field the towering gates of the city were completely missing; only a wide, jagged tear remained in the city wall. Beyond that, the streets of the city were obscured by raging fires and black greasy smoke that roiled into the air, the shore breeze stirring flame and smoke occasionally to reveal the massive pyramid shape of the temple in the distant heart of the city, its mass still standing amid the devastation. Now and then, Theona's shifting gaze would fall upon a dark and familiar shape lying amid the rubble: a hand or an arm, a torso with an arched back, a charred mouth gaping open in a voiceless scream. She looked away quickly, not wishing to fix her gaze on the image long enough to allow her mind to comprehend fully its meaning. She was forced to look away often as they walked, dazed at the raw edge of combat-hallowed ground. Arryk drifted listlessly in the air nearby, while the centaur glowered at the ruins—both of them reacting to the terrible scene of devastation as well as the unease of their human hosts.

Gaius emerged from the square arch leading into the ceremonial house to their right and descended the crushed, shard-strewn steps softly. He spoke with hushed puzzlement. "If there is anyone alive, they've gone. The dead are everywhere, but it looks as though the entire city was either massacred or has been deserted, man, woman, and child."

"That doesn't make sense." Treijan spoke almost to himself as he gazed around the fire-blackened square at the ruins surrounding them. "They were at peace. The island was united under the king. This nation hasn't known war in over four hundred years. They *have* no enemies. Who could have done this? Surely, they couldn't have killed everyone."

"And not just the people," Gaius observed. "Listen to the silence; there are no house dragons either."

Treijan turned sharply toward his friend. "You're right.

The silence; it's—it's almost more unsettling than the destruction."

"Unsettling or not, Queen Dwynwyn is awaiting our answer on the other side of that monstrous portal we've opened up." Gaius's voice quivered slightly, his emotions raw and near the surface. "Your friend Arryk has got to report soon, or they may come through whether we are ready for them or not. We've promised to save the faeries from their war—only to bring them into the middle of another."

A sudden sharp sound broke the air around them, causing each of them to crouch down instinctively. Treijan waved them backward to take some cover around the broken corner of the ceremonial house steps.

"Where?" Treijan mouthed toward Gaius.

His friend gestured down the left side of the open plaza, pointing toward the crushed remnants of a shop.

Treijan nodded and made to move toward the sound, but a delicate hand restrained him. Treijan turned to look at the faery.

Arryk whispered gentle rain cooling a warm evening.

Treijan smiled and nodded.

The faery's wings opened wide, and he sailed up over the top of the temple, disappearing silently from sight.

Treijan turned back to watch the plaza.

For a time they heard and saw nothing. The stillness in the air grew more oppressive with the anticipation. Gaius tried to say something, but Treijan motioned him into silence.

"Aiyeeee!" came the sudden deep yelp, accompanied by a jumble of crashing metal and shattering glass. Then the pounding of heavy feet kicked up black soot from the charred field as an entirely too familiar figure ran toward them faster than anyone would have thought possible.

"Demons er is!" the dwarf grumbled loudly to himself, his hat held firmly on his head with one hand and a bag overflowing with pearls gripped tightly to his chest with the other. "Flee for yer life, ol' Dregas! Demons er is!"

Treijan stepped easily from his hiding place and with a flick of his wrist encased the charging dwarf in a glowing lift-bubble. The dwarf floated up free from the ground, turning end over end in the translucent sphere.

"Got me as er is!" the dwarf screamed in complete panic. "Them demons got me sure er is!"

"And you said you weren't much of a dancer," Gaius said casually as he and Theona followed Treijan toward the sphere hovering above the debris-strewn field.

"Apparently, the social graces *do* occasionally come in handy. Arryk taught that one to me. He says it's all the rage in the city of the dead." Treijan smiled grimly, then turned toward where the dwarf drifted just above them. "I wonder why *you* are the only one left alive."

"Treijan! Gaius! Thank the gods of the deep!" The dwarf was nearly in tears above them. "One of them demons be in the town! Thought sure them had eaten thee!"

"Dregas Belas," Treijan said casually. "And just what brings you back to this city—especially since I thought it was clear that you weren't wanted here? And now we find that you are the *only* one who *is* here."

"But there be a demon right behind me!" Dregas bellowed.

"That is not a demon," Gaius said. "He is called a faery, and he is with us."

The centaur took several steps forward, coming to

stand next to Treijan as he gazed curiously up to where Dregas floated.

The dwarf suddenly stopped struggling in the air, but his momentum left him turning end over end as he considered what he had just heard. "Friend with the demon, are ye?"

"Yes, but I have a better question for you," Treijan said toward the spinning Dregas. "How is it that you are a dwarf who can *see*?"

The dwarf sat on the broken steps rummaging through his bag as he spoke. "Thought you dead as er is, Treijan. You, too, Master Gaius, and the lady there. Old Pe'akanu sent yer sister back er she came from. Old Dregas take er her back safe and soft. Home she be er now among her own kin. Then returned I to get my hat from that thieving Pe'akanu er I go back to my cellar in Khordsholm. Talk enough now as er is! Smart be ye to leave now while the road is clear and the weather fair."

Theona listened quietly. Treijan and Gaius stood on the steps to either side of the dwarf, bending over him in a casually threatening manner. Arryk sat on the edge of the temple tier just above them, his wings wrapped around his slight body with his head cocked to one side. Below him stood the centaur, his massive arms crossed in front of him and a look of concern on his face.

"So," Treijan said with a careful edge to his voice, "what happened here? What did you see?"

"See?" Dregas snorted. "Old Dregas blind as er is. See not er the great blackness of my bound eyes. All dwarfs er blind under the open sky, know ye not?"

"All, it would seem, except this one," Treijan said, straightening up and folding his arms across his chest.

"You're an outcast—like all your kind aboveground—but I see that you've taken to the ways of men better than most. You dress well, and while your obsession with your hat is typical, I see you chose one that matches the rest of your clothing."

"So I be guilty of good taste, then?" Dregas huffed.

"If there were ever a dwarf who dressed well, you would be the first," Gaius said with an easy sarcasm.

"But it was the faery that gave you away," Treijan said. "You told Pe'akanu that it was a demon that took us—and you ran from that same 'demon' just now."

Dregas nodded. "Aye, dangerous er is, too!"

"But if you're *blind*," Treijan asked pointedly, "how did you know they were the same? You've never touched the faery—either when he took us beside the pond or just now when you saw him coming for you here—yet you knew so much about him."

"Nay," Dregas said, panic creeping into his voice. "*Heard* I his wings moving as er is! *Smelled* his coming, did I!"

"And just now," Treijan said, "when I lifted you off the ground and told you the faery was with us, you relaxed. A dwarf gets his sense of direction from his feet being in contact with the ground. Lift them up and he panics every time; but not you, Dregas. You could *see* where you were."

"Ye be whistling in the dark," Dregas whined. "Nay true! Dregas were panicked as ever dwarf er was!"

"Say, Gaius," Treijan asked suddenly, "what do you suppose *really* is behind a dwarf's blindfold?"

"I don't know, Treijan," Gaius responded. "I've never heard of anyone taking one off before."

"Well, we could be the first." Treijan reached forward slowly, his hand hovering in front of the dwarf's face.

Dregas reached forward, too, arresting Treijan's hand at once.

"Well, Dregas?" Gaius's words were insistent.

"Black glass," Dregas groaned, putting his head in both his large hands. "Dark as midnight er is. Had 'em ground in Arazatha down the coast from Khordsholm. I fit them behind the cloth. Good business er is; much to see for a blind dwarf in my business."

"That's easy to believe," Gaius sniffed.

"'Tis my secret," Dregas whispered hoarsely. "You'll not be telling, will ye?"

"I don't really care whether you see or not," Treijan said forcefully. "But I am keenly interested in what you *have* seen, Dregas! What happened here."

"Best we leave first," Dregas said quickly. "Old Dregas gladly tell you once in Khordsholm er is!"

"No," Treijan said, stepping away from the dwarf. "You tell us now—"

"Nay!" Dregas insisted, an urgent whine once more in his voice. "You open yon gate and back in Khordsholm we be quick as er is! Sure, and I'll buy the ale!"

Treijan and Gaius looked at each other in concern.

"What is it?" Theona asked.

"Dwarves *never* buy ale for anyone!" Treijan said as his hand plunged down toward the dwarf's chest, his fist gathering up the front of the dwarf's frilled shirt. "Listen, you little wharf rat, if you're so anxious to get back through the gate, then you'll tell me what happened here and maybe—just *maybe*—I'll let you come through with us!"

"Nay!" the dwarf squealed. "Used yer magic, you did! *They* be coming sure as er is!"

"Who?" Gaius pressed his face closer to the dwarf. "Who is coming?"

"Smell the magic, they do!" Dregas began to flail, but Treijan held him fast, pressing him against the broken wall at the top of the stairs. "Sniff you out like preyhounds! Run now—and maybe you live, too!"

Theona was having trouble concentrating on the conversation. It was as though a daydream were intruding on her waking thoughts, calling her attention away. *Green demons with sharp teeth walked down the streets of a broken city carrying strange devices of brass and steel in their hands. They were following a taller demon in a robe who clasped a book to his chest while his eyes glowed an impossible deep blue . . .*

Theona blinked, trying to focus on Treijan as he shouted.

"What happened here?" Treijan demanded.

"Nay time now!"

Treijan lifted the dwarf and slammed him against the wall. "Tell me!"

"War!" the dwarf bellowed.

"Whose war?"

"Demons' war like as I know," Dregas moaned, his body going limp. "Started right after you left, it did!"

Theona found her sight focusing elsewhere, as though she were remembering a dream. *The demon in the robes passed by her, his glowing, blank eyes fixed down the road toward a clearing in the rubble beyond. The other demons that followed the robed creature clacked their teeth together in anticipation. They crouched down, mov-*

ing carefully out among the ruins in silence, their strange weapons rising in their arms.

Theona took in a sharp breath. "Treijan?"

"Demons?" Gaius asked with concern, too intent on the dwarf to heed Theona. "What demons? Where did they come from—the sea?"

"Nay from the sea," Dregas said, shaking his beard. "Nay from anywhere er is. An army appeared inside the city walls quick as death. Poured out of the library like a flood from a mine. Nay warning; nay stopping."

"By the gods," Gaius murmured. "It's a gate! Someone put a gate in the center of the city and poured an army through it."

"But whose army and from where?" Treijan wondered. "The dwarf's talking about demons—it doesn't sound like the Pir, and besides, none of the Drakonis sects have ever been able to build a gate. Dregas! Whose army? Who invaded?"

"Fought them, natives did," Dregas said, shaking his head. "Thought they might beat the devils, too—but one of them beasties would fall back and two would take its place er is!"

"Beasties?" Treijan asked. "What beasties?"

"Big metal men er is," Dregas said, his voice hushed in near reverence. "Taller than trees. Copper and iron, brass and steel. Magic in 'em sure er is!"

"Oh, he's lying again." Gaius spat the words as though they tasted ill in his mouth.

Theona's eyesight blurred once more as her attention was dragged forcefully back into her vision. She reached out, steadying herself against the stones of the wall next to her. *The robed demon smiled wickedly, baring his pointed teeth. Theona followed his gaze to the open ground beyond. There stood four figures, outlined in glowing blue.*

"Come with green demon-men er is," Dregas said, shaking his beard again. "Long ears and sharp teeth er is with blades that fly through the air and bring death."

The sound of scraping glass caused Theona and Gaius to wince. When they opened their eyes again, Treijan was staring up at the faery.

"What was *that*?" Gaius demanded.

"Arryk," Treijan answered in a voice gone suddenly hoarse. "He says he didn't create the rift-gate—he stole it from a little green demon who had abducted him to a different place altogether."

"A *different* place?" Gaius said with growing fear.

"It seems"—Treijan swallowed hard—"we aren't the only ones traveling between worlds."

Theona saw—the glowing figures. Although she could not make out their features from this distance, one of them was a centaur.

"We have to get out of here!" Theona said more loudly than she intended, her voice quivering.

"Theona?" Gaius asked. "What is it?"

"They're coming for *you*!" she said, her eyes darting about, looking at shapes that were not there, images they could not see. "They *see* you—all of you! They are hunting mystics—using the dream to find you!"

Gaius and Treijan both looked sharply at each other. Both slowly straightened up and stood casually at the top of the broken stair.

"Think they should run for the rift-gate?" Gaius asked quietly.

"Absolutely," Treijan replied with practiced ease. "Run, Theona—run right now."

"What?" she asked uncertainly.

"Run!" Treijan shouted as both he and Gaius spun around, their spells forming in their hands just as a cadre of vicious green creatures leaped from the tiles of the roof above them, their weapons discharging as they screamed.

35

To See and Not Be Seen

Arryk flew as quickly as his wings would allow, sweat pouring down off his brow. The oppressive, humid air weighed down on him; it pressed against his chest and made his wings hang heavily on their veins, making them move sluggishly. The strange trees drifted past him too slowly as he made his way through the dense growth. He had been careful to mark his path on the trees of this forest as they made their way from the rift-gate; though he trusted Treijan with his life, he also knew the importance of being able to find his own way back to the gate should anything go wrong.

And things had gone terribly wrong.

He could hear the crashing mass of Hueburlyn behind him, smashing his way through the underbrush. He could also hear the sounds of Treijan and his companion Gaius as well, their magic occasionally punctuating the air with thunderous effect. He knew that the woman and that strange dwarf-creature were somewhere, but he could not think about them now.

He could think of nothing but himself.

Fear had finally gripped him. There was nothing in the world but the danger that stalked him; there was no higher purpose than escape. His mind willingly surrendered to the lurking monster behind his conscious thought, and he fled from all his excuses: his haughty superiority and his smug condescension. His pride boiled away in white-hot terror of the monsters that he somehow sensed were at his heels and ready to devour him. He could feel the heat of their breath on the backs of his legs, sensed their teeth snapping just inches from his laden, fluttering wings, and smelled their stench creeping ever closer to envelop him.

The trees opened suddenly onto a meadow. Arryk knew in some part of his mind that they had crossed it as they walked to the city. His mark was on the tree on the other side, and getting to that mark filled his mind to the exclusion of all else.

More than halfway across the tall grasses, a new sound made him turn. It was the scream of iron and brass like the sounding of a hundred mountain harpies.

Hueburlyn was charging across the meadow directly toward him, but Arryk took no notice; his wide eyes gazed upward.

Towering above them all was a giant clad in metal, standing twice again as tall as the trees. It was faceless— its head had been plated over so that it had no mouth or nose or eyes. Its left arm was missing below the elbow, its brass skull torn open by some unimaginable force and from which dangled its shredded brass flesh and iron tissues. In the smoky distance beyond it, Arryk's mind registered the featureless shapes of two others.

Arryk knew they were all focused on him.

The monster stopped and bent over to its right. Just then the metal of its featureless face began to glow, growing rapidly from a dull orange to blinding white. The metal screamed and then exploded, the monster's head thrown back.

Arryk pressed forward faster, flying wildly between the trunks of trees, his entire being lost in panic.

Too fast. On instinct alone he curled his head under his arms, trying to dive out of the way at the last minute. He swerved, but the rough trunk of the tree barely yielded. He bowed backward with the impact and fell spinning to the ground below.

The wind left his lungs, but he was still in the grip of his mindless fear. He clawed at the ground, trying to drag himself up, to unfurl his wings, but everything happened too slowly. The ferns around him seemed to be reaching for him, wrapping their tendrils around his arms.

He screamed, tearing at the fronds, rolling across the ground, mad to get away from their reach.

Suddenly, an iron grip wrapped itself around Arryk, pulling him up from the ground.

"Ar-ryk!" came the angry voice, far away in the faery's mind. "Ar-ryk! Stop!"

The faery went limp, quivering.

"Ar-ryk!" the voice said, more insistent this time. "Which way?"

Arryk focused on the broad face floating in front of him. "Hueburlyn?"

"Which way?" the centaur said, shaking him. "Now!"

Arryk's world grew wider as he stared into the face of the centaur. Trees, smoke, cries, death, and pain. There was a new sound, too, the sound of metal scraping against metal and the thunder of footsteps that had to be made by the gods.

Arryk glanced around as he lay in Hueburlyn's outstretched arms. He was vaguely aware of the woman and the dwarf astride the centaur's back.

"There," Arryk said, pointing. "Past those trees—that way."

The centaur lunged forward, his great galloping strides carrying them through the underbrush. Something behind them was moving through the trees, making considerably more noise than the centaur. Metal screamed against metal, and the trunks of trees snapped, their tops crashing to the ground. Then came another sound: a tremendous explosion that shook the ground beneath the centaur, making his footing momentarily uncertain. Hueburlyn gathered himself up and bounded once more, regaining his balance, though the ground again shook to a cacophony of metal that crashed behind the veil of smoke filling the jungle.

Arryk felt the floor of the cavern under his feet as the centaur lowered him to the ground. He stood uncertainly before the rift-gate. He could not see them through the harsh ultraviolet of the rift-gate, but he knew that Dwynwyn and what was left of his nation lay waiting for him.

"I caused this," Arryk said aloud. "This is my fault."

The centaur reached back and grasped the human woman around her waist and lowered her carefully. His voice was angry as he spoke. "Ar-ryk *now* have fault? Too late now!"

"I—what am I going to do?" Arryk stammered. His hair fell across his eyes. He squatted down on the cavern floor, facing the rift-gate that had grown to tremendous size even in their short absence. Arryk hugged his legs, hiding his face against his knees. "They're all going to die, and I've killed them."

The dwarf-creature began to make its growling sounds again as the centaur plucked it off his back and dropped it unceremoniously to the floor. Hueburlyn grunted, "Ar-ryk always have plan. What Ar-ryk plan now?"

"I don't—I mean, I . . ."

The centaur clopped forward toward the gate, his face set. He reached to the right side of the gate, his massive hand wrapping around the Songstone. With a single swift movement, he pulled the stone free of the oval structure.

The strange glow vanished with a soft pop. The stones of the gate clattered loudly to the floor of the cavern, the oval of the gate collapsing into rubble.

Arryk looked up horrified. He stood suddenly, rage boiling over as the centaur stepped back past him with the glowing Songstone in his hand. "What have you *done*!"

"What Ar-ryk *should* have done!" the centaur growled back. He stepped quickly up to the Theona-woman. She looked at him uncertainly, but the centaur merely leaned forward and held out the Songstone in his wide, open palm.

The wingless woman reached forward tentatively and then took the softly glowing stone with her hand.

"Take that back!" Arryk commanded. "Have you gone insane? We *have* to go through the gate! In the name of Sharajentis, I *demand* that you put that back!"

Hueburlyn turned back to Arryk, his face filled with contempt. "Hueburlyn not serve Sharajentei—Hueburlyn serve Sharaj!"

Arryk seethed for a moment, then stepped toward

the wingless Theona. She saw the look on his face and stepped back away from him.

Hueburlyn's arm caught Arryk's and pulled him around to face the centaur. "Think, Ar-ryk! Hear Hueburlyn's words. War is here. Metal giants search for the Sharaj; they follow Ar-ryk and Hueburlyn here—*here* to rift-gate!"

Arryk blinked, looking into the face of the centaur, suddenly hearing his words.

"Metal giants look for Sharaj in Ar-ryk and Hueburlyn," the centaur said. "If metal giants find rift-gate, not just Sharajentei die, not just Kyree die, but all faery die, all Famadorian die."

Arryk's anger went out of him. "Hueburlyn, what do we do?"

The centaur pointed to Theona. "You tell Hueburlyn that Theona-woman no have Sharaj. Metal giants and demons not see Theona in dream. Give stone to Theona-woman, demons no find gate."

"And what about us?" Arryk asked quietly.

"We do what the hu-mans Treijan and Gaius are doing now; we make sure that metal giants and demons no find us *here*," Hueburlyn said.

"My Fae..." Arryk found it hard to speak the words. "My people will die."

"But all *other* peoples live," Hueburlyn replied.

"We can't make that decision for them!" Arryk pleaded.

"No, Ar-ryk!" Hueburlyn said with force. "We only ones who *can* make decision. No pretty. No easy. No fair. We go now or too late."

"She doesn't understand our words," Arryk said, shaking his head as he gazed back at the wingless woman. "She won't understand."

"Maybe not always important to understand," Hueburlyn said. "Maybe sometimes more important to do."

Arryk nodded, then sighed as he followed the centaur out of the cavern.

"Where do they think they're goin'?" Dregas asked in astonishment. "Here now! Insane er is!"

Theona gazed at the Songstone for a moment and then slipped it into the pouch of her traveling buckler. "No, Dregas—I suspect they are quite rational."

"Rational? Rational, says ye?" Dregas scoffed, pointing back at the pile of stones scattered across the floor of the cavern. "That were a good gate, were it not? All sung open like and ready for us to pass as er is. Them pulls the stone sure, and now we be stuck in a cavern, with them forged beasties coming for us and no back gate as er is!"

Theona stepped up to the front of the cavern and knelt down, carefully drawing aside the fronds covering the entrance. "Come look, Dregas."

The dwarf grumbled as he moved forward, adjusting his hat nervously on his head. "Yer prefer I *see* my death coming, eh?"

"Just look," Theona said quietly.

Through the trees they could make out the towering mass of a metallic giant, with another in the distance behind it. As they watched, both creatures turned, moving off toward their right.

"Well, burn my beard," the dwarf muttered in astonishment. "What magic did ye do, lass?"

"None," Theona said, her face still filled with concern. "That's what saved us."

"Eh?"

"Dwarves have no magic at all," Theona said, sitting down just inside the cave, her back resting against the wall as she closed her eyes. "Neither do I. Those creatures are using the Deep Magic to find other mystics—other creatures with magic powers. They can see them in the realm of Deep Magic—"

"But they can't see us?" the dwarf finished, though he sounded unconvinced.

"They can see us well enough," Theona replied, "just not in the dream."

"Then a chance is good er is!" The dwarf grinned through his widely spaced teeth as he clapped his hands together and rubbed them gleefully. "Theona, darlin', come with old Dregas to the *other* gate as er is! Dregas knows the way. Theona sings the gate open, and Khordsholm be as sure as er is!"

"No," Theona replied, her eyes still closed. "We need a bard to sing open that gate. I can't do it."

"Well, nay *dwarf* can it sing open neither!" Dregas grumbled. Then his face brightened. "But this old dwarf know where be someone who *can* sing a gate!"

Theona opened her eyes. "Who?"

"You see as er is!" The dwarf chuckled. "Not all dead in yon native city—and not all seen as er is!"

My Enemy's Enemy

The dwarf led Theona from the cave and into the thick jungle foliage. His course took them into a thicket, then turned sharply, following a meandering stream at the bottom with nearly vertical walls on either side. This opened onto a wide pool where the dwarf took another turn and down a barely discernible path through a sea of broad-leaved plants.

The dwarf stopped so suddenly, holding out the flat of his hand as a warning, that Theona nearly ran into him. He motioned her down as he slowly crouched among the leaves.

The dwarf pointed ahead of them. Theona tried to see through the seeming wall of foliage before them. She could just barely make out an open glade beyond the broad leaves.

She sat quietly on the ground, glancing from time to time with uncertainty at the dwarf, yet Dregas remained motionless. She was beginning to think the dwarf was having some sort of private joke at her expense when her eyes caught movement in the glade.

A group of the sharp-toothed demons—eight or perhaps more, she could not be sure—were moving across the glade, each being led by one of their book-toting masters with the strange, glowing eyes.

Theona held still. The dwarf might as well have been made of stone.

Each of the little creatures wore a vest of some sort and carried a strange-looking device. They held it casually before them as a woodcutter might hold his axe; to be sure, the circular blades fixed to it made Theona think that it was some kind of weapon. She was certain that she did not wish to see the device in operation.

Then one of the warrior demons near to where they were hiding stopped and sniffed the air pensively before taking several steps in their direction. Fortunately, its robed master with the glowing eyes called the wayward soldier back into line with a screeching noise.

They can't see us in the dream, Theona reminded herself, quivering with her back against the cool, damp wall. *Hide and they won't find us.*

The group soon moved off to Theona's right, crashing noisily through the brush. Yet even after the sound had died away completely, the dwarf remained still for many minutes. Theona did not dare move or make any sound in all that time, merely watching Dregas and trying to remember to breathe.

At last the dwarf turned toward her. "Good lass! Old Dregas get us safe as er is."

"Where are we going?"

"South er is," the dwarf said in a low voice. "Then

round seaward side gate. Them demons nay like water nor expect attack from the sea. Long way round the city, but we pass up their armies and warriors and such. Slips we in through the fish gate and then go calling on yer old friend, lass!"

"Nearly there, we be," the dwarf whispered, his back pressed against the outside of the city's western wall as they both squatted behind a thick cover of ferns.

Theona could scarcely breathe. The dwarf had kept up an unexpectedly furious pace. Though she had heard considerable noise from the gigantic metal monsters during their headlong rush through the jungle, the dwarf chose a course such that she never saw another demon, let alone another metallic giant. Yet as they neared the city wall proper, she noticed that their path became more erratic and their passage more fitful.

Now, her back against the city wall, she could see the three sets of shattered gates that led into the heart of the city. The great doors had been torn from their hinges and lay broken to splinters on the ground. Beyond them she could see a wide rubble-strewn plaza that ran almost to the base of the tallest of the stepped-pyramid temples of Tua'a-Re, its mass nearly obscured by the dark smoke billowing from fires that burned unchecked in several buildings around the plaza.

"Theona ready?" Dregas rumbled.

Theona was quite far from ready, but she knew more time would not change her condition. She nodded in the affirmative.

"Then we go now," the dwarf agreed, grabbing her hand and pulling her to her feet.

They ran into the plaza, Theona stumbling over the

rubble as they ran its length between the shattered buildings to either side. Blackened shapes that lay curled in on themselves dotted the landscape, but she could not bring herself to look at them or think too long on who they once were or the lives they might have lived. She focused on the line of blackened trees beyond the end of the plaza and on keeping her feet beneath her as she ran.

Then, almost as a surprise, the trunks of the trees were all about her, and her nostrils filled with the tang of charred wood. The dwarf did not stop, however, pulling her quickly toward the enormous fitted stones that formed the base of the temple looming above them.

"Nay much time." The dwarf spat the words out, Theona hearing an unusual urgency in his voice. He then began moving down the rock face before him, running his hands along its surface. "Patrols er is. Them demons nay smell the magic on us, but their sight in the day keen as er is!"

Theona glanced nervously about, staying close to the dwarf as he stepped down the wall. "What are you doing?"

"Dwarves be many and different"—Dregas flashed a gap-toothed smile as his hands continued to move down the stone—"but *all* know stone. Deep in the mountain—out under the sky—all stone we know, and its ways are owned by us all. Ah, here it be!"

"Here *what* be?"

The dwarf grinned as he took out his small hammer and, in a sudden movement, smashed it against the stone. Theona started at the sharp sound, but before she could fear someone hearing it, she was astonished to see an arched line appear in what she had thought to be solid stone. The rock within the line pulled backward into the temple and swung aside, revealing a narrow passageway barely three feet wide and not five feet in height. The walkway turned to pitch-blackness as it ran into the heart of the temple beyond.

"Here be the back door," Dregas said as he did a little dance. "Humans build with stone but never trust it like dwarfkind. Always want another way out."

The dwarf stepped into the claustrophobic space and gestured toward Theona. "Come quickly! Your old friend be waiting and happy to see you er is!"

Theona ducked down and cautiously entered the narrow passage. The walls seemed to close in toward her, and she could barely see the outlines of the dwarf ahead of her as she moved.

"Dregas?"

Suddenly, the stone behind her moved back into its accustomed place with a grinding boom.

Darkness, utter and complete, engulfed her. Theona was blind and helpless. She shuddered, her breath suddenly quick and short, her mind threatening to unravel into bottomless panic.

A rough hand took hold of hers.

"Nay you mind, lass," Dregas said in the darkness. "Take you through my world, old Dregas will."

With a great shove the dwarf pushed the stone out of their way. The narrow passage had proved to be a winding one and, in several places, nearly impassable, or so Theona thought in the threatening imaginings of her mind. Yet the dwarf had managed to get her through them until they had come to the final stone. Now it swung open before them with a rush of cool, fresh air that washed away the heavy fear that Theona had been carrying.

The passageway opened onto a corridor that was lit by several burning torches set into sconces on the walls. Theona eyed them curiously; torches had not been used by the mystics for lighting for nearly a century. They were a poor light source, unsteady and generally dirty and foul-smelling.

The dwarf turned to their left and then went down a winding passage. There were several archways to either side of the hall leading into darkened rooms and cells, but the dwarf seemed intent on his course. Theona followed him and soon discovered why: one of the rooms near the end of the corridor was lit.

"Eh! Hello!" the dwarf shouted from up ahead. "Friends come to call er is! A proposition has we as grand as er is!"

Theona followed, eyeing the illuminated archway suspiciously.

"Hello! Hello!" the dwarf bellowed. "'Tis only old Dregas come to call with yon Mistress Theona. Nay harm; come to chat all friendlike and peaceful as er is! Sorry sure as er is for the trouble we caused."

Theona slowed, anxious at the silence from the room before them. "Dregas, I don't—"

Suddenly, a shadow rushed at her from the darkened archway at her side. Arms curled around her throat, pulling her backward. She reached up instinctively, clawing at the arm. She could not turn, could not see who held her.

Dregas spun around, his hammer in hand, but the dwarf relaxed almost at once. "Nay call for that now! Told ye, friendlike and peaceful we be. Let the lass go, she be no threat to ye."

The arm released her, and Theona tripped forward,

spinning to face her assailant. The figure was stooped in pain, drawing in a sharp breath.

"Meklos?" Theona croaked.

Aboth Meklos Jefard stood hunched before them, leaning heavily on his dragonstaff. He breathed with sharp, staccato intakes, and the lines of his pain were etched in the corners of his eyes. "You shouldn't—shouldn't have come like that."

"Aye, and just how should we be coming?" Dregas demanded with annoyance. "Announced ourselves louder than the heralds of a dragon in a full gale, we did! This dwarf nay live so long as to know ye don't sneak up on wizard-folk. Like to get oneself turned into something unpleasant as er is!"

"Oh, shut up," Meklos snapped. He straightened up slowly, a grimace fixed on his face. "I didn't ask you to come, and I certainly didn't expect you."

"Told you I'd come back, I did," Dregas protested. "Trust old Dregas; honest a dwarf as er is!"

"You're a liar and a thief," Meklos responded, limping past them toward the lit room beyond. "If you are as honest a dwarf as your people offers, then woe betide the entire dwarven nation. And you've brought Mistress Theona Conlan with you—I don't suppose you'd care to tell me just what you did that put me in my present state?"

Theona eyed him carefully as he passed. Bone-white bracers caught her eye from under the cuff of Meklos's sleeve. "You are still without your magic."

"A mixed blessing at best," Meklos replied with a sarcastic edge. He stepped into the room, his back toward them. "My jailers have robbed me of my powers, but then, those same jailers all appear to be dead or gone. I have the run of my prison. More than that, the very absence of my power seemed to keep these monstrous goblins from finding my little sanctuary—as I'm sure you are aware."

Theona followed Meklos into the room. The ceiling was nearly twelve feet above them and supported by half-pillars against the walls. It might have seemed like a large space—perhaps thirty feet square on a side—had it not been filled with a number of large jars, foods, and other materials. It was a storeroom, Theona thought, and a perfect place to hide from the world.

"Goblins?" Theona asked. "Is that what they're called?"

"That's what they call themselves," Meklos replied, lowering carefully into an ornate chair.

"True er is you understand yon demons speak?" the dwarf asked in wonder.

"Yes, 'true er is' I understand—at least I understand one of their number." Meklos sighed. "A fellow named Skramak; he appears to be the one in charge of this . . . this invasion. It was difficult not to overhear him, too. He was screaming at the top of his lungs about spies being captured with a pair of gods."

"Gods?" Dregas snorted in surprise.

Meklos nodded. "Yes, gods. A winged creature and some half-man monstrosity. They're holding them down in the King's Palace until Conqueror Skramak decides if it's a good idea to kill a god or not."

Theona's eyes widened. "Spies? Two men—with a winged creature and a four-legged man?"

Meklos's eyes narrowed. "Yes. They were taken this morning."

"They're alive," Theona murmured, closing her eyes in relief.

"Who?" Meklos asked.

"Treijan—Treijan and Gaius." Theona smiled, a tear rolling unbidden down her cheek. "I—there's hope, after all."

"Oh, yes, hope indeed," Meklos sniffed. "The great Calsandric bards to the rescue once more. Well, those heroes are locked up in the mansion and will probably be executed the moment Skramak decides whether he cares if he offends his 'gods' or not. They're in there and I'm in here, and I'd even bet a dwarf that I'll be alive by dawn and they won't."

"We've got to get them out!"

"Mistress Conlan," Meklos said pointedly, "I came here to *kill* them. Rescuing them would be, shall we say, counterproductive."

"Please," Theona said as she sat wearily down on a box nearby. "We just returned—and we don't know what happened here."

"I don't *know* what happened," Meklos returned. "At least not all of it. I doubt that anyone will know—although I would certainly be interested in hearing from where it was that you returned."

"That would be . . . a bit difficult to explain," Theona said, biting softly at her lower lip.

"Indeed?" Meklos chuckled, then winced, closing his eyes for a moment as he fought to win over the pain. A moment later he opened his eyes and continued. "Those goblin-creatures: even a commoner such as you must be aware that they are from the Deep Magic of the dream—manifestations in the flesh of beings previously only seen in the spiritual realms."

"Where we have been," Theona said in soft, halting tones, "is a place where other creatures from the dream exist—lithe beings with wings like moths or butterflies."

Meklos leaned forward slowly, his eyes suddenly bright. "And a city—a black city with terrible gates flanked by monstrous statues of black glass."

"I have walked its streets," Theona said. "It is called Sharajentis by its inhabitants—a winged race who call themselves the Fae."

"And you, a commoner, walked its streets?"

"I felt the cobblestones under my feet. I saw their Army of the Dead pass before me toward certain doom. I stood before the Queen of the Dead and wept to hear her voice."

Meklos gripped his staff so hard that his knuckles had gone bone-white. "And she spoke of doom and the end of her world."

Theona nodded. "They stand at the gate, Meklos. Even now their entire nation waits on us and what we do. Their survival depends upon us."

Dregas glanced back and forth between the two humans. His voice, too, was hushed in awe and wonder. "What here er be?"

"Then it *was* a gate that I saw take you," Meklos said. "A very special gate."

"Yes," Theona agreed sadly. "And apparently, not the only one."

Dregas spoke up quickly, wedging his words into a conversation he was having difficulty following. "Someone mention a gate? Now we be talking right, for a gate be exactly as we need! Meklos here can sing open a gate and off we be, safe and home by supper, and leave our cares right here!"

Meklos leaned back slowly, fingering his staff as he thought. "So Treijan thought to bring an entire nation of the faeans—"

"Faeries."

"What?"

"Faeries—they call themselves faeries."

Meklos nodded and continued. "So Treijan thought he would bring an entire nation of these ... faeries ... through his special gate and into our world. Well, it seems that someone among the goblins pulled that particular trick ahead of him."

"What happened here?" Theona asked.

"Only what the mystics in Calsandria have been dreading for years—except these Hanu'ui were entirely unprepared for it," Meklos said, closing his eyes as he spoke. "It was three days ago. I was in the great room of the temple above us, recuperating from the injuries I sustained that last time someone apparently opened a gate between our world and another. It was late morning, I think, when there was a terrible sound—like thunder, but it continued rolling on and on—from somewhere in the city. I hurried as best I could, but as you can see"—he gestured to his contorted body—"I was in no position to run. The temple quickly emptied of warriors and shamans—and everyone else, for that matter—leaving me to struggle to the entrance by myself."

Meklos closed his eyes once more for a moment, gathering his will as his mind went back to relive the moment. "Even before I came out of the entrance hall, I could hear the battle—the screams of the dying and the rage of the house dragons, the chants of the warriors and the shriek of tortured metal. I kept pulling myself toward the light— telling myself that it was safer in the light—and emerged onto the platform at the top of the third tier of the pyramid. You have a pretty good view of the city from there, even though you're only a third of the way up the sides.

You can see everything, from the Temple of Fire on the south to the Temple of the Sky on the north—the whole length of the Avenue of the Kings. It's quite a sight. *Was* quite a sight."

Meklos stopped for a moment, then opened his eyes, gazing directly at Theona. "You know, they barely noticed who it was they were killing. Warriors, shamans, women, children, house dragons—it didn't seem to matter to them. Everyone was a target; everyone was an enemy—everyone died. And me? I just stood there on the temple porch watching it all happen—watched mothers trying to shield their children from harm, but it was pointless because they both died anyway—all because *these* bracers, these *chains* with which they had hobbled me, kept me from doing *anything*."

Theona looked at the dwarf. Dregas had gone silent, his eyes downcast on the floor.

"You said that was three days ago," Theona said quietly.

"Yes," Meklos replied, his voice suddenly tired. "Since then the battle has moved off to the north. King Pe'akanu has apparently rallied a number of the northern cities to his aid. I think the goblins may have taken some place called Pe'i-Re, about eighty miles to the north of here. The goblins are pushing them pretty hard, but the local warriors are giving as good as they're getting, maybe a little better. They have a strong form of the Deep Magic here, though it's unlike any I've seen. Even during the initial attack they were able to bring down several of those metallic giants the goblins have doing their battle for them. I've gone up now and then to take a look, and every time I do, there is a stream of those metal monsters limping back into town and down toward the library. And there's an equally impressive stream of them coming back the other way."

"So they're what—*fixing* them?"

"That's my guess—and doing so just about as fast as they can be brought down." Meklos shifted uncomfortably in his chair. "You can't beat an army that can't die. I believe they're going back through the gate that brought them here, getting fixed up, and then returning to fight again."

"So all we need to do is close the gate?" Theona asked.

"Wait a beat there, lass," Dregas jumped in. "We need to get *through* a gate, nay close one."

"Yes, that would go a long way toward defeating them—eventually," Meklos agreed, ignoring the dwarf. "Close the gate to their own supplies and repair resources, and they'll start losing to attrition—if you don't run out of warriors yourself first. There are just a few problems with your little plan. First, you'd have to get near enough to the gate to close it. You may not have noticed it, considering how you got in here, but between you and this gate is a mass of goblins and their giant metal warriors. They call them titans, by the way. They have technomancers, whatever they are, constantly on guard for *anyone* that has any presence in the dream."

"Then the three of us are perfect for the task," Theona replied. "None of us appear in the dream—we're invisible to them."

"To the technomancers, yes," Meklos said as though to a child, "but there are literally *thousands* of regular goblin troops out there with perfectly good eyes just waiting for an excuse to separate your flesh from your bones. You'd never get close enough, mystic or not."

"Then—then we need a diversion," Theona said. "If we were to free Treijan and the others, we could send Arryk and Hueburlyn—"

"Wait," Meklos said, holding up his hand. "Who?"

"The faery and the centaur—half-man and half four-legged animal—who came from the other world," Theona continued. "They could bring the faery nation through the rift-gate right into the goblins' backyard, just as they did here. That could cause enough confusion that one of us could get to the enemy's rift-gate and close it."

Meklos nodded, considering for a moment. "My compliments, Theona; you would have made a fair tactician. A most reasonable plan."

Theona drew in a deep breath. "So when do we begin?"

"We don't."

"What?"

"I'm not helping you, Mistress Conlan. I choose to let Treijan and his entire world die with him. He and his kind destroyed my family, forced me into exile, and ruined my life. I long ago vowed to exact my vengeance and regain my family's honor. This may not be the way I had hoped for it—I certainly would have preferred some grand confrontation—but as Treijan sat back and watched my family wither, I suppose there is some justice in my sitting back and watching his die in much the same way."

"You cannot be serious," Theona said in open astonishment. "Whatever Treijan or the bards have done to you in the past, the threat now is *here*—with this army of conquest. Don't you feel anything for these people? They've tried to help you!"

"Help me?" Meklos scoffed. "They made me a cripple!"

"You were a cripple long before they found you,"

Theona shot back. "All you see is vengeance. You live in the past, breathing in its hate, its mistakes, and its prejudices as though *those* were the source of life itself. These people of the island could have let you die, but they saw something in you that still needed to live. They deserve your respect for their lives, as they respected yours."

"They are *not* my concern!" Meklos yelled.

"We are *all* one another's concern," Theona shouted back. "I have *seen* it, Meklos; this army will not be content with this land. They will find the bards' gates and erupt like a plague on the continent from Khordsholm. No one will be spared, because conquest alone is their only desire. No one—not the mystics or the Pir—will be spared their endless thirst for war. But *right here* and *right now* you can change that. You stand at the crossroads, Meklos, and from you the future is decided. Help us free the others—help us close the gate—if for no other reason than to save each other from destruction."

"So my enemy's enemy is now my friend?" Meklos said, quietly standing, leaning heavily on his dragonstaff. "No, Theona; I have sworn my family's oath against the bards of House Arvad."

"Don't do this, Meklos," Theona said, standing to face the Aboth. "Sometimes we do not get to choose our destiny—sometimes it chooses us. You cannot change the wrongs of the past; they are immovable by our will, etched into time and dead. You cannot change the future just by dreaming of it either. All our choice, all the force of our will, is in the *now*—right *now*. You must choose now the road on which your destiny will take us all."

Meklos gazed at Theona, his face a mask of thought.

"Which destiny do you choose?" she asked softly. "Right here; right now."

Meklos winced against his pain, stooping over slightly to relieve it.

The dwarf folded his thick arms across his chest, listening intently.

"As I told you, your friends are being held in the King's Palace," Meklos said at last. "It is the large building to the southeast of the corner of this same pyramid. I've no doubt that the goblins will be more than happy to show you the way—if you can get as far as asking them."

Theona sighed in disgust. "So you'd rather let these people die than let go of your own hate."

"It's all I have left to me," Meklos replied.

37

Choices

Lord Skramak strode down the broad avenue of the City of the Gods with a scowl on his face, his one eye shifting from side to side. He was the undisputed master of all he surveyed, but it was not enough—it was never enough.

To either side of the avenue, ranks of goblins moved quickly northward toward the front line of the assault, many of them raising both of their fists to their chests as they passed him. He did not bother returning their salutes, nor did he cast a single glance at the war-titans that lumbered over him, their colossal feet rising and falling, cracking the carefully fitted cobblestones beneath them. His eye was intent on something else: a dreadfully noisy procession coming back from the battlefront that he could see just above the broken ridgelines of the city's buildings east of the avenue. He could only catch glimpses of it between the buildings and occasionally above them, but what he was seeing was deepening the frown on his craggy face.

"Lord Skramak, please slow down," squeaked the unusually pinched voice behind him. Big-funder Thwick was having difficulty keeping up with the Dong Mahaj Skramak. Though he was a full head taller than the Dong, Thwick's robes kept his stride in check. "I'm sure that whatever the problem is, I can find someone to blame for it!"

Thwick certainly did not want to be here. It was bad enough that the Dong had demanded the Big-funder himself cross through the dreadful rift-gate and into the realm of the gods, but the conqueror had returned from the battle in order to speak with the Big-funder personally. Thwick did not dare refuse and had been so stunned at the order that he could not think of a way out of obeying it, even though such a summons could not be anything but bad news.

"I've already got plenty of goblins to blame!" Skramak seethed. "And you're first on my list! Look at that! Just look at it!"

Thwick looked, following Skramak's emphatic gesture. They had stopped in the center of a large plaza on the avenue that extended eastward toward another of the odd pointy-shaped buildings these gods seemed so fond of building. To its right were three other, smaller buildings of similar construction, one of which had been nearly demolished to its foundations. Where it had once been there now stood a great ring of light, and through it passed the Grand Army of the Conquest: titans rising out of its light, while goblin warriors scurried about their feet trying to re-form their ranks and follow their directions forward.

Yet Thwick could see at once that there was a second, more disconcerting flow: in a steady procession of retreat came a line of shattered titans, several of them dragging other fallen titans behind them, that were pushing their way across the land back through the gate. The scraping of their metal against the stones rang all across the city—and there were far more of them returning into the gate than were going out.

"Where are my titans?" Skramak shouted.

"They are being repaired as quickly as possible, my lord," Thwick replied, though his voice sounded less soothing than he would have hoped. "It isn't just the physical damage that the gods are doing to the titans—though *that* damage is certainly bad enough—but the more recent returns have had something new gone wrong with them."

"New?" Skramak snapped. "New like a weapon?"

"Something like that," Thwick said, running his long-fingered hand up through the luxurious lock of hair atop his head. He feared it would be impossible to keep it standing properly in this dreadfully wet climate. "It is as though the gods found a way of unraveling the technomancy that binds the titans' parts together and brings them life. We try to put them back together, but for some reason they don't stick."

"Well, you had better find a way to *make* them stick," Skramak bellowed, "or I'm going to start greasing those gears myself with the blood of academics, is that clear enough for you?"

Thwick nodded quickly. "Yes, my lord. Vividly clear. I shall return at once and see to it personally—back on the other side of the rift-gate."

"You're not going anywhere just yet!" Skramak grabbed the Big-funder by the arm and urged him toward a large building facing the west side of the plaza. Several ranks of goblins were forming up before the steps of the building, but one look at Skramak and they parted well out of his way. "I've got bigger problems, some of which are about to become *your* problem."

Skramak propelled Thwick up the broad steps of the structure with a grip so tight that Thwick felt sure he would lose the use of his arm. They passed through a shattered colonnade and heedlessly crossed a shallow pool, Skramak's wide feet splashing water upon Thwick's robes. Thwick passed through a succession of antechambers before being thrust forcefully through an archway.

"There!" Skramak growled. "There is the problem."

Thwick looked in astonishment on a scene his wizened goblin eyes could barely comprehend. The room was enormous—a throne room, perhaps, of the local god—lined with parallel colonnades of pillars and with a great seat on a platform at the end of the hall.

Yet it was the cage in the center of the hall that attracted his immediate attention. Thwick saw that it had been crudely and hastily wrought by goblin hands, though it glowed with the unmistakable aura of technomancy. Indeed, four robed technomancers stood at the corners of the cage, their books in hand and their sharp gaze fixed on their captives. Two of the captive figures inside the cage looked like the local gods: tall and sickeningly pale in skin color with small feet and hands and horribly rounded ears. The other two . . .

Thwick caught his breath.

"*Now* do you see our problem?" Skramak roared.

"Aren't they—those are *Lunid's* gods!" Thwick sputtered in astonishment. "I recognize the winged one! He's the one Lunid was all upset about losing. Urk, I think she called him."

"Yes, Urk!" Skramak spat on the floor. "Of all the gods to meet, it *would* have to be him."

"Well, this is *good* news, isn't it?" Thwick said, considering for a moment. "I mean, Lunid will be so pleased to hear that you actually found her god—"

"That she'll close the gate," Skramak finished angrily. "The only reason she opened the rift-gate in the first place was to find this ugly stick. Here I am on the greatest war of conquest in the history of all goblinkind—the subjugation of the gods themselves—and the whole glorious campaign is threatened by an academic's adolescent crush on a hideous winged monstrosity that would make any sane goblin child hide under their bed of rocks in terror. I tell you it's obscene."

"But you promised Lunid you would—"

"If I deliver her winged creature, she'll close the gate," Skramak said again, jabbing his long, bony green finger into the academic's chest. "What do you think happens then? Tell me, O great scholar with all the wisdom of that academy of yours, what happens to me then?"

"Well, I—"

"I'll tell you exactly what will happen and teach *you* something for a change," Skramak said. "My army is paid on spoils. They've seen the books and the wealth here. If I drag them all back through the gate now, I won't last until sunset. My own army will be using my skin as a banner for whoever comes after me."

"Well, then, the solution is simple," Thwick said, rubbing his sharp chin between his long fingers.

"And?"

"Kill them."

"Don't you think I've tried that?" Skramak seethed. "What kind of an idiot do you take me for? Killing them would have made all our lives easier, but the troops that were on patrol around the city didn't know that. *They* got the word from one of my late gen-reels to *capture* anyone in the back area for interrogation—and were given specially built cages for the job."

"Specially built? By whom?"

Skramak sighed. "Lunid."

"Lunid?"

"Yes," Skramak replied, grinding his sharp teeth together. "And apparently, Lunid was concerned about the safety of anyone in her cages. Not only can they not escape, but apparently, so long as the cage is closed, we cannot get in either. Our weapons pass through it without touching anyone inside, and our technomancy does the same."

Thwick nodded, then considered for a few moments. "I believe I have the answer for you."

Skramak looked over at the academic with his single eye. "Well?"

Thwick gazed at the cage, his thin eyebrows rising. "Well, I'd say they aren't going anywhere. Nothing is going in, and they aren't coming out."

"And?"

"Let them starve," Thwick replied with a shrug. "Don't feed them or give them anything to drink, and I should think your problem will be solved for you inside of a week."

"You don't look well," Gaius said quietly.

Treijan looked up from where he sat, his knees drawn up to his chest and his head bowed down. "I'll be all right. We've just got to find a way out of this cage."

"What about a gate?" Gaius asked. "You've got other Songstones from other places. We could—"

"I've tried," Treijan replied in a whisper. "It's this

damn cage. I can't sing the gate open here. It's as though they knew exactly how to stop us—almost as though they *knew* us."

Outside the cage, Gaius spotted two new robed figures entering the hall, each carrying a large, heavy book across his chest with both arms.

"Well, here comes the relief guard," Gaius said. "So much for waiting until they're tired. I can't believe that it's going to end like this—that this is what Theona saw."

"Theona?" Treijan chuckled. "So you believe in her visions, after all?"

Gaius watched as the squat demon tugged at the robe of one of the guards he was relieving and shoved him toward the door. "I've seen a lot of things these last few days, Trei. Is it so amazing that Theona may be seeing things that we don't?"

Treijan nodded. "You might be right—although we may never know. This hasn't turned out quite the way I planned for my wedding day."

"Well, what about Arryk?" Gaius spoke softly, leaning in closer, his eyes shifting to keep an eye on the robed demons replacing two of their former captors at one end of the cage. One of them walked with a strange waddle; Gaius noted that he could probably outpace it in a flat run. "Does he have any ideas? What about his centaur friend?"

Treijan drew in a deep breath. "Arryk is certain that he has condemned his entire nation to extinction, and Hueburlyn is so disgusted with our faery friend that he isn't talking to anybody—not that I'd understand him if he did. It seems, however, that they both broke out of a cage similar to this one just before they dragged us into their own world."

Gaius looked up hopefully. "And?"

"And whoever built that cage apparently learned from their mistakes," Treijan concluded, resting his chin back on his knees, his arms wrapped around his curled-up legs. "We are imprisoned in the new and improved version of Deep Magic dungeons."

"Maybe when they feed us," Gaius considered aloud, still keeping an eye on the waddling demon, its face hidden from him. He noticed that the creature was making an effort at not being seen—and there was a large dark stain on the back of its hood. "They've got to open the cage to get the food in. We could…"

Gaius froze.

The goblin's face turned toward him. It was still mostly obscured by the deeply hooded robe, but he distinctly saw a patch of smooth, tan skin around a gloriously bright and beautiful eye.

The robe turned from him once more as it began waddling toward the guard at the other end of the cage.

"By the jests of Skurea," Gaius said, nearly choking.

Treijan looked up sharply. "What is it?"

Gaius stood up. The newly arrived squat guard was also moving toward the guards at the far end of the cage.

"Hey, ugly!" Gaius shouted, his eyes fixing on the guard still watching him in the corner. Gaius pointed directly at the robed demon and shouted as he walked toward him, "Yeah, you! I think you are about the most revoltingly hideous creature ever spawned! I think you and your entire family should be dropped back in the maggot pile you came from!"

Treijan stood up in surprise. "Uh, Gaius—they can't understand a word you're saying."

"Oh, right!" Gaius shouted angrily. "But I'm betting

they get my tone! And if you know what's good for you, you'll do the same with that other slime-skinned puke-face in that other corner right now!"

Treijan stood up, a questioning look crossing his face before he, too, started shouting angrily, stepping toward the second guard in the other corner. "I suppose this is all part of some plan, isn't it, dragon-cheese?" he bellowed, shaking his fist at the demon, who took a step back and raised his book in front of him, his eyes fixed on Treijan. "Yeah, you heard me, garden-skin! I'm yelling at you, and you haven't any more of a clue what I'm saying than I do! I wish *someone* would tell me *why I'm yelling!*"

"Because we have *visitors!*" Gaius barked toward the guard. The waddling guard was nearly behind him now, rising up taller and taller over the short demon, the heavy book rising higher still in both slender, tan arms.

"Oh, yeah?" Treijan screamed, now noticing the squat figure standing behind his own guard. "Like *who?*"

"I *think*—it's your *wife!*"

Both books crashed down simultaneously.

The robed goblins fell senseless to the floor.

Theona tossed back the hood of her robe, eyed the book in her hands, and then dropped it on the still form at her feet. "At last," she said, "I've found a use for magic."

The squat figure tore at his robes, revealing himself as Dregas. "Done as promised er is! Now a bargain be a bargain, lass! Where be my hat?"

"Theona!" Treijan laughed. "Hrea be praised! How did you manage it? The city is overrun by goblins."

"Yes," Theona said, looking around the room, searching for something. "They've been pouring out of their own rift-gate for days."

"What?" Gaius asked.

"You were right, Treijan; they came from yet another world," Theona said, then stepped over to the dwarf. "Give me your hammer."

"I'll do nay the like!" shouted the indignant dwarf.

"Your hat is right where we left it," Theona said, her voice no longer a request. "Now, give me your hammer; you'll get it right back."

The dwarf gaped but reached around his back and produced the heavy steel mallet. Theona lifted it with effort and turned back toward the cage.

"But how did you get past this—this goblin army?" Treijan asked. "I mean, it's incredible that you should just walk in here without any—I mean—"

"Without any *magic*," Theona said as her brown eyes flashed at the prince. "Wizards and mystics—Hrea save us all! You're all so bound up in your 'powers' and your 'symbols'—your petty secrets and clannish snobbery—that you don't see us common people. You're so afraid of each other and the glorious raw energies of the Deep Magic you wield that you never notice the quiet, simple power of the rest of us making life as best we can. Well, I've a voice, Prince Rennes-Arvad, and a mind that will choose which path I take and which future I want! It's not the power that you have, Treijan—it's what you *choose* to do with it that sets the future!"

Theona lifted the hammer high, her stance wide.

"Theona, don't!" Gaius shouted. "It's magic!"

"I'm sick of hearing it!" She shouted out her fury, and she swung the hammer wide and level, all her weight and strength going into the blow. The hammer slammed against the metal bands, the cage ringing loudly from the blow. The hammer rebounded, its weight pulling Theona away. But she stepped up once more, focused only on releasing her rage.

"I'm sick of being worthless! I'm sick of the magic!" She raised the hammer again, her swings coming more frequently now, her blows raining down on the metal cage. "I choose my future here and now! I won't be anyone's slave!"

The bands, still glowing, bent inward slightly with each successive strike.

"I've *seen* what the future can be! I've *seen* the roads our choices take us!" Theona wept openly now, blinking through her tears as she beat incessantly against the metal. "I *choose*! I *choose*! I—"

The metallic bands bent inward, snapping.

The blue aura flickered and vanished.

Theona dropped the hammer to the floor, suddenly spent.

Gaius reached up, the Deep Magic now flowing into the cage, and found Dwynwyn in the dream. The connection was there again, and the metal of the cage evaporated around them. Arryk flitted up into the ceiling, stretching his wings, as Hueburlyn stepped nervously in a circle around them, eyeing the exits with suspicion.

Gaius took a step toward Theona, but Treijan was already gathering her into his arms. Gaius looked away and stepped back. "What do we do now, Your Highness?"

"After that racket I suspect we'd better be prepared for more guards," Treijan replied lightly.

"I be getting my hat er is!" Dregas spoke up.

"Meklos has been watching them," Theona said, her voice tinged with sadness. "Your friend King Pe'akanu is losing his battle because the goblins can fix their warrior giants—their titans, they call them—faster than the

Hanu'ui's magic can wreck them. They just drag their damaged titans back through their gate, patch them up, and send them back through."

"But if we close the goblins' gate . . . ," Gaius began.

"Then we have a chance to defeat this army," Treijan finished, nodding his head.

"We have to close the goblins' gate," Theona said. "It's just down the plaza from here in a broken building to our right."

"But the entire goblin army is between us and the gate," Gaius said. "Even if their book-toting monsters aren't looking for us, they're sure to spot you if you get anywhere near the gate."

"We're so close!" Treijan growled. "What we need is a distraction—something that can confuse these goblins long enough for us to get to the gate."

The sound falling around Gaius reminded him of fire burning through a plain of dried grasses. He looked up at Arryk as the faery spoke, then to his companion. "What did he say?"

Treijan's brows were raised in puzzled surprise. "He says that we need an army to get through an army—and that Theona has one in her pocket. Theona?"

They all stared at the woman for a moment.

"There is a path"—Theona sighed—"but it is not an easy one, and it is not our choice to make." She reached into her pouch and held out her hand.

In it she held the Songstone of Sharajentis.

Into the
Unknown

Dwynwyn, Queen of the Dead, sat upon the stairs at the base of the fallen rift-gate, stoically surveying the wide paved court between her and the towering walls of her dread palace. Her personal protectors—the Shadow Guard—stood arrayed, as she ordered, on either side of the stairs. Peleron sat next to her so that together they might look out over the last of the Sharajin now sitting on the stones of the courtyard awaiting the final battle.

The day had begun with such hopes. Following what, to Dwynwyn, seemed to be an entirely too hasty wedding ceremony, Arryk and his strange companions had opened the fabulous gate that bridged their worlds and by all appearances passed through it just as they had described it to her. All that remained of Sharajentis, including Dwynwyn herself, waited patiently in the courtyard, their ranks ordered naturally by family according to their station in the Sharaj. Their wealth—such as it was—lay arrayed on a series of carts behind them. All were waiting patiently and in silence, facing the great shimmering surface within the gigantic ring of the magical portal.

And so the silence continued into the afternoon.

While the faeries were not known for patience, they were known for the single-mindedness of their thinking. To them, there were only two choices: pass through the gate and live, or remain and die. So they watched the shimmering images of the dark place with the patch of light and waited for Arryk to return.

When the gate collapsed, Dwynwyn's spirit went with it. There were no more options, no more choices to be made. Her city was encircled by the Kyree-Nykira, and their vengeance would be most terrible. Her armies of the dead had fought fiercely and bravely, and so they now were nearly gone. The last of their number now stood outside her walls prepared to defend her to their last glory. The end was coming; there was no other course for them to take.

So they remained as the hours of the day lengthened, and the armies of the Kyree-Nykira closed toward them with murderous intent.

"My queen?"

Dwynwyn turned toward a voice that seemed to be speaking at her from a great distance.

"Yes, Peleron."

"Word has come from the Deathlords," Peleron said quietly. "The Kyree are in the Margoth Woods and approaching down the main road from the south. The Deathlords have made probing attacks to the northeast, southeast, and west. All reported back with heavy losses sustained. We remain surrounded and without avenue of retreat."

Dwynwyn nodded. "As expected."

"Still, it was worthy of the Deathlords to make the attempt."

"And no doubt many of the dead in our service found release to the Enlightenment in their doomed attempt," Dwynwyn added. Her Deathlords led her armies and had never failed her before. "Yet for us it changes nothing. The Kyree are artists when it comes to war; having so carefully constructed our trap, I would have been disappointed had they proved themselves so stupid as to let us escape. How strong are the Kyree from the south?"

"The Deathlords offer us their observations of three or, perhaps, four qintalons,"* Peleron said, averting his eyes as he spoke, "at least one of which is full strength and each being comprised of mixed dekacian units. There is also nearly a full dekacian of siege machines observed coming up behind the main force."

Dwynwyn rubbed her hand hard across her forehead, as though trying to push the thought out of her mind. "That must be nearly forty thousand strong. How long until they arrive?"

"Two hours—perhaps three, if they take their time," Peleron replied.

"They won't," Dwynwyn scoffed. "They smell our blood."

"So I take it you think it's too late to negotiate?"

Dwynwyn laughed darkly. "Peleron, you have the oddest sense of humor."

---

*A Kyree word referring to one of their largest units of war—an army of approximately ten thousand warriors. The word is also an honorable title given to the commander of such a force.

"I married the Queen of the Dead," Peleron said, smiling wistfully. "I was told that a sense of humor was a requirement for the position. So what are your thoughts on this rather auspicious occasion, my dear queen?"

"I was thinking—I was thinking about that wingless woman who came with Arryk and the others."

"Theona?"

"Yes, that's her name. She gave me a message through Gaius—strange now to think that I ever actually met him outside of the Sharaj—"

"A message?" Peleron inserted.

Dwynwyn shook her head. "I suppose it doesn't matter now, but I can't seem to get it out of . . . my . . ."

A murmur was building in the great crowd before her, growing moment by moment. First one, then five, and then hundreds rose to their feet, their wings unfurling and fluttering in anxious anticipation. Dwynwyn stood, watching them pointing in her direction, their voices rising louder and louder until astonished shouts filled the enormous courtyard with sound.

"Syldaran's eye!" Peleron swore in amazement.

Dwynwyn turned. Her mouth opened, but she could not find words of her own.

The stones of the rift-gate were rolling back across the courtyard, bounding upward over the steps of the platform, and falling into place. One by one, shard by shard, the gate was re-forming itself around the Songstone at its base, the terrible onyx limbs, veins, and sinews re-formed just as they had been before.

Dwynwyn took a cautious step back, reaching out for the support of Peleron's arm. "Is it true?"

"It is a truth, Dwynwyn!" Peleron exclaimed. "It most certainly is a truth!"

The final shards from the peak of the oval leaped into the air, collapsing into their position. In that instant the air within the oval flashed with brilliant light and then became subdued into the shimmering, odd deep blue surface that they had seen before.

The air within the circle flared brightly once more—and before her on the platform stood the centaur . . .

. . . And Arryk.

Dwynwyn rushed forward, throwing her arms around the young faery as tears flooded down her cheeks.

Arryk blinked uncertainly, his hands and arms reaching around the queen in an awkward embrace. "Queen Dwynwyn—I am—I am so sorry—for everything. I—"

"It's all right now, my child," Dwynwyn said, her exuberance boundless. "You came back. I was sure you would, but when the gate collapsed . . ."

Arryk shook his head. "My queen—Dwynwyn—we don't have a lot of time."

"No, of course not," Dwynwyn agreed. "We've got to get our people through the gate. The Kyree will be here within hours and—"

"Please, you've got to listen to me." Arryk's voice rose.

"There will be plenty of time to speak once our nation is safe," Dwynwyn said, turning back to face the crowd.

"No!" Arryk shouted.

He grabbed Dwynwyn by the wrist, pulling her around to face him.

The quick sound of steel sliding on steel was followed by several flecks of light. An instant later Arryk was facing the tip of six blades at his throat.

"Hold!"

Dwynwyn's arm was still held firmly in Arryk's grasp

even as the Shadow Guard surrounded them, their cold dead eyes fixed on Arryk.

Arryk chose to look at Dwynwyn as he spoke, taking great care not to move.

"There is war on the other side of this gate," Arryk's words rang.

Dwynwyn eyed him carefully for a moment. "Guards—withdraw."

The blades vanished as quickly as they had come, the dead guardians stepping back to their places. Arryk let go of the queen's arm.

"What do you mean?" Dwynwyn demanded. "There is war here!"

"And there is war there," Arryk said, his bowed head causing his long bangs to fall across his eyes. "I've—I've *caused* all this. If I hadn't let Hueburlyn into the city in the first place—if I hadn't escaped and brought the gate here, I—"

"No, son," Dwynwyn said, reaching out to him, picking up his chin and raising his eyes to meet hers. "Look at me and listen to truth. If it had not been this centaur, it would have been another of the Famadorians. If it had not been your disappearance, then the Kyree would have found another excuse that suited them. Our problems are not one man's folly, but the folly of many of us over time. You cannot carry the burden of so many others' mistakes—nor, come to think of it, can I. We only get to choose for ourselves..." Dwynwyn paused. *Two roads*. "Tell me why they fight."

"What?"

"Tell me why the wingless men fight beyond this rift-gate."

"There is—there is another gate from the world of the

demons," Arryk said. "The wingless men fight to save their peace and their lives."

"The demons," Dwynwyn asked, "what do they want?"

"They want death—like the Kyree."

"And what of Gaius and your friend Treijan? What do they advise?"

"They need our help to save their world—but, in truth, my queen, I do not think any of them know the ends of what will happen or have any assurance that any of us will survive their war."

Dwynwyn stood for a moment considering.

Two roads—and a time when she must risk everything on the unknown.

"Dwynwyn?" Peleron asked with concern.

Dwynwyn refocused and turned to face the enormous assembly, holding her hands high for silence. Slowly, quiet fell over the crowd, and at last she spoke.

"Arryk has returned from a far land—a distant world where our brothers and sisters in the Sharaj, too, fight wars against those who would take their lives, rob them of their breath and their spirit and their future. War, it seems, is not the special province of the Kyree or, indeed, the faery.

"But we know this truth: if we stay and do nothing, we shall surely die. The Kyree thirst for our blood and offer nothing in exchange but our annihilation. Should we stay, our lives will pass for naught."

Dwynwyn turned to Peleron and offered him her hand. He took it and stood beside her as once more she faced what remained of her nation.

"Every life has worth if we but spend it wisely. It is our choice to do so, and it is your choice now. Here is death, certain and without value; there—there beyond this gate is also war and death, but *there,* too, is the hope for meaning, the hope for life. We asked for a new land and a home in a new world, but it seems we must purchase our right to such a place with our blood. It has ever been so. We cannot be given another home—we must earn it. *There* through that gate is a road uncertain, but it is the road I *choose* to take!"

With that, the Queen of the Dead turned her back on her palace and her city. She drew her staff in front of her, conjuring a spell of dreadful power at its apex, and charged through the gate.

39

Two Roads

Meklos pulled himself forward painfully with his staff, making his way through the convoluted halls of the Temple of the Dragon and, with agonizing slowness, up the steep, rough steps into the great ceremonial hall.

The vast room was deserted; the goblins had already murdered the shaman priests who had defended it with their last breaths, and stripped the place of its books and other objects they deemed of value before moving on to better pickings. Nevertheless, as Meklos neared the top of the stairs, he grew quiet, listening intently to the farthest reaches of the dark hall for any sign that he was not alone.

Flickering light from the fires in the city outside still penetrated the wide opening arch of the ceremonial hall. No sound alarmed him, and nothing moved save the shadows from the flames. The bodies of the shamans remained where they had fallen. Meklos knew better than to engage in any formal honoring of these desecrated dead; whatever he did for them would not put their souls to rest, and moving them might put the continuity of his own breath in question. The fewer traces Meklos left of his passage, he reminded himself, the better his chances of living through all this. Someone else would have to send these poor souls into eternity.

So he made his way to the temple porch, because something inside of him wanted to see—wanted to be a part of, even from a distance—what was happening outside. He cursed himself for his own curiosity and cursed Theona, too, for it was she, after all, who had disturbed his thread of rationality and brought him to question himself.

They'll die here, Meklos thought as he came at last to the archway that led from the dark interior to the temple porch beyond. *Even if Theona manages to talk that liar of a dwarf into helping her, they are only two bards against an army that has already brought an entire nation of shamans to its knees. But I know Treijan; he'll try anyway, right here in the center of the city.*

He lowered himself with the help of his dragonstaff, sitting behind a statue and gazing out over the city. Steep steps ran down from the porch past two lower tiers of the pyramid and onto the wide plaza below. Winds from offshore blew the billowing smoke inland, affording him a clear view of the entire plaza from the Avenue of the Kings at the eastern end of the plaza, north to the smaller Temple of the Sky and south to the Temple of Fire. Three titans stood in the plaza before him, their heads higher than where Meklos sat, while countless goblins swarmed beneath the titans' gigantic legs. Their masters were urging the goblin warriors back into the avenue so that they might join the seemingly endless stream of warriors making their way to the north. Meklos counted seven titans alone passing down the avenue, their arms and legs patched with burned welds and mismatched scraps of metal. Meklos could not see the Temple of the Sea to the southeast, now hidden behind a veil of thick smoke, but he knew that the army was coming from that direction. It was, no doubt, the location of this special "gate," as Theona called it.

Theona. Meklos frowned at the thought. The woman had a singularly disturbing way of speaking to a man, he decided. "Well, Mistress Conlan," he muttered to himself, "if I'm not exactly *at* the crossroads, I certainly have a good view of them. The entire world will die at last—right here in front of me."

Meklos looked up at the enormous bulk of the temple rising up behind him. The steep stairs on either side of the archway into the ceremonial room continued up the face of the stepped pyramid from concourse to concourse. At the top, illuminated by the flames of the city below, he could make out the entrance to the topmost room. The goblin invasion had left King Pe'akanu no time to mount the thousand steps and sound the Voice of Rhai-Kuna, as he had called it. In the moment of their greatest need, all their plans had failed the king and his people.

Just as I have failed, Meklos thought.

"I've got to get back to the front," Skramak yelled, his voice barely carrying over the terrible sound all around them. "You know what to do?"

Big-funder Thwick nodded, though, in truth, he was not all that certain of what it was Skramak wanted. The continuous clamor of the slogging goblin troops, the whip cracks of their sar-gant and left-nat masters, and the groaning and clanging titans all pressing forward through the rift-gate behind him were overwhelming. He just knew it was a bad idea to disagree with the Conqueror of Gods—as Skramak now preferred to be called—whether you understood him or not.

"It's your job to keep these titans coming!" Skramak screamed. "I don't care who you threaten or kill to make it happen; just keep them coming. This is the most glorious war that goblins have ever fought, and I'm not going to lose it just because some weak-kneed, round-eared, flat-faced academic can't find his nerve. You keep the titans coming—keep the technomancers supplied and working and, above all, this gate open—and I'll make you the richest Big-funder to ever own an academy, you understand?"

This much Thwick certainly got, and he nodded enthusiastically. Here was a goal he could understand: to be in power forever, lording over lesser Deep Tinkers and approving acquisitions for personal use. It was not the riches exactly that attracted him—he had a healthy disdain for wealth that suited his position—but to continue to tell everyone else exactly how and what to think was too seductive a thought to be ignored. "I will, Lord Skramak! You may rely on me to support you every moment of this campaign!"

A robed figure ran toward them, pushing his way against the stream of warriors as he shouted, "Warlord Skramak!"

Skramak's single eye narrowed, but he nodded at Thwick anyway. "See that you do. I'll be directing the battle to the north personally, and the last thing I need is to have to come all the way back here to deal with—oh, what is it!"

Skramak wheeled around, grabbing the young technomancer by his robes and shaking him before tossing him to the ground with such force that he dropped his small book. The hood of the technomancer fell back to reveal a face so young as to be barely mottled and ears without tufts. At once the Big-funder guessed that this creature was bearing bad news; the master engineers that ruled the technomancers always sent their youngest with bad news. If he was killed by Skramak, the loss of training investment would be minimal.

"Warlord Skramak!" the technomancer yelped. "It wasn't my fault! It was Techno-steel Gudunk, he sent me!"

"What's your name?" Skramak snarled.

"Me? Nobody, master—really, I'm just another of your worshipful servants. It's that guy Gudunk you really need to remember. He's the one who knows about it."

He may be young, Thwick thought, *but this technomancer is no fool.*

"Knows about *what*?" Skramak bellowed.

"Magic!" the technomancer whimpered. "They've detected *magic* in that big palace building down at the end of this courtyard."

"You idiot!" Skramak shouted, his big hand grabbing the young messenger by the hank of hair at the top of his head and shaking it from side to side. With his other hand he reached down and drew his long curved sword from its sheath. "Of course, they've detected magic—we're holding prisoners in there! Gudunk's own goblins are guarding them and—"

"No, master!" the messenger whined. "A *lot* of magic. Not just one technomancer or two-feet-full-of-toes numbers of technomancers, but—but more than all the numbers he can count!"

Skramak looked up suddenly. "Here?"

"There's more coming by the moment, master!"

Skramak released the messenger's hair, dropping him to the ground at once.

The Big-funder was perplexed. "What is it, Warlord Skramak?"

"Thwick, go back and move the rest of the army through the gate as quickly as you can." Skramak turned around, searching the stream of warriors until he saw his quarry standing to the side of the road. "Gen-reel Piew! Contact the left-nats of those three phalanxes of titans and turn them around. I want them set all around the gate in two ranks—the first one about three strides out and the second ten away from the gate."

"At once, my lord!" Piew replied, slamming both fists to his chest.

"And the ground warriors—pull them back, too!" Skramak added. "Have them prepare to defend the gate!"

"What of Gen-reel Ekee at the front?" Piew asked, probably to avoid responsibility for whatever disaster had caught Lord Skramak's eye. "Should he withdraw to support us?"

"Not yet. Not until I'm sure!"

"Sure of what, my lord?" Big-funder Thwick asked, his eyes wide with concern.

"By Malak, get back through the gate and do as you're told!" Skramak shouted, his face flushing a deep green as he ran toward his titan, kneeling next to the raging power of the gate, its six tall banners flapping noisily in the wind. "I smell a trap!"

Dwynwyn was the first to come through the gate, and though her dark face was drawn from the horror of the transit, her eyes remained bright and determined.

Then followed Peleron with Arryk at his side. The elder faery's jaw was set in resignation, the younger already reaching into the Deep Magic of the other world and calling its force to his will.

Then came the Sharajin, first in ranks of two or four, but then in ranks of ten abreast, marching out of the shimmering portal in perfect unison.

Dwynwyn stepped quickly to Gaius and spoke, her words sounding like gentle rain weeping from a midnight sky. "We offer our strength to you, that we may purchase our new land with our blood."

The ranks of faery men and women were filling the hall to bursting. "How many of you are there?"

"Of the Sharajin we have one thousand two hundred and fourteen," Dwynwyn replied. "Of able men and women willing to fight with weapons at hand, I do not know but perhaps no more than three thousand. There are another six thousand beyond that in families and children—"

"Children!" Gaius exclaimed. "Queen Dwynwyn, there is *war* here!"

"There is war beyond the gate, too, as you well know," Dwynwyn countered in a voice like iron. "*That* war's end was predestined—the complete destruction of our people assured—but *here,* right here, our fate is uncertain. To stay *there* is to die, to come *here* is to hope. My nation is coming through that gate *right now*—and this tiny hall will not hold them all."

"What are you saying?" Gaius asked, wide-eyed.

"If war is our only hope," Dwynwyn said as an electric ball of force steadily grew in her upraised hand, "then let us make war *now*!"

*   *   *

Meklos sat uneasily with his thoughts, shifting from time to time to alleviate his pains.

He looked across the city through the evening haze. The Hanu'ui loved straight lines, he thought as he gazed over the rooftops and trees from his perch on the side of the temple. The city itself was laid out in straight lines and right angles around two offset plazas connected to a single broad avenue. The Avenue of the Kings ran straight north from the Temple of Fire on the south edge of the city to the Temple of the Sky near the northern wall. The Plaza of the Dragon—a great rectangle below Meklos—extended from the foot of the Temple of the Dragon, where he was hiding, down to the avenue. The Plaza of Spirits was farther to the south, branching from the avenue eastward to the base of the Temple of the Sea. Each was set along perfect lines—ordered and sure—that reflected the way the Hanu'ui viewed the world around them.

Life was not that clearly defined, Meklos thought. Life, he knew, was as twisted and contorted as himself.

Theona had said that he was a cripple long before she returned—what did she know about him? She had lived her life among freight haulers! How dared she call *him* a cripple? It was obvious to him that she knew *nothing* of ambition or politics or the lies of bards who destroyed generations of families all in the name of their supposedly higher ideals!

Higher ideals, he thought bitterly, glancing up at the Voice of Rhai-Kuna. It was all just talk: a symbol that the lords of power sold like stale bread to the masses so that they would quietly ignore the injustices being done to them.

He would have changed all that, he thought bitterly. He would have *made* them see the truth! He would have put their faces flat against what they had done to him and his family and make them suffer as he had suffered.

Why couldn't the Conlan woman see that? He did not ask for her approval and loathed her apparent pity. For that matter, he had not asked for or wanted help from King Pe'akanu, yet the old king had brought him back from death.

"We are all one another's concern." Theona's words floated up into his mind.

Something was changing in the city arrayed below him. Through the haze Meklos could see the Temple of the Sea at the eastern edge of the city. Across the tops of the buildings and at the foot of that temple was a mass of confusion. The steady stream of titans and warriors that had been emerging from the goblins' rift-gate seemed to have fallen into disarray, with the phalanx of titans dissolving and moving out into the city. The larger titan he had seen earlier—the one with the banners—stood up and was gesturing with its arms to the other metal giants around it. Below, in the Plaza of the Dragon, the goblin ground troops were scurrying about in a panic. More interesting still, one of the phalanxes of titans moving off to the north at the end of the avenue hesitated and actually turned around.

There came a terrible silence, as though sound itself had been pulled from the air, its energies sucked into a single center below him. The world seemed to hold its breath and Meklos with it, teetering on the edge of some unseen abyss.

Light exploded outward in waves from the palace to the south, and the streets below were suddenly filled with the sound of tortured metal mixed with the high-pitched screams of goblins. In moments the first of the waves passed over Meklos, the moisture in the air flashing into fog as the temperature dropped astoundingly fast. Meklos pulled his robe around him, trying to shield himself just as the second wave and then a third passed over him. The fog crystallized across the city, falling to the ground as ice.

Then the air became incredibly clear, revealing a city whose previous fires were largely snuffed out by the glacial blast. Thick ice coated the city, the goblins in the plaza below him falling over in obvious terror and panic. Perhaps, Meklos thought, they came from warmer climates and had no experience with such a freeze. Meanwhile, the titans tried to shake themselves free of their icy encasements, sending a shower of frozen shards down on the hapless goblins at their feet and killing many.

In that moment the palace erupted like a fallen hive, and Meklos's jaw dropped in astonishment.

Faeries. Thousands of the winged, lithe creatures straight from his Deep Magic dreams poured out of the palace and washed into the air like a wave of death. The goblins in the courtyard below tried to flee, but the ice underfoot gave their feet no place to step. Lightning crackled across the plaza, sweeping over its surface with deadly effect. The mass of faeries in the air wheeled as one, pressing toward the Temple of the Sea on the other side of the city.

They were driving directly toward the goblin rift-gate.

The titans rallied to their gate in the distance, urged by the tall titan, its banners now stiff from the cold. But though the titans moved quickly, the faeries continued their rush forward.

The titans reached down and dug their enormous metal hands into the cobblestones at their feet, tearing them up and raising huge piles of shattered stone in their grasp. With impossible speed the great arms began throwing their handfuls of rock, hurling tons of broken ground at a time.

The debris tore through the faery swarm, dismantling as it flew, creating an expanding pattern of death. Wherever the rock and dirt passed, enormous gaps would appear in the faery formation. Still, the Fae charged headlong, trying to weather the assault, but eventually, they broke apart so as to present a less dense target.

When the faeries reached the six titans at the gate, they enveloped the metal beasts. One titan suddenly imploded, its metal collapsing inward on itself until it looked ridiculously thin. The monster toppled over, falling against the side of the Temple of the Sea, and did not move again. The head of a second titan exploded, as did a third, leaving the lead titan and two others alone in the square.

But not for long, Meklos noted. Four titans that had turned around on the Avenue of the Kings were approaching the combat area. Another group of six more titans was emerging from the goblins' rift-gate and entering the Plaza of Spirits in the distance.

Below Meklos the goblins were regrouping. He could see them raising their strange mechanical weapons, aiming them overhead and launching blades into the sky.

The faeries can't push through the plaza to the rift-gate, Meklos noted to himself as he watched. *They need a real concentration of power. They need—*

Meklos glanced behind him once more.

The Voice of Rhai-Kuna.

"No," he growled at himself.

"My enemy's enemy is now my friend?" the words came unbidden into his mind.

"Right here and right now you can change that!"

Meklos pulled himself to his feet with his dragonstaff and staggered across the stone platform, falling against the stone stairs leading up the side of the pyramid. He was a man who longed to have a life of his own. No one knew that—no one understood it. His family had been proud and powerful among the Sea-kings of the Crescent Coast. They had been a great clan, and the greatness that was lost became a stone they carried on their backs every day. But what he yearned for was a home and the warmth of loving companionship—the life that every common man hoped for his future—but not *him;* never *him.*

He reached up, gripping the step with his fingers while still holding on to his staff. The pain nearly overwhelmed him when he lifted his leg to the stair and pushed himself upward.

His ancestors would not allow for his own happiness. How many times had his own father told him—beat into him—the story of his grandfather's stand against the dragon? He could see his father now, slumped against the wall of that slumhole his mother called home, his speech slurred with drink until Meklos could not understand him. But understand him Meklos did. For to *not* understand was to be beaten or, when Meklos got old and strong enough to fend off the raging drunk, to invite a beating on his mother. The old man had carried the burden of the family honor on his back year after year until it broke him and buried him.

Meklos had reached the third tier of the temple steps. The battle continued below, but the sounds seemed distant in his ears; Meklos was hearing other voices.

"You live in the past, breathing in its hate, its mistakes,

and its prejudices as though that *was the source of life itself."*

"Liar!" Meklos screamed, the word becoming a cry of pain. His hands were shaking now as he reached for another step.

He did what he had to do, he thought. He took on the family honor and knew that he would be the one to reclaim it. He would succeed where his old man had failed. Then Meklos found the talent in him for the Deep Magic and hated it; it tied him to the bards of Calsandria—the very ones who had spread the lies about his family and their past! But there were other paths for that magic—other disciplines among the Pir. He worked with a zealot's will, became a Dragon-Talker, and, in time, returned to his beloved Khordsholm. Meklos knew that this time—*this* time—a Jefard would stand on the ruins of the city and bring the dragon Ulruk to heel!

He hunted Ulruk, confronting the old monster in the north hills beyond Khordsholm, almost ten years before. He presented his staff, called the powers of it into play, and demanded the dragon cower before him.

He failed.

"You're weak, Meklos!" It was his father's voice now. *"Never reconsider your position once you take it! You are a Jefard! Act like one!"*

"Damn you!" Meklos shouted as he reached with agonizing effort for the next step. "You weren't always right! I don't need you anymore! You always wanted someone else to take care of your problems—always wanted someone else to blame! I won't do it anymore!"

"Let go of your demons. Let go of your fear. Let go of your past."

"I have a life!" Meklos said quietly, spent. "I—I want to choose."

"Sometimes we do not get to choose our destiny . . . sometimes it chooses us."

Meklos stood panting and realized only then that he had reached the top of the long stairs. His pain was fading, and he stood up, stretched, and turned.

The top tier of the pyramid consisted of a platform with a stone roof supported by four corner pillars. Suspended from the ceiling was a large ornate instrument of curious design, its horn curling around, ending in a mouthpiece.

Meklos approached the horn and considered it for a moment. The ways of the gods are strange, he thought, that he might search the known world and come to find salvation in such a place.

He looked at his dragonstaff. Dragon-Talkers of the Pir had commanded the Dragonkings themselves to kneel before them through its power. If he were to call Rhai-Kuna and force the beast to do his will, this was the tool he would need.

He grabbed it with both hands and, in a single strong motion, broke it over his knee, tossing the pieces over the side of the pyramid.

He was done with forcing anyone to do anything.

With that, he leaned forward and blew into the horn.

Dragon-Talker

Theona ran onto the grand portico of Pe'akanu's palace as stones from the titans at the far end of the Plaza of Spirits began raining down on the building. She fell heavily behind a pillar just as the crossbeam supporting the roof crumbled, so she covered her head with her arms while stones crashed down next to her. She screamed, the sound lost in the din of battle, shaking from the fury around her and then choking on the dust she sucked into her lungs.

She had seen it all in her visions, but the experience of it was vastly different. Her dreams could not capture the smell of death, the cries of the dying, and the overwhelming sounds of panic and despair. Worst of all, in the midst of the terror washing around her like the tide, was the sudden thought that she had been wrong; that she had not just foreseen this catastrophe but had somehow caused it. Perhaps Hrea had not come to her at all. Perhaps the visions were merely echoes of her own desires wreaking a madness within her as terrible as any afflicting those of the Asylum.

The faeries continued to pour out of the crumbling palace, now the center of the goblin army's attentions. The great titan machines hurled both raw stone and their own magic toward the building against which she cowered. The ceiling had collapsed in places, and the walls were beginning to shift. The faeries answered back with magic of their own: ice, wind, hail, and lightning. The plants and trees lining the sides of the Plaza of Spirits became their allies, twisting and writhing in unnatural ways and with frightening speed. Goblins were suddenly dragged by these plants downward below the ground, their shrill screams choked off. One set of whipping palm trees encumbered a titan by pulling its feet out from under it, lifting it in the air, and repeatedly slamming it against the ground. Then it swatted at the goblins on the ground as though they were insects to be smashed. The little green demons retaliated with magic and brute force: the palms were assaulted with disease and withered by blight, while smaller plants were simply torn from the ground.

Theona rolled her shoulders and glanced beyond the pillar that shielded her. She cowered at the top of the palace steps and had a clear view down the length of the Plaza of Spirits toward the Temple of the Sea. The faeries were stopped less than a third of the way across the plaza by a growing line of wounded titans that moved in from the north as well as goblin warriors pouring through the gate next to the temple. The fate of those warriors was terrible indeed, for they were being constantly urged forward by their commanders, forced to throw themselves bodily against the ever-entrenching line of faeries. The goblin dead were mounting so quickly that Theona could literally see piles growing across the center of the vast plaza. Still they came, draining the powers of the faeries who struggled to press forward.

No less piteous was the fate of the faeries who could find no way either to advance east toward the goblin gate or to flank the goblin position to the north or south. Though Dwynwyn herself led the north-flank faeries and Peleron the south, both their advances were forced to a halt. The initial assault had been broken, if only just, by the titans defending the gate. Now the faeries were forced to commit their reinforcements into the fray, fighting to advance eastward toward the rift-gate and to protect their flanks from separate goblin forces encroaching on them from both the northern and southern ends of the Avenue of the Kings. Though they had the advantage of flight, the faeries were frequently knocked to the ground by goblins armed with a terrible weapon that shot blades into the air with deadly accuracy.

Brilliant light flared again and again from the eastern skirmish line. Gaius, Theona realized, and Treijan were there doing everything they could to break through and close the gate—to stop the flow of goblin warriors that was bleeding away their own forces one drop at a time.

She closed her eyes. *Please, Hrea,* she prayed, *please show us the road.*

In that moment she heard the deep, thunderous rumble of a great horn.

Meklos stood back in awe. The deep vibrations of the horn shook the stones beneath his feet. The entire temple seemed to resonate with the sound, amplifying it, adding to it in mystic sympathy. Even after Meklos released the instrument, the sound was building, stronger and stronger.

The island itself trembled.

* * *

King Pe'akanu, his face smeared with soot for war, looked on angrily with red, sleepless eyes at the line of titans striding toward them. He had called for warriors from across the island to defend against these demons. Many were coming from the farthest cities of his kingdom, but their roads were long. Already he had given his totems to a runner—the symbols of his office and power—so that his brother in Omanahue-Re could continue the fight when Pe'akanu had gone to his father's house among the stars. He would go with honor, for he had fought with his brother warriors for three days now and had killed hundreds of the demons with his arms and many with even his bare hands. Now he stood overlooking a wide patch of grassland from the ridgeline, his warriors arrayed next to him down its length. Each easily swung his warrior's club, his house dragon perched on a shoulder. When the demons and their cursed metal giants reached the bottom of the ridge, they would rain death upon them.

The lead monster of iron clanked to a stop at a stream that wandered across the field, waiting for the four others of its kind to catch up. The grasses shifted with the green demons that moved through it.

Pe'akanu raised his left hand, his right swinging his war club faster and faster.

Then he heard the sound.

The monsters at the bottom of the ravine stopped, turning to face the noise that rolled toward them from the distance.

"The Voice of Rhai-Kuna!" the king whispered in wonder. "The Voice is sounded!"

The metallic man turned at once and began running in great loping strides away from them, its gait so fast that it was shaking great pieces of itself from its shoulders. One entire arm fell to the ground, but the creature did not slow its steps, it merely continued its headlong retreat.

The other four giants turned with it, moving uncertainly back in pursuit.

"The Voice is sounded!" Pe'akanu screamed with the full fury of his voice. "Rise up, warriors of Rhai-Tuah! The Voice is sounded!"

The warriors cried out in glorious cheer, their gathered magic unleashed before them as they charged down the slope. The spirits of their ancestors formed to charge with them.

The green demons suddenly broke ranks, fleeing in squealing panic after their metallic giants, who had abandoned them.

"The Voice is sounded!" cried Pe'akanu at the top of his lungs.

The plaza shook with the sound of a great horn.

"What was that?" Gaius shouted as he pulled one of the strange weapons from the dead hand of a goblin. Another goblin leaped over the street stones which Gaius had conjured upward into a barricade, falling on the bard before he could raise the device. The creature curled its incredibly strong hands around Gaius's throat. The bard had a blurred impression of the creature grinning at him, baring its sharp teeth, when suddenly the head vanished and the grip loosened.

Treijan stood over him with a bloodied axe. "I have no idea," he said, raising it up just as two more of the enemy prepared to leap on him. Three faeries, however, swooped down out of the sky and whisked them into the air, dropping them after soaring upward nearly thirty feet.

Gaius scrambled to his feet, his mind searching the other realm of the dream for another mystic connection. They were getting tenuous and more difficult. "Whatever it was, I hope it was a good sign—I don't know how much longer I can keep this up."

"*I'm* doing just fine." Treijan smiled, glancing over at Arryk standing next to him. The faery spread his fingers out in front of him, searing light fanning outward into the wall of approaching goblins, each of whom collapsed at its touch. Arryk's face was rapturous. "But something's got to change. If we don't get advancing soon and get that gate closed, we're dead."

Gaius heard a terrible scream overhead. He looked up and shuddered. "We may be dead anyway!"

Meklos stepped to the edge at the top of the pyramid temple and caught his breath.

Soaring over the Plaza of Spirits was a dragon larger than any he had ever heard about, let alone seen. Its great wings were nearly twice as wide as the plaza itself, and its mass moved with a grace belying its size. The membranes between the veins of the wings were blotched and thinning, while the horns of its massive head were long, weathered, and curled back in long hooks to either side of its eyes. The multicolored scales of its body had lost their luminescent quality, but its haunches were still obviously powerful, and there was a depthless quality to his eyes.

Eyes that were watching the Aboth.

Meklos stood still as the dragon approached. Part of his mind was screaming at him to act, to follow his training and subdue the dragon with the power of his magic or to find a weapon with which to defeat his enemy.

"I cannot force it to do my will," he said to the wind around him.

Meklos opened his arms wide as the dragon soared over the shattered palace, its roar shaking the mortar from between the stones of the remaining buildings in the city below. Its talons, razor-sharp and stained, extended from its foreclaws, reaching toward him.

Meklos waited.

The dragon landed on the side of the stepped pyramid, its impact shaking the structure and causing Meklos nearly to lose his footing. The massive head of the dragon craned forward, its lips curling back from its yellowed, ancient teeth as its depthless eyes opened wide.

Meklos was a Dragon-Talker—and so he spoke.

"A dragon! By the gods!" Treijan cursed. "That monster is huge! Now what?"

"The goblins," Gaius said breathlessly. "They're backing off. I don't think they like the dragon any more than we do."

The faery spoke with the sound of winter wind on a gray day.

"Arryk wants to know what it is," Treijan said in astonishment. "Apparently, the faery don't have dragons either. What's going on?"

Rhai-Kuna was an old dragon even as his kind measured the years, and his understanding of the Dragon-Talker was not as good as that of others who were more practiced. The ways of dragons were strange, and their thoughts were not the thoughts of men, yet Rhai-Kuna had come to look upon the people of his island with something akin to fondness, for they had ever been kind to him. Above all, he objected to invasion of his peace by those who would harm him or his island. So he considered the words of this creature who had sounded the Voice to call him from his peace, and though he did not understand all that the man had said, and was not much moved by what he *did* understand, Rhai-Kuna knew that the peace of his island rest was threatened and his joy would be lessened until it was ended.

He did not understand the ways of the humans, so he did not understand what needed to be done. However, one thought came to him like a voice from afar, and it was the one thing he understood clearly.

This tiny, insignificant, harmless creature knew what to do even if he, the great Rhai-Kuna, did not.

So the dragon bowed his head down and, to Meklos's wonder, urged him to climb between his lengthy, curled horns.

Theona watched from behind the pillar as the dragon rose from the temple and wheeled in the sky. He circled around the back of the pyramid and then reappeared above the palace, his wings scooping at the air with strokes so powerful that ice and broken stones flew into the air behind him.

Everyone has chosen their road, Theona thought. *And now I must take mine.*

The goblins were already fleeing from the onrushing monster, piling up over their own dead, the faery dead, and into their own troops behind them. The titans at the end of the plaza, now seven in number, shifted uncertainly from side to side, while the tallest of them, his banners tangled on themselves, reached out with his mismatched arms, motioning emphatically to them to remain where they stood.

The faeries in the air darted away in panic, diving for cover as the enormous creature bore down on them, his mouth gaping wide as he drew in a terrible lungful of air.

The dragon's breath erupted from his open maw, an inferno so hot that its flame burned blue for nearly a hundred feet. The goblins in its path exploded, their organs boiling then charring in an instant and their flesh reducing to ash. The dragon swung his head from side to side, his breath coating the plaza in deadly flame.

The goblins situated on the avenue from the north and south panicked, dissolving into a mob that fled away from the center of the city. Seeing this, the embattled faeries began to cheer, rallying from their barricades, rising up, charging across the ash-laden plaza, to follow the path burned clear by the dragon soaring before them.

The colossal dragon spewed his blaze toward the titans at the end of the plaza.

Theona sucked in a deep breath.

It was time.

She sprang from behind the pillar, raced down the steps, then leaped into a dead run down the length of the plaza.

Little Sacrifices

Meklos held tightly to the rough horns of the old dragon, blinking furiously from the onslaught of wind. He had asked Rhai-Kuna for aid, and when the dragon responded, it nearly broke the Aboth's heart for joy. Now, riding on the ridges of the ancient dragon, his head bobbing beneath his bent legs as together they hurtled through the heart of battle, he began to wonder if he had made a mistake.

But he said none of this to the dragon. Rhai-Kuna did not understand him well enough, so it was essential not to let any human doubt enter into his words. Meklos spoke simply to the dragon as they flew, his voice clicking and hissing awkwardly in the tongue of the dragons. He hoped he could be understood over the rushing wind and through what was probably an atrocious human accent. Still, it was good to hear his own voice and confirm he still lived. *"Rhai-Kuna Lord! Ore melted giant many face-wind striking! Giant blood-stealing! Claw-breath to death!"*

The flames boiled up before him as they passed over the plaza, the dragon dropping his head.

A line of titans was arrayed at the end of the plaza just before the foot of the Temple of the Sea. As he and Rhai-Kuna flew closer, Meklos watched the titans seem to grow in his vision, and he noticed that one of the metal giants was fitted at the shoulder with several tall banners. It was taller than the rest and seemed to be taking its place behind the other five.

Rhai-Kuna turned his breath up from the ground, its searing jet blasting against the chestplate of the foremost titan. The metal glowed, then flashed white-hot before it sagged like butter on a warm day. An instant later the creature shattered, its arms and head exploding away from the dissolving torso and crashing to the ground. The creature's legs tottered for a moment before they, too, fell against the stone of the plaza.

Meklos's eyes widened. The titans were reaching up, trying to grab the dragon and pull him down from the sky, so the Aboth yelled for the dragon to turn. The creature's massive head lifted under him as they rose together, climbing skyward on their momentum.

Dregas stood with his back against the gate and gazed fearfully from behind his bandages at the procession of the faery Sharajin as they stepped out of the shifting, shimmering gate next to him and rushed forward. The floor rocked under his feet as sand and dust sifted down from the ceiling overhead. Occasionally, a large section of the roof would crash downward, smashing into the floor.

He had no intention of following anyone into battle, and though he had only the vaguest of notions about where this particular gate ended, he knew he wanted to be anywhere but here.

So he waited, keeping himself as inconspicuous as possible while the grim winged people passed him through the collapsing room and marched to their doom. In due time the families began arriving, frightened-looking children tended by their mothers, who folded their wings protectively around their charges. These groups filled the vast hall to overflowing, taking cover as best they could, which caused many of those in more exposed areas to seek places elsewhere in the building despite the dangerous shaking and crumbling of its walls.

Dregas decided that enough was enough. A gate to *anywhere* was better than here.

So when a gap opened between families coming through the gate, Dregas quietly stepped through it going the other way.

Tears streamed from Meklos's eyes as he blinked furiously at the wind. He hugged the left horn and tucked his head behind it hoping to get his face out of the direct wind. The streets of the city turned below him as he looked down on the battle from a thousand feet overhead. What a marvel! Here was a perspective that few generals had ever enjoyed. It seemed to him as though he were looking down on a play battlefield. He could see the goblins on the Avenue of the Kings trying to regroup and hide at the same time that the faeries pushed them back to the north. More faeries continued to pour out of the palace, but even from this height he could tell that the strength of their force was trailing off.

Beyond the line of titans at the southwest corner of the Temple of the Sea, Meklos saw the gate for the first time. The goblin rift-gate! Through it once again charged more of the goblin warriors, streaming northward toward the titans. There seemed to be no end to them, and they were heading directly toward the plaza, where Treijan and Gaius and the faeries charged over debris and barricades toward the titans. Meklos could see that a collision with the goblin reinforcements was about to come.

Treijan has to get the gate closed, Meklos thought, *or any victory will be short-lived.* The dragon could take out the titans one at a time, but by then Treijan and the faeries would be lost.

Meklos yelled once more in the clacking sounds of the dragonspeak. Rhai-Kuna responded, rolled to his left, and, in a sweeping curve, dove toward the plaza.

Treijan and Gaius hurtled headlong down the length of the plaza with Arryk flying beside. Following on their heels were the rest of the faeries, whose own cries sounded like a hurricane.

After the dragon had soared upward above the remaining titans, Gaius saw that two of the metal giants were missing. One lay in scattered, smoldering parts around the feet of its brothers, while the other was staggering backward, the arm of the exploded titan having been driven through its midsection. Gaius watched it turn to the south, stumbling awkwardly toward . . .

The goblin rift-gate! Gaius could see it now beyond the fleeing titan: an oval of shimmering light fixed in the center of the library's ruins. It was astonishing; this was not the rippling black surface of the bard gates, but a clear window into another world. And the vista shocked him. On a large plain at the foot of a range of distant mountains he could see an enormous army waiting to be unleashed on his world.

They see me, too, he realized, just as a flood of goblins poured through the gate, screaming wildly and charging. The remaining four metallic monsters stood between them and the gate, their arms rising as they prepared for battle.

"Treijan!" Gaius yelled. "What do we do?"

"Keep running!" Treijan yelled back.

"*Toward* the giants?" Gaius yelped.

"This is our only chance," Treijan said, his eye on the gate beyond.

Lightning flashed from the arms of the titans, raking through the faeries overhead. They fell limp from the sky by the dozens, smashing into others below them and thudding to the ground.

"Keep running!" Treijan yelled.

"This won't work!" Gaius shot back, but he ran anyway. "We're being flanked from the gate!"

He heard the roaring of the dragon approaching behind him before he saw anything. The faeries were scattering once more around him, but Gaius didn't dare look back.

Meklos drew in a deep breath, wondering at his own calm. The dragon was moving much faster than he had in their first pass over the plaza. The dragon could do the most damage against the warriors, the Aboth reasoned, so he called Rhai-Kuna's attention to the goblins flooding through the rift-gate. It meant that they would have to fly directly past the remaining giants, who, he did not doubt, would try to pull them out of the sky. Whether the monsters succeeded or not, the one thing that Meklos was sure of was that he probably would not live through it, either way.

Dragons, however, do things for their own reasons, and despite his years of studying these creatures and learning their ways, what happened next shocked and astonished Meklos.

The dragon reached up with his powerful foreclaws at the last moment and snatched Meklos from his head inside his great fist. Then the dragon, his wing membranes trembling in his terrible speed, curled his head under at the last moment, throwing his weight directly into the assembled titans.

Arryk glanced upward just as the dragon slammed bodily into the titans. The first two crumpled inward at the impact and seemed to have little effect on the momentum of the huge mass of the creature. Then all the titans as well as the dragon vanished in an explosion of rubble as they were carried into the stones of the temple behind them. The temple itself collapsed from the impact, its stones raining down on the titans and the dragon alike.

"The goblins! They're coming from the gate!" Arryk shouted to the stunned faeries around him. "Charge them! We must close that gate!"

He ran forward with Treijan and Gaius, but many of the faeries flew ahead of them, sweeping down into the goblin line. Still, the goblins advanced as though driven by blind zeal. Arryk reached within himself as the goblins charged, searching for the magic—searching for Treijan in the City of Dreams.

Skramak pulled himself out of the shattered head of his titan and stood uncertainly atop the rubble around him.

Though dazed, he was a warrior first, so he looked down to examine what was rapidly becoming a bad situation.

His line of titans had been crushed by some enormous flying beast, and the winged gods had fought their way to his gate, after all.

Through his spinning mind he grasped one clear thought: he had to protect the gate.

He began making his way off the side of the shattered temple, slowly at first but with growing momentum, driven by that single thought. He reached the foundations of the ruined building, and there, still clutched in the fist of a dead goblin warrior, was a blade-caster.

Skramak reached down and pulled the weapon free from the dead goblin's grasp. The poor idiot never even got off a shot, Skramak observed before turning toward the gate.

Three of the gods were behind the line of battle, directing the others forward. *Leaders.* Skramak nodded, recognizing that one of them was all too familiar.

He raised his weapon, advancing quietly from behind them.

Lunid stood on the hillside next to the gate, wringing her hands. The search for Urk was just not working out the way she had envisioned. Titans, which had been returning for repairs in a constant stream since they had entered the gate two days before, were exploding in plain sight on the other side of it.

She was exhausted from anxious days by the rift-gate, but she dared not leave—Urk might be found at any moment. She wanted to be here to explain to him why he should never leave her again.

It was after the flying monster smashed into the titans,

driving them into the building, that Lunid saw through the gate an army of the gods come around the corner. Winged creatures just like her Urk! Perhaps one of the other gods would know where he could be found.

She glanced around. The gen-reels were being yelled at by Thwick, who was trying to get them to send more of the warriors through the gate. No one would notice her, she thought, no one ever did.

Lunid ran down the slope toward the crowded gate.

Treijan glanced back just as the one-eyed goblin released his first blade. Instinctively, the bard raised his hand, freezing an arc of air between them, deflecting the shot. Three more followed in quick succession before Treijan reached forward and with a flick of his right hand, lifted the one-eyed goblin into the air in a bubble of magic.

The vicious little creature was bleeding from a head wound and screeching incoherently. Treijan chuckled to himself. "Well, little fellow, you look rather upset to be here all alone." He took a step toward the goblin, who, though he floated upside down, was still trying to train his weapon on the prince. "Hey, Gaius! Look what I—"

Treijan's face fell.

"Gaius?"

With a shudder Treijan collapsed, to writhe senselessly on the ground.

The bubble holding the one-eyed goblin vanished, too.

Suddenly, the magic poured into Arryk with a force he had never known. He compressed the very air around him and blew it outward in a hazy wave, pushing it through the skirmish line. The goblins before him flew apart, blowing away from the cobblestones as though they were leaves before an angry gust of autumn wind. The parting of the demons left the way clear leading up to the gate.

"Treijan! A path is clear!" Arryk cried out, the power of the magic coursing through him barely controlled. "We did it! They cannot stop us now! Close the gate, Treijan! Treijan?"

The goblin warriors swarmed around Gaius, trying to press him and a group of faeries against the wall of broken buildings.

Gaius countered, trying to set a wall of his own around him from which he could defend and attack, but the goblins moved too quickly, and he soon found himself surrounded by the creatures, lashing out at them with rods of deadly light.

"Treijan!" he called out. "Where are you?"

Lunid stood flattened against the side of the gate, watching in astonishment as the goblin army started backing away, refusing to pass through to the battle. Dozens of other goblins returned through the gate with less order, being catapulted through the air to land on their fellow troops.

She turned and peeked, suddenly seeing why. Urk! Her beloved winged god was standing in the street pushing the army back. Lunid's eyes filled up with tears. *He's trying to come back to me,* she thought. *He's coming this way, and he's trying to come back to me!*

The gate was clear now, the army backing away uncertainly.

Lunid could not wait.

She stepped through the gate.

* * *

Theona ran across the plaza. She did not think about the bodies over which she stumbled or the ash that choked her breath. She could only see Treijan, lying helplessly on the ground at the foot of the ruined temple, and the one-eyed goblin that stood raising his weapon.

She had seen it in her vision of Treijan's paths—and it was the most hateful thing she had seen. She ran knowing what was coming next—dreading what was coming next.

The weapon now no more than a foot from Treijan's quivering body, the one-eyed goblin pulled the release.

Arryk's head jerked back, and he fell to his knees. The magic that had been flowing through him with a raging force had suddenly, shockingly stopped. The power of it rebounded in his soul.

Lunid saw Urk collapse and ran all the harder toward him, oblivious to the battle between the gods and Skramak's warriors around her. Urk needed her. Urk had come back for her, and now she would make it all right. She would take care of him, and they would always be together because she would never let anything happen to him ever again.

She had almost reached her beloved winged god when she saw Skramak standing over the body of one of the wingless creatures from the dream. His face was a terrible mask, and he swung his blade-caster around, taking aim at Urk.

"No!" Lunid screamed, but her words were muffled by the sounds of battle. She rushed forward. "He's the one! He's the one you're looking for!"

Skramak apparently didn't see her, and he once again tripped the release.

The six-blade cluster shot from the weapon, cutting the air with a swish.

Lunid leaped between Skramak and Urk.

Skramak stood up in horror as the blades sank into the goblin woman.

The goblin rift-gate, in a great roar, collapsed.

The goblins panicked when the gate collapsed. They fled down the alleyways of the city, vanishing from the square. Gaius was suddenly free of them, and only then saw Treijan where he lay still on the ground, a goblin standing over his cousin with his weapon still held high.

Arryk knelt nearby in the square, gazing down in horror at a little goblin female that lay dead at his feet. Looking up, he saw the one-eyed demon sneering at him from behind the weapon. Faeries began to close in on the single goblin but were warned off by the sight of his weapon trained on Arryk.

Gaius quickly ran toward where Treijan lay, but when he saw the goblin shift his weapon and stare him in the eye, he stopped. Theona, too, approached the prince but was held off by the goblin, who threatened her with the weapon in turn.

A strange quiet descended in which all they could hear were the stones in the shattered temple settling slightly.

"Kree-an tagakh!" the creature screeched from behind the weapon.

Gaius raised his hands out from his sides, showing his palms forward, swallowing hard. "I don't understand you, you unspeakably vile little monster."

"Don't provoke him," Theona said quickly.

"Kree-an tagakh echuk!" the ancient goblin said emphatically, gesturing with his weapon toward where the gate had been.

Arryk spoke slowly but calmly. "I can't understand you."

Treijan suddenly screamed in agony.

The goblin's eye narrowed as he bared his teeth.

In that instant the goblin's head jerked back and he dropped his weapon. He snarled once and then fell facedown; his back was riddled with blades.

From behind the fallen goblin came the dust-covered form of Meklos, a blade-casting goblin weapon in his hands.

Theona leaped forward, falling next to Treijan. She began speaking to him at once. "It's all right, my lord. It's done."

Gaius stood his ground, watching the approach of his old enemy.

"What the goblin said was that he wanted you to reopen the gate," Meklos said.

"You understood him?" Gaius said warily.

Meklos sighed. "He was my link in the dream. Now I'm going to have to find another, I suppose—but I've come to believe that there are many things in my life that need to change."

And as the Aboth knelt next to Treijan, the bracers on Meklos's wrists suddenly fell away. Gaius moved forward and joined Meklos and Theona as they tended to his friend.

Treijan looked up, trying to focus. "Hey, Meklos! Where's your—your dragon?"

"Right over there." Meklos, his eyes filled with concern, pointed his thumb toward the broken temple. "Lie still. I'll show him to you later if you like."

"I think—I think I'll have to take your word on that," Treijan said, wincing. He turned his head, his eyes unfocused. "Theona? Are you there?"

"Yes, my lord," she responded.

"Did I choose well?" Treijan asked. "Is this the right road?"

"Yes, my lord." Theona's tears streamed down her cheeks. "Everything will be all right now."

"Give me your hand," Treijan said, his breaths quickening.

"Treijan, I—"

"Quickly!"

She took his bloodied hand. He gripped it and pulled it to his chest, bringing it to rest on his tally.

"It doesn't end here," he said to her. "You cannot let it end here. Finish it for me—finish it for all of us."

Treijan's back suddenly arched, his hand slipping from hers.

Theona closed her eyes and slumped forward.

When at last she raised her head, Gaius drew in a sudden breath.

Treijan's tally lay around Theona's neck.

Songstone

Big-funder Thwick stood staring at the fallen gate, unable to take his eyes from it. Lunid, his most lucrative Deep Tinker, was on the other side—somewhere—as was his greatest patron, Dong Mahaj Skramak. The gate lay in ruins, and he had no idea how to open it again.

Lunid would fix it, he thought. She was just on the other side, and she would take care of everything. All he needed to do was wait awhile.

Soon the Grand Army of the Conquest, bereft of its unifying Dong, broke into factions under each of the remaining gen-reels. By the following morning they were attacking one another. Several of them decided to attack the ogre city of Og—home of the Big-funder's academy— just out of nervous energy. The ogres responded gladly, anxious for an excuse to go to war again.

All this Thwick ignored as he watched the broken pieces of the gate. Lunid would take care of it. Lunid would open the gate, and everything would be back the way it was before.

Thwick waited a long time.

Hueburlyn stood in the ruins of the palace hall. The space was empty; the faeries had all moved out of the building, and no one had returned. The floor no longer shook, and the walls had ceased to move. All that remained was a profound silence, the rippling motion of the rift-gate, and the centaur standing guard.

Hueburlyn chose to believe that the faeries had won their battle because no one had returned. He took the silence as a blessed sign.

Now, he knew, it was his turn to do his duty—perhaps the most important duty of all. He believed that the gods had brought him into the world for this purpose, and he would not fail now.

"The end of one is the beginning of another," he said to himself.

The centaur turned and stepped back through the rift-gate.

Dregas could not believe his luck.

He did not know what this place was, but these winged demons must have been the dumbest creatures ever. They seemed to have dropped everything of value in their haste to meet their own death. The wealth of an entire nation, deposited right here on the other side of the gate, and they just left it behind like it was rocks or dirt.

Admittedly, the passage through this particular gate was dreadful. Enough perhaps to put most folks off traveling through gates permanently. But once he came out the other side, the dwarf caught the smell of gold and jewels and enough finery to satisfy even his seemingly bottomless lusts.

He could see the gleaming shapes through the gloom of his black glass, although his smell, taste, and touch served better in evaluating what was around him. When he first came through, he could still hear the sounds of faeries trekking through the gate. But it had been quiet for some time now, and the only sounds remaining were his own shufflings from pile to glorious pile. It was the greatest find in his entire life, perhaps in the life of any dwarf. He began to think that it would be enough to buy respect in the dwarven halls and have his past—and any ill steps in the future—forgotten.

He moved with casual ease between the piles, keeping himself hidden from the single-minded march of the faeries as he picked the finest of their wealth and placed it in his hip pouches almost without a thought. He was so intent on inventorying the ornate and beautiful golden carvings—and recalculating their worth based on their raw smelted weight—that he was surprised when a terrible crashing sound echoed off the walls of the black city around him, and even more surprised by the clomping footfalls that followed.

"Hello?" Dregas called softly.

The footfalls receded, replaced by the sound of a distant trumpet.

"Hello?" he ventured a little more boldly.

No sound but the wind in his ears.

Dregas stepped slowly toward the gate, his speed checked by the weight in his bulging pockets. "Maybe old Dregas go back now," he said to himself. "See if everyone all right er is."

He waddled up the steps to the gate and stepped through.

Nothing happened.

The dimming light conspired with the black glass, making it hard for him to see. He felt to his right for the edge of the gate, found it, and ran his hand up its smooth surface.

"Ouch!" Dregas quickly sucked on his finger, tasting the iron in his blood.

The stone ended in sharp onyx shards.

The gate was gone.

Dregas stepped back, dread rising from deep within him. He had come through the gate, and now the gate was gone. He did not know where he was and had no one to tell him.

He sat down on the steps and sobbed into his wide hands. He took no notice that the horns were getting louder and closer by the moment.

When the first dekacian of Kyree warriors entered the city, they were wary and terrified. The dead warriors of Sharajentis had fought to the last soul, and when they were defeated at last on the grass moat surrounding the city, the gates opened of their own accord. Now the Kyree warriors fluttered nervously through the winding and convoluted streets of the city of the dead, but were greeted only by silence. They suspected a trap: the Sharajin would still make a terrible last stand before their utter defeat and captivity. And with every darkened window they passed, the warriors' fear grew. The magic-wielding people of this city must have something unimaginably terrible planned. Yet there was simply no one to be found.

Dekacian Skahk was the first commander to enter the

central plaza of the city. Like the troops around him, he was made nervous by the silence.

"Warmaster Khithish!"

A young Kyree warrior stepped forward, saluting at once.

"By your command, Dekacian!"

"Is there *no one* in this city?"

"We have one captive, sire!"

"One?" Skahk scoffed. "In this entire city?"

"Yes, Dekacian." Khithish was uneasy. "We found him in the city center—a squat Famadorian from a race none of us have encountered before. His pouches were filled with looted objects, sire."

"Well, see to it that he's taken back in chains," Skahk snapped. "We've got to have *something* for the emperor to lord over at the victory parade."

"I suspect he'll be happy to lord over *this*," Khithish replied, gesturing to the piles of valuables covering the floor of the vast inner courtyard.

Skahk nodded as he considered. "The wealth of the kingdom without having to deal with its subjugation, eh? I rather like making war on the faeries."

"But where do you think they went, sire?" Khithish asked quickly. "I mean, sire, for an entire nation to simply *vanish*..."

"Let the politicians worry about that one," Skahk replied testily. "What matters is that the Sharajentei and all their perverted magic have gone with them. Not even the other faeries will care where they went—just so long as they are gone!"

Hueburlyn stood on the hillside north of Sharajentis and gazed sadly down over the city below.

"Have we failed?" asked the satyr standing at his right.

"No failed," Hueburlyn answered in a voice heavy with emotion. "Succeed in unforeseen way."

"The Sharajin are gone from our world, Master Hueburlyn," observed the Mantacorian standing at the centaur's left. "What hope is there now for us?"

"We shall have to be our own hope," Hueburlyn replied. He reached into the pouch that hung over his shoulder and pulled something from it, holding it in his hand.

"What is that?" asked the satyr.

"It is a Songstone," Hueburlyn answered. "It is a key that we must guard and keep safe from the world until the time is right for the Sharajin to return."

"And if the time is never right?" the Mantacorian asked.

"Then we must take the burden on for ourselves and our children."

With that, Hueburlyn placed the Songstone carefully in his pouch, and the three travelers turned and melted into the Margoth Woods.

Rylmar Conlan stood uncomfortably under the morning sun and leaned over to his agent. "Zolan! Are you certain of the message—that it came from my daughter?"

"Oh, yes, my master!" replied the man, his olive-tanned jowls shaking as he vigorously nodded. "She came to me only last night, weary though she was, although still most attractive, Your Grandness, for both of your daughters are, without doubt, beauties that would favor any—"

Rylmar remembered why he had sent Zolan to Khordsholm and why he so seldom called him back.

"Master Conlan!"

Rylmar stiffened at the sound behind him, swallowed hard, and then turned wearing a gracious face. "Lord Rennes-Arvad, what an unexpected pleasure."

"I seriously doubt whether it is either unexpected or a pleasure," Dirc Rennes-Arvad responded in a low, seething tone. "I do not know what game it is you think you are playing at, but should you move against me, I assure you that you and your entire grubby house will be finished!"

"My lord, if that is your pleasure, you are free to try, though we Conlans are not known for going quietly," Rylmar replied in soft, clear tones. "But the truth is that I have no idea what you are talking about."

"Then why are you here, Conlan?"

Conlan lowered his voice further. "A message from my daughter; Theona is coming home. So what are you doing here?"

Dirc Rennes-Arvad blinked.

"Well?"

"A message from Gaius," the Lord of the Empire grumbled. "He says he is bringing Treijan home."

Rylmar took in a quick breath, then began speaking in a rush. "We said that Valana was married to your son. The entire empire knows about it!"

"Everyone *except* my son," Dirc agreed.

"We've got to keep this quiet," Rylmar muttered, "contain it until we can think of something."

"Smile, Conlan," Dirc said, "and take a good look around you."

Rylmar forced a smile and, nodding slightly, looked about. With a shock he realized that the courtyard of the Citadel was coincidentally filled with the heads of all the high-ranking families in the city. They milled near the forty-first gate talking amicably and paying only the most cursory attention to the head of House Conlan. Rylmar smiled at each in turn but eyed them all suspiciously, as a dying man might eye vultures.

Now he stood next to the gate numbered forty-one based on a message from his daughter, and obviously, it was not the only message sent.

Rylmar leaned toward the fawning Zolan. "And you said they would be returning this hour?"

"So she informed me, although, master, she was most vague in answering my questions, while being most insistent that I make special arrangements for the gates into the city, which, of course, I have done in her name, as I believed you would have wanted me to do, as if her words were spoken entirely by yourself—although, if my master wishes it, I could alter the arrangements even at so late a moment as this…"

The Songstone gate resounded, chords echoing between its stones. It flashed once, and then a familiar shimmering blackness filled its interior.

Rylmar heard a murmur sweep through the crowd of great and powerful Calsandrians.

The gate flashed once more—and through it stepped Theona Conlan.

Her clothing was a terrible mess, smeared with ash and stained with blood, but her hair was pulled back carefully, and her eyes, though shot with red and turned down in sadness, were bright.

"Theona!" Rylmar shouted, rushing forward.

She embraced him warmly, closing her eyes for a moment and sending a tear down her dirty cheek. She pulled away and looked up wistfully into his face.

"What is it, child?" Rylmar asked softly.

"It's just—just that I'll miss the way things were," she

said through a sad smile. "It will be all right now, father—just different."

Rylmar gazed at her, not comprehending.

"Mistress Conlan," Dirc said, stepping forward, "where is my son?"

Theona turned to the master of House Rennes-Arvad and looked into his eyes. "Lord Dirc—Gaius Petros follows me and—and I am sorry to bring you such news."

"What news, child?"

Theona reached into her tunic and gently pulled out Treijan's tally that hung about her neck. "He has left us, Your Majesty."

Rylmar stepped forward in shock. "Theona! What have you done!"

Dirc Rennes-Arvad stared at the tally, its intricate marks of his house and the personal marks of his son. He gaped for a moment. "No! No, this *cannot* be true!"

"I am sorry, Your Majesty," Theona said gently.

The Songstone gate flashed once more, and a sarcophagus of glowing crystal emerged into the light of the courtyard, floating above the pedestal of the gate. Gaius Petros appeared at last, his hands on the surface of the transparent coffin as it drifted down the stairs of the platform, stopping before the stunned Dirc.

The flag of House Arvad that lay across the sarcophagus was folded back.

Preserved within for all to see was the body of Treijan Rennes-Arvad.

The assembly in the courtyard gasped.

Gaius stepped over to the shaken Dirc. "He died valiantly, Your Majesty," he said in leaden tones. "He died defending Calsandria—and the honor of your house."

"My son . . . my son . . . ," Dirc said softly. He gently pulled the flag up to hide the face of the prince.

Rylmar bit at his lip as he stepped forward, putting his arm around the grieving man. His words were quiet so as not to carry. "Lord—Dirc! The eyes of the empire are on you right now. Let's retire to your keep, my lord—take our sorrows behind your walls and deal with our problems privately."

"No, father."

Rylmar turned. "Theona?"

"There will be no private deals, no secret deals, and no special favors," Theona said in clear tones, her voice carrying into the courtyard.

"Theona!" Rylmar said urgently. "Keep your voice down!"

"I'm sorry, father, but I bear the tally of Treijan and I must be heard. That is why I invited all these people to be present today."

"*You* invited them!"

Theona nodded. "So that everyone will know."

Gaius stepped forward. "Things have changed, Master Conlan."

Dirc's eyes suddenly fixed on Theona. "How do you come by my son's tally?"

Theona did not hesitate. "I am his wife."

The murmur through the crowd was more intense. Rylmar's eyes grew large as saucers.

"She is the wife of Treijan, prince of Rennes-Arvad," Gaius said firmly, stepping back up to stand next to her. "I was witness to this and so swear before this assembly."

"*You* swear?" Dirc bellowed. "You who took my son—who *kidnapped* him for your own selfish purposes?"

"My dear uncle, this was *your* plan, not mine!" Gaius

shouted. "You sent us away, and I allowed your lies about me, but you own me no longer. I've paid my debt to my cousin—and he to me." Gaius glanced at the sarcophagus, then back to Dirc. "She is wed into the bloodlines of Rennes-Arvad," Gaius asserted. "His tally is hers—you cannot deny it!"

"Can I not?" Dirc railed. "Do you think I do not see through your plan, Gaius of House Petros? Her bloodline and that of Rennes-Arvad would bring her before the Council itself and you along with it, no doubt! It is *you* who have killed my son—you who have fabricated this sham so that you might put this *commoner* on my throne!"

"She is no commoner," Gaius shouted. "She has a talent unknown to us—*that* is why we never saw it—why she did not find it until these terrible events brought it out in her."

"What talent?" Rylmar asked in earnest.

"She is a prophetess," Gaius responded.

Dirc spoke with angry conviction. "There is no such power in all the Deep Magics!"

Theona spoke quietly and simply. "I see the paths of the future, and I hear the words of the gods."

"Blasphemy!" someone shouted from the crowd. The murmuring grew angrier.

"Believe or not," Gaius shouted back, "but one fact remains: she *is* the wife of our fallen Treijan and deserves her place on the Council!"

"And we have to accept your word for this!" spat Dirc.

"No, not my word alone," Gaius said. "Zolan?"

"Y-yes, Master Gaius?" the dark man responded.

"Will you pass back through the gate and instruct our—our 'witnesses' to come through?"

Zolan glanced at Rylmar, who nodded his permission. The servant flashed through the still-open gate.

Time passed.

"I wonder what's keeping him?" Gaius said to Theona.

"Perhaps we might have warned him," Theona replied.

Dirc, still resting his hand on the sarcophagus of his son, glared at Gaius. "I will see you dead for this treason."

The gate flashed, and Zolan, now pale and quivering, held a hastily written scroll in his shaking hands.

Then the gate flashed again, and two willowy figures of incredible beauty appeared. One was female, the other slightly taller and male. Their clothing was stained and torn, though its elegance in workmanship was beyond anything the finest houses of Calsandria had ever produced.

And both of them had beautiful, enormous wings.

The assembled mystics took in a collective breath and then fell into stunned silence. Every mystic of the Deep Magic knew these creatures, but none of them suspected them to exist other than in their dreams.

Zolan found his shaky voice. "I—I beg to announce Queen Dwynwyn and Prince Peleron, masters of the Sharajentei—a faery kingdom in exile."

Dwynwyn stepped past Theona with a smile and moved lightly down the steps from the gate to stand on the other side of the sarcophagus from the stunned Dirc. Her large dark eyes stared into his, searching his soul.

The gate flared once more, and another of the faery

stepped onto the gate's platform. This one was thinner still with midnight skin. He ran his fingers upward, pushing the bangs of his disheveled hair out of his face.

"I beg to announce Arryk, prince of Sharajentei and witness to the wedding of Theona and Treijan in their kingdom and by the authority of Queen Dwynwyn."

Arryk stepped down quickly and came to Dwynwyn's side. He spoke to Lord Dirc, even though the human's gaze remained fixed on the faery queen. The tone carried with it the warmth of shoots in the spring and blossoms, but the words, while obviously rehearsed and heavily accented, were clearly Rhamasian.

"Queen—sorrows for you," Arryk said to Dirc.

Dwynwyn laid her delicate hand on Treijan's sarcophagus, her eyes expressing an infinite sorrow.

Dirc drew in a sobbing breath.

Dwynwyn turned and then stepped back to the platform where Theona still stood. Peleron stepped down to join her and took her hand.

Together they bowed before Theona.

Arryk knelt, then spoke loudly, his words like trumpets and bells resounding through the courtyard. "Sharajentei bows to Theona, Prophetess of Mystics, wife of Treijan hero! We ask sanctuary, as Treijan promise!"

The gate flashed, and faeries began to walk into the courtyard in a silent procession. All were battered—many could barely move—but come they did, quickly filing into the courtyard of the Citadel.

Theona looked up and saw the guardians of the Citadel moving along the tops of the walls and the towers, their staves at the ready.

But one by one, the faeries entered the courtyard, and each in turn bowed to Theona.

Gaius stepped down next to Dirc Rennes-Arvad and spoke quietly to him. "How long would the House of Rennes-Arvad—or the empire itself—stand without the willing cooperation of these, our partners in the dream?"

Gaius turned and bowed.

Lord Dirc Rennes-Arvad drew in a deep breath and bowed to Theona.

Then, one by one, the other masters of the houses of the Mystic Empire bowed as well, and though it would be an hour before the faeries would all have passed through the gate, the issue had long been settled.

Theona, Prophetess of Calsandria, would rule the Council of Thirty-six.

The Seer

It was called the Pillar of the Sky long before the mystics came to Calsandria and claimed it as their own. The great dome overhead lay open to the sky on one side, having fallen eight decades before during Caelith Arvad's legendary battle with Satinka. Though the debris had been removed from the floor of the enormous rotunda, the great gash in the dome remained, sunlight streaming through in a column that illuminated the central dais. There a bronze globe of curious workmanship sat pierced by a single spindle atop a short pillar, and before it knelt two people.

Facing them from the perimeter of the room were the usual ranks of mystics from all the guilds and clans across Calsandria. They still bickered and vied for position against one another, but now among their number were many commoners, who had suddenly found a voice and place in Calsandria the likes of which they had not enjoyed before. Old customs die hardest of all, so they stood somewhat apart from their "betters" in the hall, yet the fact that they were invited—and, better still, had come—was a sign of how much things had changed in so short a time.

Stranger still was the contingent of faeries—those creatures who stepped from the world of dreams and became real. They stood in regal elegance together at the east edge of the hall, their dark skin an alluring counterpoint to their elegant formal dress, which outshone even the finest efforts of the human clans.

The two figures on the dais stood slowly, the ceremony of their wedding nearly complete. The groom wore a special rose-colored vest and white long coat. The bride wore a magnificent red dress with a long train. Such ceremonies were often carried out in the Citadel of Calsandria, but this wedding called for the unusual and grand. The groom took the bride's hand, and they walked around the altar before the assembly, stopping to bow before the three enormous statues in the hall—statues which on this day had new and wondrous meaning. When they were done, the groom took the bride's hand and pressed it to his tally as she took his hand and pressed it to her own. For a moment light flared gloriously around them, and in that moment they were wed.

The bride, Valana Rhami-Conlan, lifted her eyes to the crowd as her new husband, Jesth Rhami-Conlan, grinned foolishly.

The crowd erupted into cheers and applause, joined somewhat belatedly by the faeries, who seemed startled at the practice.

Theona, Empress of Calsandria, First Seer of the Clans, and Mistress of the Council of Thirty-six, stood resplendent in her deep blue gown with silver trim and smiled at her sister, shedding a few tears of joy as she joined in the applause. Next to her, Gaius of House Petros applauded as well, his narrow face splitting into a warm grin.

Valana rushed forward, her arms open to embrace her sister.

Theona held her tight. "Oh, Valana! I am so happy for you!"

"It's a fine match, isn't it?" Valana gushed. "His bloodlines are a perfect counterpoint with ours. Between us we've got nearly all the clans covered!"

Theona laughed. "Yes, Valana—you've done very well for us all, although I suspect his twin brother is not nearly so pleased with the outcome."

"Danth?" Valana's eyebrow rose rakishly. "Well, they're both so handsome; I just hope I can find a way to tell them apart."

Theona laughed in mock outrage.

But by then her sister had spun away into the pressing crowd, her husband now holding her as close to him as possible.

Theona gazed at her sister for a time, watching the bright red dress swirl away. It had been difficult between them when she returned, but in the end it was Theona who had made the match for Valana—offering her a socially acceptable way around the awkward business of both of them being widows of the same prince. In this it was also Theona who came to appreciate her sister's strength and resilience.

"Empress?"

Theona looked up at the tall, older man whose long gray hair was drawn back from a high forehead. Her face softened at once. "Meklos! I am delighted that you could come."

"How could I refuse you?" Meklos smiled. "Besides, I

find travel not nearly as burdensome as I once did. I take a lot of delight in beauty—it's a world that I never saw."

"The world has not changed," Theona said with a breath of sadness.

"No, but the way I see it has," Meklos replied. "It is surprising to me, even at my age, that the world can look so different when viewed without . . . the past shadowing over it."

Theona merely nodded, though the comment gave her much to think about. Still, she decided it better to change the subject. "So will you be staying for the feast tonight? Please say you are."

"I regretfully cannot," Meklos replied. "King Pe'akanu and his people still suffer, and there is much to be done. The goblins have mostly been routed, but there are hold-outs up in the mountains of the island. The destruction of Tua'a-Re was devastating; the aid of Calsandria has been much appreciated."

"It wasn't their war," Theona said sadly.

"No, it was our war, but they fought it for us and are still paying for it." Meklos extended his hand, grasping Theona's forearm as she offered it. "King Pe'akanu sends his blessing and that of all his people. He hopes that you will grace his island before too many seasons pass."

Theona smiled. "Tell him I shall do exactly that."

Meklos released her arm, bowed, and left the hall.

"Is it just me, or is his step lighter?" Gaius commented as he sauntered up behind Theona.

"He is a new man," Theona said. "He sees the world through different eyes. Where have you been?"

"Speaking with Queen Dwynwyn," Gaius said, clasping his hands behind his back. "She was startled by the statues in the hall."

Theona looked up. The three gargantuan statues stood holding up what remained of the dome at three equally spaced points around the hall. One was a beautiful woman, Hrea, who held three globes together in her joined hands. The next was what she now recognized as a goblin—a big-eared demon balancing two globes in his hands while keeping a third floating in the air. The third was definitely a faery, an exquisite man with astounding wings who pondered three globes in his left hand.

"Aren't we all." Theona nodded, a chill running down her spine. "Has the queen decided on where she wishes to settle?"

"She considered Vestadia but does not trust the dwarves to the north," Gaius reported. "I believe she wants to settle her people in Meadowland on the border between our Provinces and the Eastern Marches."

"I heartily approve of that." Theona chuckled. "I would appreciate some buffer between the Provinces and the Pir expansion from the north."

Gaius nodded, raising his eyebrow. "That's just what she said, too. I'll speak with Lord Dirc about getting everything arranged."

"He makes a fine chancellor, don't you think?"

"Yes . . . but after everything he's done . . ."

"We need House Arvad to remain strong to balance out the other houses," Theona said easily. "Besides, it's easier to keep an eye on him when he's close-by."

"Easier, perhaps," Gaius replied, "but not nearly as satisfying as dealing him the justice he deserves."

Theona continued to stare at the statues. "Meklos said the world looks different when viewed without fear and pain."

"Indeed," Gaius said with a smile. "Then tell me, Theona, what do you see now?"

I stand at the fork of two roads and walk one path before me.

It brings me to stand atop the highest tower of the Citadel of the city. All of Calsandria lies beneath me. I watch the white towers, walls, and roofs as they grow with miraculous speed from the seeds of former ages out of the rich earth below. The sun shines on my city; Calsandria matures, glowing with its own light across the face of the world.

A shadowed man stands above the western hills. He walks out of the Desolation, and with him comes a disease that drifts across the landscape toward me. The trees of the orchards wither at its touch, the waters it enters become brackish, and the air fouls at its breath.

I call out to the city below, but they do not hear me above their own squabbling. They do not see the danger for their own blindness. The pestilence touches the city, shriveling its roots and poisoning its stone. The alabaster walls become stained and pitted, rotting from within, and the city stinks of it. The Citadel falls from beneath me, collapsing on its side.

The dragons circle above and dive onto the dying city, feasting on it as though it were carrion.

I step back, tears streaming down my face. The world is dying around me as three worlds tear one another apart at the Binding, each devouring the other, and the city I had grown and nurtured as a sanctuary is dead and with it the hope of our world.

I stand at the fork of two roads . . .

DIARY OF THEONA CONLAN, VOLUME 4, PAGES 10–11

* * *

"Tell me, Theona."

Theona drew in her breath and then turned to look at Gaius.

He watched her, his face puzzled. "What *did* you see?"

Theona glanced up at the statue of Hrea that seemed to be looking back at her as the goddess's words returned to her mind. *"It is for you to know and to see. It is up to your own wisdom how you use this sight—for the greatest road is never the easiest, and few would take it if they knew the price."*

Theona smiled at Gaius, reached out, and enfolded his hands in hers. "I see—that you and I could be very happy walking our roads together."

Thrice upon a time . . .
came the Binding of the Worlds.
Not even the gods knew
. . . which world would reign . . .
. . . which world would submit . . .
. . . and which world would die.

Song of the Worlds
Bronze Canticles, Tome 1, Folio 1, Leaf 6

THE END OF BOOK III

Appendix A:
Genealogies

Genealogies became of paramount importance to the mystics after the Patents of the Bloodline were established in 547 DK. It was thought at the time that mystic ability was inherited from one's ancestors, and thus family relations became the all-consuming preoccupation of power and politics in the early eras of the Mystic Empire. This was complicated by the unfounded (and unwarranted) belief that patriarchal bloodlines were superior to matriarchal.

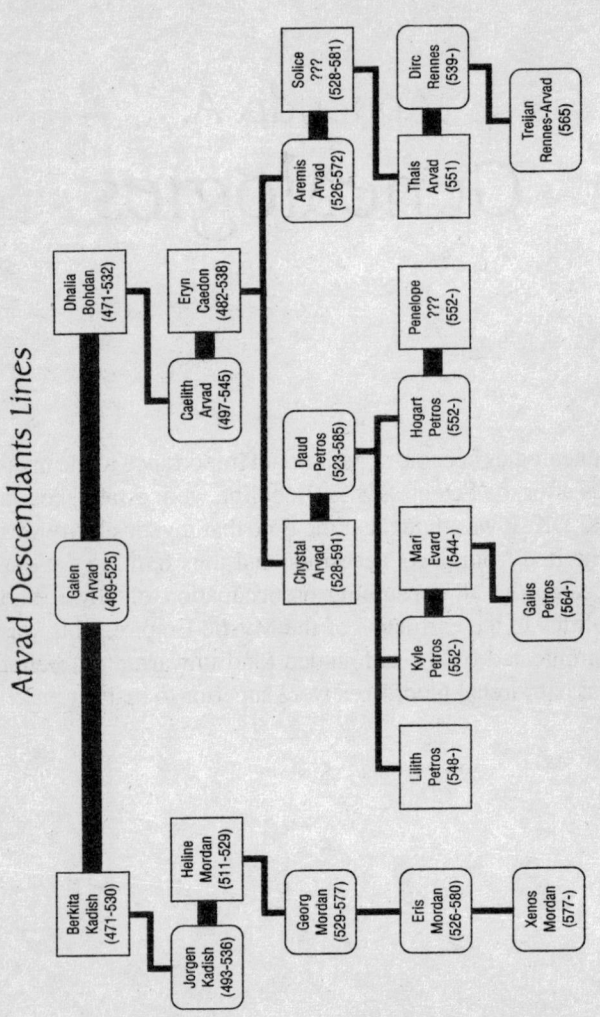

Conlan, Myyrdin, and Harm Lines

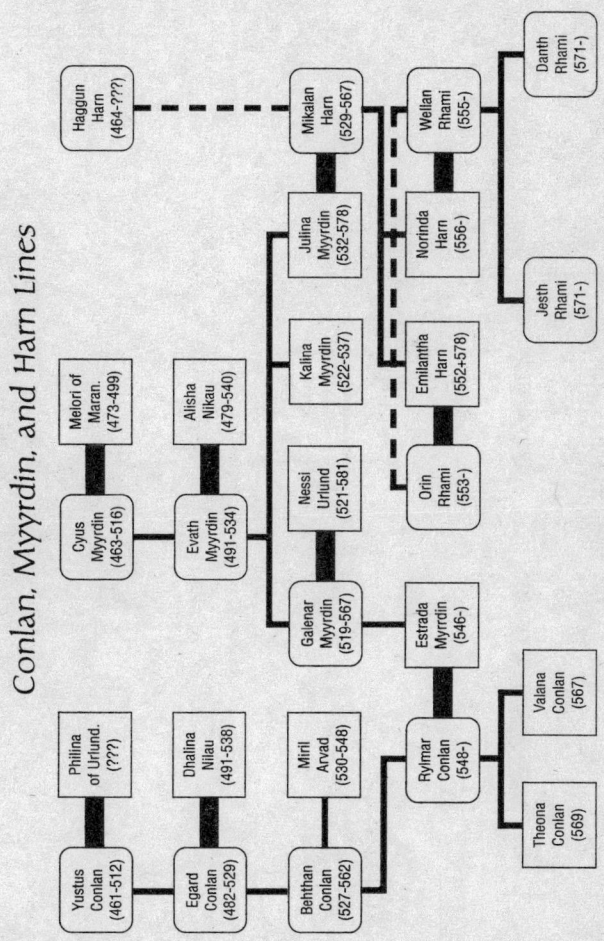

Appendix B:
The Disciplines

By 547 DK the Arvadian mystics had formalized their magical systems along both clan lines symbolized by the six ancient gods of Rhamas. This was partly in honor of Caelith Arvad's encounter with the gods at the Pillar of the Sky. The divisions of both the houses and their magical guilds were along the following lines.

Rhamasic
(Magic of the Firmament/Clan Mistal)

This magic is the realm of the physical. This is divided into subdisciplines, or guilds, which include the following:

Transmutation
- Woodshapers
- Stoneshapers
- Cloudminders

- Claymolders
- Armorers/Metalsmiths
- Alchemists

Enchantment
- Enchanters
- Catalysts (Combiners)

Hreatic
(Magic of Dreams/Clan Arvad)

This magic primarily deals with the realm between intellect and spirit—pure creation. The subdisciplines, or guilds, include but are not limited to:

Evocation
- Enforcers
- Warriors

Illusion
- Watersculptors
- Smokedancers
- Enchanters
- Muses
- Bards

Mnemeatic
(Magic of the Day/Clan Nikau)

This magic primarily deals with the realm of ideas and information. Subdisciplines, or guilds, include:

Divination
- Diviners
- Craft Talkers
- Forest Talkers
- Creature Talkers
- Loremasters
- Dowsers

Ekteiatic
(Magic of the Night/Clan Myyrdin)

This magic deals with force and power. Subdisciplines, or guilds, include:

Abjuration
- Guardians

Conjuration
- Conjurors

Theleic
(Living Magic/Clan Caedon)

This magic is the realm of healing and life, motion and animation. Subdisciplines, or guilds, include but are not limited to:

Flora
- Forest Healers
- Crop Healers
- River and Sea Healers

Fauna
- Empaths
- Torusk Healers
- Range Healers
- Fish Healers

Anthropomorphist
- Animators
- Imbuers

Healer/Magipathic
- Healers

Skureatic
(Still Magic/Clan Harn)

This magic is the realm of death and pain. In its early history this discipline was seen as a simple balancing force—just another part of the complete whole that made up the complete sum of Deep Magic. This view would change within a single generation.

Necromancy
- Reanimators
- Death Magic
- Transmuters

ABOUT THE AUTHORS

TRACY AND LAURA HICKMAN, the creators of Dragonlance™, have been publishing game designs and stories together for over twenty-five years. Tracy Hickman is the coauthor of international bestsellers including the Dragonlance Chronicles trilogy, Dragonlance Legends trilogy, Darksword trilogy, Rose of the Prophet trilogy, and the Deathgate Cycle septology. Tracy and Laura Hickman live in Utah.